The Best
AMERICAN
MYSTERY &
SUSPENSE
2023

The Best AMERICAN MYSTERY & SUSPENSE™ 2023

Edited and with an Introduction by LISA UNGER

STEPH CHA, Series Editor

MARINER BOOKS
New York   Boston

FIRST EDITION

Library of Congress Cataloging-in-Publication Data has been applied for.

ISSN 2768-1920
ISBN 978-0-06-331581-5

23 24 25 26 27 LBC 5 4 3 2 1

Contents

Foreword

OVER THIS LAST WEEK, millions of civically engaged Americans have visited two separate courtrooms to witness important legal proceedings from the comfort of our own homes. One was of inarguable historic significance: the former president's arraignment in a Manhattan criminal court, where he pled not guilty to thirty-four felonies. The other involved a skiing accident, an opportunistic optometrist, and famous actor and lifestyle influencer Gwyneth Paltrow.

I watched these dramas unfold on my phone in some of the precious blank time when I wasn't working or taking care of my two children, both born during my three years as series editor for *The Best American Mystery and Suspense*. I was, I have to admit, more interested in the Gwyneth Paltrow ski trial, with its colorful cast and delicious little details (the optometrist claimed that his injuries prevented him from enjoying wine tastings!). I spent so much energy following the constant reality show of the Trump presidency that I'm no longer willing to immerse myself in these post-presidency seasons.

Not everyone reads fiction, but we all seek out stories to enrich and ornament our time on earth, confined as we are to our own bodies and our own lives. Sometimes we lose ourselves in grand, multigenerational epics, and sometimes we just want to enjoy fun, petty episodes, where we can get gleefully invested in the lowest of stakes. The main thing is to visit other people's lives, worry about their jobs, their families, their problems for a while.

Of course, you and I read fiction, and specifically crime fiction—

stories that are, almost by definition, about bad things happening to other people. This is my third *Best American* anthology, so I can't even count the number of mystery and suspense stories I've read in the past few years. The number of dead bodies must be in the thousands. But it's not all murder and mayhem—the stories are full of juice, full of color, depicting the broad sprawl of human experience.

It's such an honor and pleasure to edit this series, to sift through the enormous trove of American crime stories and share my favorites with you. Since its inception as *The Best American Mystery Stories* in 1997, this anthology has published short fiction by many of your favorite writers at different points in their careers. It also boasts an illustrious roster of guest editors: Robert B. Parker, Sue Grafton, Ed McBain, Donald E. Westlake, Lawrence Block, James Ellroy, Michael Connelly, Nelson DeMille, Joyce Carol Oates, Scott Turow, Carl Hiaasen, George Pelecanos, Jeffery Deaver, Lee Child, Harlan Coben, Robert Crais, Lisa Scottoline, Laura Lippman, James Patterson, Elizabeth George, John Sandford, Louise Penny, Jonathan Lethem, C. J. Box, Alafair Burke, and Jess Walter.

For *The Best American Mystery and Suspense 2023*, I got to work with Lisa Unger, an author I have known and admired for many years. I first met Lisa at ThrillerFest 2013, a conference for crime writers in New York City. I was a debut author no one had ever heard of, and I will never forget how warm and welcoming she was when I introduced myself outside the book room. Lisa was already a luminary of the mystery world then, and has only become more accomplished over the last decade. She's the *New York Times* best-selling author of twenty novels published in thirty-three languages, with millions of copies sold worldwide. *Secluded Cabin Sleeps Six*—a story about a relaxing weekend getaway with friends; what could possibly go wrong?—is her latest international bestseller. *Confessions on the 7:45* is in development at Netflix, with Jessica Alba attached to star. Her books are regulars on every best book list in the business, and she's won or been nominated for numerous awards, including the Strand Critics, Audie, Macavity, ITW Thriller, and Goodreads Choice Awards as well as the Hammett Prize. She is also a recent contributor to this series: Alafair Burke and I selected her story, "Let Her Be," for inclusion in *The Best American Mystery and Suspense 2021.*

Lisa has been an active, enthusiastic partner in this process.

We're both faithful fans of the genre, and it was so fun sharing stories with someone I knew would enjoy them. I've said this before, but one of my favorite parts of this job is the two-person book club with my guest editors. I was once a total author groupie (I still am, honestly, I'm just more chill about it now) and I still get such pleasure from sharing this experience with writers I've always admired.

Three anthologies in, I've gotten a decent handle on where and how to find eligible stories. I sought them out from a variety of sources, though I still started with the usual suspects. I read through every issue of *Ellery Queen Mystery Magazine* and *Alfred Hitchcock's Mystery Magazine* as well as Akashic's collections of noir and genre stories. I tracked down the crime anthologies published in 2022, many of them after receiving submissions from individual authors or editors, and kept tabs on the various mystery publications, both in print and online. I also hit up editors of literary journals I thought might have a few stories that would fit comfortably under the crime umbrella. I sifted through all these stories and picked around fifty of the best (or more accurately, my favorites), which I passed on to Lisa. She read them as fast as I could get them to her (which, this year, was not fast, as I had a baby in August), and she chose her favorites. We met in person once—such a pleasure—and finalized the list, gushing about this or that story. Twenty of them made it into this volume, but you can find the remaining thirty candidates in the honorable mentions at the back of this book. All the writers and stories on that list are worth seeking out.

As you read this volume, I should be well into my reading for *The Best American Mystery and Suspense 2024.* I still worry about missing eligible stories (and this year, I took on the additional, very stupid task of judging for the National Book Awards), so authors and editors, please do send me your work. To qualify, stories must be originally written in English (or translated by the original authors) by writers born or permanently residing in America or Canada—yes, Canadians, you kept emailing me, and I've started considering your stories. They need to be independent stories (not excerpts) published in the calendar year 2023 in American (or Canadian) publications, either print or online. I have a strong preference for web submissions, which you can send in any reasonable format to bestamericanmysterysuspense@gmail.com. If you would like to send printed materials, you can email me for a mailing address. The submissions deadline is December 31, and when possible, several months earlier. I promise to look at every story sent to me before that deadline. After that, it's between reading your story and wrangling my two small, demanding sons.

I'm proud of all of our work here, and grateful for the chance to share these outstanding stories. I hope you enjoy them as much as I did.

STEPH CHA

Introduction

MOST WRITERS FIND THEMSELVES on the outside looking in, at least some of the time. We are observers, often standing in the margins. From that vantage point, though it's not often a view we choose, we can see clearly what others miss. When I was young, my family moved every few years, and I often felt like an outsider, the new kid, the one who didn't quite belong. But in stories, those written by others, or those I created myself, I found a home. Then, and sometimes even now, unpredictable, unkind reality was far less appealing than the richly imagined lives and loves and worlds created by writers.

It was in a collection of short fiction and nonfiction, *Music for Chameleons* by Truman Capote, where I found myself as a writer. Transported by those vignettes, taken to new places, listening to strange, vibrant voices, I remember thinking of them as "word pictures." Capote, like most writers, had a complicated relationship with the truth—his fiction often painfully autobiographical, his nonfiction frequently departing from the facts. But he used his formidable gifts to capture character, place, and mystery vividly, drawing readers in with his secrets and lies and intimate confessions. Each story in that collection is a glittering gem in a mosaic that reveals a genius and flawed and difficult writer, in brief colorful bursts of light.

It's no surprise then that my first stabs at writing—other than the obligatory terrible poetry and rambling diary entries—were in short stories. Terrifyingly, my parents still have these buried in a drawer somewhere. I remember my early efforts as being fantastical and maudlin. Perhaps there were fairies involved, and adolescent angst. I seem to recall trains and airplanes, magical creatures, journeys without end, longing, and probably some sort of mystery since I already had a taste for the dark side. If you call my mom, I'm sure she'll happily share them with you. But please don't.

I wasn't old enough (or smart or talented enough, certainly with nothing enough to say) to write a novel, wouldn't be for many years. But I remember thinking I could create these little spaces for myself, for characters, and dwell in them completely. I could lose myself and the world around me, live inside an imagined universe which somehow seemed more real than anything else. And I did.

Later, when I was still studying at Eugene Lang College, the undergraduate division of the New School for Social Research in New York City, I started writing my first novel. And it was a long time before I found my way back to short works. It's only in recent years that I have fallen back in love with the form.

Short fiction has a rich literary history, and yet it is often overlooked by contemporary readers. When I publish my short stories (one of them, "Let Her Be," selected for inclusion in the 2021 edition of this iconic series), I often hear from readers things like "I wanted more" or "this should have been a novel" or "I don't like short stories." I puzzle over this because this form has a special kind of magic, the ability to transport you quickly, intensely, to capture character, time, place, and story with immediacy and deliver it all with a punch.

As a writer, I have a different relationship with short fiction now than I do with my novels. The writing—and reading—of a novel is a long relationship. You sink in and get to know it. There are good days and bad, side roads and joyful surprises, missteps and ecstatic discovery. But a short story is like a breezy jaunt away, a transporting fling, fast, passionate, immersive, and then gone. There's such pleasure in that, in the momentary escape. You can't compare a short story to a novel, in the way that you can't compare your hometown to an exotic weekend destination.

I was honored when the immensely talented Steph Cha asked me to guest edit *The Best American Mystery and Suspense 2023* anthology. More than that, I was overcome by reader joy. The professional writer spends so much time, you know, *writing*, that the kid who used to read under the covers after lights-out often gets neglected. It was an exciting proposition to dive into the best short fiction written last year, just for the pure enjoyment of losing myself in the work of the most talented people writing today.

The journey was richer and more thrilling than I imagined, though choosing the "best" of what I read was a challenge. After all, reader joy is utterly subjective; one person's masterpiece is another's doorstop. But for me as a reader, it's about feeling something, losing myself for a while, going somewhere. Ultimately, it seemed important that each story in this collection was a doorway. I want you to open each and walk inside to find yourself someplace you did not expect to go. Someplace new and fresh, weird, or wonderful. If you allow yourself to be transported, you'll go into orbit, visit a hidden world of misfits deep below city streets, jet off to the tropics. You'll buy a Popsicle, deliver a baby, fall in love a little with a former movie star.

The gifted and inventive writers gathered here take a deep dive into strange worlds and altered states. They explore big themes like love, grief, community, family, identity, as well as those small moments of choice and circumstance that dictate the course of our lives. Crime fiction is a crucible, a place where human nature is revealed under the most intense of circumstances. Every story here will have you holding your breath, flipping the pages, will leave you thinking about people and why they do the dark, dangerous, frightening things that they do.

Many of the collected authors stretch the conventions of genre to offer an outing wholly unique and without category, offering us creative escapes from the world's most troubling problems.

Adam Meyer, in his poignant and moving "Mr. Filbert's Classroom," imagines a magical place that is safe for our children, accessed through a devoted second-grade teacher's whiteboard. "The Blood-Red Leaves of Autumn," Annie Reed's darkly observed and propulsive entry, launches us into the heart of a murder investigation on a space station circling our dying planet. The great Walter Mosley invites us down into a secret, subterranean network of tunnels where folks unwanted by society find a home in his wildly imaginative and twisting "Not Exit." In the rich and vibrantly told "Ripen" by Ashley-Ruth M. Bernier, we climb a mango tree in the Virgin Islands as a crime is about to rock a peaceful island community. The haunting and unsettling "When We Remembered

Zion" by A. J. Jacono asks that we watch a murderer and abductor deliver a baby.

Another theme that comes up again and again in these stories in different ways is the idea of the outsider, the person separated from life as they would like it by circumstance, emotion, culture, or desire.

Capturing character and voice in the ways that only a true master can, Joyce Carol Oates takes us deep into the inner life of the complex and difficult Gigi, who is struggling with the loss of idolized Marguerite, even as she tries to piece together what is left behind in the hypnotic "33 Clues into the Disappearance of My Sister." A haunted veteran turned career criminal on the run from a job gone wrong returns to the only place he ever felt safe and loved in James A. Hearn's beautifully told "Home Is the Hunter." Grief and regret loom large in S. A. Cosby's gripping, atmospheric "The Mayor of Dukes City," where an injured fighter turned bouncer seeks vengeance for his lost love. In the evocative and atmospheric "The Land of Milk and Honey," Silvia Moreno-Garcia reveals a young woman who has a chance to escape the oppressive world created by her controlling father but finds herself trapped all the same. The darkly funny and character rich "New York Blues Redux" by William Boyle introduces us to a cast of misfits on a collision course all headed for the same Brooklyn dive bar. "Flight" by Thaai Walker is the brutal but gorgeous story of a Washington Heights girl struggling with the harshness of life, friendship, and growing up, even as she looks to the stars. Grief, inner pain, and dislocation make outsiders of the characters in the dreamlike and elegant "Flip Lady" by Ladee Hubbard when a young girl seeks a replacement for her dropped Popsicle.

Hope is a slippery thing in crime fiction, yet some of these outings strike that note, even from the depths of darkness. When all seems lost in Anthony Neil Smith's tense and utterly immersive "The Ticks Will Eat You Whole," a man who is helping spread the ashes of his father-in-law on an isolated property gets a surprising rescue. Two close friends run a gauntlet of bad people in a dangerous neighborhood while trying to care for an infant in Jervey Tervalon's moving and exquisitely drawn "How Hope Found Chauncey." In the buoyant and layered "Love Interest," Jess Walter gives a thoroughly modern edge to an old-school noir detective story when a former movie star has an unusual request of a nerdy

PI. Leigh Newman takes us to Alaska in the lyrical and dreamy "Valley of the Moon," where sister love manages to overcome all.

In her inventive and involving "The Invitation," Margaret Randall invites us to consider another recurring theme in the collection, the consequences of choice, when a college student about to embark on an important internship receives an enticing invitation from an old boyfriend. A widow makes a deadly decision when she picks up the fight that obsessed her late husband in the deep and surprising "The Obsession of Abel Tangier" by Faye Snowden. In Joseph S. Walker's compelling and twisting "Crime Scene," an assassin on his last job finds himself questioning his life choices and breaks all the rules to understand his final victim. In a brilliantly original and tantalizingly clever outing, repeat contributor Jacqueline Freimor uses the form of a fictional "Foreword" to reveal the buried secrets of a marriage and a murder.

Regardless of theme or setting, behind each of these doorways is a surprise. I gasped. I yelled at characters. I laughed out loud. I suspect you'll have similarly powerful reactions. I hope you do because that's what reader joy is all about. We are so immersed, so transported, that fiction seems more real than reality.

As guest editor, I'm just a visitor here. Steph Cha did all the heavy lifting of perusing journals, anthologies, magazines, and everywhere short fiction is published to send me the work that most stood out. Everything that I read was exceptional, with something that made it special enough to be a part of this collection. I wish that we could have included them all. And so, the final cut was difficult.

So much talent, so many unique, exciting voices—experimental, risk-taking, fresh, and original. Truly, we are in a golden age of mystery and suspense. Some of our finest writers are working in this form and pushing it in important new directions. We finally settled on twenty, but there were many more that could have easily been featured as well. Be sure to seek out the stories listed at the end in the Other Distinguished Mystery and Suspense of 2022. There is nothing on that list that could not also have been featured here, as well.

The act of compressing suspense, action, and mystery into short fiction is no small feat. Suspense can take time to build. It might be pages and pages before we get to know a character well enough to care about him or her. A twist must seem like a surprise, but also that it was inevitable, not a gimmick or trick. Every single selection here accomplishes something masterful. Each story is a unique, perfectly placed piece in a mosaic that reveals some of our greatest talents.

Of Capote's *Music for Chameleons*, *The New Republic* said, "Everything is displayed in this book: insights and recollections . . . ; old jokes and fresh wit. . . . These stories and vignettes will endure." When I was writing this, I went back again to my yellowed, dog-eared, and scribbled-in copy of Capote's collection, often getting lost in the rereading of this or that story or paragraph. I hope this collection finds a similar home on your shelf and in your heart, and that you return again and again to the stories within.

My huge thanks to Steph Cha for inviting me through these doorways. To the writers featured here who gave me hours of reader joy, I offer my deepest gratitude and congratulations. And to you, the lucky reader about to embark on this journey, happy reading.

I'll ask one thing as you read. Accept each story for exactly what it is. Don't wish it were a novel, or that you could spend more time with this character or that. Just open the door and allow yourself to disappear into its brief, powerful perfection.

LISA UNGER

The Best
AMERICAN
MYSTERY &
SUSPENSE
2023

Ripen

FROM *Black Cat Weekly*

SOMETIMES I IMAGINE what tourists do with their first few hours after stepping off the plane into paradise. I bet it involves a scenic ride to their hotel or villa, some gasps at the view and no-filter-needed selfies being uploaded to social media; perhaps a sip of something flooded with rum or an ecstatic plunge into the Caribbean Sea. For me, on my visits back home to St. Thomas every couple of months, those first two hours always find me in the same place: at my mother's insistence, I'll be ten feet high in whatever fruit tree is currently blooming in her garden, avoiding antisocial iguanas and blighted branches. This visit, it's mango season. I bet my fellow passengers are ordering daiquiris from the hotel bar. I'm shimmying down a bough a couple fathoms above my mom's herb garden, trying my best not to get twigs tangled up in my skinny sisterlocks and tossing mangoes down to my mother below. Well. Tossing mangoes and weighted questions.

"Ma," I try, pulling a particularly sappy fruit from a branch. "Jus' now, in the car, it seemed like he couldn't figure out how to turn on the radio. Maybe you and I should—"

"Iss fine, Naomi. It's a new radio, is all. All deh features in the new car are confusing for both of us," my mother says. She smiles up at me. "See if you could get those to the top of the tree, love. If the birds ain' get to dem yet."

This is what she does best. My mother fills spaces with plants. There's her garden, of course, but here in the little house on the Northside of St. Thomas where I grew up, there isn't a windowsill or a bedside table that doesn't have a tiny aloe or a spindly orchid quietly growing on top of it. There are fruited *passiflora* vines that wind along her gates and crotons in decorated pots in the corners of rooms. There's a need somewhere deep inside of her to plug every hole she sees with something green and growing, even if that hole is in the middle of a conversation. *Especially* when that hole is in the middle of a conversation.

I sigh and take the picker, reaching as high as I can into the mango tree leaves and angling the metal fingers around the dewy fruit ripening up top. "Okay, but then, when it came time to make the turn off St. Peter Mountain Road, I saw that you had to remind him where and when to turn. Into our own—"

"Honey, I know you saw the storm we had las' week knocked down the Flamboyant tree at the end of the road. You didn't see how different the turnoff from the road looks? Your father's still getting used to the new landscape," she interrupts. "Barely even June, an' the storms already comin'. You should've seen the garden after the one las' week. It's a wonder there's still fruit hangin' from the tree."

Oh, there are plenty of things left hanging. Just as I'm getting ready to drop some more—mangoes, and probing questions too— I feel a buzz in my back pocket that, thankfully, has nothing to do with the fat bumblebees that are making their daily rounds through the leaves. I wrap one arm around the thick bough and ease my phone out of my pocket.

"Yuh pickin' fruit, love? Or you on your phone?" Ma calls up to me.

"It's Mateo," I answer.

"Oh," she says. She's trying her best to sound nonchalant, but I can see the look on her face clearly, even from twelve feet up— excitement, and perhaps a bit of relief, that this beautiful thing growing between my former classmate Mateo and me over the past six months hasn't been wilted by distance and time since I was last on island. "He's good? He on his way up?"

The texts are buzzing in furiously. *You here? Meet me at Brewers when you can. Please, Nay. You need to be here. Won't believe what's happened,* they say.

"I think I'm on my way down," I say instead. "Teo's working. He's asking me to meet him at Brewers Bay. Something's going on down there."

"Lord. Well, take the car. Bring him some mangoes too," she

says as I shimmy down the tree. She's got a bucketful ready for me by the time I'm back on solid ground and dusted off appropriately. "Tell him not to wait too long with these. Too much time, and things spoil. He might want to keep that in mind." A pause. "You both might."

"Right, Ma." I decide to meet her thinly veiled insinuations with some of my own. "There are other things that probably shouldn't wait for too much longer, either. We still need to talk. About Daddy and his—"

"Right," she echoes, cutting me off. She links her arm through mine, and I'm struck by the matching tones of our skin, like polished mahogany, as she rubs some sap off of the back of my hand. "Oh! Before I forget. Look for some Flamboyant flowers while you're down there, please? I like to keep a bunch in my vases, and since the tree down the street is gone see if you could find some for me, love."

All I can do is stare—at the bucket of mangoes by her feet, at the pleading behind the smile on her face.

"We'll have plenty of time to talk later," she assures me. "Go on down to Brewers. And don't forget meh flowers, eh?"

I mutter my own reassurances to her while I pile the mangoes into a bag. Mateo and I have both been looking forward to my visit for weeks, but his texts are never filled with this level of urgency, and he almost never sends them when he's on a shift. I wonder what this is about—and why he would think that whatever's happened down on the bay would require the services of a food journalist like me.

But, hey. At least for once, in my first hours back, I get to go to the beach.

I note as I drive down the hill to Brewers that finding Flamboyant flowers for my mother won't be a problem at all. The hillsides look like Christmas trees—rich greens dotted with spots of vibrant red. When I was little, my father told me the story of two Virgin Islanders decades before, flying over the St. Thomian hills in a tiny airplane and scattering hundreds of Flamboyant seeds across the island. I loved the idea of them tossing out seeds they'd probably never get to see grow entirely, leaving those gifts for those who'll come afterward. I loved the idea of a plant being a legacy.

Brewers Bay is lit up with an entirely different color. Both lanes are filled with blue police Chevys, most of which are flashing their neon lights. Officers and EMTs like Mateo fill the beach, talking into their radios and milling around on the sand. There's a group of them hovered down at the water's edge, crowded around a rescue boat. Their deep blue uniforms are a soft contrast against the aquamarine water, and their very presence—and all the reasons that could be behind it—a sharper contrast against the waves and white sand.

I pull my parents' Explorer against the curb, making sure not to scratch or smudge Daddy's new tires, and look out over the shoreline. There must be at least twenty first responders on the beach, as well as a sizable crowd of onlookers and—I'm noticing cameras on tripods and audio equipment, so these must be my people: press. There's a police officer keeping the civilian crowd closer to the road, away from the rescue boat anchored close to the shore. Mateo was right, this certainly is something. I'm starving, and it takes everything in me to ignore the bunches of fuzzy sea grapes growing along the edges of the beach and make my way down toward the crowd on the sand. I'm halfway there when I hear someone calling my name.

It's been a while since I've seen Coziah Hodge, but she's only become more unmistakable than ever. In the decade since I interned at her fledgling online newspaper, she's doubled in size, cut off all but three inches of her hair and dyed it a deep red, and traded in her contacts for wide frames the same color as her hair. Her newspaper's grown too. Back when I'd interned for her the summer before I'd left for college, she was struggling to get reporters, to get interviews; to get readers to check out her page. Now the *Conchshell Chronicle* boasts thousands of readers—with paid subscriptions— from all over the islands and the world. She walks up from the crowd and greets me with a hug that feels as soft and giving as the mangoes in my mother's tree. Yeah, Cozi's presence has grown plenty, but to me, she'll always be the person who welcomed a curious seventeen-year-old into her one-room "office" in the back of her sister's nail salon and gave all the advice and experience she could. Like those two men on the plane—scattering seeds for later.

"Nay-Nay! Wait, you been on island an' you ain' call me?" she greets me.

"Meh plane jus' land, Cozi. Not even three hours ago."

A healthy guffaw. "An' you already down here? Already found the action? Look you!"

"What can I say? I only learn from the best."

"Well, I only teach the best, okay, love?" She takes a step back and grins at me. "I've been watching your show on EAT TV, Naomi. Oh, I love it so much. The interviews are truly something."

"Easy to ask questions when we're talking about food and drinks and seasoning."

"Yes, but you always ask the right ones. I really did teach you well." The smile fades. "Seriously, though. Were you jus' driving by and got curious? Or did you hear about what's happening down here?"

"Mateo called me. I . . . don't know if I've told you how close he and I have grown in the past few months . . ."

"You haven't," Cozi says. Her words are straightforward, but there's a question in her voice and a sparkle in her eyes.

"Yeah. I . . . well, I'm down here to see him, and to deal with some other things with my parents. Mateo's an EMT. He texted me to come here to Brewers, but he didn't give me any details, Cozi. What is all this?"

Coziah exhales slowly, then links her arm through mine and begins to walk us toward the crowd. "Li'l background. I assume you know about the storm last week."

"Yeah, Tropical Storm Blaine, right?"

"Yup. Formed right over us. It was just a barely organized tropical depression until—bam, just like that, it's a named storm with a little eye and all. This all happened within five hours of it hitting us. No one was prepared. 'S a blessing it wasn't any worse."

"Same thing my parents said. They hadn't boarded up or anything. They had trees down and some flooding in the back, but it could've been a lot worse. My . . . uh, Mateo; he worked for like, three days straight."

"So, he's 'my Mateo'? Well, sah! We gon' circle back to he, okay?" Cozi says suggestively as we walk. "Lemme finish telling you about this here. About a day after the storm passed, some people cleaning up Lindbergh Bay found a small fishing boat that drifted in from the sea. Flipped over, no one inside. Police checked out the boat's registration number and they learned the boat's owner was Lewiston 'Lucky' Simons." She spits out the name like a bitter piece of fruit. "Lord. Ah sorry. *Senator* Lewiston 'Lucky' Simons."

My eyes are already rolling. "Um. *Former* senator Lewiston 'Lucky' Simons. Unless I missed something."

"You didn't. 'Former' is right. Not to hear him tell it, though. Talking to him, it's clear he thinks he never left. And by 'left,' I mean 'got thoroughly rejected by hundreds of voters.' He came in like—tenth in the last two election cycles. You've met him before, right?"

I have. It's an experience I still regret. I'd first met him when he still went by Lewiston "De Sign Man" Simons and his biggest claim to fame was running a sign shop in town on one of the narrow streets behind the Market Square pavilion. Daddy took me with him there once when I was fourteen, when he was trying to order some colorful business cards and a car decal for his tour and sightseeing service. "De Sign Man" had originally charged one price, but after catching a glimpse of Daddy's tricked-out, brand-new tour van, an extra two hundred dollars got added to the final bill—something he'd tried to pass off as a typo due to "slippery fingers." Once Daddy threatened to use his own slippery fingers to call the Department of Consumer Affairs, the charge was taken off. The sleaze associated with him in our minds remained. Seemed like everyone on island had a story like that about "De Sign Man"— but then, about two years after Daddy and I walked into his shop, the man got struck by lightning and survived. He was playing golf on St. Croix and didn't clear the course quickly enough. I'd seen it as kind of a divine indictment, but other people saw it as a sign of strength; of him being "chosen" or something like that. Man changed his nickname to "Lucky" and served—poorly—as a senator for years.

"Unfortunately," is all I say to Coziah. "Shit. Did he drown out there at sea?"

"Well, he wasn't at his shop or his home. His girlfriend said she hadn't seen him since the day of the storm. Then a couple of fishermen said they saw him launch in Frenchtown the same day the storm hit. Coast guard's been searching for him for five days now. First as a rescue, then they started to hint that it might wind up being a recovery. So, when we got the call to come down here—"

"You're thinking they found him. His body."

"We don't know what they found. But with a presence this big, what else could it be?" Coziah flashes her Press badge at the cop standing between the crowd and the action down at the shoreline, and casually walks me to the front of the group. "Look behind us," Cozi whispers. "Bunch of them are wearing his campaign T-shirts."

There's another police officer, big guy sweating his light blue uniform shirt a couple shades darker, making his way up the sand toward us—so the glance I take behind me is quick. Cozi is right. Besides the ten or so who are obviously reporters, most people in the crowd are wearing gray shirts with "Time to get LUCKY! . . . into the Senate" printed across the back in bright green letters. It takes everything in me not to roll my eyes, not when so many of them look distraught.

"Ahem. Can I get everyone's attention?" the officer calls out. The low chatter stops, and several microphones and cameras click on. "Some of you done know—ah, *already* know I'm Lieutenant Emery Oliver. I've been authorized to speak to you all about the events that transpired here today."

The lieutenant looks like he's trying his best to balance formal speaking in front of the cameras with the desire to hurl every expletive he can think of at the heat and the sand. He takes a moment to mop his brow with a handkerchief that already looks soaked and continues. "Ah. Okay. So, this morning, 'round five A.M., the pilot of a plane delivering newspapers from St. Croix noticed something unusual on Saba Island as she was flying over it to our airport. She made an official call to the—"

"'Scuse me, can I interrupt?" An older guy with blondish hair calls out from behind Coziah. "Nolan Kirby, *Daily News*. Why was a plane leaving St. Croix flying all the way over Saba to get to St. Thomas? Isn't the island of Saba a good three, four hours eastward by ferry, over by St. Eustatius and St. Barths?"

Lieutenant Oliver sucks his teeth and gives Nolan Kirby an especially nasty stare for keeping him in the heat for an extra ten seconds. "You ain' been here long, eh? Clearly you don't know—" He seems to remember the cameras in the middle of his sentence and tries again with a sheepish smile. "Apologies. As a—a clarification, I'm not referring to Saba, Dutch Caribbean; I'm talking about Saba Island, one of deh—ah, deh cays out there that we can see far out in the distance from the shore. It's the bigger one. The one to the west." He gestures to the peaks way out on the horizon, two of the tiny uninhabited islands that surround the West End. "The pilot thought that there may be a person in distress on the cay. The coast guard and VIPD jointly deployed two rescue boats. In the early morning light, one of the rescue boats struck some low-lying rocks. Three EMTs were thrown into the water."

A murmur goes through the crowd like a breeze through leaves. Lieutenant Oliver takes the opportunity to run the dripping kerchief over his face again, and then continues. "More rescue teams were deployed. In the end, one person was rescued from the shoreline of Saba Island. That individual is former senator Lewiston Simons."

The screams begin before Lieutenant Oliver finishes saying the name. "Praise GOD!" someone yells, and there's applause and happy wailing behind me. They're all reacting somehow, even the reporters are scribbling on pads or talking hurriedly into their recorders, and in the middle of that is when I finally see Mateo.

He's ten yards behind Lieutenant Oliver with a group of other EMTs. They're all standing close together, listening to the officer as intently as the rest of us are, but it's their posture—it's Mateo's posture—that hits me hard. He's always been sturdy, as long as I've known him—firm and rooted and upright, with a crown of wild curls grafted from his Trini Indian father and Crucian mother. But right now, he looks like my mother's plants when they haven't been watered nearly enough. They all do. They aren't cheering with the rest of the crowd. I think that's why I call out to Lieutenant Oliver. I think that's how I know there's more to the story.

"Excuse me—Lieutenant?" I shout. Cozi turns to me, confused, and I grab her hand. "Naomi Sinclair, for—um—special reporter for the *Conchshell Chronicle*. Sir, can you please elaborate on the condition of the three EMTs who fell off the rescue boat?"

"Good one, Nay," Cozi whispers as the crowd quiets down.

Lieutenant Oliver lets out a long breath. "I'm not authorized to give too much detail about that at this point. But. I can share that the rescue fleets were able to rescue two of the EMTs thrown from the boat. Um. We . . . jus' learned—not even fifteen minutes ago now—we jus' learned that the third individual, uh, unfortunately expired despite the best efforts of the emergency personnel. And it's always rough when we lose someone, you know, in the line of duty. We're, uh, we gon' be dealing with that. Overall, though, the goal of the rescue mission was a success. Like I said, we brought Mr. Simons back."

"Cory Venzen, Channel 5 News. Can you tell us more about Senator Simons's condition?" a voice yells out from behind me, as if he didn't hear the first part of the lieutenant's statement.

"Is Lucky okay?" screeches one of the supporters.

Lieutenant Oliver doesn't get a chance to respond. He opens his mouth, but before he's able to say anything, applause and whoops ring out from the crowd. I immediately see the reason why. Limping up the sand from the rescue boat, holding on to a stocky police officer for support but grinning triumphantly, is former senator Lucky Simons.

I've always thought that Lewiston Simons looked more like a skinny circus clown than a statesman. He's awkwardly bony and has a hairline that pulls back more than the waves at low tide. The years haven't exactly been kind to his mismatched features and the hair he still has left, which is decidedly more salt than pepper at this point. But he's grinning like he's expecting his face on headline news and the front page—which, at this point, might not be such a wild expectation. Lieutenant Oliver steps back and grins.

"Perhaps, uh, Senator Simons can tell you heself," the lieutenant says, clapping a little as his colleague helps Lucky to the central spot in front of the crowd.

"Nuttin' could stop you, Lucky!" a man in the crowd bellows, which starts another round of cheering and whistling. Coziah mutters something ugly under her breath.

"Thank you, thank all of you for being here for me today," Lucky Simons addresses the crowd. His voice is raspy, but I sense that the energy in the crowd is powering the electricity that crackles through it. "I . . . was blown off course during Tropical Storm Blaine las' week when I went out fishin'. Wound up spendin' some time out there on . . . on Saba. Thanks to the determination of our first responders, I'm here today. 'S a shame about the one young man, deh . . . EMT; may he res' in peace. His bravery won't be forgotten. As fuh me, I'm a li'l dehydrated an' all, but I spent my fair share of time in the bush as a child. Lots of time outdoors. I was able to keep mehself fed from some of the local flora that—"

"HER bravery," a voice cuts him off. I look off to Lucky's right, and my eyes go wide. It's Mateo. He's walked away from the rest of the EMTs to address the former senator. His face is twisted like an angry vine. "The EMT that died today on your rescue mission, she was a woman. HER rest. HER peace. An' she had a name too, sir. It was—"

"Teo!" I call out. I step away from Coziah and the rest of the crowd and run across the sand to him. "Mateo, you can't—you need to stop now, love. Please—"

"I understan' you're upset, son," Lucky Simons says to the crowd as I slip my arm around Mateo's waist.

"Naomi." Mateo's voice is quiet, but his words are hot. "He has to know. He's talking about her like she's—like her life was just a necessary sacrifice for him to be here today. He has no idea who she was."

"He doesn't. He has no clue," I whisper back. "But you can't say her name, love; not here, not now. Not in front of the cameras. Her family probably doesn't even know yet, Teo. Please, just walk away with me, okay?"

He runs a hand over his face and lets out a long breath. "Okay. Yeah. Let's—I can't listen to this anymore. I can't stay here. I need to—"

"We're walking," I cut him off, pulling him away from the crowd in the direction of the quiet end of the beach.

"Let's give a hand to that young man; the lieutenant says his name is Matthew Ramakumar—ah, Mattoo Ramkyumar—an' to all of our hardworking first responders," Lucky Simons's nauseating voice rings out behind me.

And they do. They clap for Mateo and for all the other uniformed helpers on the beach. I doubt Teo hears any of it. I hold him tight as we walk away. I let him cover his face and sob. It makes me think, as we walk away from the circus behind us, about how these past few months with Mateo have been all toasts and twilight. They've been dancing and dinners when we're together and hours-long phone and video calls when we're not. Surprise visits. Jokes. Gifts in the mail. There's been nothing like . . . this. And I think about how wonderfully things can sprout and grow when there's abundant sunshine, but how it's the rain that makes them bloom.

In the end, we drive. We get in Daddy's new car and leave the beach behind. Twenty minutes later and with half the island between us and Brewers, we finally stop under the enormous Flamboyant tree at the Drake's Seat overlook, which is blooming in all its crimson glory. The full red flowers mean we can barely see the expanse of Magens Bay and the Atlantic way out beyond us, but that's okay. It's fine. I gather flowers for my mother while Mateo gathers his composure. And when he's ready and my arms are full of foliage, he and I talk about Consuelo Rivera.

"She was young. Think she graduated high school two, three years ago," he says quietly from where we sit on the stone wall. "Sway lived for this job, though. Put her all into it, every day. She didn't deserve to go out like this, mehn . . ."

"I know, Teo. I know."

"Yeah. She and I were real cool too. She had a girlfriend, Nessa. We'd—um—help each other out, give each other advice. Those earrings I sent for your birthday? She helped me pick those."

"She had good taste," I tell him.

"Damn good taste. She did." He sniffs. "She was tired, I think. Overtired. She and I, we'd done a long, tough rescue after the storm. That's the one I told you about. The two tourists on the inflatables."

"The ones you were looking for on the wrong island?"

"Yes! They got swept over from Morningstar Beach to the other side of Water Island. We looked all over the east side of Hassel Island. They were way, way farther west than we'd thought. Anyway, Sway worked with me on that one too. You know I had las' night off—until I got called in this morning for this whole situation with Lucky Simons—but she worked. She'd been working. To the point of exhaustion. I think when she hit the water, she just couldn't . . ." He clears his throat. "Giovanni and Jehron barely made it out alive."

"Were you on the crew that rescued them?" I ask.

He makes a sound that—under different circumstances—might have been considered a laugh. A hollow one. "Nah. Nope. I was on the crew that rescued Lucky Simons from Saba Island."

"No way."

He shrugs. "The coast guard boat wound up having to stop and help Giovanni's team when their boat hit the rocks and capsized. So, four others plus me, we got called in to finish going out to Saba for Lucky. His name did him good, boy. There's no fresh water on Saba. No trees . . . just a lot of low bush. Another twenty-four to forty-eight hours, and we might have been having a very different conversation." He pauses for a beat. Two. "Naomi. We *should* be having a very different conversation. Sway should be the one walkin' up the beach with everyone cheering, and Lucky should be the one lyin' up there in . . . in . . . my God, I jus' . . .

I keep thinking about all her plans. Everything she wanted to do. All she was supposed to become. That she's gone and he still here, it jus' ain' right."

My phone is buzzing again, and I look down at the texts on my screen. "Looks like he's feeling well enough to give interviews. Coziah just texted me. *Conchshell Chronicle* got the first interview slot with him first thing tomorrow morning. She asked if I want to join her. I never liked the man, but . . . I mean, I gotta admit, I am curious about what he ate over there those four days. I have a show planned for next month about survival food."

"You think you'll do it?"

"I don't know. I . . . still haven't gotten to talk to my parents yet. You know. About—"

"Aw. Man. I called you down to the beach; of course you didn't have time. I'm sorry." He slides an arm around my waist. "Just remember, please, don't tell them that I was the one who told you, all right? When we showed up with the ambulance that day, they both begged me not to tell you about the accident. It could've been so much worse, and I'm glad it wasn't. But Nay, he doesn't need to be behind the wheel of anything anymore. The tree and their car, they were both wrecked."

"They're trying to blame the tree being gone on the storm, and they're saying the new car is their anniversary gift to themselves. But—God, those pics you sent me, Teo . . ."

"Yeah. Going on three weeks ago now, so their tree didn't look anything like—you know, like *this*." He gestures to the canopy of red above our heads. "The hood and windshield of your dad's car, they were covered in the branches and the leaves and . . . must've been hundreds of green buds. I kept thinking . . . I dunno, jus' how sad it was that your mom wouldn't get to have her flowers this year. They never got their chance. And—shit, I'm making a mess of this, but—today, with Sway, I'm feeling the same thing. She'll never—she won't get the chance to—"

He reaches out and touches the flowers in my arms, and I nod. I know how the sentence is supposed to end. "I'll do the interview tomorrow with Lucky, Mateo. I'll tell him who Consuelo was. He should know."

"Thank you," he says quietly. I let my head settle on his shoulder. We can't see the sun above us through the thick bunches of flowers and branches, but we can feel it on the tops of our heads, on our shoulders and legs. Warming us from above. Growing us into our very best selves.

Daddy isn't having it the next morning. "If you're going out Fortuna to talk to that thief Lucky Simons, I'm driving you, Naomi. You already put a dent in the trunk of my car," he fires at me as I scoop the rest of my oats into the trash bin.

"I absolutely didn't, Daddy. That dent was already there. It lines up with the handle on the gate. And I always pull in forward. I don't reverse," I tell him.

He snorts. "Well, I didn't back into the gate. I might get close, but I never touch."

"You want to drive me? Fine. I need to talk to you about a few things anyway."

"You know what? I need to go to the nursery today. I want to add some color to the garden and replace the lime tree that blew over," Ma interjects. The grin she flashes at us is more desperate than pleasant. "We can all go, right, Val? We'll drive Naomi to the interview, and then afterwards you both can help me pick some new flowers."

"That dent isn't new," I whisper to her as we follow him outside.

"Maybe not, dear. You want to bring Senator Simons some plums? They jus' got ripe. So sweet this year. And filling," she answers. Right. Filling. In more ways than one—that hole in our conversation, plugged right up.

This is how all three of us wind up driving out west to Lucky Simons's house, with me reminding Daddy to stay off the yellow lines and mind the stop signs while my mother jabbers on about her guava crop from the back seat. I think we're all relieved when we finally pull into a driveway with a tall iron fence twenty minutes later. Lucky Simons's house sits at the top of a small knoll, one that faces south down the mountain to the open Caribbean Sea and the tiny cays way out beyond the airport runway. As I walk up the driveway to where Coziah waits for me on the covered porch, I can see Saba Island way out in the distance, and another smaller rock off to the east, Flat Cay. They rise out of the choppy blue water like enormous sea monsters. I wonder if they've haunted Lucky in the few hours since he's been home.

"Family field trip today?" Cozi greets me as I walk up the tiled stairs to Lucky's porch. She's in bright yellow today.

"Let's not even get into that," I mutter. "Damn. Lucky's house is nicer than I thought it would be. Looks new. Look at that roof."

"If you're impressed by the house, wait till you see his girlfriend," Cozi whispers. "I mean—it don't take much to be out of Lucky's league, but she look like she playin' a whole different sport."

Cozi isn't exaggerating, I realize, when the front door opens. The woman behind it can't be much older than I am. Short haircut, flawless makeup, huge earrings. One could probably mistake her for Lucky's daughter, except she has none of the unfortunate features Lucky's saddled with. She breaks into a cool smile and nods at us.

"Oh! I know you, Ms. Sinclair. I watch your show," the woman says when Cozi tries to explain who we are. "And *you*—I remember you from Tradewinds Bless. Asian shrimp salad and a Hummingbird, no cherry."

"Ah. Yes. Lynelle, right? Bartender?" Cozi asks.

"Close. Lydia. And I used to waitress," the woman answers as we follow her through the front door into an expansive living room. The house has a lovely open floor plan, with dark granite in the kitchen and furniture I know couldn't have been purchased on island. "That was before I met Lucky, though."

"You're not at the restaurant anymore?" I ask. She leads us down a hallway. Eight-foot doors, fourteen-foot ceilings; dishwasher in the kitchen—a *dishwasher*, on an island where wasting water could easily count as the eighth cardinal sin. No money was spared on this place. Damn.

"Lucky lets me work on my YouTube channel full time," she says. "That way, when he gets back into the Senate, we can be a . . . Lord, what was it he came up with? Oh, yes—a 'power couple.' His own words, han' to God."

I open my mouth to respond to that, but she's grinning so proudly that I bite my words back. "Wow. That's unbelievable," I try instead. Cozi looks like she's trying to stifle a laugh.

"Right? He's always coming up with li'l phrases like that. Such a mind. Listen, Ms. Sinclair, don't let me forget to give you my information before you leave. In case you ever want to work together on a project."

"Come in!" The voice ringing out from behind a door saves me from having to fake agreement. It's the same raspy-but-powerful voice from yesterday on the beach. Lydia pushes the door open, and there, sitting behind a large mahogany table in a home office that looks out over the water, is Lucky Simons.

"Thank you for coming," he says. He stands to greet us. Man's got on a suit, which only makes him look like a formal potato. "I see you've met Lydia. Go on, dear. Tell them what you do on your Twitter—your, ah, YouTube show."

"I make trail mix," she tells us. "From scratch. With seeds and dried fruits and stuff like that."

"Seeds and fruits you grow yourself?" I ask.

Lydia wrinkles her nose. "I get them from the store," she says to me as if I've suggested she flies them in from Neptune. "I jus' . . . you know, I put it all together myself. From scratch. Oh, and then I add my . . . what did you call it, Lucky? My personal . . . ?"

"Signature," Lucky supplies.

"Yes! My signature seasoning blend. It jus' means it's a recipe I came up with myself. Lucky gets me the best cinnamon, the best turmeric, the best lemongrass and cloves and cayenne and garlic and—"

"She's very talented," Lucky tells me, breaking into a slimy smile. He gestures to two plush chairs on the other side of the table. "You'd be very prudent to have her on your show sometime."

"We appreciate you giving us this interview this morning," Coziah says, saving me again from having to say something I don't mean. "You'll be telling this story all day. I'm happy I'll get to hear it first."

"Of course, dahlin'. I'm just thrilled to have two such . . . exquisite young ladies in my presence. Definitely a sight for these ol' eyes."

I'm not sure I can hide my revulsion so well, so I turn to take a glance over at Lydia instead. She's standing before an enormous professional-grade printer in the corner, taking small slips of paper out and packing them into a box. If she heard Lucky, she doesn't react.

"I imagine you're exhausted, Mr. Simons. Why don't you start by telling me your story? What happened that morning when you got into your boat?" Coziah asks.

"As you may know, I've been an avid fisherman for decades," Lucky begins. "Saturday morning began jus' like any other. I like to get out on my boat ahead of storms—I always seem to catch the best fish a few hours before things really get out of hand with the weather. Do either of you girls fish?"

He's asked the question in the same voice men have used to

buy me drinks at clubs. My father taught me how to fish when I was barely old enough to walk, but Cozi and I both respond with headshakes. "You should come out with me sometime. It's truly an invigorating experience. Anyway, the storm blew in fast an' hard. I was pretty far out. Couldn't get back to shore. The waves pulled me out, and then threw the boat over and I went with it. I was wearing my life vest, but the current—the waves kept crashing over me an' pulling me this way and that. Felt like I was in the water forever."

"When did you get to Saba?" Cozi asks.

"Later that day. Almos' night. The storm had mostly passed by then. I was still in the life vest, but exhausted and cold. I fought to get to that shore, though. And I made it. They don't call me 'Lucky' for nothing."

It's twenty more minutes of the same—Cozi, asking questions about Lucky's experience in the water, and Lucky, purring answers back to her like a slippery cat. He's in the middle of answering a question about yesterday's rescue when he turns his skinny body in the chair and settles his eyes on me.

"What about you, dear? Haven't heard much from you. You jus' here for moral support?" he asks.

"Um, no . . . I'm here to learn about what you ate when you were on the island," I answer. "I'm not a reporter, like Ms. Hodge. I write about food."

"I see. Then let's talk. I know how to get what I need from the land. I believe the correct term for that, honey, is a . . . environmentalist."

"Uh, sure. If you say so." I clear my throat. "So, there doesn't seem to be much to eat on Saba Island. Tell me about what you were able to find."

"There's plenty to eat if you have the know-how, love. I always keep a small bag of nuts in the pocket of my life jacket. I made those last me the first day. Second day the storm brought in some sargassum."

"Oh, that makes sense," I say. "Eating the sargassum. You know, some people—"

"No, no, chile, you can't eat that stuff! No, no, no. You say you write about food? You can't eat seaweed. There are all kinds of toxins in ocean plants. What I did was find some li'l crabs and fish that had been tangled up in them. Protein, you know?"

All I can do is nod. The gulp of water Cozi's taking from her canteen seems conveniently timed.

"By day four, though, my resources were getting slim. I was feeling a little desperate, so I went for a walk over the main part of the island to see if I could find any fruit trees or so on. There were none to be found. Except . . ."

"Except . . . ?"

"You're young but are you familiar with what the ol' people call 'lizard food'?" he asks.

I am. Small, warty orange pods with bitter red seeds inside. My mother still grows them—intentionally—to keep pests away from the more palatable fruits in her garden. "You ate those?" I ask him. "How many?"

He chuckles. "You young people don't realize those are edible, do you? They're certainly not poisonous. I ate several of them. They're not tasty, but they are what kept me alive for those last few hours before the rescuers arrived. You know, I should—"

"Luck. Remember you have that man from Channel 12 coming by in a few minutes," Lydia pipes up from her spot by the printer.

"Ah, yes," Lucky says. She pads over to him and puts something into his outstretched palm. "Sadly, it looks like our time together is through. But before you leave, let me congratulate you both on being the first to receive these. They're my new campaign cards. I jus' took the picture at dawn this morning over at Drake's Seat, an' printed the cards jus' now. Anything I can do at the shop, I can do here at home too. So here. Take one. Take several, for your friends. Let's make lightning strike twice, together!"

I leave Lucky's house disgusted. Disgusted by the man himself and by the ostentatious card he's shoved into my hand—a gorgeous, unobstructed view of the entire expanse of Magens Bay, marred only by Lucky's mismatched face and the huge Lightning Can Strike Twice sign he's holding. Disgusted by myself for not doing what I'd promised Mateo, for not even bringing up Consuelo Rivera. After saying my goodbyes to Cozi and making plans to meet up for drinks later, I slide into the passenger seat of the car next to Daddy and sigh.

"Can you believe this?" I hand him one of Lucky's cards. "Man barely crawled off that island alive, and he's already campaigning this morning. Already turning his ordeal into a—an election plat-form. God. He's so gross."

"Well, they're always campaigning, love. Did you give him the plums?" my mother asks from the back seat.

My father sits silently in his seat studying the card. Long enough for me to notice he's engaged the emergency brake, but the car's in neutral instead of park. "This just isn't right," he mutters, handing the card back to me.

"I know, right? He's such a—" I stop midway. Daddy most likely meant Lucky's political ambitions, but something about his words strike me hard. Something about that card *isn't right.* I take a closer look at the slip of card stock in my hand. Lucky, the beach, the sign . . . and then it hits me. A truth that's been growing quietly in my mind since yesterday afternoon. One that's been rounding out and losing its green; one that's finally thick and full and ready to be picked. "Dammit, Daddy, you're right," I whisper. "Don't drive yet. I need to call Teo."

The next time I knock on Lucky's door—six hours later—Lucky himself is the one who answers, not Lydia.

"Ms. Sinclair?" he asks through the crack. He's looking at me the way iguanas look at my mother's mangoes. "Well, well. I didn't think I'd see you again so soon. Mus' admit, it's quite a pleasant surprise. Perhaps you an' I could—"

"Mr. Simons. I—think Lieutenant Oliver has some questions he'd like answered first," I say quietly. Lucky opens the crack a little wider to see Emery Oliver and two other officers standing beside me, and his face falls. He opens the door wider, and the four of them head inside toward Lucky's living room.

Cozi's behind me on the steps. Her bright red lips—made up to match the scarlet color of her hair—twist into a smile. "You know once this breaks, everyone is going to be calling you for interviews."

"Glad I could give you the scoop. They'll call, but I . . . I came down to spend time with Mateo and to deal with some stuff with my parents. I don't really want to spend the rest of my trip talking to the media," I tell her.

"I see your parents waiting in the car for you. So, let's make this quick, then," she tells me, pulling out her phone and easing herself down onto the steps. I settle next to her and nod. She pulls up her recording app and hits start.

"Tell me what made you suspect something wasn't right about Senator Simons's account," she asks.

"It was the card, Cozi. His campaign card, the one he gave me this morning during the interview. It's a picture of him standing at Drake's Seat, looking out over Magens Bay. He's holding a huge sign that says Lightning Strikes Twice."

"You think the sign referred to his ordeal on the golf course twelve years ago, and then also to his rescue from Saba Island."

"Exactly," I tell her. "The thing is, he told us he printed those cards this morning. Took the picture at dawn. And the card does show a sunrise. He was wearing the same suit at our interview. It all looked right. Except for the tree."

"The tree?"

"The Flamboyant tree at Drake's Seat. It's blooming now. The flowers are everywhere—you can barely see anything past them. But in the picture, the tree wasn't in bloom. The seeds weren't ripe. The buds were still green. You can see the beach in full. And so . . . I started to think that maybe, Mr. Simons took this picture a few weeks ago. Which means that his whole ordeal was planned."

"That's a big accusation to make, Naomi."

"Yeah. It was a big hunch. So, I called Mateo. I talked to my parents. And we . . . um . . . we put some things together." I pause. "That storm last week, Blaine, it was unexpected. The intensity and the organization. Everyone said it was supposed to be weaker than it turned out to be. Mateo and some other EMTs, including Sway Rivera, had a rescue the other night that involved two tourists who had drifted away on their inflatables during the storm. They were looking for them all over Hassel Island, but the storm had pulled them much farther west than anyone expected. I started to think that . . . well, maybe Lucky intended to get shipwrecked for a day or two. For the attention. He knew the storm was coming and it was the perfect situation. But he didn't count on it being as strong as it wound up being, and maybe he hadn't intended to wind up on Saba."

"So . . ."

"So, Mateo and a couple of officers went out there on Teo's boat this afternoon. They didn't go to Saba, though. They went to the little rock east of it. Flat Rock Cay. And they found something. A bag." I pull out my phone and show her the photos Mateo sent to me earlier that day . . . a small brown bag, carefully stashed in a hollow under a tree on the rocky shoreline of Flat Rock. A couple bottles of water inside. A flare. A bag of chips and a few bags of what looks like homemade trail mix—cashews, almonds, pretzels, and chocolate, all covered in specks of a myriad of spices. "It sure looks like a 'just in case' bag. They haven't proved it's Lucky's . . . yet. But they'll be looking for prints. His and Lydia's, especially if that trail mix has her—you know, her 'signature spice blend' all over it."

"If they can make a case against him, they can convict him for fraud. Wasting police resources and such," Cozi says.

"Worse. They can charge him with Consuelo Rivera's murder," I say. "If he knowingly caused this situation, he put all those police officers and EMTs in danger when they rescued him. If she died as a result of that, it's his fault."

The door behind us swings open, and the officers walk out along with Lydia and Lucky, who looks decidedly less smarmy than he had earlier. I watch as they head toward the two Trailblazers at the bottom of the driveway next to my parents' car. Right before he opens the back door to one of them, Lucky turns his head and takes a long look over at Lydia, and then back at the house. I'm still trying to make sense of the expression on his face when Emery Oliver speaks up.

"Mr. Simons and Ms. Porter have agreed to continue our conversation down at Bournefield station," the lieutenant says to me with a tight nod.

"Are they—" Cozi begins, but Lieutenant Oliver waves her quiet.

"No arrests have been made yet. Thank you," he says.

"You may want to bring a change of clothes for him," I call out to him.

He turns back to me. "Sorry?"

"Lucky. I interviewed him earlier about what he ate over on Saba. He seemed to be pretty confident about his choices. But . . ."

Lieutenant Oliver wrinkles his nose. "But what?"

"He made the wrong ones. He should've eaten the damn sargassum. People eat it all the time. Hawaiians serve it with fish. It's edible right out of the sea. But the 'lizard food' . . . it's not jus' native to us over here. It grows in Asia too. It's called a bitter melon. The seeds taste awful, but they are edible. It's just that . . . well . . . if you eat too much of it, it can cause massive abdominal cramps and explosive diarrhea. I'm thinking those cramps should start hitting Lucky right about now."

Now the lieutenant's entire face is twisted. "Oh. Damn. Maybe I should . . . although, if he really did that shit, if he cause that girl Sway to die out there in the water like that, maybe he deserves what he gets." He nods and heads out to the squad car behind the others. "You have a nice night, ladies."

Cozi's already having trouble containing her laughter. "Wait, Nay. Are you—are you saying that Lewiston Simons is, at this very moment, full of—"

"Coziah! Your recording app's still on," I giggle. "Turn it off, and then finish your thought." She does. Both. And we laugh until we can no longer see the blue police lights heading down the mountain.

The light's low and the sun's setting by the time I finally make it back to my parents' car at the bottom of Lucky's driveway. "So, it's done," my father says as I slide into the passenger seat.

"Almost. They took Lucky down to the station to talk to him more. He might have to choose a different nickname after this, though."

"Right." My father sighs. Squints out into the distance. "Got a call when you were in there jus' now. From that boy."

"From . . . Mateo?" I ask.

"He was looking for you. But he an' I got to talking, and he thinks I should . . ." He stops talking. Sighs again.

"You know, he mentioned the mangoes. He said they were so tasty, and . . ." my mother begins. And then she stops too. "Val. Please, jus' tell her."

"Daddy?" I ask.

"It's my memory. My mind," he says to me. His eyes are still on the wheel, not on my face. "I know I'm not . . . an old man yet, but sometimes these things happen sooner than later. The doc . . . she called it early-on or something like that."

"Early onset Alzheimer's?" I ask quietly. My mother nods.

"Whatever. It means there are things I don't always remember or understand. It means I . . . there have been a few issues with things that were never a problem for me. Uh. In the house. Sometimes in the car." He pushes open his door. "So. Maybe it means we go back home an' talk about some things over dinner. Couple of things happened recently you should know about . . . the story of what really happened with our tree and our old car. And. Ah, maybe . . . maybe you drive."

My father isn't looking at me, but I'm looking at him, and I see it. Lucky's the epitome of rotten fruit, but there, on Daddy's face, is a milder version of what I'd noticed on Lucky's face earlier, what I'd seen in his eyes when he'd glanced back at Lydia and his sharp new home right before he'd climbed into the back of the police car. I think back to being in my mother's trees, picking overripe fruits, and I think I understand. It's what it feels like to be a day or two too long on the vine. It's the droop, the shrivel, the sickening sweetness of the beginning of decomposition. It's the realization that the prime has passed. It's the knowledge that you can only look back on your very best days in the sun.

WILLIAM BOYLE

New York Blues Redux

FROM *Black Is the Night*

Southern Brooklyn
August 1986

JANE THE STAIN takes her usual stool at the bar, and Widow
Marie brings over a shot glass, slops some rye in there, and then
grabs a cold beer out of the cooler. A cold beer on a hot day. Jane's
been waiting for it. Nothing better. First, she puts back the shot to
loosen herself up, to get rid of that feeling of hardness that fills
her while she's waiting. One sip and her insides go mushy. It always
feels like a miracle. Loaves and fishes–type shit. Turn the misery
into joy. Religion.

She follows the rye with a long swig of beer, while Widow Marie
pours her another shot. This is their routine. Bath Bar is home.

"How was the day?" Widow Marie asks.

"Three times I had to tell Duke to quit talking to me and go
back to work," Jane the Stain says, shaking her head.

"A bona fide chooch, that's what that guy is."

That's the extent of the conversation for now. There's no pressure to talk with Widow Marie, even though she likes her gossip.
A gift.

Jane the Stain works in the office at Duke's Garage on Harway
Avenue. Been there eight years now. Mostly she answers phones,
writes receipts, and orders parts. Duke's a well-seasoned douche-
bag. He hired her for her looks. He said he wanted his customers
greeted by a neighborhood beauty.

She was twenty-two when she started working at Duke's, and

she's thirty now. Before that, she worked at the Roulette Diner. She started drinking when she was a junior at Bishop Kearney. Joanne Genetti shared a six-pack of wine coolers with her after school in the park one day and got her hooked on the feeling. By senior year, she was going to bars in Bay Ridge. She tried college for four semesters, first SUNY Purchase and then SUNY Oneonta, but she skipped classes and drank in shitholes. She got straight As at drinking in shitholes. Other than that, college was a bust.

She came home to Brooklyn, moved back on the block with her mom and grandma, and got the job at the Roulette. Disco fries, rusty nails, torn Naugahyde booths—those few years passed in a blur, but booze was her constant companion. Pints secreted in her purse. Shots and beers here at Bath Bar after her shift ended.

Then there was Duke's, a job she got thanks to the bar gods. Duke had come in one night with his pal Sully. Duke was unhappily married to an angry little water bug of a woman named Linda. He set his sights on Jane and offered her a job. He'd flirted unabashedly with her since. He's suggested they sleep together at the Shore Motel. But he's never gone farther than talk, not in all these years.

It's her opinion that Duke just likes being around her, likes the promise of her, but he doesn't really want to sleep with her. He likes the rejection. It's like those ladies who wear high heels and stomp on the hands of hairy businessmen. *Look but don't touch. Let your temptation haunt you.* She's fine with playing that part.

The job's easy. She's in the office from eight until five Monday through Friday. She keeps a couple of fifths of rye in her bottom desk drawer just in case she really needs it, but she tries not to drink at work. She likes waiting until she's off the clock to drink. That's her personal code. It also gives her something to look forward to. Much of her morning is usually spent wrangling with a hangover anyhow, and she's not—strangely enough—a believer in the hair of the dog philosophy. Coffee's all that sets her right, even if it's just Folgers from that dirty old office drip machine.

Duke knows she drinks hard and doesn't give a damn when she's hungover. After all, she's not operating on hearts or trying not to misplace a kid. She's just fielding calls and scribbling on pads. She's never rude. The customers love her. Of course they do. Mr. Evangelista from up the block, who just croaked actually, used to bring his Buick Skylark in for oil changes monthly just to see her even though he never drove anywhere. He'd always bring her a gift too. Candies or a bottle of wine. There were others like that. Heartsick old-timers, for the most part. Occasionally there was a scrubby guy in his thirties who tried to talk sweet and flopped.

This beer's a rarity. She desires it now because of the heat. Usually, she sticks with rye and gin. And she doesn't eat much. She looks pretty much the same at thirty as she did at eighteen, give or take. She knows that won't last, but there's no use in worrying about it. Fact of the matter is that Alkie Eleanor down at the other end of the bar—slumped there, toothless, the only other person currently present in this unholy dive on this hot August night—well, that's her future and she's okay with it.

Jane the Stain is a nickname that, all told, she doesn't mind. Most of the guys who come around think it's something sexual. Like she walked into the bar with come stains all over her dress and never lived it down. Other bums think it's a period thing. Maybe she wore a pair of white pants to work and bled through. Men are fucking idiots, that's just a true fact.

It's actually a handle she got dealt as a kid. She was twelve. It was an August day in 1968 not unlike this August day. She was in the P.S. 101 schoolyard with Caroline Cavalcanti, Ocean Avenue Annie, and Half-Jewish Janice. They were riding bikes and playing with chalk, hanging out on the far end of the yard, which was like the deep end of the pool. A bunch of big girls came swaggering through the hole in the chain-link fence that served as an entrance, smoking, wearing cool jackets. Rita from the Benson Arms apartment building was their leader. She had buckteeth and wore a frayed plaid skirt, and the two Ellens, Carmela Mercado, and Tiny Nunziata flanked her. The rumors around the block were that Rita was a sex fiend and a junkie, that she'd screwed Dickie Sorel in someone's backyard and let Pasquale Pizzimenti film it with his brand-new Super 8 camera. She was there to start trouble. Trouble was her fun.

What happened was that Rita approached her and her friends under the guise of scoring a smoke. When Caroline, Annie, and Janice all shook their heads no to the question, ready to hop on their bikes and speed away, Rita looked ready to blow. But Jane wasn't intimidated. She isn't sure what exactly made her tough out of the gate, but she was most definitely born that way. Maybe something about just growing up with her mom and grandma, her old man out of the picture and on the skids somewhere far away. Instead of a simple no, she got up in Rita's face and told her to go buy her own cigarettes. She knew this wasn't about cigarettes at all, that it was a turf thing. Rita and her crew had dominion over this part of the schoolyard, and they didn't want these younger girls moving in. Jane knew that her only choices were to stand up now or to cower away forever. When Rita went for her bike, trying to kick the chain loose, Jane exploded. The short of it was that she was a scrappy little fighter. Her uncle Tony had taught her a few moves. The Ellens, Carmela, Tiny, Caroline, Annie, and Janice all watched, shocked as hell, as she beat the meanness out of Rita.

Jane was wearing a plain white cotton T-shirt that day. The last shot she landed bloodied her knuckles. Somehow, in the act of then setting her bike upright after leaving Rita defeated on the ground, she ran that hand across her chest, leaving a smear of bright blood. It looked like the mark of a warrior. She felt like a warrior. The Ellens carried Rita away. Caroline crowned Jane queen of the neighborhood. This part of the schoolyard was theirs forever, no beef from the older girls. Jane wore the T-shirt around with pride, never washing it. Kids started calling her Jane the Bloodstain. Eventually, they shortened it to Jane the Stain.

She still has the shirt too. She framed it the way you might frame a favorite worn-out band T-shirt and kept it hanging on her bedroom wall like a saint's relic. When she needed strength, having early on lost faith in God, she bowed at the altar of that bloody shirt, remembering that she was capable of slaying giants. Or at least bucktoothed sex fiends.

Sometimes she wonders whatever became of Rita. She only saw her a couple of times after that, never up close, her swagger deflated, and her status on the block and in the neighborhood hobbled. You don't just survive a beatdown like that. Rita got the shit end of the legend stick. *Some twelve-year-olds have nothing to lose,* the legend went. *The pecking order doesn't mean anything. Crazy trumps seniority. Watch out for Jane the Stain.* She wonders if Rita had to scurry away to Long Island or New Jersey, had to try to rebuild her reputation there.

When Widow Marie returns to pour Jane more rye, she comes bearing a gift. A scratch-off from Benny's and a dirty little nickel to do the necessary work. It's the kind made to look like a slot machine, scratching off the numbers as if pulling a lever. Gunning for Lucky Sevens or cherries or whatever.

This is also part of their routine. Instead of helping the poor or visiting old-timers at a nursing home, Widow Marie sometimes gives scratch-offs to her favorite customers to check off her good deed for the day.

Jane thanks her and starts rubbing at the scratch-off with the nickel. The black scrapings edge the ticket, and she blows them onto the bar.

She scratches slowly, purposefully.

This is a highlight of the night.

"Well?" Widow Marie asks. "How's it looking?"

"I won," Jane says. "It's not a big win, just the most basic one. Five bucks."

"There you go. Now you're on easy street. With five bucks you can move to the Bahamas."

"I'd miss this place too much." Jane tucks the ticket in her pocket. What she'll do with her winnings is buy a couple of packs of smokes. She'd been trying to quit but then she had a little sit-down with herself and really interrogated that decision. Why quit? What was she afraid of? What does she have to lose by smoking? She could use one now, actually.

She doesn't have a pack, so she goes down to the other end of the bar and snags one from Alkie Eleanor's pack of Pall Malls. Alkie Eleanor's head is down, and she's really sawing wood. People always borrow cigarettes from her. It is an acceptable thing to do at Bath Bar. Less a form of theft and more just Alkie Eleanor's contribution to the proceedings. Least she could do since her modus operandi is to black out, wake up occasionally and scream something incomprehensible, maybe fart or belch for good measure. The joint collectively puts up with a lot from her.

Widow Marie keeps a row of unlit religious candles back by the register. She fires one up now—the Virgin Mary glowing powder blue from the flame—and brings it to Jane. A lot of people are superstitious about lighting smokes from candles, saying it brings bad luck, but Widow Marie encourages it. She thinks the opposite's true. She thinks lighting a cigarette from a candle can change your whole day for the better. Jane is not sure how she ever came to such a conclusion, but she doesn't buy any stupid superstitious stuff anyway. How could lighting a cigarette from a candle or breaking

a mirror or spilling salt impact the world? Imagine. Like there's somebody up in the sky, keeping track of dumb shit. *We've got another monster lighting her cigarette from a candle. Better kill a sailor.*
Jane lights the cigarette and studies what the flames do to Mary in the dark bar. The shadows they make. She likes a good religious candle even though she's no longer religious. She also has a sweet spot for the old Virgin Mary.

The door to the bar swings open and in walks Double Stevie Scivetti. If Jane was asked to make a list of who she didn't want to see, Double Stevie would be at the top. But he's as unavoidable as bad weather. You might get a streak of nice days but then it's going to rain and rain hard. That's how it is with Double Stevie. She might go a stretch without seeing him at Bath Bar but their paths would cross at some point. He actually lives in the same apartment building that Rita used to live in, the Benson Arms, but he's older than Jane. She asked him once if he remembered Rita and he said he didn't, that he and his mom didn't move into the Benson Arms until '71.

Jane's had enough to drink now that she gets caught up thinking about what the fuck *Benson Arms* even means. The arms of Benson Avenue?

"Just exactly who I didn't want to see," Double Stevie says to her. He looks more frazzled and on edge than usual.

"Don't ruin my night," she says, taking a long drag off the Pall Mall.

Double Stevie runs with Sav Franzone these days. Sav would also be high on the list of guys she'd rather not encounter who are unavoidable. A block fixture. Married with a kid but always on the hunt for a piece. They'd hooked up once, a couple of years ago, when he didn't have the kid yet and his wife, Risa, was very pregnant. It was one of Jane's biggest regrets in that department. She'd gotten with a lot of guys she didn't like and even guys who had wives, but this was different because of that kid and because Risa was sweet. It had been in the midst of a bad drunk weekend for Jane. She remembered it only in flashes because she was buzzing on the edges of a blackout. He wanted to just borrow someone's car and go down to the dark stretch by Nellie Bly Park on Shore Parkway. They couldn't go to his apartment, obviously. Hers was tough too since she lived with her mom. They settled on the ladies' room in Bath Bar. She knew it was a mistake as it was happening.

A worse mistake than usual. But sometimes she's guided by a kind of hot loneliness in the totally wrong direction. This was one of those times. It was like closing your eyes while driving and drifting onto the opposite side of the road.

Even though her head was swirling from the booze, she remembers a lot about being up close in that dirty little stall with Sav. The smell of bad cologne dabbed on his neck. His rough hands, tugging and pulling. The way he tried to talk like a porno. How he'd called her a *puttana*. How she'd slapped him, and he begged to be slapped again. He lasted a minute and then left the stall. She threw up in the toilet, fixed herself up, and went out the back door into the alley, setting off the fire alarm. She dragged herself home and cried. The hot loneliness—the desperate yearning for physical connection with someone, anyone, the worst fucking person possible—had led to total despair, as it so often did. She didn't go back to the bar for a couple of weeks after that. The next time she saw Sav they barely acknowledged each other. Now she'd settled into feeling a seething hate toward him. Watching him with Sandra Carbonari some nights made her want to spit on him and tell him to go home to his wife and kid. Sandra was more than just young and stupid, seeming to get off on the cheating. She'd probably be in too at some point soon, in her cut-off shorts and halter top, hair done up nice at Bensonhurst Dolls, hours spent on makeup.

Double Stevie trudges past Jane down to where Alkie Eleanor is slumped, sitting on the stool next to her.

"You're back already," Widow Marie says to him.

He takes a twenty-dollar bill out of his pocket, puts it on the bar, and flattens it out with his fingers.

Jane watches through her cigarette smoke as he stares at the bill.

"Fuck's that?" Widow Marie says. "Your mom give that to you for snacks? You want a beer and a shot? You could buy a round for the whole joint." She motions around from one end of the bar to the other. Laughing. "Actually, I think Eleanor's good, so you could just get Jane."

"Twenty bucks," Double Stevie says, shaking his head. "You said there'd be more at Gilly's. A lot more."

"What're you on about, kid?"

"I want money. You said there'd be money, and you were wrong. Way I figure it is you owe me for the bad information."

"I don't even know what you're talking about." Widow Marie reaches under the bar and comes out with a Louisville Slugger. She pounds it in her hand.

This isn't an empty threat. Jane's seen her use the bat a couple of times. Once on Carlo Purpura, who'd pissed on the little Christmas tree that Widow Marie put in the corner every year. "You don't piss on Christmas," she'd said, dinging him in the knee. That was last call for Carlo. Marie banned him from Bath Bar, which took a special kind of hatred on her part. The other time was Johnny Saint Fort. He'd gotten up on the bar, pulled his pants down, and was swinging his wang around for a laugh. He had a pretty good rope on him, the tall bastard, and he could get some real movement on the thing. For all her degeneracy, Widow Marie was conservative when it came to bodies, so she took out the bat and slammed him in the ass with it. Johnny wasn't banned, but that was the last time he took out his wang at the bar.

"How much you got in the register?" Double Stevie asks.

"You're gonna rob me? I've got a bat, and you've got nothing but your pea brain."

Double Stevie stuffs the twenty back in his pocket, hops up on the bar, and then dives onto Widow Marie, fighting for possession of the bat.

Alkie Eleanor sits up, her eyes still half-closed, and says, "The goddamn raisins went bad two months ago. You can't use bad raisins. Every kid's gonna be puking on his shoes. Get new raisins, would you?"

Jane sighs and takes a pull of beer.

Double Stevie has overpowered Widow Marie and taken the bat from her. This is unusual, sure, but nothing much surprises Jane in a wild-card place like this. Widow Marie has been held up before, just never by a regular. Is that even what's going on? Or has Double Stevie just snapped? Maybe he's coming down off drugs. This is that kind of behavior. He stands, holding the bat at his side, and gets to work trying to open the register.

Widow Marie is splayed on the floor, groaning. "Oh, you fucker," she says.

This is a definite ban, Jane thinks.

"How do you open this old piece of shit register?" Double Stevie says.

It's a classic register. One of the big, old dramatic ones. Swimming with buttons and numbers and a locked till. Widow Marie always looks so small next to it.

"Put the bad raisins in the garbage," Alkie Eleanor says. "Don't worry about the wasted money."

Jane gets up.

"How do you open this thing?" Double Stevie says again. He pokes Widow Marie with the bat. "Come on. Open it."

"Go shit in the river," Widow Marie says from the floor.

Jane walks past Alkie Eleanor and crosses through the open space where the bar flap is turned up on its hinge. She sidesteps Widow Marie and makes her way next to Double Stevie. He holds the bat in a threatening way.

"Whoa, boy," she says. "I'm here to help."

"You know how to open it?" he says.

She nods.

"So open it."

She positions herself in front of the register as if she's about to get to work, like Duke under the hood of a car. Double Stevie's breathing hard. He's hungry for whatever's in the till. Instead of reaching out and popping the drawer, which is so easy that Double Stevie must be even dumber than she thought, she turns quickly and stomps his foot with her heel. He yelps in pain, drops the bat, and jumps back. She picks the bat up and swings it at him. Another doggish yelp. He climbs up on the bar, holding his elbow, cursing under his breath. Jane moves toward him, starts to swing again but pulls it back. "You should go," she says.

He jumps off the bar, taking down a stool, and slams his way out the door.

Jane sets the bat on the floor and helps Widow Marie up. "You okay?" she says.

"I'm good," Widow Marie says. "I didn't know I had my own security detail sitting right here."

"I'm pretty scrappy."

"Jane the Stain, a hero for our times. Drinks are on me."

"Double Stevie's banned, right?"

"Forever. I'm putting his name in the notebook now." Widow Marie follows through on that promise, scribbling Double Stevie's name in block letters in her Book of Bans.

Jane smiles and goes back to her side of the bar. A winning

scratch-off and her most triumphant defeat of a shitheel since taking down Rita in the schoolyard eighteen years ago.

Widow Marie puts on the radio. They listen to traffic, weather, and sports. The night hums along stupidly. Double Stevie's charades are in the rearview mirror.

Martina has come this far, so she might as well go all the way. Her grief has led her here. To this nothing block in end-of-the-line Brooklyn. To the man who'd shot Jerry. Sav Franzone. The name like glass in her mouth. It had all gone so wrong, this man getting into Jerry's life right after she'd come back to him. How'd it all get so wrong? She guesses it started wrong for her and Jerry. Maybe Sav killing Jerry was God's punishment.

How deeply she loved Jerry. Idolizing him as her stepbrother, turning into something else. Something unnatural, her mother and stepfather said. Something that needed to be hidden away. Making her a nun was their answer. They paid for shortcuts. The surprise of it was that she liked being a nun. She liked the solitude and the sisterhood. She liked letting go of *things*. There was a library at the convent, and she spent her time reading when she wasn't praying or working. She liked being in the garden most of all, tending to the fruits and vegetables. The convent is upstate in a town called Highland, close to the Hudson River. Nearby are apple orchards. The river is serene. She misses watching the river. It had been almost perfect there except that she kept on loving Jerry in her heart—she loved him more than she loved God and the other sisters—and that resulted in a sort of spiritual anguish that was always hiding under the surface. She saw Jerry in the trees, in the dirt, in the water. His voice came to her in storms. Her prayers to God turned into prayers to Jerry.

She went and found him in the city. His loft on Avenue A. They stayed tangled together for weeks. And then Jerry met Sav at a bar. They cooked up a scheme together to make money. Martina was against it; she had a bad feeling about Sav from the start. She was right. He found out about her and Jerry—what their relationship was—and threatened to blackmail them, to go to their rich parents in Connecticut. Jerry fought back. Or tried to.

That stupid gun. Sav wrestled it away from Jerry and shot him. Martina was stunned. She watched from the window as Sav ran away, dropping the gun in a sewer drain out on the street. Martina

had begged Jerry to get rid of the gun, but he'd had enough trouble
with junkies and muggers that he felt safer with it around. If he
didn't have it, nothing would have played out the way it did. Sav
didn't bring a gun. He would've tried and failed with his blackmail
scheme. So many sins. The sin of their relationship. Lust, pride.
The immorality of it. She knows. She knows forever. It's their relationship, the mess of it, the rottenness at its center, that really led
to all of this. Without their love, Jerry would be alive. Without their
love, Jerry would've likely never even moved to the city and got his
gun and crossed paths with Sav.

It hadn't been hard to find out where exactly Sav grew up. She
knew Brooklyn, but she didn't know the neighborhood. She called
a contact of hers at the diocese office to find out where he'd been
baptized. Her contact told her Sav had been baptized at St. Mary
Mother of Jesus on Eighty-Fourth Street. Once she had the name
of the church, it was easy enough to track him down. She called
the rectory at St. Mary's, spoke to a nice woman named Peggy who
answered the phones there, and asked if she had a number for
Sav's mother. The woman said, "Lola?"

Martina said, "Right. Lola."

"Around here, we think of Sav as Lola's son, not Lola as Sav's
mother." Peggy laughed, as if it were a joke only she understood,
but she gave Martina the number.

Next Martina started to ask a question and then purposefully let
it drift off: "Is Lola still over there on . . ."

"Bay Thirty-Fifth. Between Bath and Benson. A few houses
down from Sav and Risa. God bless Lola. She's got a lot on her
plate with Sav."

Martina got the exact house number and then thanked Peggy.
That Sav lived on the same block was pure luck. She hadn't imagined him as the kind of person with a house or an apartment. She
guessed that Risa was his wife, though she couldn't picture him
with a wife. He had blown into Jerry's life, into her life, a straggling
thing, a strange stranger.

Those calls were made while sitting next to Jerry's body. She
blessed him. She touched his head with holy water. She cleaned
away the blood and surrounded him with flowers she bought from
a market a couple of blocks away. She said the prayers she needed
to say. She turned the loft into a tomb.

It wasn't hard to fish the gun out of the sewer where Sav dumped it. He hadn't been careful. It was lodged on an outcropping of broken blacktop that had somehow affixed itself to the wall just below the grate. She reached it without much effort. She knew she needed that gun. She has it now in the black clutch she's carrying. The gun is small. She doesn't know anything about guns. She feels certain it will work when she needs it to.

She tries again to reconcile her desire for revenge with her vision of a loving, tender God. She can't. She feels so much rage as her feet move along the sidewalk on Sav's block. It's like electricity entering her from below. She's from the Old Testament. She's a flood, crashing over the concrete. Sav doesn't know it yet, but the water's gathering in his name. He won't have her pegged as the kind to come for blood, but here she is. She's wearing one of Jerry's plain black T-shirts and black pants she bought at a thrift store on Second Avenue. The shirt smells like him. God bless Jerry Malloy.

She says the address over and over in her head until she's standing in front of Sav's mother's house. The lights are on in the front window. It looks similar to other houses on the block. White siding. A brick front porch with a few wooden chairs set in a row. A black mailbox next to the door. Garbage cans inside the gate. A garden in the small front yard overseen by a plaster statue of the Virgin Mother. Our Lady of Sorrows. Heart pierced seven ways. The blue of her robe so vivid. Hands clasped across her stomach. Looking down at the dirt in the garden. Grieving. Lola. Dolores. Our Lady of Dolours. The Sorrowful Mother.

The sight of the statue stops Martina from reaching out and opening the gate. She, Mary, is a warning and a sign. Others grieve. Lola grieves. What would it be like to lose her son? What would it be like to be the person who strips her son from her? This is not Martina. She's no flood. She's a sad starfish clinging to a piling as waves crash around her.

Martina backs away from the front gate. What was she even going to do? Confront Lola about Sav? She scurries away down the block. She wonders which house is Sav's. She looks for his name on mailboxes.

When Martina comes to the bar on the far corner of the block, she thinks a drink might take the edge off. Drinking has never been something she's been against. She's always liked it, even— maybe especially—at the convent, where it wasn't allowed. She associated drinking with Jerry too. Those early days where they'd share a bottle of wine and go into the woods.

It's called Bath Bar, this little dive, which conjures the image of someone bathing in booze in some sort of tenement washtub. The sign out front is hand painted. *Bath Bar* in red curlicue script on a blue background. A cocktail glass painted next to the words. In the window is a neon beer sign with almost half the letters blown. It says GSEE AM ALE. The letters that aren't lit are still visible in the fading daylight.

Martina goes in and hunkers down at the bar. It's a bar full of women. *Full* is the wrong word. A mostly empty bar that happens to be inhabited by three other women and her. There's the bartender, a bulky woman, slouching and sturdy at the same time. Sitting not far from the bartender is a passed-out drunk. Martina can tell she's a lady by her shoes and ragged clothes. Then there's a somewhat normal-looking woman in her thirties on a stool nearby, looking like she just got off work and is already in the midst of really tying one on. She speaks first to Martina: "All they have here is Genny Cream Ale and cheap whiskey, so if you're thinking about one of those cocktails on the sign out there, think again."

"Whiskey's all I want," Martina says.

"You talk like a cowboy," the woman says. "I like you. My name's Jane."

The bartender brings over a bottle and a shot glass. She pours one for Martina.

Jane continues: "That's Widow Marie slinging drinks. And that's Alkie Eleanor down there, sawing wood." She points to the slumped-over drunk.

Martina puts the clutch on the bar and downs the whiskey. It loosens her up immediately. She lets out a breath.

"You a hit man or a jewel thief?" Jane asks. "I can't tell."

"What do you mean?"

"Take it easy. Just a joke. You've got this all-black thing going on. Let me guess your name. I'm good at this."

"You won't guess it," Martina says. She motions for another drink, and Widow Marie pours, slopping it over the edges of the glass. She still hasn't spoken, this strange widow of a bartender, this sloppy pourer of cheap whiskey.

"Five bucks says I guess it in five tries," Jane says.

"Okay."

Jane claps her hands together and then thrums her fingers against the bar top. "Set me up, Marie," she says. "I need some booze to help me think."

Marie goes over and refills her glass. "For the hero of the night, sure thing," she says, the first words she's spoken.

"I'm having a good night already, stranger," Jane says to Martina. "I won five bucks on a scratch-off and I saved the day when Double Stevie tried to rob the register, so I'm drinking on the arm. You stumbled in here on a real thriller of an evening. And I'm coming for your five bucks next. Okay? Buckle up." She tosses back the drink and seems to search the ceiling for an answer. "Let me ask you one thing first?"

"Okay."

"You're not from around here, right? Definitely not from the block but not from the neighborhood either. Not even from Brooklyn."

Martina shakes her head. She's trying not to give herself away. She shouldn't have come into this bar. She shouldn't have come after Sav. She's no killer. What does it matter if Sav lives or dies? Jerry's dead no matter what. He's never coming back. Every interaction will be like this one. Forced. Like she's trying to fit in to a world that won't have her, that never wanted her. Banter at a bar. Handshakes and kisses. Strange names written or said. Everything is wrong.

She thinks about where she's from. Greenwich. Horrible place. What she should do is drink two more drinks and write a letter to her mother and stepdad, whose name she took. She'll write it all down. Her love for Jerry, the way he was murdered, where he is and how she left him there with flowers. Say goodbye herself. Say there'll be peace on the other side. On her way in, she noticed a mailbox on the corner. She'll see if she can borrow a piece of paper, an envelope, and a stamp from Widow Marie. She'll sit here, have a few more drinks, and write her letter. She'll go out and drop it in the mailbox when she's done, and she'll forget all about Sav. Then she'll go back into the bar, pay her tab, disappear to the bathroom, and blow her head off. Not suicide. Mercy.

"Drumroll," Jane says, pounding the bar a little harder. "My first guess is . . . Anne."

"Anne?" Widow Marie says. "That's the best you've got?"

"What? She looks like an Anne." She gives Martina the once-over.

"Okay, fine, she's not an Anne. Strike one. You're not an Anne, correct?"

"I did think about making Anne my confirmation name," Martina says.

"There you go. Right track. Okay, here goes. Try two." Jane closes her eyes and taps her temples this time, takes a nip of whiskey. "Elizabeth. Or any of its variants. Betty. Betsy. Liz. Beth."

Martina shakes her head.

"Damn," Jane says, genuinely seeming pissed.

Martina wonders what it'd be like to be this way. Loose. Easy. Fun. She only ever felt fun with Jerry and even then she wasn't sure if she was actually fun or if she was playing the role of someone who understands what fun is. She envies this Jane. She's a regular on the sitcom that is this bar. She *fits*.

Jane's next three attempts to guess her name come rapidly. Almost making Anne her confirmation name must've seemed like some sort of clue because she sticks with saints' names. "Catherine? Joan? Mary?"

Martina shakes her head again. She thinks of the statue of Mary outside of Lola's house that warned her away, that steered her to this bar.

"Fuck me," Jane says. "I guess my luck's run cold. What is it?"

"Martina."

"Shit. Really. You're not Irish? You seem Irish. Black Irish but Irish."

"I'm Italian." She thinks of her stepfather, Jerry Malloy Senior. A bond trader. His big gleaming bald head. His large appetite for Manhattans. When she was younger and he'd order a Manhattan, she thought he was ordering the juice of the city. Like someone had to squeeze the borough itself to make that reddish glowing drink. How stupid. Maybe if she hadn't taken his name when he married her mother. She wanted so badly to take his name, though. To be a Malloy. She hated her actual father, Carmine Cammarosano, who split when she was a baby. Maybe if she stayed as Martina Cammarosano people would've recognized that she and Jerry weren't blood. What will her stepfather look like when he gets her letter, when he knows she and Jerry Junior are gone?

And her Italian mother. Poor Rosie. The way she put blush on in the car mirror. Dancing to Dean Martin in the living room. On her knees scrubbing the cabinets clean. How disgusted she was

when she found out about Martina and Jerry. How she wailed. She
knew things like that happened in the world, but she didn't want
to believe that they happened between her daughter and step-
son. She'd tried. She'd really tried. She'll wail at the funeral too.
Funerals. They'll probably be kept separate. Buried apart.

Maybe word of her death and of Jerry's death will reach her
mother and stepfather before the letter does. Maybe getting the letter will put things into perspective at least a little. The way the world
hands you love and then says it's wrong.

Speaking of. The letter.

Martina turns away from Jane and speaks to Widow Marie: "Do
you have a piece of paper and maybe an envelope and a stamp I
can buy?"

"Sure," Widow Marie says. "No charge." She gathers the supplies,
ripping a page from a marble notebook stuffed into a nook next to
the register, removing an envelope and a roll of stamps from a cabinet under the bar. She hands Martina the paper and the battered
envelope and then rips off one of the stamps, licks it, and applies
it crookedly to the upper-right-hand corner of the envelope. She
gives her a little golf pencil too, the eraser rubbed raw.

Martina looks at the stamp. Widow Marie's spit has dampened
the edges, the paper beneath a little grainy. Something about it
makes her even sadder. She thinks of scrawling the Greenwich address. She imagines dropping the envelope in the mailbox. She
thinks of it being picked up by a mailman, stuffed in a sack, carried
on a truck across the city and up into Connecticut. Over into Connecticut. Whatever. The world that letter might know. Its journey.
She thinks of Jerry dead in his loft. The flashes are coming hard
and fast now.

Jane shakes her out of it by slapping a scratch-off lottery ticket
on the bar. "There you go," Jane says. "That's worth five American
dollars. Cash it on the corner. You won it fair and square. I choked.
I'm usually good at guessing, I swear. An off day. I feel like Jesse
Orosco blowing a save."

"Martina's a tough one to guess."

"You're right about that. You're my first Martina. I've met a
million Marys, Joans, Annes, and Betsys. Never a Martina. Must
be nice to be unique. I'm just a Jane. Jane's nothing. Jane's the
'Happy Birthday' song of names. Jane. It's white toast, burnt a
little."

"I like the name Jane," Martina says.

"Think of one famous Jane worth anything. Don't say Jane Fonda or Jane Curtin."

"Saint Jane Frances de Chantal. Jane Austen. Calamity Jane."

"You got a stockpile of Janes for this very moment? Impressive. I've heard the names, but I don't know anything about them. They're good, these Janes?"

"A saint, a great writer, and a compassionate frontierswoman."

"Huh. Well, Martina, you've woken me up to the possibilities of being a good Jane. I need another drink. You need one?"

Martina nods.

Widow Marie pours another round for them and one for herself too. The drunk down at the end of the bar stirs, sitting up and saying in a growl, "The goddamn raisins don't go in that drawer."

"Never mind Alkie Eleanor," Jane says. "What do we drink to?"

Martina picks up her glass, clinks it against Jane's and then against Widow Marie's. "God Bless Jerry Malloy," she says. The whiskey goes down like fire.

Widow Marie shrugs and drinks her drink. Jane follows suit and then motions to the paper that's in front of Martina. "Widow Marie ripped that out of her Book of Bans. She must like you. Is Jerry Malloy who you're writing to?"

Martina looks at the paper, the darkness of the bar top visible through it. She swears she sees Jerry's face there. Like a vision of Christ or a Marian apparition. Jerry as he was in life. Those eyes. She ignores Jane's question and starts to write, almost clawing at the paper with the stubby pencil, avoiding rings of condensation on the bar. Where did the condensation come from? She didn't have a beer. Maybe it's tears from Jerry.

She has her own tears now. The whiskey has helped her cry. Jane puts a hand on her shoulder and gives her a look of deep compassion as she works on her letter.

Jane gets nervous when the stranger leaves to mail her letter and then comes back and disappears into the bathroom with her bag. Something's off. She's distraught, this Martina. Beyond distraught.

"Maybe I should go check on her," Jane says to Widow Marie.

"What's she gonna do in there?"

"Maybe she's a junkie. Maybe she's shooting up. I go back there, the door's locked, and she's OD'ing on the bowl, what the fuck do we do? She's okay in my book, but a lot of junkies are okay until they're a problem you've gotta deal with."

"You think she's a doper?"

"She brought her bag with her. She looks lost in the eyes. I've seen that before. The far-off thing. She's somewhere else. Wants to be. I never told you about Junkie Jennifer?"

"Who's Junkie Jennifer?"

"Junkie Jennifer was like the Alkie Eleanor of one of my previous hangouts, the Beauty Box. Bath Bar, Beauty Box. I guess I like double B places. This was seven, eight years ago. She was a normal girl from Lake Street, and then she got deep into dope and she just became a shooting-up machine. You'd walk in on her wherever and she'd have her arm tied, needle hanging out. Track marks everywhere. She OD'd on toilets and kitchen floors, in basements and attics and once under a pool table at the Beauty Box. She'd shit herself when the dope hit. She shit herself a lot. She was like a baby. Tiny Fat Fannie started a collection for adult diapers for Jennifer. We used to joke that we were gonna strap one on her before she got high. But nobody wants to blow that kind of dough on diapers for a junkie."

"You're saying she's gonna shit herself in my bathroom?" Widow Marie asks. "Just forego the toilet in front of her and let the load fly in her drawers?"

"That's one possible outcome."

"If junkies shit themselves like that, why don't they just pull their pants down before shooting up?"

"One of life's greatest fucking mysteries. You can never tell what's in a junkie's heart."

"And you think this kid in my bathroom's a junkie?"

"Fifty-fifty, I'd say. Either that or some kind of deranged religious nut who hands out pamphlets. Doesn't she have that quality to her? Like she's the kind of person who rings your doorbell at eight o'clock at night to give you a little pamphlet about how Jesus would like to take a dumb fuck like you for a walk. Not a dumb fuck like *you*. You know what I mean. Just dumb fucks in general. She could be shooting up Jesus in there. That's even worse. Talk about shitting yourself." Jane pauses. "Don't get me wrong. I like her. She's loaded with information about Janes. That's special."

When the front door opens, Jane's not sure who to expect. Her luck, Sav will probably come charging in. Sandra too. But it's not either of them. It's Donnie Parascandolo. Crazy shit. Donnie the cop *never* comes in here. A fucked-up horse doesn't drink so close to home. Plus, one of the few times he was in here, Widow Marie said she was going to ban him for finishing her crossword puzzle when she wasn't looking. His main haunt is Blue Sticks Bar, where the cops have the run of the place. Sometimes he'll hang at the Wrong Number. She steers clear of both. She steers clear of Donnie too. His wife Donna's okay but he's got the look of someone ready to snap. Like an old pipe ready to burst at the seams and send a river of shit out into the world. He came into Duke's once when he was on the outs with his usual mechanics, Frankie and Sal at Flash. "I'm looking for Sav Franzone," Donnie says.

Jane turns her attention to Widow Marie, who's probably trying to remember Donnie's status at the bar. Maybe she remembers the crossword puzzle incident, though it was long ago. Guys like him are often in the Book of Bans, but he's not because he's a cop and no cops generally drink here. It clicks for her exactly who he is. Widow Marie hates cops. She doesn't like the look of them or the smell of them or any goddamn thing about them. What she hates most, Jane guesses, is the swagger. A cop thinks he's above everything, thinks he's doing God's work or some shit, but really most of them are chumps. Roman fucking soldiers. Betrayers of codes. There's good ones here and there, guys with decent hearts, and Jane has encountered them, but they're few and far between. Mostly, they start okay and go downhill fast, ruined by other cops or drained clean by the city, or letting the dark driver take the wheel. "He's not here," Jane says.

"He was here earlier," Widow Marie says. "Just for a minute."

"Maybe he went to Double Stevie's, the dumb fuck?" Donnie asks.

"I don't keep track."

A loud noise from the back of the bar startles them. Sounds like a truck backfiring. A gunshot. Definitely a gunshot. Came from the bathroom. Jane had the girl wrong. Not a junkie or a religious nut. A suicide. She just ate a bullet in the Bath Bar ladies' room.

Donnie's quick to react. His hand is under his shirt and then he's got a gun out in front of him, sweeping across the room. "What was that?" he asks.

"I don't know," Widow Marie says.

"Girl in the bathroom," Jane says. "She's been in there awhile.

She was looking down in the dumps. Must've brought a piece in there with her and plugged herself."

"Jesus Christ," Donnie says.

"I gotta clean up a suicide again?" Widow Marie says. "I swore after '82 I'd never clean up another suicide."

What Widow Marie's referring to is the suicide of former Altar Boy Dante Scipione. Dante had actually been an altar boy at St. Mary's, but he'd also been a member of the Altar Boys, a denim-jacketed gang of Italian kids from the neighborhood that thirsted to bust the balls of every non-Italian gang in the city. Dante had his heart broken by some girl from the city and never got over it. He drank too much and cut his own neck in the back of the bar one night. Slashed at his jugular with a bottle he broke on the edge of the pool table. Bled out pretty good. It was a mess. Widow Marie was mopping for a month. The Altar Boys made a memorial on the wall outside the bar. They kept it up for a while. Flowers and pictures and cards. Dante liked Twinkies. All these Twinkies were piled up on the cement. Kids would pass by and grab a package of Twinkies. Jane wasn't there the night Dante cut himself. Widow Marie didn't ever talk about it. Now, Jane's imagining, she's probably thinking there's more than blood on the floor. There's blood *and* brains on the wall *and* floor. And there's still a chance the loopy little letter-writer actually shit herself.

"You've got the gun, you make the rules," Jane says to Donnie.

Donnie shrugs and lets out an exhausted breath, letting them all know he doesn't need this. "Yeah, I'm on it," he says, in that derisive, thick cop voice.

Jane imagines that Donnie's envisioning the hassle that could unfold. Calling it in, paperwork, being on the clock when he's off the clock.

As Donnie heads to the bathroom—*heads to the head,* Jane thinks to herself, almost laughing—he's mumbling under his breath: "Now I've gotta deal with this. Not bad enough Pags put the Leo Manzi thing on my shoulders." He's cursing Christ and George Steinbrenner and Ed Koch and any other motherfucker he can think of. "Who is it in there?" he asks Jane and Widow Marie.

"No one we know," Jane says. "New blood."

"Never seen her before," Widow Marie confirms.

Alkie Eleanor pops up like a former champ whose still got a little fight left in her blood. "I told you to put the raisins in the baby carriage," she says. "Wheel them around like they're precious. They *are* precious."

"Jesus Christ," Donnie says, surprised by Alkie Eleanor's zombie routine. "Now we've got raisins. That's what I need. Raisins."

Jane moves next to Alkie Eleanor and puts her hand on her back, rubbing in a circle and then flattening out the wrinkles in her starchy jacket that smells of lottery ticket rubbings, sad bacon, and sour booze. "We've got it, Eleanor," Jane says. "Don't you worry."

Alkie Eleanor settles down, her head drifting back to the bar where it belongs, where there seems to be a groove in the wood for her, clasped arms folded under her forehead, chin in a notch of darkness. Like a needle on a record.

Donnie gets to the ladies' room door and knocks, keeping the gun at the ready, not trusting the information he's been given. *Could be anyone in there with a gun* is probably what he's thinking. Could be Sav. He knocks with the heel of his hand. "Hey in there," he says, pausing to yawn. "You alive or dead?"

No answer.

Donnie knocks harder, a rattling cop knock, the kind that shocks the whole block, that vibrates through the bones of old-timers and dumb enchanted kids alike. He homes in on Jane as he speaks, grinning. "Open up, come on. I've gotta make a deposit. Men's room's on the fritz. Gonna be a three-flush operation. Need you to clear out."

No answer again.

Donnie huffs, exasperated, no doubt bummed at the prospect of spending one more second of time doing something he doesn't want to do. "Lady, I ain't got all night. Answer me. Open up." He doesn't even wait for her to not answer this time. He shrugs again, says to Widow Marie and Jane, "I guess she croaked in there. I tried. Just call nine-one-one. They'll deal with it."

Martina's voice sludges out from behind the door. A shattered hush. "Don't. I'm in here. I'm alive."

"Oh, the so-called suicide speaks," Donnie says.

"Can I talk to Jane? I want to talk to Jane."

"Hey, Jane the Stain, swap spots with me, huh? She wants to talk to you. And I want a drink. I'm gonna be strong-armed into lingering in this shithole, I'm gonna need some booze. Marie, you hear me? Set me up a double of that bathroom rye you serve. Rocks. I'm hot.

It's hot. I hate August. Least favorite month. My feet get burnt on the sidewalks. I can't wipe the stink of the city off me."

Jane drains her whiskey and goes to the bathroom, passing Donnie on his way to the bar. He clanks the gun up in front of him and waits on his drink. Alkie Eleanor slumps forward again, back to dreamland, caught up in whatever raisin-driven nightmare she's usually caught up in. Jane wonders what in the fuck involving raisins happened in her life to make it a go-to thing to shout when being shaken from her blackout.

"Always an adventure in this dive, huh?" Donnie says to Marie, as she sets him up with a double.

At the ladies' room door, Jane speaks softly: "You okay in there? What happened?"

"I tried to shoot myself. I missed."

"Why'd you do that?"

"Despair."

Jane's wondering what to say to that. She's got this stranger Martina behind the door, gun in hand, having flopped at suicide. Flopping at suicide's no joke. It's like there's another basement below the basement you're in. Jane was suicidal once or twice. Hard not to be when you let booze rule your life and occasionally find yourself clunking up against a terrible darkness. There was the time with her mother's sleeping pills. She drank them down—the whole bottle—with a screwdriver and puked some hellish fountain. Orange juice everywhere. The other time was sadder. She tried to make herself choke on a hunk of food. She doesn't even remember what. Stale bread. A grape maybe. She thought choking was the way to go. It wasn't. She had to save herself by flinging her body desperately over the hard back of a dining room chair. For her, coming down after being drunk always brings the scrapings of despair. She can feel the ghost of all she's never been coursing through her blood. As she gets older, she knows how to deal with it better. She embraces being in that cage, lets dreams of the next drink lull her into a sense of calm.

Jane doesn't know what Martina's story is, but she knows the spot she's in. Must be rotten enough she's figured there's no other way. Must be rotten enough she's chosen the Bath Bar ladies' room. Why not the Verrazano or the Brooklyn Bridge? Why not throw herself in front of a B train? Flattened on the tracks like a penny. Lit up by the third rail. There's drama. Why not a bathtub with a rusty razor blade? Why not hopping off a tall building and knowing what it's like to fly or at least to fall from a great height? Hit that sidewalk below like a comet.

It was an impulsive decision, Jane bets. Martina wants someone to rescue her. "I'm glad you missed," Jane says finally.

"I'm not. What kind of idiot misses trying to shoot herself in the head?"

"You ever think it's divine intervention maybe?"

Nothing.

"Talk to me," Jane says. "Come on out. A drink's what you need. Feel better tonight, worse tomorrow. Deal with it then. That's what I always say. You need someone to listen to you, I'm pretty good at that. Not the best but not bad. I've been down in plenty of holes myself. Been on the edge."

"Yeah?"

"Of course. Come on, drinks are on me. You give Widow Marie the gun for safekeeping, and we'll have a heart-to-heart. How's that sound? Not the worst, right? You've got a new pal."

"We ought to get you a gig as a hostage negotiator," Donnie says between slurps of whiskey.

Jane puts her thumb in her mouth and mimes likes she's blowing up her middle finger until she's flipping Donnie the full bird. It's something her mother's best friend, Melinda, used to do. Jane called her Aunt Melinda even though she wasn't her aunt. She got cancer when Jane was thirteen. The news wrecked her mother. The cancer moved quickly. When she got put in hospice care, they used to go every day to sit with her. Aunt Melinda always found the strength to blow up a bird for them. Jane laughed. The woman was dying but still goofing off. Jane liked that kind of courage. She wasn't there when Aunt Melinda died, but her mother was. Aunt Melinda's last words were *Fuck it,* a fact that her mother reported with tears in her eyes, laughing. "That was Melinda," her mother said. "What a way to go."

The sound of a lock being unlatched. Feet moving on the floor. Jane tries to imagine Martina in that skanky little bathroom with its two stalls, one forever bombed out. The graffiti on the doors. The chipped porcelain sink. Black-and-white tile walls, grout all wormy and weathered. A mirror covered in lipstick messages: *DON'T FUCK FREDDIE; FREDDIE'S A THIEF; FRY FREDDIE FRY; ENZIO'S A PIG BASTARD.* Half-scrubbed toilets ringed with dark

residue. The unwieldy spools of sandpapery toilet tissue. Base-
board heaters fringed with deep threads of dust. A tiny, frosted
window to nowhere. The stink of it. Ammonia, Lysol, mildew,
piss. Of all places. Might as well be the alley next door. End it all
among the overstuffed garbage cans and scurrying rats.

Martina pulls the door slowly and she's there, facing Jane. Over
her shoulder, Jane can see a hunk of wall tile just above the sink,
shattered where the bullet must've hit. She can't figure on the
trajectory of it. Where was Martina standing when she pulled
the trigger? How'd she miss? How'd the bullet hit *there*? Doesn't
matter. A real possibility she just fired into the wall, wanting this.
Someone to guide her to the next thing. Martina's black clutch is
open, balanced on the edge of the sink.

"You okay?" Jane says.

Martina half-shrugs.

"Give me the gun," Jane says.

Martina hands the gun over. Jane holds it between her thumb
and index finger like it's a stranger's vibrator. The gun doesn't feel
like anything. The only other gun she's ever touched is the one
Duke keeps in the safe at work. She brings it to Widow Marie, who
drops it in a dark recess next to the register behind a couple of
her saint candles.

Martina struggles to make it to the bar, but Jane helps her, a
hand across her back, seeming to prop her up. Jane gets her settled on a stool.

Martina takes momentary notice of Donnie, who she must realize was the man trying to talk her down, and then focuses her
energy on the whiskey that Widow Marie pours for her.

Jane clinks her glass and tells her to drink up.

The door to the bar opens. Sav Franzone comes loping in. He's
wearing bell-bottoms, his bare stomach and chest covered in Saran Wrap, blood darkening the waist of his jeans, blood encased
behind the plastic. He's got on worn old sneakers that are untied.

"What in the everloving fuck?" Widow Marie says.

Jane must admit it's a strange, strange sight.

He's hurt, Sav. Looks like he just escaped from a serial killer
who tried to dress him like a mix of a hippie and leftovers.

Martina's up now. She's moving toward Sav. "You killed Jerry.
You killed him."

Jane remembers Martina's toast: *God bless Jerry Malloy.*

Sav doesn't seem to hear her. He's moving like a man in shock. He runs straight ahead and hits the wall full force. *Plop.* Collapses to the floor in a heap. He's making sounds that fall somewhere between breathing and snorting.

"Jesus Christ almighty," Donnie says. "Call the cops, Marie."

"You are the cops," Jane says. "You were looking for Sav and now he's here."

"What am I gonna do, unwrap this fuck? Like Christmas in August. I'll pass. I was doing a favor for Lola. This, I didn't bargain for."

"He's hurt bad." Jane wonders what exactly happened. Was he knifed and wrapped up? Shot and wrapped up? Or maybe this is some weird prank? Double Stevie's pulling the strings, outside on the sidewalk, hoping everyone will be distracted so he can pounce on the register. A stupid idea but not the stupidest. And what the fuck is up with Martina and Sav? There's a connection she didn't see coming. Unless that's why Martina's on the block. She's hunting Sav for whatever he did to Jerry. But she chickened out and tried to off herself instead. Makes sense.

Martina lashes out at Sav now, scratching and clawing at him even though he's bleeding and out cold. "I came here to kill you," Martina says, and Jane's immediately glad she got the gun away from her before she saw Sav.

Jane's not unhappy about any of it. If there's anybody on the block everybody would like to see hurt, it's Sav. "Leave him," Jane says to Martina. She kneels next to Sav and prods him. "He looks shot. I think he's shot."

The door opens again, and Sandra Carbonari sidles her way into the proceedings. Wearing a neon pink halter top and cut-off denim shorts. Her high hair stiff, sweat resistant from the can of Aqua Net they've used on her at Bensonhurst Dolls. She's a bright blur of color and smells in the dark little dive.

"This place is like a fucking clown car," Donnie says.

Sandra's all smiles for a second before seeing Sav on the floor. Despite the bell-bottoms and Saran Wrap, she makes out his face right away. "My poor Sav. What happened to him?" She's looking to anybody for an answer. Jane. Widow Marie. Martina, who she's no doubt never seen before. Donnie.

"We don't know," Jane says. "I think he was shot."

"Sav?" Sandra says to him, poking his hip. "Can you hear me?
Are you hurt?"

Sav stirs a little. Moans. His eyes open.

"Call an ambulance," Sandra says.

"You better get on the horn, Marie," Donnie says, finishing off
his whiskey and trailing his index finger over the butt of the gun
on the bar in front of him.

Marie finally picks up the receiver on the black phone behind
the bar. Her call to the nine-one-one dispatcher is less than enthusiastic. "A shot guy ran into my place of business," she says. She
gives the address. "Not dead yet, no. Being tended to by his slut
girlfriend."

Jane can tell Marie fears trouble raining down on her humble
little dive. In ten minutes or less, the place will be full of cops and
EMS workers. That's Sav's fault. No doubt, if he makes it, he'll
wind up in the Book of Bans. Widow Marie is put the fuck out.

"Who did this to you?" Sandra asks Sav.

He struggles to make words but finally spits it out: "Double Stevie
shot me. Gilly the Gambler dressed me up."

"Jesus Christ," Sandra says, leaning over him so her shorts ride
halfway up her ass. "What the hell?"

"I wanted to run away with you," Sav says.

Martina goes over and picks up the bat that Jane used on Double
Stevie earlier. She runs to Sav and starts pounding on him. Her
swings are savage. She seems bent on putting the finishing touches
on him. He never had any dignity to lose but has descended into
some special hell where he's wound up wearing bell-bottoms,
wrapped in Saran Wrap, shot, and is now being beat to a pulp by a
bat-wielding flopped bathroom suicide.

Sandra tries to stop Martina but takes a hit to the shoulder and
backs off. She's screeching. Her hands over her mouth, those long
pink nails crawling up her cheeks.

"A fucking clown car," Donnie says and splits.

He's not wrong. Jane feels like she's under a circus tent. Seven
of them in this joint, including Alkie Eleanor, who's due to pop
up any second and scream about raisins. Martina's really going
to town on Sav now, Jane deciding not to step in. Sometimes, she
decides, a woman's just got to let another woman beat a piece of

shit man to death with a baseball bat. Sandra's screeching rattles the walls and windows of the bar. She sounds like a bus accident.

Alkie Eleanor is awake and quiet for once. The scene's even got her flustered.

Widow Marie has her hands over her ears. She wants it all to end. She wants scratch-offs and silence.

Martina pounds on Sav until she's exhausted and then drops the bat on his body. It clangs on the floor next to him. A horrible sound. Martina has opened up a gash in Sav's head.

Sandra stops screaming and collapses over Sav, clawing at the Saran Wrap with those godforsaken nails.

Sirens ride the night air. They're coming for Sav, to haul him away or resuscitate him. Jane pictures the ambulance guys trying to piece together the puzzle of what went on here. She puts a hand on Martina's back and walks her back to the bar. Martina is weeping. Crying's not the right word. Weeping like someone weeps at a funeral. It might very well be holy water erupting from her eyes. "There you go," Jane says, setting the stranger up on a stool. "You belong right here. You belong with us."

"He killed Jerry," Martina says. "He didn't have to, but he killed him."

"I know he did," Jane says, buzzing with ecstasy. Such madness in the air. City-thick, steaming. Red lights fall over them. Sounds bloom. Sandra chirping to Sav. The bat rolling away on the floor. Glasses thumping on the bar. This suddenly feels like the last night of the world.

The Mayor of Dukes City

FROM *The Perfect Crime*

MARCUS PULLED OUT his ink stamp with one hand and a wad of ones with the other. He'd glanced at the girl's ID with his good eye while she and her two friends took selfies and debated whether the pics should be tagged "Girls Night Out" or "Birthday Celebration" on Instagram.

"Eight dollars is your change. Have a good night, ladies," Marcus said.

"You gonna buy me a shot? I'm doing twenty-one for my twenty-first," the birthday girl said. She smiled at him and for the briefest of moments he felt the leather skin around his heart pulsate. She was small-town pretty in that way that made the local boys forget about condoms and nineteen years of child support. She was seven years younger than Marcus. Their ages were close enough to avoid any concerns about impropriety. Except it was bad news if a bouncer got too friendly with the patrons. Especially in a small town. Especially if bouncing was the only job you could get because you were blind in one eye. And especially if the last time you got involved with someone you got heartbroken.

"Maybe later. Have a good night," Marcus said. The girls slipped by him, all giggles and swagger. Birthday Girl made sure to touch his bicep as she made her way into the bar. She got close and Marcus could smell her perfume. A bellicose, fruity scent that lingered long after she had clicked away on her stiletto heels.

"Shit, she did everything but drop her drawers, Mayor," Trent said. Trent was the other bouncer working tonight. He was shorter than Marcus but built like a fire hydrant. Two hundred pounds of muscle packed on a five-six frame. Trent walked around strung up as tight as an over-tuned guitar begging for someone to strum him the wrong way. Marcus didn't like working with Trent. He was fairly sure the kid was juicing. Add that to the two-by-four chip he had on his shoulder and that all but guaranteed they'd end the night with blood on the floor. But Lonny was the owner and Trent's uncle, so that pretty much meant Trent had carte blanche to take out his little man frustrations on drunk rednecks every other weekend.

"Not good to piss where you eat," Marcus said, conveniently ignoring the fact he had fallen in love with a girl who was in the bar five days out of seven, until the day he found her . . .

No. Marcus wouldn't think of that yet. Those memories would be waiting for him later tonight when he fell across his bed and closed his eyes. They waited in that Stygian darkness to be rendered in Day-Glo garishness. Neon reds and blues that spilled across the backs of his eyes.

"Well, let me get your leftovers. I ain't got none since before the Fourth of July. Shit, I'd bang the crack of dawn right now if it stood still long enough," Trent said with such bitterness Marcus winced.

"Get the door. I'm gonna take a lap inside," Marcus said.

"Ha! Go get her, big boy," Trent said. He winked at him. Marcus shook his head and went inside. Marcus wasn't shocked that Trent thought he was going in to stalk Birthday Girl. It never occurred to Trent to do his job, so he thought everyone else felt the same.

The interior of The Lookout Bar and Grill was laid out in an exaggerated upper-case L. The bar was in the center of the L with a bandstand near the bottom. Weathered leather booths lined the walls and twelve rickety tables with uneven legs filled the main causeway. It was still early but most of the tables were occupied, as were a lot of the booths. Pittsville County only had two bars, The Lookout and Coppers. But Coppers could never seem to keep their liquor license current, so most people ended up at The Lookout if they didn't take the two-hour drive to Richmond.

The lights were low and someone had played the latest country pop confection on the jukebox as the band set up, but Marcus could still read the crowd. It was all about body language and posture. Imminent violence charged the air like a thunderstorm. Marcus had learned how to read currents and prevailing winds. Often he would defuse a confrontation before a blow was thrown. It didn't hurt he had a legitimate rep as a bone breaker. When he'd first come home and started working for Lonny, he was sure his rep would mean endless duels with guys he'd gone to high school with, trying to show off for their girlfriends or wives. If anything, it was the opposite. Since he'd come back with his tail between his legs, he was welcomed into the fold with open arms and knowing nods. He was just another big fish who had left his small pond. Life had judged him wanting and thrown him back.

Desiree didn't feel that way.

"Why don't you get surgery for your eye? Get back in the ring."

"The cage," he'd corrected her as she lay across his chest like a lounging cat.

"Whatever. You should do it. I know you don't want to spend the rest of your life tossing Tylers and Chads out into the parking lot."

"It pays the bills."

"More to life than bills, Marcus."

She'd been right. There was love. There was death. He'd found both with her.

"Mayor! Da Mayor of Dukes City! When we gonna spar, big man?" Jody Mickens said. He stumbled, caught himself, then held his hand up palm out, waiting for a high five. Marcus slapped his palm with a touch more vigor than was necessary. The more Jody drank, the more invincible he thought he became. Marcus wanted to remind him, even if it was subconsciously, that he wasn't invincible. He was frail and soft, and if Marcus felt like it, he could break him as easily as he broke an egg for his morning omelet.

"Damn, man. You trying to break my damn hand?" Jody said. He laughed but it was hollow around the edges.

"My bad, Jody. Don't know my own strength sometimes," Marcus said.

"Yeah, I see that. Let me buy you a drink, man," Jody said.

"Maybe later. Darlene waving for you," Marcus said.

"She just want another margarita. She trying to outdrink me," Jody said, before lurching over to his wife and her sister. Marcus had seen Jody and his sister-in-law in The Lookout without Darlene more than once. It amazed him how people thought they could keep a secret in a town with less than ten thousand people. But then again, people kept the secrets that really mattered. The kind of secrets that got you the needle in your arm or a ride in Ol' Sparky.

"Why does everyone call you Mayor?" a voice said behind him. He turned and saw Birthday Girl leaning against the bar. Her pupils were as big as dinner plates. The brown ringlets of her hair framed her face and gave her a doll-like countenance. By the look of it, she was at the crest of a high from a ferocious bump of coke.

"It's just a nickname," Marcus said.

"I can see that. But why do they call you that?"

"I used to fight. MMA fighting. During my first fight a commentator said I was taking the guy to Dukes City and the other commentator said I was the Mayor. Name just stuck," Marcus said.

"You used to fight?" Birthday Girl said. Marcus shrugged.

"Yeah, for real. Mostly regional stuff."

"Nah, I believe you. You look like you could snap me in half like a breadstick," Birthday Girl said.

"I don't hit women. I've never hit a woman in my life," Marcus said.

But somebody around here does, Marcus thought. Desiree's face floated up from the depths and danced in front of him. He could almost see the maroon string lights illuminating her honey brown eyes.

"I mean, if you used to fight, what you doing here? No offense," Birthday Girl asked. Marcus stared past her to a couple in the corner of the bar. The woman took her index and middle finger and pushed them against the man's temple. The man rolled his eyes and stared up into the ceiling. Marcus hoped he was looking for the angels of his better nature. If the guy raised his hand, Marcus could close the distance in two long strides. A few of the more unruly patrons of The Lookout had found out he was deceptively quick.

"Huh?" Marcus asked.

"I said, what are you doing here if you're some big bad MMA fighter? I mean, unless you don't want to talk about it," Birthday Girl said.

"You could always google it, but the short version is I got poked in the eye during a fight. Everybody pretty much knew the winner was going to the big leagues. I had the guy. Like, I had him. One more body shot, he would've folded, but I tried to show off. I went in for a slam and he jammed his thumb in my eye damn near to the knuckle."

"Oh God."

"Yeah. Detached my retina and damaged the nerve. So, no big leagues for me. I came back home," Marcus said.

"Aw, I'm sure that's not true."

"You sound like my ex," Marcus said, instantly regretting it.

"Your ex? If she your ex that means you're single. Unless y'all still friends with benefits," Birthday Girl said.

Marcus sucked his teeth.

"No. She's dead. Been dead for almost a year."

"Jesus Christ. I'm so sorry. I'm such an idiot."

"You didn't know. You probably heard about it though. She was Desiree Bowles."

"Oh shit. That's the girl they found in the creek behind the building here. Damn. I mean damn, that's so messed up."

"They didn't find her. I found her. We'd been broke up for a month. No one had heard from her for a couple days. I was taking the trash out before we opened for the night, and I saw a whole flock of buzzards in the trees back there. I don't know why I went to check it out. Maybe I kinda knew? Subconsciously, you know? This was the last place she'd been seen. On my night off. My one night off," Marcus said. He wondered if Birthday Girl could feel the guilt emanating from him, the insatiable regret that filled him like sand in an hourglass. Tick tick ticking away every day. Each grain inscribed with the idea that if he'd been there, he could have saved her.

"You wanna drink?"

"It's your birthday."

"Yeah, but I think you need it more than I do. I can't imagine finding my ex de . . . finding them like that. Come on, do a shot with me."

"Maybe later," Marcus said. The Temple Pusher was now in the personal space of a woman standing near the hall that led to the bathrooms. The guy was nowhere to be seen.

"All right, Mayor. Don't leave me hanging."

"Okay, Birthday Girl. I gotta go handle something," Marcus said.

"Kristen!" she yelled as he went to disentangle the two women near the bathroom.

The band started up a few minutes after he and Trent tossed the two women and the guy. The three of them continued to argue in the parking lot The Lookout shared with Pets A Million and Beads Beads Beads, Linda Danvers's craft shop.

"Should we call the cops? Or do you want me to go over there?" Trent asked. Marcus looked up at the night sky. The stars looked like pinpricks in a bolt of black suede.

"No. They just yelling. It'll be okay," Marcus said. Would it be okay, though? Or would it escalate? Transform from a simple romantic squabble to a deadly encounter in the blink of an eye?

"Kiss my ass, Lavon. You told me y'all was just friends!" a voice said from the far end of the parking lot. A few seconds later a two-door sports coupé with BRWN SGAR on the license plate went roaring past Marcus and Trent. The car paused for the briefest of moments before it merged into traffic.

"That took care of itself, I guess. I wouldn't want to be Lavon tonight, though," Trent said. Marcus caught a note of disappointment in his voice. They were halfway through the night and he hadn't had a chance to really flex his muscles. Tossing the love triangle had been light work.

"Yeah, he gonna be on the couch tonight. I'm gonna take another lap," Marcus said.

"Just ask her for her number, man," Trent said. Marcus shook his head. The atmosphere in the bar had shifted significantly in the last hour. Bodies gyrated on the dance floor in desperate rhythm. Strangers had become friends and friends were trying to find the path to lovers. The band was tearing through a bluesy number that only threw more logs on the fire of sexual tension that was slowly consuming The Lookout. Marcus posted up near the bar and scanned the dance floor. He wasn't looking for Kristen to get her number. There was a wildness and a willingness about her that reminded him of Desiree. Not a naivete but a hedonistic sensibility that attracted lovers and predators in equal measure.

He heard a throaty laugh that rose over the music like an opera singer hitting a high note. He flicked his eyes over to the corner where the laugh had come from. Kristen and her two girlfriends were in a booth with the Larson brothers. Jaime and Justin were a couple of good ol' boys whose family owned the paper pulp mill that employed 50 percent of Pittsville's citizens. They were all laughing but Kristen was the star of that show. Jaime Larson appeared particularly smitten with her.

Marcus let out a sigh. She wasn't Desiree. She was just a girl having a good time on her birthday. She would go home with Jaime or Justin, or with the beginnings of a hangover. Regardless, she was going to be all right. At least for tonight.

Marcus cut through the crowd and headed for the bathroom. He needed to take a leak. As he turned the corner at the bottom of the L he saw Jody standing in the hallway that led to the bathrooms. He was in front of the bulletin board that Lonny used to advertise upcoming events. Lonny was convinced placing it near the bathroom was a brilliant marketing move. Marcus didn't have the heart to tell him drunk people trying not to piss themselves didn't pause to peruse the coming attractions.

Except here was Jody doing just that. Marcus stopped. Jody wasn't just reading the announcements. He was drawing a little bit of graffiti. He had a pen in his hand and was adding his own artistic contribution to the board. Marcus watched him as he chuckled to himself and put the pen back in his pocket.

He slipped past Marcus without raising his head. The liquor was pulling his chin down into his chest. Marcus walked along the short hall and stopped in front of the bulletin board. If Jody had drawn a vulgar work of art, he'd have to take it down and toss it in the trash. He couldn't do anything about what people drew on the stalls, but he could keep the hallway clean.

Marcus peered at Jody's handiwork. He felt his guts twist into a cold knot of despair. The entire length of his intestinal tract felt like it was being crocheted by a demon. Marcus fell back against the wall and put his hand to his mouth.

Later, as Trent was helping Charlene and Mandy, the two bartenders, clean up, Marcus pushed the crowd toward the door.

"Drink 'em up! You ain't gotta go home but you gotta get the hell out of here!" Marcus said. For the most part the crowd followed his directions. A few stragglers chugged their beers. A few late-night lotharios tried in vain to seal the deal before the light came up and their true faces were laid bare.

"Hey, man, I gotta dip. Can you finish shutting things down?" Marcus asked Trent.

"Yeah, man, I gotcha. Going to catch up with that little hottie, huh?" Trent said.

But Marcus was already out the door.

*

Jody lived out near Iron Bucket Road in a double-wide trailer down a long dirt lane about sixty yards from the main road. Marcus had driven him home a couple of times over the last few years. His own trailer was five miles away. Since Jody's house was on his way, he didn't mind dropping him off if he was too pie-eyed to drive.

Marcus couldn't ignore the irony. He'd taken better care of Jody than he'd taken care of Desiree.

Jody's truck was parked haphazardly in front of his steps. Marcus went up to the door and gave it three sharp knocks with one hand while waving away the moths and June bugs gathered around Jody's porch light with the other.

"Who the fuck is it?" Jody yelled.

"Jody, it's Marcus. You forgot your ID. I'm just dropping it off," Marcus said. He could hear Jody clomping and stomping toward the door.

When he finally appeared in the doorway his pale moon face was dripping with confusion.

"You sure, man? I swear I got it," Jody slurred.

"Yeah. Come on out to the car," Marcus said. Clarity made a brief appearance in Jody's eyes. Marcus wondered, was it a latent form of reptilian survival instinct? An animalistic sense of self-preservation left over from the days of caves and mastodons? If it was, it found no purchase in Jody's mind. It flickered out like a candle in a rainstorm.

"Okay, sure. Nice of you to bring it," Jody mumbled.

When they got to the car Marcus leaned in the passenger window. He came back up with his fingerless fighting gloves on his hands.

"What you doing, Mayor?"

"I thought we'd get that sparring session in," Marcus said. Jody laughed.

"Tonight? You must be drunker than me."

"Darlene at her mom's?" Marcus asked.

"Yeah, she got pissed at me for flirting with Jennifer Lowe. Why are you here again? Where is my ID?" Jody said. Marcus rolled his neck.

"When I found her, she was on her back. One of her pants legs had caught on a root on the bank of the creek. Cops told me people who drowned almost always float face down. Then they found out she hadn't drowned. Her head had been cracked open.

Her mama told me the mortician said she had bruises all over her body. Bruised everywhere. The person who did it had even knocked out her front teeth. The cops kept that back."

"Mayor, I'm sorry about Desiree, but if you ain't got my ID I'm going back inside. I got the bubble guts, man," Jody said. He started for the trailer. Marcus spun on the balls of his feet and gave him a stiff rabbit punch to the back of the neck. Jody dropped to his knees. He keened like a baby goat.

"Nobody knew about her teeth except the cops and the mortician and me and the person who killed her."

"You damn near broke my neck, man," Jody gasped.

"Lonny lets me keep the poster up on the bulletin board even though nobody has come forward. Nobody talks about her anymore. It's like she was never here. But that poster's still up there. She's still with me. She's still in my heart," Marcus said. He grabbed Jody by his shirt and pulled him to his feet.

"So, you wanna tell me why I watched you black out her teeth on that poster? You blacked 'em out and laughed about it. Explain that to me, Jody. EXPLAIN IT TO ME!" Marcus roared.

"You're crazy. It was just a joke. I didn't cave the back of that girl's head in. Crazy fucker," Jody said. His breath was coming in ragged bursts. Each exhalation smelled like the exhaust from a car that ran on whiskey.

"Jody."

"What, Marcus? Let me go, man," Jody said.

"I never said the back of her head was caved in. But somehow you know that too," Marcus said quietly.

Jody's face went from alabaster to chartreuse.

"It was an accident, Marcus. I swear it was."

Marcus hit him with a one-two combination to the ribs. Jody fell to the ground. He coughed once, then twice. Blood, as red as a melted crayon, spilled over his thin lips.

"Time to go to Dukes City, Jody."

Marcus hit him again.

And again.

And again . . .

JACQUELINE FREIMOR

Foreword

FROM *Vautrin*

ALL TOO OFTEN in this hyperbolic and linguistically imprecise age, the adjective *great* is used to describe that which is merely adequate or good. When I say that Edbert Reid was a great writer, however, I am using the word deliberately to convey not only that he was a remarkable writer but also that he was, arguably, superior to most, if not all, other twentieth-century American authors. (I hope the reader will indulge me when I note that Edbert Reid also embodied—literally—yet another definition of the word *great:* that of large size, hugeness [ME *grete,* fr. OE *grēat;* akin to OHG *grōz,* large].*) Consequently, when in 1980 my graduate academic adviser and mentor, noted scholar and literary critic A. L. Sticklee, suggested that I make Reid's work the subject of my doctoral dissertation, I regarded the project with tremendous trepidation. In the end, however, and to my everlasting gratitude, A. L. helped me overcome my fears, and my first book† was in due time brought forth, dare I say birthed, into the world, with the same pain and pride, I imagine, that might have attended the arrival of its human counterpart.‡

---

* At 14 years of age, the young Reid attained his adult height of 6 feet 6 inches, and at the time of his death he weighed nearly 300 pounds.

† Dunster, William P. *Mirrors, Memory, and Meaning in Reid's* Memoranda (Harvard University Press, 1987).

‡ I am using this metaphor intentionally because it is very much a Reidian trope. Both Phillip Weston (*Gender and Sexuality in the Works of Edbert Reid,* University of Wisconsin Press, 2008) and Francesca DiGiulio (*A Feminist Reads Reid,* Ohio State University Press, 2011) have discussed the feminine sensibility that pervades much

Little then did I know that a critical appreciation of Edbert Reid's *oeuvre* was to become my own life's work (and some say, obsession*). Whence sprang my fascination? the reader may ask, and it's a fair question. I would like to be able to say that the sole attraction for me, as for so many other literary critics, lay in the sheer brilliance of Reid's writing, his unique style, which may well be described as muscular yet lithe, tender yet brutal. Every year, I reread each of the author's five novels in its original Alfred A. Knopf edition—*Memoranda* (1961), *The Aching Sky* (1965), *Eyes of the Owl* (1968), *Lissette* (1977), and *The Last Enchantments* (1979)—and my appreciation of the crystalline perfection of certain passages only continues to grow. That Reid gave us only five novels before his untimely death is an almost unutterable tragedy.[†] How many more masterpieces might Reid have bequeathed the world had he been allowed to live out his allotted threescore and ten?[‡]

And yet, I would be perpetrating a grievous lie—not of commission, but of omission—were I not to confess that the life of Edbert Reid, or, more precisely, the contradictions between the man and his art, have been for me as compelling as his fiction. For example, two of his novels contain some of the most exquisite gastronomical descriptions in the history of American letters; I refer specifically to the banquet scene in chapter 5 of *The Aching Sky* and the wedding scene in chapter 17 of *Eyes of the Owl*. However, according to Reid's official biographer, Ryan Michaelson, Reid was not a gourmet but, in the word's original usage, a *gourmand*—that is to say, a glutton—and his favorite meals consisted almost entirely of fast food.[§]

---

of Reid's work, notable for its contradistinction to the "man's man" sensibility that he projected in his filmed interviews and correspondence.

* See Pears, Robert. "William P. Dunster: A Metacritical Examination of an Exegete." *Dialectics and Dialogics Today*, vol. 57, no. 6, 2001, pp. 145–79.

† Edbert Francis Reid was only 53 years of age when he was murdered in 1981. The details of the crime and subsequent events are well enough known that I will not revisit them here.

‡ *KJV Bible*, Ps. 90.10.

§ In *Edbert Reid: A Life* (Simon & Schuster, 1994, p. 588), Michaelson notes that for many years, Reid's favorite restaurants were Burger King, McDonald's, and Kentucky Fried Chicken. In 1977, however, during a California book tour, Reid sampled the Enchirito at a Taco Bell in Irvine and immediately became a devotee. On returning to his home in Nyack, New York, Reid repeatedly petitioned the local governments of Clarkstown, Haverstraw, Orangetown, Ramapo, and Stony Point

In a similar vein, much has justifiably been made of the nuanced and heartrendingly poignant depictions in all of Reid's works of romantic relationships, specifically those of monogamy in the context of marriage. Unfortunately, however, it was well known among other writers and critics that in the flesh, so to speak, Reid was a notorious womanizer.* Famously, three female authors—Georgia Barrett, Felice Touissant, and Rosemary Zemecki—had long-standing affairs with Reid, with Barrett going so far as to accuse Reid in 1963 of fathering her son, Francis.† Sadly, genetic testing was not available in the years before Reid's death, and thus this accusation was never proved. What is beyond dispute, however, is that Reid was enormously attractive to women, a quality he capitalized on at every opportunity. His friends considered him a playboy or a ladies' man; his critics considered him, in the words of conservative talk-show host William F. Buckley, Jr., "a debauched libertine."‡

Which leads us to that tantalizing cipher and the reason you are now holding this tome in your hands: Mary Margaret Reid, Edbert Reid's wife. Broadly speaking, scholars can be seen to have split themselves neatly into two diametrically opposing camps: those who do not believe that Mary Margaret played any appreciable role in her husband's literary achievements, and those who believe that she was his muse, and that the relationship between them was much like that between Beatrice and Dante.§ I find myself leaning toward the latter theory; I cannot bring myself to subscribe to the former.

---

to allow a Taco Bell franchise to open in the area, but his efforts were unsuccessful. His voluminous correspondence with the officials of these municipalities—well worth reading for Reid's vernacular, even crude, epistolary style, so markedly different from his novelistic style—resides at Yale University Library and can be accessed for scholarly study by special permission.

* In this regard, Michaelson (Ibid., p. 247) notes that in 1969, at the White Horse Tavern in New York's Greenwich Village, Reid and fellow author Norman Mailer engaged in a fistfight when Mailer called Reid a "horn dog." The police were summoned to the scene, but although both men were injured—Mailer had a split lip and Reid a black eye—neither filed charges.

† "I Gave Birth to Edbert Reid's Love Child." *National Enquirer,* Dec. 8, 1963.

‡ "The Moribund Great American Novel," *Firing Line,* PBS, SCETV, Columbia, Sept. 23, 1977.

§ For a detailed examination of these viewpoints, see Dunster, William P. "Mary Margaret Reid: Heavenly Muse or Household Manager?" *Form(alism),* vol. 139, no. 2, 2013, pp. 58–72.

First, it is undeniably true that there is abundant evidence of Mary Margaret's multifarious *domestic* contributions to the Reid household—the shopping lists, appointment books, and myriad other ephemera discovered in the Reid home after Mary Margaret's death in 2010.* However, it is clear too that Mary Margaret served if not as her husband's muse, then at least as her husband's secretary. According to Reid's editor at Knopf, Samuel Wilcox, each of the original manuscripts that Reid submitted was neatly typed and free of errors,† which is consistent with the fact that whereas Reid had never learned to type, Mary Margaret had trained at New York City's Katharine Gibbs Secretarial School. Additionally, according to Wilcox, he and Reid had conducted the process of editorial revision with Mary Margaret as an intermediary. Because Reid's writing schedule was so rigorous and he so frequently could not be disturbed, Wilcox would give his comments on Reid's manuscript to Mary Margaret over the telephone, and a few days later, she would relay her husband's responses to Wilcox by return phone call. It was an unwieldy and time-consuming arrangement, but the results were sublime, and it speaks to the enormous trust Reid placed in his wife to transmit these communications accurately.

An examination of Reid's manuscripts would likely serve to illuminate the issue of Mary Margaret's influence, but sadly, there are no surviving copies. Therefore, the question remains: Did Mary Margaret serve as Reid's muse, either in the classical sense (i.e., a goddess) or even in the modernist sense (i.e., an inspiration)? Reid never spoke directly about or alluded to her functioning in either capacity (although the women in his novels are exquisitely drawn as fully dimensional and utterly believable characters, and it is likely that Mary Margaret was at the very least a model for some

---

* After Reid died, Mary Margaret was named his executrix, and after her death in 2010, the executor's duty, along with the contents of the Reid household, was passed on—astonishingly—to me. To this day I do not know why. As I have said many times before, I'd visited Edbert Reid for the first time in 1980 and for the second time on the fateful day of his death in 1981, and on each occasion, I had only fleeting contact with Mary Margaret. In any event, as executor I was forced to rent a storage facility to house the volume of paper I received and to navigate endless loops of bureaucratic red tape to have it delivered to me in monthly batches, the schedule having been delineated by Mary Margaret in her will.

† Reported by Michaelson (Ibid., p. 367).

of them). Moreover, to the contrary, there are several anecdotal yet suggestive reports of Reid's unfortunate verbal and even physical abuse of his wife.* As difficult as it is for this scholar to reconcile the two warring sides of Reid's psyche, one can only imagine how torturous were the attempts by the writer himself to do so.

On the other hand, however, the significance of the following fact cannot be overstated: Reid and Mary Margaret were formally separated for eight years, from 1967 through 1975, and in that time Reid did not write a single word.† By all accounts, Reid's mental health deteriorated precipitously during this period, and he took to drinking to great excess, arriving intoxicated or not at all to book signings and interviews, and insulting his hosts and readers.‡ In addition, according to Wilcox, Reid was in the habit of calling him in the middle of the night, sobbing and wailing, "She's left me, Sam. It's all gone. Everything's gone."§ Ultimately, a particularly severe alcoholic blackout in late 1975 persuaded Reid to check himself into a rehabilitation facility and to endeavor to win back Mary Margaret's affections, a gambit at which he succeeded, as Mary Margaret allowed him to move back into the family home. Now I ask you: Was the publication of the masterful *Lissette* two years later a coincidence, or does the confluence of these events suggest that Mary Margaret inspired Reid to write? It's certainly a compelling interpretation. Even if her mere presence alone served as a stabilizing influence on Reid and *enabled* him to write, we needn't split hairs; in either case, Reid was able to gift us two more literary masterpieces before he died.

---

* I refer specifically to the documents I received from the Reid estate upon assuming its executorship, which include both Mary Margaret's personal diaries (an example from Mar. 22, 1962: "Ed is in rare form today; he called me a bitch and a shrew") and her hospital bills for the treatment of three separate injuries: a sprained wrist (June 20, 1962); a dislocated shoulder (Feb. 2, 1964); and a broken jaw (Oct. 17, 1967).

† Reported by Michaelson (Ibid., p. 919).

‡ The most egregious of these episodes occurred on April 27, 1968. Reid had to be escorted by police from The Elliott Bay Book Company in Seattle, Washington, when at a book signing he inscribed a female reader's copy of *Eyes of the Owl* with "Dear Theresa, you are a cunt" and thereafter refused to leave the premises (McKenzie, John. "Author Ousted From Elliott Bay Book Co." *Seattle Post-Intelligencer*, Apr. 27, 1968, p. 14). Happily, an antiwar protest in the city that same day overshadowed this incident, and no other newspapers picked up the story.

§ Reported by Michaelson (Ibid., p. 952).

Which brings us back to the enigmatic Mary Margaret Reid. By virtue of holding this volume in your hands, you know that at some point after Reid's death in 1981, Mary Margaret herself eventually took up writing. What you may not know is that in the almost thirty years until her own death in 2010, Mary Margaret also published twenty-seven mystery novels under the pseudonym M. M. Flanagan, her maiden name.* It is unclear whence the authorial impetus originated; certainly Mary Margaret had no need of extra income, as Reid bequeathed his entire estate, including his considerable royalties, to his wife.†

Although Mary Margaret was a more prolific writer than her husband, I am compelled to note that as in all things, quality is preferable to quantity. I have recently read the two "award-winning" Flanagan novels featuring private detective Ellie Kidd,‡ and it gives me no pleasure to report that although both are tales competently told and rife with amusing wordplay such as puns and anagrams of characters' names, I have not been persuaded to read further. I do not share the antipathy toward mystery stories professed by many literary critics, such as Vladimir Nabokov, who famously abhorred them. However, one simply cannot compare the quality of writing one usually finds in genre fiction with that one finds in the more elevated literary forms.

The Ellie Kidd series was not Mary Margaret's first attempt at becoming an authoress. In addition to the neatly catalogued drafts of each manuscript I discovered among her papers§ were dozens of rejection letters dating between 1951 and 1955 from the editors of magazines such as *Harper's, The Atlantic,* and *The New Yorker,* to

---

* Wikipedia, accessed June 4, 2019.

† Reid's five novels were all literary sensations, and each has been reprinted numerous times in English and translated into as many as 17 other languages. None has ever gone out of print.

‡ *All Kidding Aside* (1986) won the Edgar Allan Poe Award (Mystery Writers of America) for Best Mystery Novel in 1987, and *Don't Kid a Kidder* (1998) won the Shamus Award (Private Eye Writers of America) for Best PI Paperback Original in 1999.

§ The literary estate bequeathed to me by Mary Margaret Reid was almost ruthlessly organized. She was once quoted as saying, "A disordered desk bespeaks a disordered mind. I am a meticulous planner" (McGovern, Nicole Z. "Oh, You Kidd! Interview With MWA Grandmaster Mary Margaret Reid." *Mystery Scene,* no. 89, Spring 2005, pp. 7–10). Had she ever attended university, Mary Margaret might have trained as a librarian.

whom she had apparently submitted short stories.* No copies of these stories exist, but the magazines to which they were submitted, as well as the story titles—for example, "Ways and Means," "Nothing Short of Everything," and "Remembrances"—suggest they were attempts at the literary short form, not the genre fiction Mary Margaret was later to embrace. That there are no rejection letters dated after 1955 would lead one to speculate that these rejections caused Mary Margaret to give up on the idea of a writing career in favor of pursuing other interests. Indeed, she and Reid met in early 1956 and shortly thereafter she became his wife.†

When, then—and why—did Mary Margaret write the novel that you will shortly have the pleasure of reading? For it was undoubtedly written by Mary Margaret, even though there was no byline on *In the Frame,* the manuscript I discovered almost exactly one year ago in the very last batch of papers I received from the Reid estate.‡ The manuscript was undated and, as I said, had no byline, and I was quite sure I had never seen a reference to it in Reid's or Mary Margaret's literary effects. I confess that for one heart-stopping moment I entertained the outlandish idea that this manuscript was a long-lost work by Reid, but for reasons that I will soon detail, it became apparent to me as the novel unfolded that

---

* Although most of the rejection letters were tactfully phrased, a handful referred to her writing style as "frilly," "florid," and "inconsequential." One mentioned specifically "the general unsuitability of women's minds for the hard, unforgiving labor of putting pen to paper." Interestingly, Reid himself published two short stories, both in *Harper's:* "Means to an End" (vol. 268, no. 1296, May 1958) and "Reminiscences" (vol. 270, no. 1347, July 1960). An examination of these stories lies beyond the scope of this "Foreword"; suffice it to say that the stories were, as one would expect, small masterpieces in their own right, and each was met with much approbation from literary critics at the time (see Michaelson [Ibid., p. 55]).

† In her 1956 diary, Mary Margaret describes having met Reid in the drugstore in New York City's Barbizon Hotel for Women, where as a Katharine Gibbs student, or "Gibblet," she was living at the time. After a whirlwind courtship of six weeks, they were married in Las Vegas.

‡ By that time—10 years since Mary Margaret's death—I had received the bulk of Mary Margaret's inexplicable bequest to me, and I had spent my copious idle hours in the study of its contents. The batch of papers containing the manuscript, however, was, according to the timetable specified in Mary Margaret's will, the final cache of material, and I was increasingly aware that the inevitable denouement to this absorbing chapter of my life was fast approaching. Enter *In the Frame,* just in the nick—as it were—of time. (As the reader will appreciate, I am still capable of seeing the humor in my situation, even after all these years!)

although a cleverly wrought story, *In the Frame* had indeed been written not by Reid but by his wife.

I have no wish to deprive readers of the consummately enjoyable experience of engaging with the work on their own, but in summary, the plot concerns the commission of a monstrous crime and the various means by which the responsible person seeks to avoid justice. If I am characterizing the book as a mystery novel, that is because it can be labeled as such—but, I hasten to add, it is a mystery novel in the same way that Fyodor Dostoevsky's *Crime and Punishment* is a mystery novel. *In the Frame* is not a pedestrian whodunnit of the type that, say, M. M. Flanagan might have written, but more of what might be called a willshegetawaywithit, an examination of guilt, shame, and moral ambiguity; that is, it grapples, as literature does, with the pressing philosophical problems of our age.

There are, it is true, certain tropes and stylistic similarities between *In the Frame* and Reid's works, notably in the depiction of food and in the portrayal of the female characters. In chapter 3, the description of the funerary feast approaches the best of Reid's gastronomical descriptions in *The Aching Sky* and *Eyes of the Owl.* One can also argue that the women are drawn with an equally fine hand, particularly the protagonist, who manages to elicit sympathy even as she embarks upon her criminal enterprises. To what might one attribute these similarities in writing style? Perhaps instead of asking whether Mary Margaret served as Reid's muse, one should ask whether Reid served as Mary Margaret's. It seems ridiculous when phrased this way—male muses are as rare as unicorns—but in all seriousness, it is possible that having typed Reid's works for so many years, Mary Margaret's style had come to mimic her husband's.

Despite the stylistic similarities between Reid's works and *In the Frame,* there are clear differences. For example, in the latter there is something of a rageful and even sadistic sensibility in the female characters' attitudes toward the male characters that is entirely lacking in any of Reid's novels. Moreover, the women's dialogue, particularly that of the protagonist, is rendered as harsher and more direct than that in the Reidian canon, a phenomenon that hints at, though does not explicitly state, the existence of suppressed sapphic tendencies among several of the female characters. In this way, *In the Frame* less resembles the works of Edbert Reid than it does the works of suspense writer Patricia Highsmith.[*]

No less a critic than Edbert Reid himself has opined on this book, for his handwritten comments can be found throughout the first seventy-eight pages of the manuscript of *In the Frame,* comments that grow increasingly scathing page by page.[†] Interestingly, the pages after this are unmarked.[‡] Who can say why Reid stopped commenting on the work? Perhaps he had no desire to read further and pushed the manuscript aside. Perhaps Mary Margaret was displeased with his responses and refused to let him read the remainder of the book. At any rate, it should now be clear that Mary Margaret, not Reid, wrote *In the Frame,* and despite Reid's emphatic reservations—in contradistinction to my own—it is a thought-provoking work that will prove a source of enjoyable diversion for female readers and indeed some men as well.

I won't keep you from the delights that await you much longer, but I must note that when you turn the page, you will see that in addition to literary executorship, Mary Margaret conferred upon me the dedication to *In the Frame.* I was, and I remain, both honored and enormously puzzled. I encountered Mary Margaret only twice, and on neither occasion was she, shall we say, favorably impressed. To wit, during my first visit to the Reid home in 1980, I made the lamentable faux pas of assuming that Mary Margaret was Reid's maid, and rather imperiously demanded that she bring Reid and

---

[*] Patricia Highsmith was an excellent writer, albeit of genre fiction. Her works, like Mary Margaret's, also touched upon homosexuality and issues of artistic authenticity and forgery (viz., the Tom Ripley novels). The similarities are even more pronounced when one notes that the victim in *In the Frame* is a painter, and even the title is an obvious reference to the milieu of the world of art.

[†] It is disappointing to note that in this way, Reid's comments are, from the standpoint of critique, less than helpful. He begins with relatively nonjudgmental strike-throughs of various turns of phrase, noting "Diction!" in the margins, but progresses to heavily underscored and capitalized exclamations of "RIDICULOUS!!!" and "THIS IS SHIT!!!" scribbled across entire paragraphs.

[‡] Unmarked, that is, by Reid's hand. Diagonally across page 78, however, there is a spray of small, dark droplets—wine? If Reid was drinking heavily while reading Mary Margaret's work (and according to the notes I took during the trial, the pathologist who testified in court reported that Reid's blood alcohol level at the time of his murder was exceptionally high), then he might have spilled his libation on this page.

myself a cup of tea—a misunderstanding that caused Reid no end
of hilarity and Mary Margaret observable distress.[*] My second visit,
on the day of Reid's death in 1981, was occasioned by a summons
from the author via typewritten note.[†] This visit proved even more
disastrous than the first, for when I arrived at the designated time
to find the front door hanging open and Reid slumped over his
desk, I stupidly, in retrospect, thought to help him by pulling the
knife from his chest, thereby covering my hands in blood and the
knife handle with my fingerprints. Just then Mary Margaret came
into the room with a bag of groceries, whereupon she dropped
them, screamed, and fled.[‡]

Nevertheless, Mary Margaret's dedication to me remains: "For
William P. Dunster: I hope he finally knows why." I regret to say
that I don't. But now I have quite a mystery to unravel to occupy
my remaining years, and for that, I am forever grateful.

WILLIAM P. DUNSTER
Sing Sing Correctional Facility
Ossining, New York
June 26, 2021

---

[*]   In my defense, I was a callow youth, and finding myself in the presence of a
literary titan, I was desperate to appear more sophisticated and worldly than I
actually was.

[†]   As no carbon copy of the typewritten invitation was found in Reid's files, during
the trial the prosecutor insisted I must have typed the letter after the fact to explain
my presence in the Reid home.

[‡]   My ostensible motive for the crime was provided by a carbon copy of a letter
from Reid to me that was found in his files in which he, "for the last time," warned
that unless I ceased bombarding him with daily requests for additional interviews,
he would call A. L. Sticklee and terminate my academic career. Needless to say, I
had neither been hounding Reid nor ever received this letter. I professed my innocence throughout the trial and have continued to do so countless times since, but
even I have had to admit that the circumstantial evidence was damning.

JAMES A. HEARN

Home Is the Hunter

FROM *Mickey Finn*

Under the wide and starry sky,
Dig the grave and let me lie.
Glad did I live and gladly die,
And I laid me down with a will.

This is the verse you grave for me:
Here he lies where he longed to be;
Here is the sailor, home from the sea,
And the hunter home from the hill.

REQUIEM *by Robert Louis Stevenson*

THE OUTSIDE of the hunting cabin was a shambles, a dilapidated ruin of sagging eaves, askew shutters, and broken windows. Tattered curtains stirred fitfully in the autumnal wind, yellowed ghosts beckoning to the old man in the truck parked out front. *You've been away for so long, Joe. Come inside and join us. See what fifty years of neglect has wrought.*

Joe Easterbrook sat in his Ford pickup, weathered hands on the steering wheel, bleary eyes swimming with memories. He cut the engine and stared at the brambles crawling up the cabin's walls and the weeds sprouting between the porch's floorboards. For a wonder, his father's hickory rocking chair was still by the front door, its slow back-and-forth motion sending a chill down his spine.

Joe roughly wiped a tear from his cheek. *Crying again, old man? For the second time in as many days? You didn't even cry at your mother's funeral.*

As a boy, the cabin had seemed as strong as the red oak trees overshadowing it. He and his father had built the cabin from the ground up, using white pine timbers harvested from the surrounding woods. On a nameless mountainside of West Virginia, on three hundred acres of family land bordering the Monongahela National Forest, a young Joe watched as Howard Easterbrook imposed his will on the land.

Upon a foundation of exposed bedrock that seemed ordained for the purpose, father and son began by constructing a fireplace of white river rocks. Around the chimney and spacious hearth at its base, they laid solid wood floor joists, erected four log walls joined by saddle-notch corners, and finished with scissors-style trusses overlaid by planks and a galvanized steel roof. It was a small but sturdy structure, three hundred square feet of comfort.

During construction, Joe and his father had slept in a tent beneath the splash of the Milky Way. Meals were supplemented with game roasted over a firepit or fresh-caught golden rainbow trout from a stream behind the cabin, its water as clear and cold as the mountain air.

That was the summer of 1966.

Fifty-five years later, the once stalwart cabin looked like a strong breeze could knock it down, and the sight smote Joe's aging heart. He popped his last nitroglycerin pill under his tongue, let it dissolve, and washed out the burning taste with the dregs of a warm Coors Banquet.

Joe crumpled the can, then took out a flip phone and switched it on. He'd picked up the burner for cash at a Korean market on Detroit's east side, in the hours before the disastrous shootout with the Jamaicans. That was yesterday morning and a lifetime ago.

Joe held up the phone and watched the screen expectantly. No signal, roaming or otherwise. Just as he'd hoped. Smiling, he switched the phone off and put it in the glove compartment. It was a paperweight now, a useless assemblage of circuits and plastic that had no meaning out here. If his heart gave out, if he fell from a ladder and broke a leg, there would be no rescue from the outside world. Only the wolves would hear his cries for help.

No one owned this land anymore, not really. It was in the middle of nowhere, down miles of dirt roads that were marked only on paper maps—driving apps couldn't navigate roads where there was no signal. But Joe hadn't needed a GPS navigation app or even a map. He had found the cabin purely from memory. *Turn left at the abandoned windmill; after crossing the wooden suspension bridge, take the next right; five miles up the logging road, turn left.*

The land had passed out of the family the day Saigon fell, when Joe's stepmother donated it to some nature conservatory. The act was her punishment for Joe's voluntary participation in what she called "an illegal war of American imperialism." At least Shelby Watson Easterbrook had the decency to die before he returned from the jungles of Vietnam.

A brain aneurysm had saved Joe the trouble and expense of burying his querulous stepmother, though he had been dismayed to find her grave beside his father's. Howard Wilson Easterbrook— retired schoolteacher, huntsman, craftsman, veteran of the Second World War, and the best father a boy could hope for—reposed in eternal slumber between his two wives.

What are you waiting for, Joe? "Wait" broke the wagon down. That was his father's favorite aphorism whenever he saw his only son idling about.

With an audible creak, Joe eased himself out of the pickup and rubbed futilely at the ache in his back. Eleven hours behind the wheel had been murder on his arthritic joints, and he'd stopped only once for gas at a one-stoplight town east of Columbus. While filling up, he'd half-expected to see black Hummer H2s pulling up behind him, then grim-faced men with guns emerging into the flickering sodium lights. Would young Hector Ortega be among the men sent to kill him? And if so, would Joe's aim falter in the ensuing gun battle?

But William Donovan's assassins had not followed him from Detroit in the dead of night. They'd never stop looking for him, Joe knew, not after what he'd done. They'd find him; maybe next month, maybe in five years.

In the meantime, there was work to be done.

With a deep sigh, Joe went to his trailer and unlatched the back. He'd get no work done tonight—the sun was sinking behind the mountain, and the temperature was starting to drop—but he could at least set up his work area for tomorrow.

Joe unloaded a generator, filled it with gasoline, and plugged in a lantern. The gloom settling around the mountainside was pushed back a few yards, a tiny spark of civilization in an otherwise desolate wilderness. Insects drifted in and out of the light as Joe staked a canvas canopy, unfolded a table and chair, and then laid out his father's tools. They'd been in storage for decades, undisturbed, as if waiting for the day he returned to West Virginia.

In the moments after yesterday's shootout, as Joe stared at the six bodies around him—four Jamaican gangbangers, William Donovan's worthless nephew Sean O'Connell, and the pregnant girl the idiot had casually shot for seeing his face—Joe had considered leaving his father's things behind. Just grabbing his emergency cache and leaving Detroit as fast as possible.

But that seemed wrong. Cowardly. So, he'd taken the time to go home, grab his money and guns, hitch his trailer, and drive as calmly as he could to the storage unit.

By the time Joe unloaded his equipment and supplies, it was well past midnight. He looked up at the countless stars in the sky, his breath steaming in the September air. There was Jupiter passing into Aquarius, and winged Pegasus taking flight. So beautiful. With a satisfied grin, Joe set up his tent and switched off the generator and the lantern.

Tomorrow morning, he'd go into the nearest town and buy everything he needed. He might go to several towns, so as not to raise suspicion by spending thousands of dollars in cash in one place. Yes, that would be best.

Before turning in, Joe looked again at the old cabin, now a dark shape silhouetted against the deeper darkness of the mountain. How strange to feel such a bone-deep sadness over times gone past, the innumerable hunts through the wilderness tracking deer and other game. Those were happy days of youth growing into manhood, of learning what the mountain could provide.

Inside the tent, Joe unrolled his sleeping bag and eventually drifted to a fitful sleep, his Winchester Model 1892 lever-action rifle within easy reach. Carrying the Glock 19, his preferred firearm for so many years, just didn't seem right anymore. Not after yesterday, and certainly not in these sacred woods.

Joe's last thought as he listened to the wind sighing through the boughs of the red oaks was disquieting, yet oddly comforting: *This place is as good a place as any to die.*

"The old man ain't here, Hector. We're wasting our time."

Hector Ortega didn't look up from the desk drawer he was rifling through. He hadn't found much of interest in Joe Easterbrook's quaint home on the outskirts of Detroit, besides some letters and a few Polaroids.

The letters were from the '60s and '70s—something the writers called a "Round Robin" that was apparently circulated via snail mail to family members in an endless chain. As for the Polaroids, one with a lean man holding a lever-action rifle caught Hector's eye. The rifle had a short barrel and no scope, the kind John Wayne carried in a hundred Westerns. A buck lay at the man's feet, a blue mountain landscape behind.

Hector studied the picture and said, "*Isn't*. The old man *isn't* here. And we are not wasting our time, Blinky. We are looking for clues to where Easterbrook may have gone."

Blinky Simons opened a closet door and rummaged around half-heartedly, a frown on his square face. The big man was an aging street tough who followed orders without question, and Hector suspected he was along to ensure that if they did find Joe Easterbrook, Hector would actually kill his former partner.

As he had sworn to do.

"Clues?" Blinky said. "It's hard to know what's a clue when I don't even know what I'm looking for."

Hector closed the drawer and slipped the letters and the Polaroid into a pocket. He brought a slender hand to his dark beard and studied Easterbrook's home. He'd never been here, despite working with Joe for years.

The home was Spartan bordering on austere, everything arranged with a military precision. Even the leftovers in the refrigerator were labeled according to contents and date. There was nothing, aside from a vintage record player, to say what kind of man lived here. But that was a clue in itself, wasn't it?

"Easterbrook's been here," Hector announced. He went over to the record player and opened the plastic dust cover. John Denver's *Poems, Prayers & Promises* lay on the turntable, flipped to Side B. Interesting. Hector picked up a stack of records and began flipping through them.

Blinky scratched his bald head. "How do you figure?"

"It's what we *haven't* found that's important. No cash. No guns, ammo, or personal effects. He took his pillows from the bed but left his phone charger behind. He came home after the . . . incident with Sean. Grabbed his emergency cache, a few personal items, and left."

Blinky cracked a beer he'd found in the fridge and was helping himself to leftover fried chicken. He sat down in a recliner opposite Hector and said, "Incident? Killing the boss's favorite nephew ain't—I mean *isn't*—an incident. It's suicide."

Hector put down the records. More country artists: Waylon Jennings, Johnny Cash, and Willie Nelson. Outlaws. But no new country, none of the synthesized pop-trash Nashville churned out nowadays. That said something too.

"Get me a beer, Blinky."

"Sure. Can we watch some TV?"

"No TV," Hector said. "I need to think for a few minutes."

Blinky set a Coors Banquet in front of Hector and a plate with more fried chicken, then returned to his recliner.

Hector cracked the beer and took a long swallow to steady his nerves. Yesterday, for a moment, he'd thought Joe would actually shoot him the way Joe had shot Sean. But the older man stood motionless over Sean's body and the dead pregnant girl, his face unreadable.

Hector went over the scene in his methodical mind, point by point. He had waited for the Jamaicans in an out-of-the-way alley for a supposed drug buy, while Joe and Sean hid behind concrete stairs, guns drawn.

The Jamaicans arrived wearing surgical masks, hands open. Hector pulled up his own mask and waved them over. Come closer. We're friends. When the men cleared the stairwell, Joe and Sean stepped from the shadows and opened fire, dropping them in moments.

For good measure, Sean O'Connell kicked the bodies and spat upon them. The boy always seemed like he was hopped up, but Sean never touched the poison he peddled. Whatever the demons were that fired his brain, they came from within.

Some people were naturally rotten, Hector supposed.

After the gunfight, Joe and Hector had to grab the animated Sean by the arms, pulling him away from the bloody scene and toward the street. As they turned, all three men stopped dead in their tracks. There was a girl standing in the mouth of the alley, a dark figure with a swollen belly.

The mother-to-be was maybe nineteen, an evocative silhouette against the brightness beyond. To Hector, she looked so pretty in her red dress, a bag of groceries clutched to her chest. Though a mask covered her mouth, pleasingly color-coordinated to match her purse, Hector could clearly see the "O" of surprise on her lips. She was looking right at Sean's face.

Sean, who wasn't wearing a mask. According to him, masks and vaccines were for *sheeple*, and the pandemic gripping the planet (the Kung Flu, as Sean called it) was part of some nefarious world government scheme. It had something to do with chemtrails in the sky and sterilization and taking people's guns.

"She's seen my face," Sean said, as if this were the girl's fault. Before Hector knew what was happening, Sean shot the girl three times—once in the chest, then a double-tap to the head when she was down.

An instant later, Joe's Glock 19 spoke at point-blank range, inches from the base of Sean's skull. The boy fell, his head caved in on itself like a rotten melon.

As Sean's body thudded to the ground, Hector found he couldn't move. There was a dead civilian, the kind to make police and politicians scream for blood, and there was Sean beside her. Granted, the world was a better place without him in it, but there would be a reckoning for him too. A more severe reckoning.

And there was Joe holding his Glock, his eyes on Hector. Fight or flight waged war in Hector for a split second. Run? Draw my Beretta? Joe's quiet calmness decided the matter; Hector ran for it. Before he rounded the corner, he caught sight of Joe bending over the girl's body, head bowed.

"This chicken's tasty," Blinky said. "Can I turn on the TV?"

Hector sighed and stared daggers at the other man. Why not shoot this simpleton, like Joe had done to Sean, and disappear? It would be so easy and quick, three seconds, tops. But the man's perpetually red-rimmed eyes unnerved Hector, and he let the moment pass. Blinky was an ironic nickname, like calling a fat man Slim or a bald man Curly. The big man never, ever blinked.

"No TV. How about I play a record for you?"

"Like what?"

Hector went to the phonograph. "John Denver."

"Huh. I didn't know Gilligan was a singer too."

Hector shook his head and didn't bother to correct Blinky. He sat back down on the couch and listened to "Take Me Home, Country Roads" while he drank his beer.

There was something significant about this album, Hector

thought. For one thing, it didn't *belong* in this collection with the others. John Denver was no country music outlaw like Waylon and Willie; he was a bespectacled folk singer, a favorite of his beloved grandmother. There was personality and nuance in these lyrics, a longing for things past.

A homesickness.

Hector pulled out Joe's family letters and began to read them. Pecan pie recipes. The baby kicked today. Mundane details, tears, and quiet triumphs. His mind began to wander, and he thought of William Donovan standing over him, fat fists clenched.

"Your partner killed my sister's boy," Donovan had told him. "And you didn't do a thing, Hector. You ran like a coward and let Sean's killer go free."

Hector hadn't dared to rise from the floor. He was thanking his lucky stars to come out of this with only a beating.

Donovan delivered a swift kick to his ribs and said, "You're going to get justice for my Sean. You will find Joe Easterbrook and kill him. Or your precious grandmother will die."

The first time Joe saw the dog, Joe was on the cabin's roof with a bucket of mortar and a trowel. He'd been sealing up cracks in the chimney, enjoying the sting of cold air in his eyes, when he sensed someone—or some*thing*—watching him.

He glanced around warily, cursing himself for leaving his Winchester by the ladder. There. Down the winding dirt road, at the foot of a gnarled oak, a ragged-looking dog sat on its haunches. It was the wrong color and shape to be a coyote, and it was certainly no wolf. A hound of some kind, by the look of its floppy ears, and it was far from home.

Slowly, Joe put down his tools and descended the ladder. The dog continued staring at him, but its ears were back now, and a low growl sounded deep in its throat.

Once on the ground, Joe spread his hands to show they were empty. "Easy there, fella. Easy. Nothing here to hurt you." He took a cautious step forward, but the dog bolted into the woods.

The next evening, Joe saw the dog again, this time sitting much closer to his camp. A male beagle, Joe noticed, probably nine or ten years old from the white in his face. Had a hunter met with an accident in the wilderness, leaving his faithful dog to fend for himself? Or had some heartless bastard dumped him by the roadside?

Regardless of where he came from, there was dried blood at the dog's throat, and the tip of his left ear ended in a jagged line.

This time, Joe did not approach the dog. Instead, he maintained his seated position by the firepit, where a rabbit was roasting on a spit.

"You look like hell, old-timer. But from the blood around your mouth, you gave as good as you got."

The beagle's tail thumped the ground once.

"By the fur stretched over your ribs, you could use a meal," Joe said. "Hungry?"

The beagle leaned forward, brown eyes flicking from Joe's face to the rabbit. Back and forth, back and forth. Joe could almost hear his thoughts.

Joe took the sizzling rabbit from the spit, placed it on a wooden plank, and carved it with his hunting knife. The beagle's tail betrayed his hunger, for it began to thump the ground repeatedly.

Joe sliced off the hind legs for himself, then held up the remaining carcass. The beagle was on his feet now, his entire being focused on the meal in Joe's hand. "This is for you, old-timer. Eat hearty."

The beagle caught the carcass before it hit the ground, then tore into the meat with a will.

Joe laughed aloud for the first time in weeks. "Now I'll never get rid of you, I suppose."

The dog wagged his tail as if agreeing with this statement, though he retreated to the woods once his meal was done. Their relationship continued this way for another few weeks. At dinnertime, the dog would show up at camp and watch Joe cook his one meal of the day, then eat whatever Joe threw to him: rabbit, fried bacon and eggs, venison.

Joe continued his work on the cabin, the dog watching from the woods. He'd started outside first, working from the top down. For the roof, he'd mortared the cracks in the chimney and caulked any holes in the galvanized steel. Replacing the eaves proved tricky for one man to do, but Joe managed it by positioning multiple ladders beneath his work area to prop up unsupported boards. After clearing away the climbing brambles from the walls, he vigorously cleaned the white pine timbers and resealed them. Finally, he rehung the shutters and replaced the loose boards on the porch.

Inside, the damage was not as bad as he'd feared. Aside from some boards that had popped loose from their joists, the cabin's floor was solid, its construction fundamentally sound. It was just utterly filthy.

Joe began by sweeping away the cobwebs and animal nests, a process that gagged him with the stench of rat urine. The surgical-grade masks he'd picked up in town kept his lungs clear of dust, animal dander, and feces stirred up by his broom.

All that remained was to clean and disinfect the floor, repair the loose floorboards, replace the broken windows, hang new curtains, and reseal the floor. The work was exhausting but refreshing, and there were times he forgot about Detroit.

Then one evening in late October, when a waning gibbous moon was cresting the eastern horizon and the wind had died to nothing, something wonderful happened. As Joe sat before his cooking fire and felt the peace of the West Virginian wilderness penetrate his soul, the beagle walked up and put his chin on Joe's knee.

Joe scratched the dog's ears, and the animal closed his eyes and seemed to relax. "Your name," Joe said after a moment of deep contemplation, "is Old Timer."

The dog's eyes snapped open, and the two locked gazes. This was the primal bond, Joe thought, bred in the bone, a friendship between man and beast since the world began.

"Old Timer."

A playful bark, and Old Timer's paw came up and worried at Joe's hand. *Keep scratching me.* After dinner, when both had eaten all the roasted grouse they could, the beagle curled up at Joe's feet and went to sleep before the fire.

Joe sighed contentedly. "That's the ultimate show of trust, isn't it? Whether it's between two lovers or a man and a dog. You can fall asleep beside me. We are pack, now."

Old Timer kicked his legs in a dream.

"Chasing a rabbit?" Joe asked. "Wish I could sleep as deeply, as peacefully. But I keep seeing a dead girl's face when I close my eyes. She reminds me of something I've tried to forget." Whether it was in a Detroit alley or a rice paddy in Vietnam, the bodies of civilians looked the same.

"I was my best self here, Old Timer. In these woods, with this very rifle. Before I went to war to defend my country. Before Dad died and the family land was sold out from under me."

In the dying firelight, Joe spun a tale for his new companion.

He told the dog how he'd gone to war and learned to kill, then returned home to a country that hated him. Spat on him. With a heavy heart, he left West Virginia and hitchhiked to Detroit, where he perfected his trade on the streets—murder. Joe left nothing out, confessing everything—the men he'd killed, the women he'd loved and ultimately disappointed. A cheap life of money, booze, and decades wasted in the service of evil men.

Wolves howled in the distance as night covered the mountain like a shroud. Joe looked into the darkness beyond his fire, his hackles rising. Sound was a funny thing out here. The wolves might be just over the next ridge, or miles away.

Old Timer raised his head at the howls.

"They're out there, all right. The wolves are always out there." Joe took up his Winchester and checked the action. The weapon had a twelve-round capacity, and the only ammo Joe used was Winchester's 100 Years of John Wayne; in his vest pocket above his heart, Joe kept another thirty-eight rounds in the box bearing The Duke's likeness.

As a kid, Joe imagined riding the range with his rifle at his side. The gun had no scope, but that was no matter; the buckhorn-style rear sight and the front sight dovetailed into the twenty-four-inch octagonal barrel were all Joe needed. Chambered for .44–40 rounds, he could still drop a deer—or a wolf, if need be—at 150 yards.

The wind shifted, blowing from the north. Joe threw another log on the fire, held out his hands to the flames. It hadn't snowed yet, thank God. The first snow usually fell by mid-November, but it was not unheard-of to have snow in late October. A man caught outdoors in a snowstorm might freeze to death by morning.

"Soon, maybe next week, the cabin will be done. We can sleep with a roof over our heads, build our first fire in the fireplace, and cook our meals inside like civilized folk. What do you say to that?"

Old Timer snored in reply. *Whatever you say, Joe. The hearth sounds nice and warm.*

Joe looked to the cabin. In the dancing light of the fire, he could discern his father's rocking chair on the porch. He had a vision of himself in the chair, his guitar in hand and an Irish whiskey on an upturned barrel, with Old Timer asleep at his feet.

When my labors are done, Joe thought. *When the cabin is fully restored to its former glory.*

*

La vida no es justa, Hector told himself as he drove the Hummer H2 past an abandoned windmill. That was his grandmother's favorite saying, and Hector agreed. Life wasn't fair. It wasn't fair that a heart attack struck down his father in his prime, or that his mother succumbed to breast cancer the following year, leaving Hector as a burden to a loving but aged grandmother.

It wasn't fair that he'd been pressed into the service of a drug lord to pay the family's enormous medical bills, or for Donovan to seek vengeance for the death of a monster like Sean O'Connell.

And it wasn't fair that ten men were coming to kill one.

"Beautiful country," Donovan said from the passenger's seat. The middle-aged Irishman had insisted on coming to witness what he called *justice.* Whatever this was, it wasn't just. "Take me home, country roads." The man began humming John Denver's ballad to West Virginia.

"It's colder than a penguin's turd," Blinky said from the back seat. The big man wore a thin jogging suit like he was Vladimir Putin about to go for a run. The other men in Donovan's entourage were dressed no better. They would be out of their element in these woods.

"You should've worn something warmer," Hector chided.

"It was fifty degrees in Detroit," Blinky complained. "Can we turn on the Thanksgiving game? The Lions are playing. I want to hear the score."

Donovan's eyes flashed. The man was irritable at the best of times, and the cross-country drive had not helped his mood. "Shut up, Blinky. Find the score on your phone."

"No signal out here," Blinky muttered. "Just trees."

Hector drove across a wooden suspension bridge, praying to God that it would support two Hummers and ten men, then took the next right. His map called this the Old Logging Road, and it twisted for miles into the mountains. Somewhere ahead, they'd find Joe in the middle of a wilderness.

At least, that's what a private investigator named Rainsford promised—a man who specialized in finding people in so-called witness protection programs. Hector had supplied the man with a starting point based on Joe's family letters and the Polaroid picture. Rainsford had done the rest.

Up the Hummers drove, higher and higher into the mountains,

on meandering dirt roads. The air was thinning out, Hector felt, and the temperature was dropping. The bright sky overhead—at least what he could see through the pine trees—was clouding over.

Maybe they wouldn't find Joe, Hector hoped. Not that he felt any special kinship with his former partner. Between jobs, they drank together and spoke of trivialities, of women and football. No, it wasn't friendship holding Hector back, and it wasn't quite fear either.

There was a Greek word for it, something he remembered from high school when reading about Achilles and the Trojan War. When mere mortals dared too much, tried to go beyond the boundaries set by the gods. And the gods struck them down for pride. What was the word?

"Something troubling you, Hector?" Donovan asked.

We are coming to Joe's country. His turf. The sun's about to go down, and the weather report is bad. Men will die today. But Hector kept this to himself and said, "Nothing." He pushed the accelerator.

Old Timer heard the Hummers coming before Joe did. The beagle had been relaxing on the porch by Joe's feet, listening to Joe pluck Johnny Cash's version of "Ghost Riders in the Sky" on his guitar. The cabin was done at last, and the sun was sinking behind the mountain. Above, dark clouds told of a coming snowstorm to mirror the song.

Suddenly, the beagle raised his head, alert.

Joe stopped playing. "What is it?"

The dog growled, his eyes trained on the road, as if he smelled a wolf. Then Joe heard an answering growl, mechanical in nature. An approaching vehicle, perhaps several, and they'd be here within minutes.

Joe put down his guitar and belted the last of his whiskey. Then he put on his warmest coat and hat, grabbed his Winchester and a pair of night-vision binoculars, and sprinted to the woods as fast as his heart would tolerate. Old Timer followed soundlessly. About 150 yards up the mountain, there was a tree stand Joe used for hunting deer. And it had a perfect view of the clearing in front of the cabin.

Hector stood by the H2, his Beretta drawn. He didn't like the look of the cabin in the gloom, with its windows like eyes staring accusingly at the trespassers. Smoke was curling out of the stone chimney, and inside was a half-eaten dinner on the hearth. On the front porch, they'd found a rocking chair, a guitar, and an upturned rain barrel with an opened whiskey bottle.

Joe's truck was here, but apparently its owner wasn't. Had he gone for a walk in the woods? Was he fishing somewhere up that stream?

The other men were nervous, even Blinky. But not Donovan. The ruddy-faced man was drinking Joe's whiskey, a haughty look on his face.

"He's trapped up here, gents," Donovan said. "Oscar, slash the tires on that truck. Jamal, pass out the flashlights. Ramsey, give me your jacket."

"Boss, it's getting cold," Ramsey whined. Hector watched a single snowflake hit the burly man's face and melt like a tear. More snow began to fall, a gentle but steady drift.

"Exactly. That's why I need your jacket."

"Joe knows we're here," Hector said. "We should take the H2s and fall back. Get away from this cabin."

Donovan drained the whiskey bottle and said, "Don't worry about the cabin, coward." He nodded to a gas canister beside Joe's truck. "Blinky, get the gas can by that generator. Torch this place."

The big man hesitated. He glanced apprehensively at the trees and said, "What about forest fires?"

"Smokey Bear can kiss my arse," Donovan hissed. "Do it. We'll hide the H2s down the road. When Joe sees the smoke, he'll come racing back. Then, Hector, you'll kill him."

As Blinky approached the cabin, gas can in hand, a shot rang out from the woods. The man collapsed bonelessly to the ground, his open eyes glazed with death.

Donovan and his men scrambled for cover behind the H2s. More shots rang out, each followed by a familiar ratcheting sound Hector had heard in a dozen Westerns. *Joe's out there with that blasted rifle!*

"Sound off!" Donovan called out. "Who's hit?"

Hector heard eight voices for eight men, including himself. Only Blinky was down. Joe was a crack shot, so what was going on? Could the old man even see in this swirling snow and dying daylight?

Donovan chuckled. He slapped Hector on the shoulder and

said, "The bastard can't shoot straight in this, any more than we could! He's firing blind. We'll drive away in the darkness and find him when the sun comes up."

Hector laughed bitterly when he realized what Joe's true targets were. *Hubris.* That was the Greek word he was trying to recall.

"He isn't shooting at us." Hector pointed with his Beretta to what was left of their vehicles' tires. Each H2 was lopsidedly resting on two of its rims, and Joe had even shot the spares exposed on the back. "Joe's shooting the tires on the H2s. *We* are the ones trapped on this mountain, not him. We are the hunted."

Full night fell, and the snow began to come down in earnest. Every so often, the Winchester echoed across the mountains of West Virginia.

Flip Lady

FROM *Electric Literature*

History

Raymond Brown hears the sound of laughter. He puts down his book and looks out the window.

Here they come now, children of the ancient ones, the hewers of wood, the cutters of cane barreling down the sidewalk on their Huffys and Schwinns. Little legs pumping over fat rubber tires, brakes squealing as they pull into the drive, standing on tiptoes as they straddle their bikes and stare at the house with their mouths hanging open.

Just like before. Some of them he still recognizes. He made out with that girl's sister in the seventh grade, played basketball with that boy's uncle in high school. This one was all right until his brother joined the army, that one was okay until her daddy went to jail. And you see that girl in the back? The chubby one standing by the curb, next to the brand-new Schwinn? She hasn't been the same since the invasion of Grenada, nine years ago, in 1983.

The Spice Island. When the marines landed, she was three years old, living in St. George's near the medical clinic with her mother, the doctor, and Aunt Ruby, the nurse. The power went off, the hospital plunging into blue darkness while machine gunfire cackled in the distance like a bag of Jiffy Pop bubbling up on a stove. *Oh no*, Aunt Ruby said. *Just like before.*

It's all there, in the book on his lap. Colonizers fanning out across the Atlantic like a hurricane, not exactly hungry but looking for spice. They claimed the land, they built the plantations, they filled the Americas up with slaves. Sugar kept the workers happy, distracted them from grief. And four hundred years later you have your military invasions and McDonald's Happy Meals, your Ho Hos and preemptive strikes. Your Oreos and Reaganomics, your Cap'n Crunch.

And Kool-Aid. These kids can't get enough of it. They sit in the driveway, they shift in their seats, they grip the plastic streamers affixed to their handlebars. One of them kicks a kickstand and steps forward, fingers curled into a small tight fist as he knocks on the kitchen door.

"Flip Lady? You in there?"

Just like before. They roamed the entire earth in search of spice so why not here, why not now?

"Flip Lady? You home? It's me, Calvin . . ."

For the past few weeks, they've been coming almost every day.

Raymond closes the curtain. He shakes his head and turns toward the darkness of the back bedroom. "Mama? It's those fucking kids again."

2.

The squeak of old mattress coils, a single bang of a headboard against a bedroom wall. The Flip Lady wills herself upright, sets her feet on the floor, sits on the edge of her bed and stares at the chipped polish on her left big toe. She stands up, reaches for her slippers, straightens out her green housedress, and walks out the bedroom door. The Flip Lady shuffles into the living room where her nineteen-year-old son, Raymond, sits on a low couch, reading. Long brown body hunched forward, elbows resting on his knees as he peers at the page of the book on his lap. In an instant his life flashes through her mind in a series of fractured images, like a VHS tape on rewind. She sees him at sixteen, face hidden behind a comic book, then at seven when his feet barely touched the floor. And before that as a chubby toddler, gripping the cushions with fat meaty fists, laughing as he hoisted himself onto the couch. Without breaking her stride, and for want of anything else to say, she mutters, "I see you reading," and passes into the kitchen.

The Flip Lady lifts a pickle jar full of loose change from the counter and looks out the kitchen window.

"That you, Calvin?" she says to the little boy standing on her porch.

"Afternoon, ma'am." Calvin smiles.

She twists the lid off the jar, opens the kitchen door, and squints at the multitude assembled in her backyard.

Calvin plunges his hand into his pants pocket and pulls out a fistful of dimes. He drops them into her jar with a series of empty pings.

"Well, all right then," the Flip Lady says.

Calvin glances over his shoulder and winks.

She walks toward her refrigerator while Calvin stands in the doorway. He cocks his head and peers past her into the living room. Glass angel figurines and the tea set on the lace doily in the cabinet against the wall; bronzed baby shoes mounted on a wooden plaque; framed high school graduation photos and Sears portraits of her two sons sitting on top of the TV set; a stack of LPs lined up on the floor. A dark green La-Z-Boy recliner and the plaid couch where her younger son sits with a book on his lap. Calvin turns his head again and sees the Flip Lady standing in the middle of her bright yellow kitchen, easing two muffin trays stuffed with Dixie cups out of her freezer.

The Flip Lady studies Calvin's face as he scoops the cups out of the trays, licking his lips, eyes lit up like birthday candles. She smiles. Her boys were the same way when they were that age, crowding around her back door with all their friends, giddy with excitement as they sucked on her homemade Popsicles. She used to hand them out when their friends came over to play after school and on weekends; it was a way to keep them in her backyard where she could watch them from the kitchen window. A good mother, she wanted to get to know how her boys passed their time and with whom. She wanted to memorize their playmates' faces and study their gestures until she felt confident that she could tell the clever from the calculated, the dreamy-eyed from the dangerous, the quiet from the cruel. She hadn't done it for money. No one had to thank her, although her neighbors told her many times how much they appreciated her looking out for their children that way.

The Flip Lady frowns. Of course, everything does change, eventually. There comes a time when a mother has to accept that the promise of sugary sweets has lost its ability to soothe all grief. They don't want your Kool-Aid anymore. They busy, they got other things to do. One day you find yourself standing alone in the kitchen, hand wrapped around a cold cup, melting ice dripping down your fingers as you wonder to yourself when exactly the good little boys standing on your back porch became the big bad men walking out your front door.

She looks at Calvin. "How was school today, son? You studying hard, being a good boy? Doing what your mama tells you?"

"Yes, ma'am." Calvin walks around, passing out Dixie cups to his friends.

"Well, all right then," the Flip Lady says.

3.

What you get for your money is a hunk of purple ice, a Dixie cup full of frozen Kool-Aid. The girl in the back stares at hers. It's not quite what she was expecting, given how far they have come to get it. According to the black plastic Casio attached to her left wrist, they've been riding for a full twenty minutes in the opposite direction from where she was trying to get to, which was home. One minute she was in the schoolyard unlocking her bike and the next they were standing over her, the whole group of them saying, Come with us. She knew it wasn't an invitation but an order. They were taking her to wherever it was they went when they sprinted off after class, their laughter echoing in the distance long after they'd disappeared past the school gate. How could she say no? She lifts the cup to her open mouth and runs her tongue along its surface, absorbing flat sweetness and a salty aftertaste.

"It's just Kool-Aid," someone says.

The girl closes her mouth. She looks around the parking lot of Byrdie's Burgers, where they have parked their bikes to eat. Everyone is pushing the bottoms of their cups with the pads of their thumbs, making those sugar lumps rise into the air. They're tilting their cups to the side and pulling them out, melting Kool-Aid dripping down their hands as they flip them over, then carefully placing them back in the cups, bottom sides up. They're sucking on their fingers, they're licking their lips, their mouths pressed against homemade Popsicle flips.

"What's the matter? Don't they have Kool-Aid where you come from?"

The girl looks down at her cup. She pushes her thumbs against the bottom but presses too hard; the hunk of purple ice pops out too fast and soars over the rim. She tries to catch it, but her hands fumble; it dribbles down the front of her shirt, then lands with a thud on the pavement.

"Now that's a shame."

The girl wipes her hands on the front of her shorts, palms already sticky. She blames her upbringing, all those years spent stuck on that rock, how to flip a homemade popsicle was just one more thing she should have known. She got the exact same looks from the kids on Grenada, after she moved there with her mother and Aunt Ruby all those years ago: *What you come here for? What you want with this rock, when everybody trying to get off it?* As if only white people were supposed to spin in dizzy circles like that, as missionaries or volunteers or tourists on extended leave. She can still see her former playmates in the eyes of her new school's handful of immigrant kids, with their high-water pants and loud polyester shirts, huddling and whispering to each other as they move down the halls. They look tired, fagged out from the journey, but at least they have an excuse. She's not even West Indian. Everyone knows her uncle Todd lives right around the block from Henry's Bar and has been living there for at least twenty years.

"What a waste."

When her mother said they were moving back to the States she'd been like everyone else she knew, picturing New York or LA like she saw on TV, not some narrow sliver of southern suburbia wedged senselessly in between. Instead, she is surrounded by a whole parking lot full of distracted sucking children who don't like her anyway.

"Go get another one," someone says. Calvin, the boss around here, although sometimes they take turns.

"It's only ten cents. Ain't you even got another dime?"

"What's the problem? You scared to go back by yourself?"

"What's the matter? Don't you want one?"

Of course she wants one. But she wants that one there, already dissolving into a pool of purple ooze at her feet. If she can't have it then she wants to go home, sit on the couch, eat leftover Entenmann's cookies from the box, and watch *Star Trek* reruns until her mother gets home from work at the hospital.

She looks back at the Flip Lady's house, now halfway down the block. She's tired of traveling the wrong way, dragging herself in the wrong direction without real rhyme or actual reason. But she also doesn't want to cause trouble, doesn't want to make waves. She reaches for the handlebars of her bike.

"Naw, leave it." They lick their lips and smile. "We'll watch it for you."

But they lie: In a few minutes they are going to teach her a lesson about realness, about keeping it. Because even her accent is fake. Because she rides around on a Schwinn that is just like theirs, except it is brand-new.

"Go on, girl."

Plus, she's fat.

The girl nods her head. She knows they are going to start talking about her as soon as her back is turned. They're a mean bunch; she's seen them do some terrible things at school. She's already figured out that it does no good to wander in and out of earshot of this group. Either you've got to stay knuckle to knuckle, packed tight like a fist, or else give them a wide berth and do all you can to not draw attention to yourself.

She turns around and starts walking. She can hear them whispering and laughing behind her, a hot humid jungle of bad moods circling her footsteps, gathering in strength with each step she takes. A flash of fear tickles her nose, like when you're swimming and accidentally inhale water. But she does not stop walking, somehow convinced that to turn around midstride will only make things worse.

She knocks on the Flip Lady's door, expecting to see the kind face of the woman who answered it not a half hour before. Instead, it's a man, dressed in a pair of sweatpants and a blue T-shirt, a little brown Chihuahua shivering in the palm of his left hand. She stares up at flaring nostrils, dark eyes, eyebrows arched.

"What do you want?"

"I dropped mine."

Raymond shakes his head. "No. I'm not doing this. Mama's not here. Understand? Flip Lady gone. She went out. Shopping. To buy more Kool-Aid, most likely. So why don't you just come back tomorrow . . ."

A harsh peel of laughter cuts across the horizon. The girl puts her head down and reaches into her pocket. She holds out a dime like a peace offering.

Raymond recoils. "I don't want that. What am I supposed to do with that? Girl, you better just go on home."

He squints into the distance behind her. "Those your friends? Little heathens . . ."

The girl hears the harsh scrape of metal against concrete as the man steps past her, onto the porch.

"Hey, girl. Is that your bike?"

She winces at the sound of rubber soles pounding on the spokes and stares down at the mat in front of the door.

"Hey, girl . . . What the heck are they doing—"

She shuts her eyes, feels a stiff pressure in her groin, like a sudden swift kick against her bladder, then a sharp tingling sensation between her legs.

"Hey, girl, turn around . . ."

The girl looks up. "May I use your bathroom, please?"

Raymond looks at the child breathing hard with her thighs clamped together, shifting her weight from side to side. He bites his lip then nods and points down the hall, watches her sprint past his friend Tony, who is standing in the middle of the living room grinning from ear to ear.

"You from Jamaica?" Tony says as the girl rushes past. She runs into the bathroom and slams the door.

Raymond shakes his head. It's all there, in his book, he thinks. It's always the weak and the homely who get left behind. Stranded on the back porch, knees shaking as they quiver and dance, thin rivers of pee running down their ashy legs.

4.

The girl sits on the toilet in a pink-tiled bathroom, staring at a stack of *Ebony* and *Newsweek* magazines in a brass rack near the sink. She's thinking about her bike, about how much she's going to miss it. She's only had it for a few weeks, but still. It's something she begged and pleaded for, something she swore she needed to fit in at her new school. Now she doesn't even want to look at it. A few minutes before the Flip Lady's son knocked on the door and told her he would fix it so she can ride home, but it's too late. It's already ruined. She's already peed herself and run away.

Everybody's always so busy running, so busy trying to save their own skins, she remembers her aunt Ruby telling her. *That's what's wrong with this world. We've got to stand together if we're going to stand at all.* The girl had liked the sound of that even if she sensed that it didn't really apply to her. She'd seen her aunt and mother working in the clinic, stood numb and mystified by the deliberateness with which they thrust themselves into other people's wounds. Stitching a cut, dressing a burn, giving a shot, connecting an IV. It was intimidating, the steadiness of her mother's hand sometimes. Even now, in the midst of grief. Like some nights when her mother stomped into the living room and cut off the TV in the middle of the evening news, her voice damming the flood of silence that followed with the simple statement: "They lie."

The girl reaches for the roll of toilet paper and wipes off the insides of her legs. She pulls up her damp panties and zips her shorts. When she opens the door she finds Tony alone in the living room, crouched down on the floor, peering behind the stack of LPs lined up against the wall.

"You feeling better?"

When she doesn't say anything, he puts the records back. He stands up, shoves his hands into his pockets, and smiles.

"So, what, you from Jamaica?"

The girl shakes her head. "I come from here."

"Not talking like that you don't." Tony walks past her and then stops. He crosses his arms in front of his chest, puts one hand on his chin and stares down at the couch.

"I lived on Grenada for a time but—"

"What's that?"

She watches as he kneels in front of the couch. He lifts the cushion and runs his hand underneath it like he's looking for spare change.

"Another island," she says.

He puts the cushion back and sits on top of it, bouncing up and down a few times to force the cushion back into place.

Tony nods. "Y'all smoke a lot of ganja down there too?"

The girl shrugs awkwardly. She wonders what about her appearance might remind this man of a Rastafarian. Rastafarians wore dusty clothes, had calloused feet and thick clumps of matted hair. They sat in the waiting room, making the clinic smell like salt and homemade lye soap. Her mother checked their charts while Aunt Ruby rubbed their arms with cotton pads dipped in alcohol. When they saw the needle, Aunt Ruby smiled and told them it was just a pinprick. *Don't worry, it will be all right,* she promised. *Just look at me.*

But, no, she didn't smoke a lot of ganja.

"That's all right," Tony says. "You still got that sweet accent, huh?" He pulls a bouquet of plastic flowers out of a white vase, peers down inside it, and holds the flowers up to his nose.

"I like things sweet." Tony puts the flowers back in the vase and reaches underneath the table, running his hand along the wood panels. The girl stares down at the books stacked on top of it. And next to the table is an open cardboard box with still more books tucked inside.

The kitchen door swings open. Raymond walks back into the living room, tossing a wrench onto the table, next to the books.

"How far away you live?" He can already see her starting to blink rapidly. "I mean, I tried. But the body's all bent. You're going to have to just carry it or drag it or something, I don't know . . ."

"Damn." Tony shakes his head. "What's wrong with these fucking kids today? Why you think they so evil?"

Raymond looks at the girl: short, stiff plaits of hair standing up at the back of her neck, dirty white T-shirt with a pink ladybug appliqué stretched across the stomach, plaid shorts, socks spattered with purple Kool-Aid stains. He used to feel sorry for awkward, homely girls like that. But now sometimes he thinks maybe they are really better off. "I tried."

"Why they do that to you, girl?" Tony says. She just stands there, hands clasped behind her back, swaying from side to side.

"You gonna be all right?" Raymond nods toward the front door. "You want a glass of water or something, before you go?"

"Hey, Ray, man, you remember us? You remember back in the day?"

Raymond shrugs. All he knows is that the girl is not moving. She just stands there staring down at the stack of books on the table.

"I think we were just as bad," Tony says.

"Let me get you that glass of water." Raymond disappears into the kitchen. The cabinet squeaks open, followed by the sound of crushed ice crumbling into a glass.

"And your mama with them flips," Tony yells from the living room. "When'd she start up with that again? I haven't seen those things in years."

"Well, you're lucky," Raymond calls back. Just thinking about all those little kids crowding around his mama's yard is enough to make him wince. She started making those fucking popsicles again almost as soon as he came back to hold her hand at his brother Sam's funeral. He's convinced there is something wrong with it, that it is unhealthy somehow, an unnatural distraction from grief. And look at the kind of hassles it leads to. He puts the glass under the faucet and pours the girl her water. All he wants is to get the child out of his house before she has time to pee herself again.

"When did she start charging people?" Tony asks. Raymond closes his eyes and shuts the water off. He knows Tony doesn't mean anything by it but, really, that's the part that bothers him the most, all those jars of fucking dimes. He walks back into the living room.

"Man." Raymond shakes his head. He hands the girl her water. "I don't want to talk about fucking Kool-Aid."

Tony shrugs. He looks at the girl.

"They used to be free."

5.

There are too many people in the house, Raymond thinks. That's what the problem is. He can sense that, Tony and the girl filling up the space, making him feel crowded and cramped. For the past five days it's been just him and the books, the box he found hidden in the back of his brother's closet. And it shocked him because he'd never actually seen his brother read anything more substantial than a comic book. But he knew they were his brother's books and that his brother actually read them because he recognized the handwriting scribbled in the margins on almost every page.

The girl lowers her glass and nods her head toward the stack on the table. "Are all those yours?" she asks Raymond.

"Naw." He shakes his head. "They belong to someone else."

"Just a little light reading to pass the time, huh, Ray?" Tony says. He picks up a book and glances down at the cover, assessing its weight. "Looks dry."

Raymond shuts his eyes. The word "fool" bubbles up in his mind involuntarily before he can force it back down with guilt. He's known Tony for twelve years, ever since they both got assigned the same homeroom teacher in the second grade. Somehow, when

Raymond went to college, he'd imagined himself missing Tony a
lot more than he actually had. He opens his eyes and looks at the
girl.

"Why did you ask me that? About the books? I mean, what difference does it make to you who they belong to?"

She points to the one lying open. "I know that one."

"What do you mean you know it?"

"I mean I've seen it. I read it."

"That thick-ass book?" Tony glances down at it, then back up at
the girl. "Naw. Really?"

"Parts of it," the girl says. "Aunt Ruby gave it to me."

"Now you see that?" Tony says. "Another one with the books.
Now we got two . . ." He stands up and walks to the kitchen.

Raymond squints at the girl in front of him, rocking slowly from
side to side as she drinks her glass of water.

"Look, girl. You've been here for almost an hour now. What's
the problem? Don't you want to go home?" He studies her face.
"Are you scared? Worried your daddy is going to beat you or something, for letting them fuck your bike up like that?"

"I don't have a daddy."

"Then what is it?"

"It's the bike." The girl shakes her head, lower lip popping out
in a pout. "I don't want it."

"What do you mean you don't want it?" He winces at the sudden loud clatter of pots and pans being pushed aside in one of his
mother's kitchen drawers.

"You don't want to take it home?"

The girl nods.

"Well, leave it then. You just go home, and I'll keep it in the
garage and you can come back for it later, like when Mama's here
or something."

A drawer slams shut in the kitchen.

"Hey, man, what are you doing in there?" Raymond yells.

"Where she keep it?"

"What?"

"The Kool-Aid. I'm thirsty."

Raymond frowns. "I told you she went to the store," he yells
back. "What the fuck is the matter with you?"

Tony steps back into the living room, squints at Ray.

"There is no fucking Kool-Aid in this house," Raymond says.

"I hear you." Tony nods. He frowns. "Just relax. Hear me? Don't lose your cool."

Tony keeps his eyes locked on Raymond's as he walks backward to the kitchen, then disappears behind the door.

Raymond looks at the girl.

"I'm trying to be nice."

6.

Tony stands in the middle of a bright yellow kitchen, staring at the dimes in the pickle jar on the windowsill, thinking about Raymond losing his cool. Baby brother is clearly not well. Tony could see that as soon as he walked into the house, sensed it just from talking to Ray on the phone. Something about his big brother, Sam, having all those books in his closet really tripped Ray up for some reason. Maybe Ray forgot other people could read, had a right to read a fucking book when they felt like it.

Ray just needs to get out of the house for a little while, Tony thinks.

Ray just needs some fresh air. Have a beer, smoke some weed, take a walk around the neighborhood and relax. Tony has it all laid out in his mind, the speech he's going to give Ray about how fucked up everything is, how Ray needs to get back up to school before it's too late. *Anybody who likes reading books as much as you do needs to be getting a college education, can't be fucking up a chance like this.* He'll shake his head and tell Ray he understands wanting to be here for your mama and all, but sometimes you got to just put shit aside and go for yours *because how you supposed to help anybody else if you can't even help yourself?* Sam would have wanted him to say all that. Would have said, *Listen to Tony, you know Tony got plenty of sense, always has.*

He's going to tell Ray about how proud of him Sam always was. Tell him that as much as Sam rolled his eyes, everybody could see how much he liked saying it. *Naw, that doofy herb ain't here no more. He up at school.* The eye-rolling was just reflex. *My baby brother, up at college . . .* He'll make up a little lie about how one night he and Sam actually talked about it, tell Ray how ashamed Sam was for hitting him, especially that last time. Knocked his books on the

floor, slapped Ray across the face. *Now pick it up.* And really there
was something pitiful about it, big man like Sam hitting a little boy
like Ray. Tony could see that even then.

But of course, Tony wasn't the one getting slapped. Tony was
the one standing on the sidelines watching, the one who had his
hands out when it was over. The one who dusted him off, handed
him back his book, said *Here you go, Ray* and *Damn, that motherfucker
is mean.* And Ray cut his eyes and said, *Oh, that son of a bitch is probably
just high, he don't even know what planet he's on half the time,* which Tony
knew wasn't true. But he let Ray say it because it made him stop
crying and sometimes people just say things.

Tony spins around, opens the door to the pantry. Ray's mama
has got all kinds of shit in there: baked beans, Vienna sausages,
Del Monte canned peaches, SPAM, a half-full jar of Folgers crystals
that has probably been sitting there for years. Tony sucks his teeth,
thinking how his grandma is the same way. Can't throw anything
out, no matter how nasty or old. Jars of flour, baking powder, baking
soda, cornstarch, cornmeal, sugar. He can see how someone might
get confused in a pantry like that. If they were crazy, say, or couldn't
smell nothing because their nose was too stuffed up from crying all
the time.

Ray's mother is not taking very good care of herself these days.
That's what Tony's mother said when he told her he was going out
to visit Ray: *Saw her shuffling around the supermarket the other day, poor
thing with her wig on all crooked and walking around in that nasty housedress. Just grieving, poor thing. She not taking very good care of herself
these days, looks like.* If Tony's mother hadn't pointed it out to him,
he might not have even noticed. To him, Ray's mama just looks
old. But she always looked like that, even when they were kids.

Tony stands there for a minute, looking up at a jar of what appears to be powdered sugar. He glances over his shoulder and decides that if Ray walks in and asks him what he's doing he'll just
shrug and tell him he's got a sweet tooth. He twists the top off the
jar and opens a drawer near the sink, looking for something to put
it in. He is pulling out a plastic Ziploc bag when he hears a knock
on the front door.

He walks back into the living room and sees Raymond peeking
out the front window.

"I told you, man," Tony says. "It's the changing of the guard."

Raymond nods. "Just wait here . . ."

7.

The girl watches Raymond walk out the front door and shut it behind him. She puts her glass of water on the table and stands by the window. She sees Raymond heading out to a car parked by the curb. An arm spills out of the driver's-side window and it is a man's arm, thick and muscular, fingers outstretched to clasp Raymond's hand. Suddenly Raymond looks different to her: thin and awkward, like a boy.

"That's his brother Sam's friend, Sean." Tony shakes his head and sits down on the couch. "Everybody's cool now, but let's see how long that lasts."

Another man's hand appears, dangling out of the rear window, holding out a forty-ounce bottle of beer.

"Somehow they got it in their stupid heads that Sam took something that belonged to them and hid it somewhere, maybe right here in his mama's house."

The girl watches Raymond take the bottle, twist off the cap, and spill a sip onto the pavement before raising it to his lips.

"And you know what's fucked up? I mean really fucked up? I'm starting to think that too."

When the girl turns around, Tony is staring at her from the couch. He lowers his eyes, looks down at the book.

"Hey. You really read this? For real?"

The girl nods. "Aunt Ruby gave it to me."

"Well, who the hell is Aunt Ruby?"

"Mama's friend. She came down with us to Grenada, as part of the Creative Unity Brigade."

Tony picks up the book. Somehow this makes sense to him. Of course there is a Creative Unity Brigade. Somewhere. Full of the righteous, marching proudly, two by two, with their fists in the air. The book is a call to action; he can tell that just by looking at the cover.

"That why y'all moved down there, to that island? Help the needy, feed the poor? That kind of shit? What, you part of a church group or something?"

"Not really."

He flips the book over and stares at the back cover. Outside he can hear the revving of a motor, music blaring through the car's open windows, the screech of brakes as it pulls away from the curb.

"Why did you stop?" he asks the girl. "I mean, why did you all come back?"

The girl stares at him. She has to think for a moment about how to answer because in truth, no one ever asks her that. They ask why she went but never why she came back. Most people she has met here don't even know where Grenada is, except when they sometimes say, *Didn't we already bomb the shit out of that place years ago?* And everyone who hears about the Brigade seems to assume that it was bound to fail simply because it did.

"Aunt Ruby. She gone now."

"Gone where?"

"In the kitchen. She take a bottle of pills."

Tony turns away from her. Tries to picture the woman, Aunt Ruby, but can't. So instead he thinks about Sam, someone he had known all his life, someone he loved, truly. He rises to his feet and as he walks across the room he thrusts an abrupt finger toward the cardboard box. "You see all them books? The one who left them for Ray? He gone too."

He peeks out the front window. He can see Ray still standing on the sidewalk, staring down the block. He has already figured out that Ray is different, that something is not quite right. Him and his mother both stuck in the righteous purging of grief. One had history, the other had Kool-Aid, and from where Tony stood he couldn't see how either was doing them a bit of good.

He looks at the girl.

"Hey, girl. Look what I found."

Tony reaches into his pocket and pulls out the plastic bag full of white powder. He opens it up and pokes it with his finger.

"You know what this is?"

The girl stares down at it, then up at him. If she had to guess, she'd say sugar.

"It's medicinal is what it is," Tony says. "Like what the doctor give you when you got a cavity. Like Novocain. Rub it on your gums and the next thing you know, you can't feel a thing." He stands beside her and holds the bag open. "Go ahead and try it."

The girl stares back at him while he nods. She dips her finger inside the bag and rubs the powder onto her teeth.

"You see what I mean?"

A dry, metallic taste stretches up from her tongue, shoots through her nostrils, and clears a space for itself in the front of her brain.

"You see what I mean?"

All of a sudden she's dizzy. She sits down in the La-Z-Boy, struggling to keep her eyes open. Tony stands there, studying her face. After a moment he backs away from her slowly and sits down on the couch.

"I like you, girl. For real." He nods. "You just keep your head up. You'll be all right. You know why? Because you're cool. I could tell just as soon as I saw you, standing out on that porch."

He winks.

"That's why I want you to listen to me, okay? I'm gonna tell you a secret. And don't tell Ray I told you either. Because I love Ray's mama and all . . . she's like an auntie to me. But she also silly simple. You know what I mean?" He twirls his finger in the air near the side of his head. "Something not quite right. And if I were you I wouldn't drink any more of that woman's nasty Kool-Aid. You understand? Because I wouldn't . . ."

Tony shakes his head.

"Not even if you paid me."

8.

Raymond stands next to the curb, watching his mother's car pull into the driveway. When she opens the door and the light clicks on he can see the frantic look in her eyes, lips moving as she mutters to herself. She can't help him, he knows that. It's all she can do to keep herself upright, drag herself out of bed in the middle of the afternoon, open the door for her little flip babies, collect her parcel of dimes.

He helps his mother unload her grocery bags from the car and listens to her talk to herself. Blaming herself, trying to make sense of what happened. How could she have lost her son? How could things have possibly gone so wrong? What could she have done differently if only she had tried? She looks at Raymond, a quiet hysteria animating all her gestures: "Help me get these bags in the house. I've got work to do, I'm running out of time."

That is what is needed more than anything, he thinks. Time. So much history to sort through, struggling to make room for itself, scribbled in the margins of every page. The books he found in the back of his brother's closet are full of secrets, the private truths of a man talking to himself, whispering things that Raymond could scarcely imagine his brother saying out loud. Clearly Sam was standing on the precipice of a new understanding when he passed, and now there is no one to finish his thoughts but Raymond. He doesn't want to be interrupted. Not yet. He still needs time.

"Is that Tony sitting in my living room? Go tell that fool boy to come out here and help me with these bags—"

When Raymond walks back inside the house he takes one look at the girl sitting with her mouth hanging open and Tony shoving a plastic bag into the pocket of his jacket and knows that something is very wrong.

"What the fuck did you do?" he says, and Tony laughs. Tony laughs, even as Raymond pulls him up by the collar, pushes, and then hurls him toward the front door. Even in the midst of grief, Tony is still laughing.

"Remember what I told you, little girl . . ."

A door slams. The girl can hear them scuffling out on the porch. She leans back in the La-Z-Boy and stares up at the ceiling, trying to negotiate the shifting rhythms of her own heartbeat. She is in the present, she is in a suburb of the south, and everything is quieter than before. There is no fist in the air, no promise of the Creative Unity Brigade. When she looks up she does not see the words from a book or her mother's hands or Aunt Ruby's face or the kids in the yard or the Rastafarians in a clinic waiting room. She doesn't see a needle or blue lights or even the little brick house across the street from Henry's Bar, where her uncle lives. When she looks up at the ceiling, she sees something even better.

A blank page.

And just as she is about to smile Raymond appears, hovering above the chair. She stares up at his pursed lips, dark eyes, eyebrow arched. He reaches around, takes her by the arm, and gently pulls her to her feet.

"Little girl? It's time for you to go home."

9.

The Flip Lady stands in her bright yellow kitchen, unpacking a bag of groceries. She takes out a large pot, fills it up with water from the sink, and sets it on the counter. She empties a canister of

Kool-Aid and stirs. She adds a cup of sugar, watching the powder swirl through the purple liquid then disappear as it settles on the bottom. She thinks for a moment, then scoops out another cup.

"Little heathens." She chuckles. Just like Tony, always thinking she can't see past their smiles. But she watches everything from the kitchen window, and she has seen it all. Nothing has changed. It's just like before: she always could tell the good from the bad.

"Bet y'all sleep good tonight," she mutters to herself. She doesn't do it for the money. No one has to thank her.

She smiles, thinks about all the little flip babies in this world. It doesn't last, nothing does. But for now they still come running, gather around her back porch, hold their hands out for the promise of something sweet.

And she gives it to them.

When We Remembered Zion

FROM *Southeast Review*

SHE IS LYING spread-eagle on the mattress. I kneel at the edge. My shins are soaking in the mud of her amniotic fluid. She screams. Blood and mucus bead over her perineum. Her cervix is about ten centimeters dilated. I don't want to touch her vulva, so I use a set of forks to look.

Breathe from the diaphragm, I say.

She does. She reaches for my hand again. I don't let her have it. It still hurts from all the earlier squeezing. Instead, I give her the squishy ball I took from Walmart the other day. She wrings it so hard it flies out of her hand and knocks over the lamp next to us. Thankfully it doesn't set the cabin on fire. I grab the ball and give it back to her.

Warren, she moans.

This is the first time she has mentioned him in weeks. Don't think of him right now, I say. I put down the forks and dab her face with a towel.

I want him, she says.

He isn't coming back, I say. You know that. Now push.

She throttles the ball and pushes. No progress.

Harder, I say.

Another push. Blood gets all over the mattress. Fucking shit, she howls.

More.

A long breath. Another thrust. Then the tiny, conical head.

He's crowning, I say.

Don't hurt him, she says.

You know I won't, I say. Then I tell her to push again.

The engine starts to clatter. I pull over. I turn the car off and try the ignition a few times. Sputtering and then nothing. I don't have a phone, so I get out and stand under some nearby trees.

Soon a pickup truck comes down the road. I wave my hands. It stops. A woman sticks her head out the passenger window. She has brown hair and a small nose and blunt canines. The man driving has large biceps.

You okay? the woman asks.

It won't start, I say.

We can try jumping it, the man says. His eyes are hard and dark.

Once they park I open my hood and the man opens his. He takes cables out from under his seat. The woman stays in the car. He says she's pregnant and needs to rest. He lights a cigarette as he untangles the cables.

Where you headed? he coughs. I wonder when he will develop emphysema.

Just driving, I say.

You from around here?

No. Is that your wife?

Girlfriend.

In a purely observational way—I don't experience sexual attraction but admire symmetrical features—I say, She's very pleasing to look at.

He raises an eyebrow. He has a profound laryngeal prominence that bobs like a fishing lure. Are you hitting on my girlfriend in front of me? he asks.

No. I'm just remarking.

Just remarking? he hacks. He looks me up and down. His eyes widen. He walks to me with balled fists. What the fuck is wrong with you?

I put a hand up to keep him at a distance.

Fuck you think you're doing, reaching like that? he growls. Then he lunges. He puts one hand on my throat. He strikes at my beltline with the other. I punch him right under the sternum. My father taught me that this should knock a person unconscious, but he only grunts. I see drifting golden sparks. I don't want to, but if I don't I might die, so I draw my pistol and fire twice. He collapses.

I split. Meaning I start to see myself from the outside and my brain makes me do what it wants.

the basement smells of formaldehyde and human rot my father stares at me over the examination table

My body climbs into the truck. My foot presses the gas. For a while the woman just stares. Then she punches me in the ribs. My arm blocks her. Her hands plow through and strike me in the head. She is stronger than she looks.

he says Listen Close with his forceps he pokes the cadaver's abdomen the brown heart the fibrous lungs he says This Is The Small Intestine This Is The Mitral Valve These Are The Bronchi

Warren, she sobs. Oh my fucking God. Warren.

I'm sorry, my mouth says.

She pummels my shoulder. You killed him, she screams. You fucking monster.

he pinches a little nub on the large intestine he asks What Is This I say That Is The Appendix Sir he nods and even though I am correct right now I won't always be and when I am wrong he will beat me

What my brain thinks: I'm not a monster. I was defending myself.

What my brain makes me do: suggest that she breathe with her diaphragm to lower her cortisol-related stress levels.

Shut the fuck up, she says. She clutches her bump. It's not small, but it's not large. She must be twenty-four weeks along. She is wearing a maternity frock covered in flower patterns. I don't know why but that calms me, and in a few moments I regain control of my body. She trembles against the door. I have the strange feeling that I want to shield her.

Where are you taking me? she asks.

I don't know, I say.

Are you going to kill me?

No, I won't kill you.

She looks relieved. Then terrified again. Then what're you going to do? she asks.

I am about to say that I don't know. Then I realize that my split saved me. Meaning I could have frozen up and stayed put until the police came to escort me back to Quilton. Or to death row. But they don't know anything. They don't have to. I need to make a plan.

We're going to wait, I say. Then we can talk about letting you go.

She doesn't respond. But she does throw up all over the center console.

We'd been on the road for an hour when, for the first time that day, you reached over and touched my belly. You used to stroke the surface for a while—you liked the sound of skin scraping against skin—then stick your finger in my belly button and make a face, like it was an accident, and that would make me laugh, and you always said that when I laughed you felt like maybe the world wasn't so bad, and that maybe we'd all been conditioned to think it was when, really, there's proof of its goodness in the grin of the woman you loved enough to reveal all the things you hated about yourself, like your crooked teeth and your extreme impulsiveness—take the time you did a backflip out the second-story window of your frat house and broke your leg, which never fully recovered—and how much you wanted your parents to forgive you for knocking me up out of wedlock. Most of the time you tried to act proud, like nothing ever mattered, but you knew when to admit what you felt, and that's why I loved you so much.

Five minutes later, some strange man reached for his gun while you were jumping his car, and you—bravely? stupidly?—tried to disarm him, and then you were bleeding out while Rodney kicked and kicked and rolled around inside me. And the man stood over you, and he was smiling, and his pistol was coughing out smoke the color of the walls in my parents' basement, and for the first time since I met you, I thought that maybe you were wrong, that maybe the world really is as horrible as everyone says it is, and maybe the fact that you thought it wasn't and so decided to help that bizarre motherfucker with the lisp and the ugly beard and the holes in his jacket is why you're in the ground, and why five days later I'm listening to a stolen Volkswagen Jetta's radio that is always turned to the news because the man who killed you is too paranoid to listen to music, and why the authorities are announcing a multistate investigation after identifying my kidnapper as Samson Whitaker, who three years ago was admitted as an inpatient at the Quilton Psychiatric Center, and who to make things worse hardly sleeps, just stares through the windshield the whole night so I can't escape, and why the police are searching for your truck, which yesterday he forced me to push into a lake fifty miles away from where this nightmare began, and maybe it was perverted of me to think, but as the car burbled into the water, all I could think of was how one night a couple of years ago we'd fucked in the truck bed, and after we were done we cuddled under your old throw blanket and you told me that if you had to choose one moment to remember for the rest of your life, it would be that one, huddled together in the night, smelling of each other's sweat, our bodies gray under the moon, and I nuzzled into your neck and you ran your fingers through my hair and we fell asleep, and in the morning you were still there.

The protocol (inspired by my father's):

- Follow all traffic rules.
- Stay in the right lane so highway drivers don't recognize her.
- Keep my pistol on her on our way through towns.
- Wear sunglasses and dye our hair.
- Wear elevator boots.
- Only visit stores when necessary. Must have large enough windows in front to see the car.
- Bind her hands and feet (flesh-colored rope) whenever I leave the car and before she falls asleep. Knot should not be loose enough to undo or tight enough to inhibit proper circulation.
- Make sure she has no access to a phone.
- Keep her fed.
- Treat her well.

There's not much to the plan other than to keep driving and listening to the news. I don't tell her this because it would make her sad again. The last time she was sad I had another split. She'd been crying and begging for days and kept saying how much she hated having blond hair, and my brain made me veer off the road and almost crash into a tree. That hushed her. But now she just stares out the window and doesn't speak. Which is almost worse because sometimes I think that she's dead. And that would make me responsible for another killing. This time of a good person. Good because she always holds her bump. And she smiles at animals on the side of the road. And it has been two weeks and she hasn't resisted the protocol.

Her name is Cara Dyer. I know because of the radio. She didn't tell me, and so for the first few days I only called her Girl. Now when I say her name, she turns her head. She looks away when she remembers it's me.

This morning I park outside of a deli. I tie her hands and feet before I go inside. I order us breakfast sandwiches. I ask for spinach in hers because she looks anemic. Back in the car I undo her ropes and hand her her sandwich. When she unwraps it, she pokes the greens with her index finger.

Is that spinach? she asks. It's the most she has said in two days.

Yes, I say. I start to drive.

What kind of breakfast sandwich has spinach in it?

I asked for it.

Why? she asks.

You're pale. You need vitamins.

I'm naturally pale, she says.

I mean that you look paler than usual.

Her upper lip twitches. Than usual? she says. Look, guy, I'm not your daughter. I'm your fucking captive. Remember? She rolls down the window and throws out her food. It hits a passing fence. Fuck you and your spinach sandwich, she says.

This doesn't offend me because she's talking again. Though I do feel bad that she's frustrated.

I keep driving and eating my sandwich. She breathes heavily. I wonder how many liters of air her lungs can hold. Soon she looks in my direction. At first I think she's staring at my face. But then she drinks back saliva.

Do you want the rest? I ask. There are still a lot of antioxidants in this.

She glares. Like she hates every part of me. But she nods and takes the sandwich. I've noticed that she chews a lot before she swallows.

Why do you care so much? she asks.

I don't want you to feel bad, I say.

Little late to be worrying about that, don't you think?

It takes me a moment to tell that she's being sarcastic. I'm sorry about what I did, I say.

You're not. You reached for your gun for no reason. You smiled after you shot him.

I did not, I say.

You did. I saw you.

I did not, I say more firmly.

She looks like she's going to scream. Instead, she sighs and holds her belly. Whatever, she says. I won't try to convince you when you're obviously delusional.

She finishes the rest of the sandwich. She balls up the wrapper and tosses it out the window. I'm about to turn up the radio when she says, Can I ask you something?

Okay.

What happened to you?

What do you mean? I ask.

You were in a mental hospital.

I didn't think she would bring this up. I should have changed the station when the newscasters mentioned it.

I was, I say.

Why? she asks. Besides the obvious.

I don't want to think back to that time. It might make me split. So I decide to be vague. I have problems with my prefrontal cortex, I say.

Yeah, I kind of gathered that much. But what—

I don't want to talk about it, Cara, I say. It was the worst time in my life. But I'm free now.

She nods. Then she looks out the window again. I adjust my seat and merge onto the highway.

It's been six weeks. The only reason I know is because the newscasters announce the date and time before their monologues. You died on May 24, and today is July 5, and by my calculations—which I know are right, because most of the day I count the cars we pass, count the miles we've traveled, count the days since I last saw you, count the months until Rodney arrives—that is exactly six weeks of too much thinking. I haven't gotten used to all the changes and don't think I will, but sometimes what goes on in my head is easier to bear, and those moments are the ones when I can finally take a long enough breath to believe that things will be okay in the end, even when I know they won't.

I didn't realize that yesterday was the Fourth until he wished me a Happy Independence Day, and then I got to thinking about all those old summer nights when I'd drink a twelve-pack with Amy and Tara and you'd finish a handle with Derek and Killian, and we would turn on the stereo and listen to Zac Brown and Bruce Springsteen and, for some reason, Sufjan Stevens, whose music we knew was too depressing but we enjoyed anyway, as the night wound down and we gathered around the backyard firepit and watched the fireworks, their bursting colors, wondering why it took a holiday to feel so free. Or at least that's what I would think, even though I had everything I needed and could technically do whatever I wanted in this country and so should have been happy with how much freedom I had.

But I don't blame myself for having those thoughts, because there was always something restrictive in normal life. Maybe it was how we spent so many mundane days at the office or in the living room, watching the same three shows on rotation because we didn't want to start at any new beginning. Which isn't to say that life was never inspiring, because it sometimes was, especially when something unexpected happened, like when my mother called to say that she and my father had decided to move into a bungalow fifteen minutes away because they were getting too old to handle the cold up north, and so I spent the next three days planting daylilies and hydrangeas in the front yard because I wanted them to see how mature I'd become when they visited—yes, I was old enough to own a pretty house, and yes, I was wise enough to live with a man I wasn't married to. Though when I think about it now, I remember you thought that this was all a little pretentious, which hurt me, because if we couldn't support each other when it came to minor things, how would we make out when something significant happened? Isn't the trust we had in each other why we decided to have a kid, why even though I wasn't thrilled with the name you wanted for him, I yielded to Rodney, after your late uncle who, although you adored him, always struck me the wrong way, what with his creepy smile and sexual jokes that were a little too graphic for family gatherings?

This year, the Fourth was uneventful—we're on the road most of the day because he doesn't like to stay in any one place, and boredom has become as familiar to me as breathing—until about eight o'clock at night, when he stopped the car in a forest clearing filled with fireflies. He opened my door and told me to get out, and I was sure he was going to rape and kill me—he could have done it and nobody would have known—but as I stepped out, he went to the back of the car and pulled two lawn chairs out of the trunk, which surprised me because I had no idea when he'd gotten them. He opened them a couple feet away, and I just stood there not knowing what to do because he'd only ever let me out to pee or shit, but then he sat down and asked me to join. And as I did, my hands started to shake, and the air smelled like dung and the trees around us were swaying a little too much, and I was afraid that my head would explode until he smiled at me—which I'd never seen him do—and said that I should look up, because there would be fireworks soon. And ten minutes later there they were, sparkling and shimmering all over the night sky, and they were so beautiful I started to cry, and right then I felt like I was free, freer than six weeks ago when I could watch all the TV and read all the books and listen to all the music I wanted, freer than all those bad-breathed mornings you'd kiss my neck and say you loved me, freer than when I was seventeen and would speed down the highway at three o'clock in the morning, and my friends and I would stick our hands out the windows and let the air blow back all the hair we'd primped for the boys we'd seen earlier. And as the fireworks went out, I wondered why it took being stripped of all my freedom to realize that I was never as free as I thought I was, and part of me blamed you for whisking me into a life I accepted because I didn't know any better, and I wanted to punch you, to yell until fire came out of my throat, but then I remembered that you're not here any-more, and that even if we could talk, you would shake your head and say that I was being silly and should sleep off my worrying, just like you used to.

After we check out of the motel, I drive us to the diner down the road.

Don't do anything bad, I tell her.

I won't, she says. Then we get out of the car.

This will be the second time we've eaten in public. She's nervous, but I'm not. We've been staying in motels for weeks and haven't had any problems. Nobody this far west knows about us.

The diner has chipped green walls and smells like perspiration. The host is a septuagenarian man with solar lentigo on his arms. He leads us to a booth. Cara holds her lower back as she sits. Her bump pokes up over the table. She bites the cuticle of her thumb.

It feels weird to be in here, she says.

It's just a diner, I say.

Yeah, she says. Guess I've been away from people a little too long.

I've been away from people for much longer than eleven weeks before and it never bothered me. Then again we're different. For instance, she always used to ask when she could go back to her normal life. Which was strange to hear because this is my normal life. But she did stop asking that question around Independence Day.

A middle-aged waitress with strabismus brings over water. Her good eye fixes on me. I order myself an omelet and Cara a fruit bowl. Before the woman leaves she looks at Cara's bump and congratulates us. I'm about to say the baby isn't mine when Cara says, Thank you. Which surprises me. But I don't comment. I just sip my water.

Can I ask you something? Cara says.

Her questions can be intrusive. But I still say, Okay.

She taps on her glass. Have you ever felt love? she asks.

I've never been in love with anyone, I say.

I don't mean been in love. I mean felt love. There's a difference.

I can't recall ever experiencing what people describe as love. But maybe I have felt it and just didn't know what it was. I don't know, I admit.

What about your family? You must love them, right?

My heart palpitates. I don't want to talk about this, I say.

Samson, I just want to know, she says. She has only recently started to use my name, and I like how it sounds when she says it.

Why? I ask.

We've been on the road for a while, she says. I still don't know much about you.

That's not a bad thing.

Maybe not, she says. But the longer we're together, the more questions I'm going to have. So we might as well get some out of the way.

She has a point. But she doesn't know how uncomfortable I am. What if I split again? And in public? She is almost begging, though. And I don't want to disappoint her.

My mother committed suicide, I say. My father is a neurosurgeon. He's an evil man.

My head tingles. It's not a good idea to say anything else, but my brain makes me talk.

He wanted me to be a neurosurgeon too. He tried to teach me. We brought dead bodies home. He forced me to dissect them with him. I haven't seen him in years.

we lift the cadaver out of the trunk we carry it to the basement and lay it on the examination table my father points at the body which is still gasping he asks Why Are You Afraid I say Because It's A Person Sir he says Everybody Is Just Viscera And Nothing More And The Sooner You Understand That The Easier This Will Be

Samson?

he pushes the scalpel into the windpipe the body twitches and then goes still then he saws into the cranium and when he is done he points at the membrane around the cortex he says Tell Me What This Is and I say Those Are The Meninges he nods he says More Specific and I say The Dura Mater The Arachnoid Mater The Central Sulcus

Samson. Samson.

he smacks me he points at one of the brain's grooves he says This Is The Fucking Central Sulcus I say Yes Sir I Apologize he cuffs me again he screams Now Correct Yourself and I say That Is The Pia Mater Sir he nods he smiles his teeth are crooked yellow covered in dental plaque

My mouth makes noises. My brain thinks: Why does this have to happen to me?

he says So You're Not A Fucking Retard I taste blood I say No Sir he says You Could've Fooled Me Now Don't You Dare Waste My Time Again then he turns back to the cadaver he points somewhere on the brain's right hemisphere he says What Is This and I know that later on he will beat me worse

She grabs my hand. She says, It's okay. Around us people stare. Which makes me consider announcing that I was joking. But that would draw even more attention to us.

She hands me a napkin and holds my hand until the waitress returns with our food. Her strabismic eye is between us now. She asks Cara if everything is to her liking. She doesn't ask me the same. When she leaves I begin to eat my omelet. Cara prods at the fruit in her bowl.

My older cousin, she says, used to touch me when I was a kid.

I don't know what to say. But the anger is the strongest I've experienced in a long time. I want to find her cousin and hurt him badly. Maybe even kill him. Of course I don't tell her this. She wouldn't like to hear it.

We get back to eating in silence. Which usually wouldn't feel uncomfortable but does now. I'm almost done with my omelet when she points across the diner. The waitress is on the phone. She is staring at us. She cups the receiver to her mouth and turns away.

We should go, Cara says. We run out. The waitress yells something behind us. We get in the car. I put my gun in my lap and start driving. I don't know where to.

He's out getting more supplies: food, water, folic acid supplements, kerosene for the lamp, a roller to loosen my muscles. We go through most essentials in three or four days—that number will go down to a day or two once Rodney is born—so he's often out shoplifting, which is risky, but he couldn't find enough game or plants around the cabin to support us.

We don't do much when he's here—either read what he stole from the library or walk around the forest, although these days I'm not really on my feet because my legs are so swollen—but when he's gone there's even less to do, and I've had to be completely alone for most of the day, which in a place as isolated as these woods is terrifying. Sometimes I think that a bear or some other vicious animal will knock down the front door and maul me to death, which is why Samson has agreed to leave his gun behind. Even though he isn't the warmest person, he does give me the strongest sense of comfort I've had since you died.

I still think about you a lot, but I don't know if that's because I miss you more or less. Which sounds cold—how could I not still yearn for the man I loved for so many years and lost in a split second—but this isn't something I can control. And if you were to think about it like I do, then maybe you'd understand, but you did always have trouble figuring out what I thought and why, so maybe it would be stupid to expect you to do something you're not capable of. And if you believe I'm mistaken, then why don't you think back to that day on the beach, when we were lying in the sand and you said I should undo my top because it would be more comfortable, and I said no, because it wasn't a nude beach and I was already comfortable, but you said I was wrong, which struck me as absurd because I'd just told you how I felt, and then you said that if you were to lie in the sand with your shirt on it would feel scratchy and painful, and you couldn't imagine how it would feel with tits. I was pissed off, but I laughed and got back to reading my book, and a minute later you undid my knot and pulled my top out from under me, and I was too shocked and violated to explain how that made me feel, and I never told you afterward how much what you did disturbed me because you were how you were and I was how I am.

That's also why I told Samson, but never you, about what Eddie did to me. Because Samson has also been through awful things, and has never touched me, let alone looked at me sexually, so I knew that he'd never judge me if I told him the truth, and in that way he's more respectful than you ever were. I also have to admit that what you did reminded me of how Eddie used to tell me to take off my clothes and lie down even when I said no, and part of me was afraid, as you took off my top, that you could do the same, or at least that you would ignore my feelings, so I said nothing, and I'll always regret that.

But since you died, my love for you has changed, and for me to keep feeling it, I can't keep making excuses for you. So as vile as it is to say, I realize now that you're somewhat to blame for what happened to you. You didn't deserve it, of course, but you didn't think of what Samson may have been feeling, which could have been fear—you always did have a huge voice and large muscles—and you decided to be violent when he put his hand on his gun, which could have been a reflex or an accident, and maybe he smiled when you hit the ground not because he was happy that he killed you, but because he was relieved to have survived.

I'm relieved that I've survived too. Because I'm safe now, and Rodney will be here in two weeks, and Samson knows how to deliver a baby. I don't know where things will go from there, but I don't feel so worried about it all anymore.

I pick up the bulb syringe. I clear the mucus from the baby's mouth and nostrils. I tell her to push again and guide him until his shoulders emerge. I grab him by the underarms. Another push. He slides out. He is slippery with vernix, but I have a good grip. I wait for him to cry. Then I snip the umbilical cord with a pair of garden shears I've sterilized. I towel him off and wrap him in the bedsheet. He has a fat purple face and his frontal fontanelle is very wide.

Is he okay? she asks.

Yes, I say.

I lay him on her breast with his face turned to hers.

Rodney, she murmurs. It's Momma. I'm right here.

A few minutes later I help her deliver her placenta. Then I pass her my canteen. She drinks greedily. Some water drips on her neck. She drops the canteen when she's done.

Thank you, she weeps. Warren and I are so happy.

Rest, I say. You need to recover.

She closes her eyes. The baby mewls for a while, and then he's also asleep. I change into clean clothes and bury her placenta outside. When I get back I climb into my sleeping bag. I don't expect to fall asleep, but after fourteen hours of caring for her, I'm unconscious in a minute.

When I wake up she's stroking his face. I can feel the love she has for him. It's so foreign that it almost scares me. But then it soothes me.

Isn't he perfect, Warren? He has your nose, the narrow bridge and the pointy tip, and he has my eyes, big and blue and shiny in the light.

Hold him. This is your child. Remember you used to say that you wanted a son who by day you could play football with and by night you could hold close, and who over all the years of raising him you could teach to be happy no matter how cruel life is? Here is that son. He is yours. He is mine. He will always be ours.

He's crying. Can you bring him to me, Warren? He's hungry. Hello, my sweet. I know, I know. Mommy's right here. She's going to make it all better. Here, drink. Just like that.

Thank you for the water. It's refreshing. Has the hot compress gone cold again? You can take it off. Heat it up and bring it back. Hello again, my angel. Are you done? Lie with me. Look at my finger, it goes up and down and back up and down again. You like that, don't you? Mommy loves you, and so does Daddy. We love you to Pluto and back a million times over.

Where did you go, Warren? You were here a minute ago. Are you on a walk? Come back. I want you to hold me and kiss my forehead and look at our baby again. Please don't leave me. We need you. I need you.

Samson. Has Warren still not come back? Look out for him. And thank you for the food. I hope you were careful getting it. Before I forget, I want to tell you that you're not a monster. You're a good person. You have to be.

*

The baby is crying again. Can you rock him back to sleep? Samson? Where are you? Your sleeping bag is empty, and I don't hear you outside. Maybe you're getting some more food. But there's no light in the window. You're never out when it's dark. Please come back. I don't know what Rodney and I would do without you.

There are footsteps outside. They're not yours, Samson—yours are quicker, like you're always running away from something. It could be a creature, a moose or a wolf, so I clutch Rodney to my chest and point your gun at the door. There are knocks, then a man's voice saying it's the police. I tell him to get away, I've got a gun, and they say please put the weapon down, and I ask why I should, and they say because we got him, it's over, you're okay now. But I don't feel okay, Warren, and all I want right now is for you and Samson to be here with me and Rodney.

They open the door, and there are three of them carrying rifles, and I drop the gun, and Rodney is bawling because he knows I'm not strong enough to protect us. I say, Don't touch my baby, motherfuckers, and they say, We won't, we're here to save you. It's a sentence I would normally understand, but right now it means nothing, because what is safe, Samson? One of them takes my arm and brings me outside to one of their cars blaring lights all over the forest, and Rodney spits up milk on my shirt, which I know would make you nauseous, Warren, and I burp him and whisper that I love him and that we're going to be all right, even though I don't believe it. When I ask where they're taking us, they say home, and for a moment I think that they're bringing me back to Samson's car, but that wouldn't make sense, because we haven't had a car in weeks.

Is it bad that, after a few minutes of thinking, I have no idea where home is?

Do You Know Why I Am Teaching You These Things he asks he is sitting on a stool next to the cadaver I shake my head I can't open my mouth because it's swollen shut from yesterday's beating

He really think flopping around like that is gonna do anything? the officer who is driving says on the other side of the cage.

he says I Am Giving You The Keys To Think And Provide For Yourself he looks down at the scalpel in his hand he says I Do The Things I Do Because If I Didn't You Would Live Your Life As A Slave

The officer in the passenger seat stares at me through the grate. He has a blond mustache and a patch of nevus flammeus on his neck. You sure are having a fucking ball back there, he says.

I nod I wonder what it would be like to have a different father or a mother who is still alive he says You Are Too Young To Thank Me Now But One Day You Will Look Back And Say "The Things My Father Taught Me Saved My Life And I Didn't Even Know It"

My body falls on its side. My breath spasms. My eyes sting. My brain thinks: When was the last time I cried? Beyond the cage they laugh so hard they sound like they're choking.

hear Me listen to Me you must be safe with your baby you must love him your only baby he will be good he will be good and right and he will know beyond all reckoning what it means to be free

Mr. Filbert's Classroom

FROM *Magic Is Murder*

SHERIFF MAGGIE STANTON pulled up outside the elementary school, her heart pounding so hard she thought it might rip right through her chest. Her mind was still chewing over the words that every cop had come to dread—*gunman, shots fired, elementary school*—even in leafy green suburbs like Logan Hills. Or maybe especially in places like Logan Hills, where people lived in a kind of bubble, thinking it could never happen there. Until it did.

They'd gotten lucky today, she knew that. But she was the kind of cop who always believed her luck was about to run out.

Heading for the main entrance, Maggie barely saw the neatly trimmed shrubs and the close-cropped grass, the swirl of lights from emergency vehicles swishing across the well-tended lawn. It had only been twenty minutes since the 911 call came in—it had taken Maggie that long to get out of a meeting on opioid overdoses at the county seat downtown and race over. A handful of reporters from the local news stations had already camped out at the bottom of the front steps, shouting questions at her, but she ignored them.

As she neared the front door, she saw a half-dozen thirty-something women in yoga pants and oversized sweaters, edging ever closer to the yellow crime-scene tape. Their kids must be inside.

"Stand back, everyone," Deputy Frank Katz said. At sixty-five, he was the oldest member of her department, but his commitment to enforcing the rules made him invaluable.

Maggie slipped past the anxious moms and ducked under the tape, feeling all eyes shift to her.

"Sheriff, wait!" one of them called out, but Maggie kept walking. She put a hand on Deputy Katz's arm and brought him with her to the front doors.

"Make sure none of the parents get past the front lobby. Not until I know for sure what's what. And if they ask, let them know we'll give them an update soon."

"Will do, Sheriff."

As Maggie went inside, she was struck by the outlines of tiny children drawn in marker on brown butcher paper hanging on the wall under the banner LOOK HOW MUCH WE'VE GROWN. What might've been cute in other circumstances looked a little too much like the chalk outlines of bodies in old movies. A few feet away, a state police forensics tech was taking photos. A gaggle of Maggie's deputies looked over. Maggie nodded at them, heading straight for Deputy Amanda Walters, her number two.

Walters was a five-foot spark plug with pale blond hair and a round face. Maggie had been with her at brutal car accident scenes and a couple of grisly murders and had never seen her look ruffled. Until today.

"You double-checked with all the teachers?" Maggie said, fighting her own sense of anxiety. "No kids were hurt?"

"No, ma'am, not unless you count a first grader who fell trying to crawl under her desk. Guess that's where they're supposed to hide."

"Where are the kids now?"

"In the cafeteria. We're getting head counts from the teachers to make sure everyone's accounted for, and the guidance counselor's in there talking to a few kids who are shook up."

"Make sure you send the paramedics in too, just in case anyone's got an injury we missed." Giving orders, Maggie felt the fear begin to recede. A little. "Now give me the background on the shooter."

"Gerald Roach, forty-six years old, grew up in Richmond, has held a series of odd jobs over the years—mechanic, delivery driver, janitor. For years he was in a relationship with Carla Angle, a fourth-grade teacher here, but they split about three months ago."

"So he decided he wanted a little reunion. How'd he get past security?"

"That's the thing—he used to be a janitor *here*, got fired for drinking on the job back in June." Walters sighed heavily. "Anyway, the office staff knew him and when he said he was here to pick up Ms. Angle for lunch, they buzzed him in."

"Only she wasn't expecting him."

"Far from it. She'd told him she never wanted to see him again, but he wouldn't back off. Kept calling, showed up unannounced at her house a few times."

Maggie frowned. "Did she ever file a report?"

"No, she figured she could handle it herself. Then about a month ago, she finally changed her number, moved into a friend's guest room. She didn't hear from Roach and thought maybe it was over . . . only it wasn't."

"Which brings us to today. Tell me what happened."

Maggie had heard the bones of the story already, but Deputy Walters laid it out in detail: At just past ten thirty, Gerald Roach had showed up at Carla Angle's second-floor classroom. He wanted her to leave with him. When she said no, he pulled out a Ruger 9-millimeter and fired two shots into the ceiling. He told her he'd pick off her students one by one unless she left with him. Terrified, she agreed. He grabbed her by the hair and was halfway down the hall with her when another teacher, Mr. Filbert, slipped out of his classroom. He sneaked up on Roach and conked him on the head with a big fat textbook.

By all accounts, Mr. Filbert was an unlikely hero. A wiry man in his sixties who'd avoided service in Vietnam because of extreme nearsightedness, he had been teaching second grade for more than thirty-five years. He had a reputation for being stern but fair, and rarely raised his voice.

After Mr. Filbert knocked Roach down, the shooter fired at him, missing the second-grade teacher by inches. By then a half-dozen other teachers had appeared, along with the school security guard, who managed to pry the gun away from Roach. Someone had already called 911, and the first responders were on the scene within minutes. That was just over an hour ago.

"Is Roach still here?" Maggie asked now, glancing over Walters's shoulder. Deputy Rodriguez, a twenty-something former wrestler who'd only been in her department for the last six months, was speed-walking toward them.

"Yeah, we handcuffed him and locked him up in the nurse's office while we secured the premises. We were going to move him to the station, but the media's everywhere and I wasn't sure that was such a good idea."

"Let him sit tight for now. We'll take him out the back door soon."

"Sheriff?" Deputy Rodriguez shifted from foot to foot, like a first grader who needed to go to the little boy's room. "Can I talk to you?"

"In a minute." Maggie looked back at Walters. "How's Carla Angle doing?"

"She's been checked out and, except for some bruises where Roach grabbed her, she's fine—just upset and scared."

"Sheriff?"

Maggie sighed, looking impatiently at Rodriguez. "Yes, Deputy?"

"I hate to interrupt, but there's something you should know . . . we just got the head count from all the teachers and, um, well . . ."

"We got a problem?"

"Sort of. You gotta understand, when we first got here things were pretty crazy, and we didn't realize . . . anyway, we're missing some kids."

Maggie felt a tight band pull across her temples. "Okay, well, maybe a couple of them hid out in the bathroom when the shooting started."

"I, um . . ." Rodriguez studied his size-thirteen shoes before meeting Maggie's gaze. "It's more than just a couple kids missing, ma'am."

Something in his tone made the hair prickle on the back of Maggie's neck. "How many kids, Deputy Rodriguez?"

"Twenty-three, ma'am." He paused as if swallowing a lump in his throat. "Every single one of Mr. Filbert's students seems to have disappeared."

A few minutes later, Sheriff Maggie Stanton was on her way to the school library, where Mr. Filbert was being held. According to Deputy Rodriguez, the hero teacher had refused to tell anyone where his students had gone. "He just keeps saying they're fine," Rodriguez said. "And I gotta say, I don't really think he'd hurt them. I had him for second grade myself, and he was the best—

he'd always listen if someone had a problem, and he'd tell us these amazing stories about magic and stuff, and whenever it was someone's birthday he would—"

By then, Maggie had heard more than enough. "I'll talk to Mr. Filbert myself, Deputy Rodriguez. In the meantime, let's see if we can find these kids." On Maggie's orders, Deputy Amanda Walters would supervise two teams of police officers that would search the school. Maggie had told her to make sure they checked everything—"every stairwell, every bathroom, every closet"—until they found the missing children.

Maggie hurried down the silent hallway, heart thundering. The group of second graders was probably hiding in some remote corner of the building. With no adult watching over them, they must've been too scared to come out. Still, she couldn't shake a feeling of dread that plunged deeper and deeper inside her.

She was almost to the library when she heard a voice.

"Maggie! *Maggie!*" She froze, taking a deep breath before she turned. At first she thought maybe it was one of the higher-ups from the state police. Someone who didn't respect her enough to call her "Sheriff." Then she realized who it was.

"Kevin," she said, feeling her heart stutter. "What're you doing in here?"

"What the hell's going on, Maggie? Some guy with a gun goes nuts, and your people say we can't even go see our kids."

Kevin Frasier looked good in a form-fitting charcoal gray suit. He commuted from Logan Hills into the city, where he had a long track record as a successful defense attorney. Their relationship had lasted six months, a personal record for her.

Although she'd liked Kevin, she'd quickly realized that two workaholics did not make a good match . . . especially when one of them was a widowed single dad. Maggie had long known she was not cut out for motherhood. Even stepmotherhood proved too much, although Kevin's daughter, Emma, was easy to like, a petite redhead full of energy and questions. Maggie told Kevin she wanted to end things before Emma got too attached, and that was that. The breakup, she realized, had been three years ago now.

"Kevin, you shouldn't be in here, this whole school is a crime scene."

"Yeah, well, I've been asking to see my daughter since I got here, and I keep getting the runaround." He gave her a steely look, one she remembered all too well from nights when she showed up at his place late for dinner, but when he spoke his voice was soft. "We're all on goddamn pins and needles, Maggie. Please, just let me see Emma."

Maggie thought of the smile he always got when he tucked his little girl in at night. Emma had been four then, older than a baby but still chubby-cheeked and sweet in her one-piece princess pajamas, the two of them so deeply bonded Maggie knew she could never really be part of the family. Another reason she'd broken things off, or maybe she just liked being alone.

"Kevin, you said it yourself, *every* parent's gonna be on pins and needles. I let you in there, I've got to let everyone in, and we're just not ready." Maggie checked her police radio, hoping for a timely update from Walters. "Give me another ten, fifteen minutes, okay?"

He brought a hand up and Maggie was expecting to see his face flash in anger, but then she realized he was actually brushing away a tear. "Maggie, I'm sorry, it's just . . . you know that since Anna died, Em's all I've got. Please, I need to see her."

For a moment, he looked like a little kid himself, albeit one in a $500 suit. "Let me touch base with her teacher. Maybe I can at least get her on the phone for you, okay? Which class is she in?"

His smile was flawless, like the cheekbones that lifted around it, and for a moment Maggie remembered why she'd gone out with him in the first place. "Em's in Mr. Filbert's class. Man, she loves that guy, always talks about these cool stories he tells, and he's really sparked her imagination. She's always coming home with these cool pictures . . ."

Kevin kept talking, but Maggie tuned him out. Mr. Filbert's class. Of course, the cute little preschooler she remembered would be in second grade now. And like the rest of Mr. Filbert's class, Emma Frasier was missing.

Shaking her head, Maggie took off down the hall. "I've got to go, Kevin, but I'll get you in to see Emma soon. I promise."

Kevin started after her, but she was moving too fast for him to catch up. She got on the radio and told Deputy Katz to escort Kevin Frasier out of the building, and make sure that he didn't get past the police blockade again. Then she checked in with Deputy Walters.

"Nothing to report yet, Sheriff." Walters's tone was confident but there was an edge of anxiety beneath it. "We've been through the entire first and second floors. We've got teams looking at the basement and third floor right now. Also, I'm trying to get my hands on the school surveillance video. Hopefully that'll tell us something."

"Okay, keep me posted. And find those kids."

Lowering the radio, Maggie approached the school library, where she could see a small man in a bow tie seated at one of the tables. His elbows were propped on top and his fingers fidgeted nervously. The legendary Mr. Filbert.

Maggie entered the library, nodding at the two state troopers keeping watch over the second-grade teacher, and sat down at the table across from him. Late-morning sun slanted through the windows and cast shadows across the fire engine red carpet.

"I'm Sheriff Stanton." Maggie looked at the small, unassuming man, the glasses on his nose sitting slightly crooked. "You did a brave thing today. How do you feel?"

"Fine. My shoulder's a little sore, but that's a small price to pay."

"For being a hero? Absolutely. You saved a woman's life, not to mention the lives of hundreds of kids."

Filbert shrugged. "I just did what anyone would do under the circumstances. Besides, I know why you're here, Sheriff. And I'm just going to tell you what I've told everyone else—the children are safe. You don't have to worry."

"But I do. Because, Mr. Filbert, since I can't find these kids, I have to assume they're in danger. Now where are they?"

Mr. Filbert just smiled. She could see why the kids liked him. He had an impish face and his lips curled up at the corners in a way that suggested mischief. She used every ounce of willpower she had not to reach across the library table and throttle him.

"What would you like me to tell these children's parents, Mr. Filbert?"

"Exactly what I told you."

"And you think that'll be enough? These people are terrified, and they want to give their children a hug. Hold them close. Tell them they love them." She tried to keep her tone steady, even as she felt anger rising. She thought of Emma Frasier in her soft pajamas and willed the image away. "Gerald Roach is in custody. You've got nothing to worry about anymore. Just tell us where your students are hiding and you can go."

Maggie leaned in toward Filbert. But the teacher just sat there, fussing with his bow tie.

"All right, have it your way."

She got up, walked to one of the deputies. "He doesn't move until he tells us where those kids are. No food, no water, no bathroom break—nothing." She glanced back at Mr. Filbert, hoping she'd rattled him, but he showed no change in expression. Furious, Maggie marched back out into the hall.

Why was he doing this, playing this game? What was his motive? Maggie didn't know. But she'd always believed that to solve a crime, you had to understand the why. Only Mr. Filbert was now both a hero *and* a suspect in this case, and that complicated things. Heroes were easy. They did the right thing. They wanted to help.

That must be it, then. Filbert thought he was helping those kids by keeping quiet. He'd said it himself.

The children are safe. You don't have to worry.

Nice of him to say, but Maggie *was* worried. More than worried, she was terrified. Something had happened to Emma Frasier and her classmates, she just didn't know what. At least not yet.

Maggie studied every inch of Mr. Filbert's classroom: the whiteboard at the front, the bins full of crayons and scissors, the small cubbies stuffed with backpacks lined up against the wall. Crossing to the floor-to-ceiling windows, she looked down at the grass two stories below. Had Mr. Filbert sent the students down on a rope ladder or something? No, she'd already gotten a report from the groundskeeper, who'd been cutting the lawn out front when the shooting started. He hadn't seen anyone on this side of the building, let alone an entire class of second graders.

She checked the bookshelves, the colorful spines showing titles of novels that Maggie recognized but hadn't read: *Harry Potter, The Lord of the Rings, The Chronicles of Narnia.* Even as a child, she'd never had much interest in fantasy, and as an adult those stories held no interest for her. Still, there was a warmth and an energy to the room that even Maggie could feel. She bet the kids liked it here. *She* liked it here. Standing behind the desk, she looked out at the tables covered with dabs of red and yellow paint, trying to imagine herself in Mr. Filbert's place.

Impossible. She'd never been good with kids. Sure, she'd loved

Emma Frasier, the feel of her small body snuggled up against hers
at night. But she hadn't really known what to say to her, how to
connect. Now Emma was gone and only Mr. Filbert knew where.

Frustrated, Maggie flung a pile of papers across the teacher's
desk. A small blue leaf fluttered out from beneath them. It was
small and pear-shaped, the color of an early evening sky. Something the kids must've decorated on their paint-dappled tables,
maybe given to Mr. Filbert as a gift.

She started to reach for the tiny leaf when the door opened.
Before she could close her fingers around it, the leaf had fluttered
away.

Turning, Maggie faced Deputy Walters, whose broad face was
flushed red.

"Well?" Maggie asked, studying Walters. But she already knew.

"I'm sorry, Sheriff, we've covered every inch of the school.
There's no sign of them. I'm going to get the blueprints, just to
make sure there's nothing we've missed. And I've looked at surveillance video of the entryways, the hallways, and the schoolyard,
and there's no sign of the kids on that either. So it's not clear how
or when they would've gotten out."

Maggie felt herself deflate. The video showed that the kids
hadn't left this room. But she was in the room and she could see
the kids weren't here. Part of her wanted to go down and shake
Mr. Filbert until he told her the truth, however awful. But she felt
sure the harder she pushed him, the more he'd sit there with that
silent smug look on his face. Then Maggie had a thought.

"The surveillance video, does it show the attack?"

It did. Deputy Walters cued it up on her phone. The screen
was small but the resolution was good, and Maggie could see well
enough. There was the empty hallway, and all was silent. Then a
shot rang out, followed quickly by another.

Soon, a jittery man holding a Ruger 9-millimeter, Gerald Roach,
shoved a woman through a classroom doorway. He dragged her
down the hall, shouting at her to move faster. She did. As they kept
going, Roach grabbing her by the hair now, they passed the door
to Mr. Filbert's room.

A moment later, Mr. Filbert stepped out, clutching a bulky hardcover book. The woman seemed to notice him, because Mr. Filbert
shook his head as if to say, *Don't talk.* Then he raised the book over
his head and smashed it down on Roach. Immediately Roach went

down and the woman backed away. Mr. Filbert reached for the gun, but Roach knocked him back, fired. A flash of orange light across the screen. Luckily, he'd missed. Mr. Filbert backed away.

Roach moved in, the gun outstretched in his hand. Mr. Filbert bumped up against the wall. There was nowhere for him to go.

Roach took a step closer, ready to fire once more. Then a burly man in an all-blue uniform appeared and tackled Roach. They wrestled for a moment, a blur of arms and legs. Finally, the guard got the gun and aimed it at Roach, who squatted on the linoleum floor. Seeing he was no longer a threat, Mr. Filbert moved in closer and said something.

Roach turned away.

"What the hell was that?" Maggie asked. "What'd Filbert say to Roach?"

Walters shrugged. "No idea. I tried to get close enough to read his lips but the resolution's not good enough."

Maggie nodded, watched the end of the clip again and again. She felt that tingle in her fingers and toes, the way she always did when she put the pieces together on a case. At last, she had something . . . or thought she did. Finally, she turned to the door. "I'll be back. But I've got to talk to someone first."

"Who's that?"

"Gerald Roach."

Maggie's bootheels clicked on the linoleum as she made her way back down the hallway to the nurse's office. She nodded at the beefy state trooper stationed outside, then went in. There was another well-muscled state cop near the desk where Roach had been shackled.

With the burly state cop watching, Maggie sat down across from Roach.

"You're a real dirtbag, you know that?"

Roach said nothing. His face was pockmarked with acne scars, his eyes tiny black coals in his pale face. His arms were scrawny inside his faded button-down work shirt. He looked so small and pathetic, but with a gun in his hand, he must've thought he was a god.

"All this time you worked here, you saw those sweet little kids, and that didn't mean anything to you, did it? You would've just taken target practice on them unless you got what you wanted."

"They're not so sweet. Every day, they'd trash this place and expect me to clean up after them."

"That was your job. And now it's my job to clean up after you, Mr. Roach. You think I like it?"

He smiled at her. Perhaps he liked the idea of them having something in common.

"You're just lucky no one got hurt. Even so, you're going to prison for the rest of your life. How do you feel about that?"

At first Roach said nothing. Then: "She still loves me. I know she does."

"Yeah, well, then next time bring flowers instead of a nine-milli-meter."

Roach leaned back in his chair, his handcuffed wrists in front of him. Maggie could feel the trooper's eyes on her. She leaned in, dropped her voice a little. "You're in real trouble, you know that? But I could help you. Make sure you get a good lawyer, not just some public defender six months out of law school. Put in a good word for you, let the prosecutor's office know you were a cooperating witness. But first, you gotta help me. You think you can do that?"

His eyes narrowed. "Maybe."

"I saw the surveillance video. After the security guard got the gun away from you, Mr. Filbert moved in. He said something. What was it?"

Roach shrugged. "What's it matter?"

"It matters to me."

"He said . . . just something like, 'You'll never lay a hand on my kids, you hear me?'"

"His kids? Is that what he called them?"

"Yeah. He was always like that . . . his room, his kids. Guy acted like he owned the place. Back when I worked here, if he found a little speck of dirt in his classroom, he'd go running to the principal and complain. A real jerk. You know, he's the reason I got fired."

"How's that?"

Roach waved his hand. "Never mind. It doesn't matter."

"It does to me. What happened? He ratted on you for leaving too many dirty floors?"

"Nothing like that. It's just . . . I was doing my rounds after school one day, going room to room. All the kids were gone by then, the teachers too. Most of them, anyway. I opened the door to his classroom and . . ." A cloud passed over Roach's face. "Forget it. You'll think I'm crazy."

"Tell me."

"I walked in there and it was like, just like this bright light coming at me. I thought it was the sun or something, but those windows face east, and anyway . . . it wasn't sunlight. It was coming from the whiteboard, this bright beam, and through it I could sort of see these trees . . . They had these dark blue leaves, shaped kinda like pears . . . and then I passed out or something. A few seconds later, Mr. Filbert was standing there, asking me if I'm okay or whatever. I told him what I saw and he says I must've hit my head on a bookshelf, dreamed the whole thing, but that's not right. I didn't hit my head."

"What did you do?"

"I didn't argue with him, that's for sure. I was freaked out, so I raced down the hall and pulled my flask out, the one I carry for special occasions, you know. I figured I'd earned a drink. Only it turned out Principal Rodgers had forgot his keys in his office, and he was coming back and saw me. Fired me on the spot."

Maggie took all this in. Did she believe what he was telling her? She didn't think so . . . but then again, what reason did Gerald Roach have to lie?

"And what do you think it was, Mr. Roach? What you saw in Mr. Filbert's classroom that day?"

"He did something, hypnotized me or whatever, messed with my head. And if it wasn't for him I'd still have my job here and Carla and I'd still be together and none of this woulda happened. You see what I'm saying?"

After finishing with Roach, Maggie hurried down the hall toward the school's front entrance. This was crazy, what she was thinking, and the only thing crazier was the idea that it might be true.

When Maggie got to the front desk, she could see a swarm of people waiting to get inside. These weren't reporters, not with toddlers in their arms and anxious looks on their faces. They were parents. Anxious parents, about fifty of them now, all jostling to get past Deputy Katz and a couple of her part-time deputies. Maggie scanned them until she found Kevin Frasier. She waved Deputy Katz over and told him to get Kevin, then went to a quiet corner near a water fountain to wait for him.

"What the hell's going on here, Maggie?" he asked, pulling at his sweat-soaked collar. "At first I thought everything was okay, and now people are saying some of the kids have gone *missing*."

"I'm sorry. I can't say anything yet."

"You mean it's true then?" His eyes were wide with shock. "Tell me Emma's okay."

"I can't tell you anything, except it's all going to be okay. But I need you to tell *me* something. It's important." She looked at him closely. "You said Emma's made lots of art in Mr. Filbert's class, she's always making these fantasy worlds . . . Do you have any pictures of her stuff?"

"Maggie, this isn't the time for—"

She flashed him a look, and he pulled out his cell phone without another word. Swiping across the screen a few times, he finally held it up. Maggie looked at an image of Emma, looking older than she remembered but also the same. Her red hair was tied back in pigtails and she held up a hand-drawn image. The crude crayon sketch showed an image of a rich orange sky with a tall tree, the branches filled with dark blue leaves. There were bright yellow orbs, like a pair of suns, glowing on either side.

"Pretty good, right?" Even in fear, his pride showed through, as did his love for that little girl. "She makes stuff like this all the time."

Maggie nodded to herself more than Kevin. She handed him his phone back, started to hurry off.

"Wait, Maggie, where the hell are you going?"

She called back to him but didn't stop. "I'm going to get Emma."

Less than five minutes later she stood near the school library checkout counter, out of breath, and looked at Mr. Filbert, who was still sitting at the scuffed round table. It was like he hadn't moved at all since she'd last been there.

"Mr. Filbert, I want those children back."

"I told you, Sheriff. I can't help you."

Maggie sat and set her right hand on the table, fist closed. "I spoke to Gerald Roach. He told me about something he thought he saw in your classroom one afternoon. A white light, you appearing out of nowhere."

"Sounds kind of crazy. You know he drinks, don't you?"

"I do. But I was up in your classroom just now, and I found something that might interest you."

She opened her fist and held out her hand. The pear-shaped blue leaf had started to brown around the edges. Up close, she could see that what she'd assumed earlier was wrong. The kids hadn't painted this leaf, which was a color she'd never seen in nature. That strange shade of dark blue was its actual color.

"Where'd you get this, Mr. Filbert?"

Mr. Filbert didn't say anything in reply, but he shifted his gaze, refusing to look at Maggie. Crazy as this was, she knew she was onto something, and that gave her the courage to keep going.

"Let me try a theory on you. What if there was a second-grade teacher, really dedicated to his students, who loved fantasy stories. I don't know how it happened, but maybe he just read a lot of books like *The Lord of the Rings* or *Harry Potter,* or maybe his imagination was just so big he couldn't contain it, but somehow he imagined . . . another place. A world kind of like ours, but not exactly, not really. He talked about this world, and maybe he talked about it so much that—I don't know, this is where things start to get a little nuts—it became real. Or maybe it was always real, and he talked about it like it was a made-up place, just because he knew no one would believe him. What would you say if I told you that?"

"This story sounds rather far-fetched to me, Sheriff."

But there was a quiver in Mr. Filbert's voice. Maggie pressed on.

"Maybe he goes to this place sometimes, when he wants to get away. Maybe he even takes his students there once in a while, just so they can see how amazing it is. Of course it's got to be a secret, but you know kids . . . even if they say something or draw a picture of this place where they say they've been, who would believe them anyway?" Maggie leaned back in her chair, studying Mr. Filbert. "Should I keep going?"

He fussed with his bow tie. "Up to you. It's your story, not mine."

"Okay, so things go on like this, year after year. This teacher, beloved by his students, he goes to his secret place sometimes, when he wants to get away. Because it's peaceful there, and beautiful, and kind of perfect. And his kids—that's what he calls them by the way, *his kids*—they leave second grade and go on to third and fourth and fifth. They eventually go to college and out into the world, and as they get older they forget what they saw. Or maybe their minds get a little foggy and they think they just imagined it all."

"I don't know, Sheriff. Seems to me you're the one with the big imagination."

"Maybe so. Then let's imagine one day a guy with a gun bursts into the school. He used to be a janitor here, only he drinks too much and he's got a dangerous obsession with a teacher. He's got a gun this time, and he might do anything, and he fires off a couple of shots, and at that moment this second-grade teacher knows he's got to do something—he's got to do whatever he can to protect *his* *kids.* So, he opens the portal to this other world, and he takes the kids right on through, all of them. At first he probably just meant to keep them there long enough to make sure they were safe, but then maybe he got to thinking, what if they stayed there? Forever."

Mr. Filbert pressed his lips together as if he was smiling, but he wasn't. "If all this was true, and I'm not saying it is, but if it was . . . well, wouldn't it make a certain kind of sense?"

"How's that?"

"We live in an ugly world, Sheriff. Especially for a child. There's violence and pollution and terrorism and global warming and pandemics. And those are just the things we know about. What about the horrors the world has yet to unleash? It's the kind of world where innocent children could be gunned down in broad daylight. And who's going to keep us safe? People like you, with their guns and their laws. You clean up messes. You don't make the world safe."

Maggie wanted to argue but she couldn't. What he'd said was true.

"If you were honest about it, you might even say this world of ours is no place for a child. What if there was another place, one without violence or disease, one without all the horrors we face? What if it was full of untouched beauty and wonder, with clean air and endless skies and perfect weather all year long? Wouldn't the children be better off there?"

Maggie didn't answer right away. Because the man had a point, didn't he?

"Who's going to take care of them there? They're just kids."

"I wouldn't abandon them, Sheriff. They'd be looked after."

Maggie nodded. She understood. And she realized then that she might never get these children back. Mr. Filbert really thought he was going to be their caretaker and keep them in this other world. Maggie still had a hard time wrapping her mind around all this, but Mr. Filbert obviously believed in this secret place, and she had to admit that a part of her did too.

"Mr. Filbert, I can't promise you those children will be safe for the rest of their lives. I can't protect them from all the awful things in the world. No one can. No cop, no parent . . . no teacher."

Maggie leaned in and met his gaze.

"Yes, the world's a messy place," she continued. "But you don't have any right to take those kids away from their parents and grandparents, their brothers and sisters. You don't have any right to decide for them whether or not they want to make their way in this messy world. You're a grown-up, and if you've found some kind of escape, then good for you. But these are still kids. And just as it's wrong to attack them, it's equally wrong to take away their ability to choose how and where to live."

Maggie wondered if she had pushed it too far. Mr. Filbert's face seemed to shut down, his eyes squinching. He turned away, studying the picture books against the far wall, and then he looked up.

"Okay, Sheriff, I'll tell you where the kids are. On one condition."

He told her what it was and Maggie hesitated. After a moment, she nodded. What choice did she have?

Somehow, the classroom looked different than it had earlier. It was full of irregular shadows, and the desks looked small and pathetic. The sense of magic Maggie had felt here earlier was gone. She stood there, watching Mr. Filbert cross behind his desk, and then she stepped outside. She closed the door behind her, heading toward the deputies who'd brought Mr. Filbert up here.

Two minutes alone, she'd promised him, and that was all he was getting.

If she was wrong about this—if Filbert had stashed his own gun in his desk, along with the colored chalk and erasers, or if he tried to slit his wrists with a pair of childproof scissors—then she'd be kicking herself for years to come. And if she was right . . . well, what then? How would she square the idea of a secret fantasy world with the ordered, methodical life she had lived for the last forty-some years?

It had been sixty seconds already. She didn't hear a sound from inside the classroom.

She looked at the two state troopers. The taller one had his hand by his holster, ready to draw. The other one stood ramrod straight, his eyes shifting this way and that, his body frozen in place. Maggie had to fight the urge to tell them to move in right now, this very instant.

Ninety seconds.

As Maggie looked up, she noticed a faint light shining through the small window in the door. But as she'd promised, Maggie didn't go in. The taller cop took a half step toward the door, and Maggie shook her head. He edged back.

She checked her watch. Ten seconds left.

Maggie counted silently to herself and looked over.

The light behind the door had disappeared.

Maggie nodded and they all went in. The first thing she heard was the sound of laughter. Children's laughter. If there was a sweeter sound in the whole world, she didn't know what it was. But that wasn't what stayed with her for the rest of her life. It was what she saw on the far side of the room, at the end of the whiteboard, just beneath a poster about fire safety. A tiny irregular shape like a puzzle piece, only bigger, about the size of her palm. And through it, what? A bit of orange sky, water as green as anything she'd ever seen, some kind of tree shimmering with dark blue, pear-shaped leaves.

She glanced over at the other cops to see if they'd noticed it too, but it was already gone.

She turned to the children, the loud, exuberant children. She spotted Emma right away, that reddish hair, darker than she remembered. Maggie threw her arms around the girl. "You all right?" she asked.

"I'm fine. But where's Mr. Filbert?"

Maggie looked around. The students were there, loud and full of energy, but their teacher was gone.

The mess Sheriff Maggie Stanton had to clean up at the elementary school wasn't as bad as it might've been. The parents were so thrilled to have their kids back that they accepted the half-baked excuses the police department offered about the delay in letting them inside. And with Gerald Roach in custody and Mr. Filbert a hero, no one was eager to change that story and portray the missing second-grade teacher in a bad light.

Within a few days, classes returned to normal. A new second-grade teacher came in, Ms. Osgood, and she was old as the day was long, and she didn't tell any stories about imaginary worlds, but the kids liked her anyway. Not as much as they'd liked Mr. Filbert, though.

No one ever saw him again. The story was that he didn't much like publicity and had slipped out of the school when no one was looking and moved away. That didn't explain why he left his apartment and everything in it, including a collection of first edition *Lord of the Rings* novels that turned out to be worth quite a lot. Maggie personally investigated his disappearance, but there was no evidence of foul play. Officially, the disappearance of Mr. Filbert remained open, but it wasn't the kind of case that kept her up at night.

If anything kept her up late, it was some of the novels Mr. Filbert used to read to his students: *Harry Potter, The Lord of the Rings, The Chronicles of Narnia.* She'd never had much interest in fantasy stories before, but now Maggie devoured them. She liked to talk about them with Emma Frasier on Saturday afternoons at the park downtown. Maggie and Kevin Frasier weren't dating, exactly—she wasn't sure what they were doing, truth be told—but they liked spending time together. And Maggie was having fun getting to know Emma.

As for Mr. Filbert, Maggie heard stories from people around town who claimed to see him here and there, though when they looked back he just slipped off into the shadows. Others noted that he'd always said he wanted to retire and move away. A few told her he must've gone off to Florida, while others said no, he was set on going to California. No one was quite sure, though they all agreed it was definitely someplace warm.

Warmer than Logan Hills, anyway. And, Maggie suspected, much more peaceful.

SILVIA MORENO-GARCIA

The Land of Milk and Honey

FROM *The Perfect Crime*

IN THE HOUSE with the red double doors there lived an old man and six women, just them and no one else. It was a tattered casona, the zaguán leading to an interior patio with a lemon tree and potted plants. The abode had once been quite grand, but nowadays the wallpaper was peeling and the tiles around the fountain were cracked. A Studebaker Roadster had been left to decay under the onslaught of the elements in the courtyard.

The man of the house was Don Aurelio Heliodoro Vallejo Pacheco, and he did not believe in modern notions of women venturing out into the world. Ladies were supposed to be courted in the presence of their family and girls had no business attending a school. A woman's place is in the home, he said. There they could rest safe and sound and far from the dangerous glare of the city's lights. To ensure the women did not stray from the path of virtue and wouldn't be distracted by idle thoughts, he had them knit every day. They knitted booties and blankets and clothes to dress the plaster Baby Jesuses that made their appearance during Candlemas and Christmas. Aurelio sold those clothes through an intermediary, even though he hardly needed the money. The profits were placed in the safe inside the office.

The six women would sit in the living room on faded couches and chairs lined in velvet. The eldest of them was Don Aurelio's sister. Then came his wife, followed by four daughters. The girls had been born two years apart from each other. The youngest one, Ofelia, turned nineteen that spring of 1949.

Something else happened that spring: Don Aurelio broke his

leg. Early that afternoon he had gone to collect the rents. Don Aurelio owned two vecindades and he knew that if he waited until Monday the factory workers and assorted riffraff that dwelled in the cramped buildings would have spent their salary on drinks. So, he stopped by before they had the chance to hit the cantinas and then, after depositing the cash back in the safe at home, he went out to drink and play dominoes.

It was nighttime when Don Aurelio stumbled outside La Valentina, landed at an odd angle, and somehow broke his leg. Two of his drinking buddies drove him home and called for the doctor from the pharmacist's store, because Don Aurelio did not keep a telephone in his house. He said it was too pricey. Meat was also pricey, and he selected the worst and cheapest cuts for his family but bought juicy steaks for himself. Sometimes he made the women go without meat for a week to economize while he ate out.

The doctor put a cast on his leg and told him to stay in bed. Don Aurelio wailed for a whole day, railing against his bad luck while the women tended to him. Then he calmed down and, remembering that he had to collect the rents, he began to worry about how he would manage that and who would run the errands, because he was the one who bought the food and other supplies.

"Perhaps we could do it," Ofelia's mother said.

"What, go out there on your own?" Don Aurelio replied. He took the women to Mass once a month and on their birthdays he allowed them to watch a movie, but they were always at his side.

"We could hire a maid."

"Do you think I'm made of money, woman?" Don Aurelio asked, aghast.

Although every family of their class had a maid and even the poorer ones could afford a cleaning lady once a week, Don Aurelio had never considered such an expense. Besides, he knew most maids had bad habits. If they didn't steal from you, then they might bring their boyfriend to the house. When there was a maid, the louts of the neighborhood came around like dogs in heat. Don Aurelio was a righteous man, and he would not allow such a thing.

Instead, Don Aurelio sent a telegram to his cousin Trinidad. Trinidad had been widowed for several years. She was one of those poorer relations that bloom in every family. She had a son who was hoping to live in the city. A few months before she had written to Don Aurelio, hoping he could find the boy a position, but Aurelio had not bothered replying. Now he invited Arturo to live with him. He would be provided with room and board in exchange for running errands, collecting the rents, and fixing whatever needed to be fixed around the house. He promised the boy a paltry salary, which would have been half of what a decent assistant would have cost him.

This is how Ofelia found herself opening the door to Cousin Arturo one warm day in March. He walked in shyly, with a suitcase in one hand and a felt hat in another. He had straight teeth, bright eyes and parted his hair on the left side.

"Cousin O-Ofelia?" he asked. "I don't know if you remember me, I . . . ah . . . I was at Cousin Magda's wedding."

Cousin Magda's wedding had taken place six years prior. Their father had taken them to the countryside. She remembered the digging of the pit for the barbacoa, the hot coals and the scent of the smoke drifting up in the air. Her gloves had stuck to her skin under the blazing sun but her father would not allow her to take them off.

"I think I do," she said, though she really couldn't have told him apart from her other cousins.

He smiled, shy yet cheerful, and she guided him to her father's bedroom. Once he went inside, Ofelia grabbed a broom and began sweeping the hallway, trying to listen to what they were saying. She couldn't understand a single word, but still she walked up and down the hallway, sweeping the same stretch of crimson clay tiles. In the living room the women knit, preparing trousers and shirts for babies and plaster statues alike, but as long as Ofelia pretended to sweep, she could escape the confines of that space and the clicking of the needles.

At length, the door opened and Arturo stepped out. He smiled at her again.

"If you'll pardon me . . . Your father says there's a cot in the little blue room, but I'll need blankets," he said, and she smiled back.

Arturo proved himself to be an industrious, well-behaved young man. He went to fetch tortillas and vegetables and chicken for the consomés that Don Aurelio liked. The milk was delivered, so he didn't need to bother with that. He collected the rent and Ofelia counted the bills in her father's office. She had kept the books for him for a long time now because her father said her mother had grown scatterbrained.

Arturo set up bait and poison for the rats that had been nibbling at their food, decided to clear the damp rooms full of junk and broken furniture in the back, and began repairing the old car.

Don Aurelio's house was a place without tenderness. But Aurelio's father had fancied himself a poet and in the dusty books that nobody else ever bothered to clap open, Ofelia had found words of passion. When her father discarded the newspaper on the table after his breakfast, leaving coffee stains at the edges, she carefully read the pages instead of merely paying attention to the headlines as he did. And when her father took them to see a women's picture, which he thought to be suitable entertainment, rather than focusing on the moral of the story—for wickedness was punished in the last reel—Ofelia reveled in the sin.

And that is how, despite Don Aurelio's talk of temperance and morality, Ofelia found herself admiring the strong arms of her cousin, fixating on the fullness of his lips and wanting to trace the beads of sweat that slid down his throat as he worked around the house, going into rooms that Don Aurelio could never be bothered to care for despite the fact the house was damp and old and needed constant attention. For the first time in years fresh paint concealed the mold that had once bloomed by a leaky windowpane and rolls of wallpaper that had been stuffed in a corner and forgotten were carefully pasted onto naked walls.

By the end of April, Don Aurelio's leg had healed, but he didn't take up his chores again. Instead, he headed to the cantina earlier, ate out more often, and decided that Arturo would become a permanent addition to the family. For a few years now he had feared he would have to marry off at least one of the girls, to ensure someone could take care of his properties. He could not conceive that the women might manage on their own, but he also feared what a strange man would want. Although dowries were relics of yesteryears, none of his daughters was particularly pretty. Ofelia was the most attractive of the lot, but even though the gap in her teeth was more charming than off-putting, the girl was so quiet. She hardly said a word. Besides, she was as flat as a board and Aurelio, who fancied hour-glass shapes and prostitutes with large breasts, couldn't imagine that any man in his right mind would settle for a flat little thing when he could avail himself of something better.

What Aurelio feared, in short, was that any suitor would want money to accompany his bride. Now, with Arturo there, Don Aurelio could rely on a man to watch over his affairs without having to spend a fortune on securing his loyalty.

That is how, the first week of May, Don Aurelio had Arturo moved to a nicer room with a real bed instead of a cot and a wardrobe to replace the old crates where the boy had placed his clothes.

Spring turned to summer and Ofelia spied on Arturo from the shadow of the lemon tree as he stood in his undershirt, fingers dark with grease. While she scrubbed the flagstones, she watched him, looking down whenever he glanced in her direction. In the evening, when he had his coffee with milk and a few almond cookies, her eyes rested on his hands.

She hovered around Arturo when he was working, finding excuses to be in the same room as the boy. When they talked, it was a succession of quick, polite sentences. But soon they were conversing rather than just exchanging pleasantries.

Ofelia asked him what he did when he went outside, she asked him to tell her the names of the actresses that appeared on the covers of magazines.

"Well, there are many of them. I should just buy a magazine at the newsstand the next time," he said.

"My father doesn't like us reading magazines. He says they have too many ads for perfumes and makeup."

"It can be our secret."

She smiled and when he brought her a magazine, they pored over it together, looking at the glamorous ladies in their mink coats. Ofelia wondered what it would be like to get her hair done or paint her nails. She'd never owned a pair of high-heel shoes, nor a string of pearls.

"You'd look prettier than the lot of them in that dress," Arturo said when she stared at a photo. She blushed.

They began meeting at night. They didn't discuss it, but somehow Ofelia would end up walking into the interior patio and Arturo was already there, cigarette in hand. Or else she'd lean against the car and he'd come strolling outside.

If it rained, they sat in the car. Just sat and talked. He was as shy as Ofelia and well-behaved. When he spoke at the dinner table it was all *usted* and please and multiple thank-yous. In private, he was still coiled tight. Until the night when Arturo's hand crept under Ofelia's thin dress, brushing against her underwear, and he leaned forward, kissing her until they were both breathless.

"It's uncomfortable, sitting here," she complained because the car had a bad smell. A rodent or some other small animal had died somewhere inside and the scent lingered.

"I could come to your room."

"My bed squeaks," she told him, her voice a whisper.

"Mine doesn't."

She thought to grab his hand and pull him back into the house, shove him into his room and onto that bed, but there was a loud whistle outside: the noise of the man selling camotes, making his nightly rounds. It startled Ofelia and she ran from the car.

That night marked a turning point for them. If she had once sought Arturo, now she avoided him. Ofelia threw herself into her duties, her needles furiously clicking as she worked next to the other women. It was regular baby clothes that they knitted, for now. The orders for clothing for the Baby Jesuses wouldn't begin to trickle in until September, perhaps October. It was still months until the women in households across the city would lovingly dress their plaster figurines and rock them in their arms. They'd dress the child again for Candlemas in fresh shoes and clothes, and again the needles in Ofelia's house would click for that occasion, telegraphing a mute tale, following the patterns they'd knit their whole lives.

But now it was summer. She hardly spoke to her cousin and she went to bed early. If it had been winter, she might have slept soundly, but the rain kept her up at nights. When it rained, the rats came rushing out of the pipes, seeking safety and warmth, and the women set up pots and pans around the house to catch the water from the leaks. In her room, the water dripped; it wouldn't let her close her eyes.

She recalled Arturo's hand on her thigh or his voice, low against her ear. She felt warm and cold, tossing the covers aside, then huddling under three blankets for warmth. The sight of a rat in the kitchen made her cry and when she burnt her dress with the iron she giggled. She was at turns furious, woeful, distracted, serious, listless, and frenetic.

Ofelia's mother thought the girl had caught a chill and told her to rest. A chill was the only ailment Ofelia's mother understood, and they did not ask the doctor to come for a visit. Women's illnesses did not deserve scrutiny.

Thus, the girl lay swaddled under one of the many blankets stuffed around the house, staring at the ceiling while the rain leaked into her room and landed in a pot set by the bed, serenading her. Finally, Ofelia rose from her bed and walked in the dark until she found a thin strip of light emanating from under a door. She pushed the door open and walked into Arturo's room. He put aside the book he had been reading and she took off her nightgown.

The first time Arturo and Ofelia made love in that room that was blessedly distant from the other rooms in the house; they did so in silence, as though they were enacting a pantomime. They were both too terrified of being discovered to utter a single sound. She didn't even bid him goodnight when she stepped out.

They were cautious, at first. But caution was quickly discarded. If they found themselves alone, they flew into each other's arms, and not only in Arturo's room but anywhere around the house. Some nights she sat on his lap on an old couch that had been stained by the humidity and forgotten in a dusty room, arms around his neck, while on other occasions he shoved her against a wall and she bit her lip in delight. The rain drew patterns on the windows and dripped into the rooms, caressing their skin.

He began to bring her things. First, another magazine. Then a pair of stockings. A little bottle of perfume. She hid them away.

One afternoon, he sat her atop the desk in the office and merrily made love to her while a rat stared at them from a corner of the room. When they were done and he was tucking his shirt back into his trousers, he let out a loud sigh.

"I guess I'll have to put out more poison for the rats," he said. "But they never die completely. The problem is this house. It's too old and damp and dark. It's dreadful. And to think your father could simply buy a new, nicer place."

"My father would never buy a new house. He'd say it's a waste of money."

"I know. Ofelia, I'm going to tell you a secret, but you must promise not to tell your father."

"What is it?"

She was still sitting atop the desk and Arturo, who had taken a few paces from her, moved back to stand between her legs, his right hand rubbing her thigh. She shivered at his touch.

"I've been putting aside a little money and I want you to go away with me."

"My father doesn't pay you enough to squirrel away much," she said.

He chuckled. "No, he doesn't. But I still find a way to put away some cash. I increased the rents a bit and I'm pocketing the difference. I swear, it's not much per household, but it adds up."

"But that's stealing!"

"It's like you said, he doesn't pay me enough. He has so much money. That safe is crammed with bills. I bet if we took a bag full of bills he wouldn't be able to tell the difference. And some of that money is yours. He sells all those things you knit and you never see a cent of the profits."

Ofelia never thought much about what happened to the garments she knitted. She knew, of course, that her father affixed a sign outside their door that said Baby Jesuses Dressed/We Knit Clothes for Newborns and women came by and placed their order. Or else, he sold the clothes to his intermediary downtown. But the money never concerned her. This was simply something she must do, and whether the garments were pure white or brown or red, she must knit them.

"With the car fixed and a little money, we could go anywhere," Arturo said, although he hadn't bothered fiddling with the car in weeks, too busy studying the contours of her body in his spare time.

"Where?"

"I don't know. But aren't you tired of being locked inside here? I come from such a small town and I hated it there, but it almost feels worse to be in the city when I feel so trapped. And you want pretty things and to have fun, you've told me so."

She'd told him she wanted to wear makeup and satin and curl her hair. So she nodded and his hands found her face and he kissed her until her hands were at his buckle again and he was pushing into her once more.

It was in October that they began taking money from the safe. They justified it using the same principle as before: it was only a little money and her father wouldn't notice it.

By then, Arturo had become surer of himself. Gone was the shy, almost stammering boy of nineteen who had stumbled through the doorway of the house. Instead, Ofelia was greeted by a man who invariably brought her a present every time he went out, then pressed her against a wardrobe or some other piece of furniture and unbuttoned her blouse, his hands on her breasts.

How she loved the look in his eyes when he was aflame, his hair tousled. Of his gifts, she felt less certain. At first, she liked them all very much. Magazines, rice powder, books. Then underwear, a dress, a compact mirror, a necklace, lipstick so crimson it was like smearing blood across her lips.

The gifts began to fill her with a strange sense of dread.

They didn't belong in the dark casona with cracks in the walls any more than the cheerful wallpaper Arturo had put in one of the rooms or the fresh coat of white paint he'd given another. She looked at the plants growing wild in pots and the dry fountain, at the women sitting in the living room with its velvet curtains and the Victrola in the corner, and she knew Arturo's eager face and enthusiasm clashed with everything inside the house, as did his presents.

The gifts he procured for her were like artifacts from another universe, as baffling as a radio would have been to a Babylonian priestess. She hid them, fearful that her father might find them, but also terrified that the house itself might reject them, that it might expel Arturo. He was like an eyelash rubbing against an eye, almost an irritant.

She suffered from piercing headaches that would arrive early in the morning and follow her late into the night. Certain noises aggravated her: the clicking of needles, the ticking of the clock in the living room.

She checked that the gifts were safely hidden inside a chest. She checked in the morning and at night, but sometimes she felt compelled to run into the room in the middle of the day and fling the lid open, to ensure the objects hadn't somehow spilled onto her bed.

The others noticed the dark circles under her eyes.

"What is wrong with this girl?" her father asked.

"She has a chill," her mother said.

"Again? You're too idle, Ofelia. That's the problem. Knit a few more booties, that'll get your mind back on track," he said.

During supper she ate two morsels and drank but a sip of water. She felt dread crawling inside her entrails. She couldn't explain it to Arturo. When they lay tangled in his bed together, she'd press her face against his chest and she'd sob and he'd ask what was wrong.

"I don't know . . . it's the house," she said. "It frightens me."

"What frightens you?"

"The noise of the headboard scraping against the wall . . . the noise of the springs . . . our voices. What if they suspect?"

The rains, which concealed all sounds, had departed and the naked night remained.

"They don't suspect a thing. Won't you wear that nice negligee I bought you? For a few minutes," he said, pressing the piece of clothing against her hands. "It's fine. Ofelia, kiss me."

How she wanted him! And how obscene was the sight of him nude on the bed. His youth was an affront, their kisses sacrilege, but she kissed him nevertheless, searching for the warmth of his body. She thought about knitting a huge, thick blanket, large enough that they both might hide underneath it and be swallowed by darkness.

By December the room Arturo repainted had grown cheerless and mold was beginning to bloom again upon its surface. It looked almost like tiny fingerprints, gray and soft.

Don Aurelio sent Arturo and Ofelia shopping for Christmas foods, for bacalao and romeritos and guayabas for the ponche. Two people were needed to carry multiple bags filled with goods, and normally Ofelia found such shopping to be a treat. That year, Don Aurelio couldn't be bothered to go, preferring to spend his time at the cantina, where he now played endless rounds of dominoes. But that suited the lovers well enough, and she relished the thought of having a coffee with her sweetheart.

The streets downtown were a collage of multicolored piñatas, mountains of fruit, colación, and firecrackers. There were hundreds of people shopping. It didn't matter where you went, waves of humans crashed against Ofelia's body. She clutched her purse against her chest, stood on her tiptoes, tried to speak to Arturo but the crowd was like a roar.

The noises of cars honking mixed with the buzzing of all those voices and the shrieking of radios, the music of the organilleros on the corners, the paper boys yelling headlines about robbers and murderers. Ofelia wished to press her hands against her ears to muffle the sound.

Near the Alameda she saw a grotesque, poorly made Baby Jesus in a shop window, resting in its cradle filled with hay, surrounded by the Three Wise Men. The unseeing eyes and plaster limbs of the figurine made her sick and she turned away in fright, shoving her way down busy sidewalks, blind to Nativity scenes and tinsel ornaments, until Arturo caught up with her.

"Ofelia! What's wrong?" he asked.

"Arturo! Don't make me go back to the house!" she exclaimed, clutching at his arms. She thought someone was squeezing her lungs.

"But, Ofelia, we said in the summer—"

"No! Not in the summer. I want to go away this instant. Please, Arturo, please!"

"Ofelia, you're being silly. Don't cry, darling. Very well . . . don't worry, just don't," he said, hugging her and pressing a kiss upon her brow. All thoughts of having coffee were forgotten. They proceeded with their shopping in haste, and it was only when they reached the doors of the house that Ofelia felt that terrible constriction in her chest lifting.

She'd been sick every morning in December, with a sour taste in her mouth lingering until noon, but now she could hardly sleep. She heard the whizzing of fireworks outside their house, as the neighbors organized their posadas, and she recalled the crowd downtown and shuddered.

Arturo purchased a rosca de reyes from the bakery and they sat around the table, drinking chocolate.

She regarded the cutting of the bread with weary eyes. She did not wish to eat a slice, she wanted to refuse to eat, but her mother was systematically handing out plates. Ofelia looked at the bread on her plate and she saw the tiny, pale leg of the Baby Jesus sticking out from the dough.

She had eaten dozens of roscas de reyes in previous years and twice before she'd found the little porcelain Baby Jesus figurine in her slice of bread. It was such an ordinary occurrence that it should not have evoked anything but a smile. Instead, Ofelia pulled her chair back in horror and stood there, mutely, a hand clasped against her mouth.

"Child! What has gotten into you!" Don Aurelio yelled.

She could not say. All Ofelia knew was that the tiny figurine reminded her of the Baby Jesus they'd seen near the Alameda and that brought back the nauseating memory of the people shoving against each other, of the scent of gasoline and perfumes and foods, and the noises of motors.

"I saw a rat," she lied, though in her eyes she saw only the blinking lights downtown and her tongue was coated with bile.

"Damn rats. Arturo, didn't you say you had bought more poison and baited them?" her father asked.

"Yes, sir, the raticide is under the sink."

"It's the cold that makes the rats so eager. It's chilly. Someone bring me my cozy blanket," Don Aurelio grumbled, and Ofelia sat down. She clutched her hands under the table to keep them from trembling. Christmas Eve was fast approaching.

She wouldn't survive it.

She held Arturo in the dark, begged him to take her away. But the hours marched on, inexorably, until she found herself sitting in the living room, with her father half-asleep, drunk already on rum, and the women smiling. Arturo sat in a corner and she tried to look at him, only at him, erasing everyone else.

"It's time to lull the Baby Jesus to sleep," Ofelia's mother said.

Her sisters were fetching the plaster statue, which had been dressed early in the morning. Ofelia had avoided looking at it, but now they were bringing it into the room. She wished to close her eyes, fearing the horrid, leprous Baby Jesus from the store down-town had sneaked into their home. She'd heard tales of Baby Jesuses that moved at night or whose expressions changed.

Miracles, they said.

Horrors, she thought.

The women were rocking the baby in their arms and they were singing. Ofelia sat still, staring at Arturo, who she could hardly see because he was sitting in shadows. Her mother stepped forward, holding the baby up in her arms, exposing its pale face to Ofelia, and Ofelia felt a spasm of terror cleave through her body.

Her hands were closed into tight fists, which she pressed against her stomach. But it was only the old figurine they'd owned for years and years and she was able to finally breathe in relief. Ofelia's mother turned away, carrying the baby back to its crib.

Then Arturo was there, extending his arms in her direction.

"Merry Christmas," he said, and she let him embrace her, eyes bright and watery.

Ofelia lay under a thick blanket that her sisters had knitted and stared at a crack running down the wall. Children were playing with firecrackers in the street. She could hear them yelping and laughing. Outside, the scent of gunpowder perfumed the air. But the house smelled of old rains that had trickled into ancient rooms for over a century, it smelled of wax and also of forgotten things.

Arturo let himself into her room. Ofelia sat up, startled; she thought him a ghost at first.

"Why aren't you ready?" he asked.

"What do you mean?"

"We said we'd leave tonight."

She didn't recall that conversation. Ofelia was in her nightgown and he was fully dressed, with a suitcase in one hand. He sighed and set the suitcase down. "I thought you wanted to leave the house."

No, she had not wanted to return to the house. But that had been a few days before. Now she was suddenly frightened by the thought of stepping out into the street, of the noise and those firecrackers exploding.

"Ofelia, you need to change and then we have to open the safe and get a little bit more cash."

"But tonight . . . I'm so tired," she said. "And if we were to take any more money I'd feel so bad."

"Just a few more bills. Ofelia—"

"Arturo, not tonight. I know something dreadful will happen tonight."

"You're saying that because you hardly ate a thing today."

"No. I just know it. Because outside . . . and the house . . . It'll never work."

"You're giving me a headache," he muttered and pinched the bridge of his nose. "Let's go to the dining room and you can have a bite and we can go over the plan again."

She nodded. They ventured into the kitchen and she began boiling water for a couple of coffees. He stood by the door, speaking in a low soothing tone. She didn't recognize half the words he said. The naked bulb above their heads cast stark shadows on the walls.

". . . and you'll never have to come back here."

She heard that. Loud and clear. Ofelia raised her head and blinked, realizing what he was saying at last. "Leave the house forever?"

"Of course. Go someplace new. Someplace better, without nosy relatives to tell us what to do."

New, better, outside. Far from the house with its cracks on the walls, the scent of mothballs lingering in the armoire, the dry fountain, and the broken tiles. Far from Don Aurelio, her mother, her sisters and the incessant clicking of the needles.

But outside there was the terrible, hungry night and the eyes of the porcelain Baby Jesus.

Outside they'd eat her bones and chew on her marrow. She knew it, she just knew it, and she felt that hand crushing her lungs again.

She realized that it was Arturo who had invited this monstrous doom into her home. Arturo and his gifts, which collided with the house, too full of life and vibrant with promise. The house spit them out, rejected them. And Ofelia, born of the house, grown in the house, couldn't exist in the presence of such animated desire and motion.

Now Arturo wanted not only to bring all this wildness into her home but to pluck her free, to toss her into the world.

She'd be smothered.

"Love, the water's boiling," he said, tugging at her hand.

Ofelia turned her head and moved the kettle from the burner. "Sit, and we can talk while we have coffee," she said.

He stepped out of the kitchen. She arranged almond cookies on a plate. She poured the water into the cups, added a splash of milk and the sugar, making the coffee the way he liked it.

Ofelia walked into the dining room and placed the cup and the cookies before him.

"Now, what's wrong? You're all jittery. I don't understand it."

She sat in front of him. "It's not safe outside."

He nibbled at a cookie. "Not safe how?"

"My father says a woman's place is the home. I can't leave, Arturo. Just stay with me here, let's just stay and forget about going anywhere. Let's forget about the money or driving to distant places. Let's stay."

Ofelia prayed to God in that instant, begging him to change

Arturo's mind. That he might abandon all thoughts of escape and that they would remain together in the dim hallways and damp rooms of the house. Because otherwise . . .

She stretched out a hand to clutch his own. The house didn't like Arturo, but if they were careful, if they tried, maybe the house would grow to tolerate him. He needed to stop bringing those gifts and those maps and stop talking about escape. They must toss away all the things he'd bought her, dig a hole and bury them, there, under the lemon tree.

"Arturo," she whispered.

She wanted to tell him that she'd seen an abomination behind the glass—that horrible porcelain figurine in the crib. The house could protect them, it could keep their secrets. They must never try to leave it.

But Arturo shook his head and brushed her fingers away. "Ofelia, no. We're leaving. That's it. We said we would, and we will," he assured her.

He shook his head again. She watched him, unblinking, as he lifted the mug and drank the coffee laced with raticide.

Not Exit

FROM *Crime Hits Home*

I.

Tom Exit went to prison for yelling at two cops who were, in his opinion, inappropriately searching a young woman he later came to know as Patricia Neil. Because Tom was hollering and gesticulating at them Patrolman Hans Braun told him to lower his voice and then grabbed him by the wrist. Tom yanked his hand free from the cop's grasp. That was assault and so the police left off their search of Patricia Neil's person in order to batter Mr. Exit into submission.

When Tom's crime came to trial his mother testified that her son had learning disabilities that made him sometimes speak out when he experienced or saw what he thought of as an injustice.

"He loses control," she said. "But he doesn't mean anything."

She had medical papers documenting his condition, but the court ruled her evidence inadmissible because she had highlighted in yellow those sections pertaining to the possible underlying causes of Tom's actions.

Patricia Neil swore under oath that the police "had their hands all in my clothes and on my body and Mr. Exit was callin' out to them to respect my dignity."

But Patrolman Braun said that they had witnessed Miss Neil buying drugs from a known drug dealer and they needed to find the evidence in order to arrest her, and her connection.

The day before the case went to the jury Tom Exit, through his lawyer, Marcia Abraham, made a plea-bargain agreement to serve eighteen months for the class D felony.

*

During the first year of his incarceration at Rikers Island Tom was beaten, raped, and otherwise sexually assaulted by multiple assailants, and placed in solitary confinement sixteen times. He was twenty-one years old.

The only bright light to Tom's imprisonment was the more or less biweekly visits by Patricia Neil.

"You know," she told Tom across the unobstructed desk that was available to visitors who could afford the forty dollars, "you saved my ass when you told them cops to leave me alone. I had enough chems on me to be called a dealer and I already got two felony convictions on my record. I'd'a been in jail till my ass was saggin' and wrinkled if they'da reached into my drawers."

Patricia had dark skin like Tom's and one of her front teeth was edged in gold. He wished like anything that he could go home with her just to sit on her couch and watch TV. He liked cartoons and shows about the animal kingdom. He could name every species of bird and most sharks, well over a thousand different dinosaurs, and mark many of the differences between mammals, reptiles, and fishes.

In his thirteenth month of incarceration Tom asked a nurse-intern for a drink of water. They were in the infirmary, where he'd been sent for a bloody nose received in an impromptu beating. The nurse-intern, whose name was Bernard Walters, denied the request and Tom said, "But I'm thirsty."

Walters said, "Then open up and I'll piss in your mouth."

Exit didn't remember attacking Walters but when he regained consciousness he was in a straitjacket, lashed to an aluminum framed cot. Lying there, bound to the metallic frame, Tom was thinking about a thick fog that had a pinkish hue.

"Mr. Exit struck and even bit Mr. Walters for no reason whatever," prosecutor Phil Hines told the judge presiding over the case.

The prosecution had convinced the court that Exit was a danger to others and so had him dragged into court in the straitjacket.

That day he got five years tagged on to his sentence.

Tom's mother, Deborah Marsh-Exit, remarried soon after her son's second conviction. Her new husband, Lance Ferragut, said he didn't like his wife going down to Rikers so often and from then on she only came to see her son on his birthday.

Patricia Neil decreased her visits to once a month because she kicked her habit and had taken a job in a small assembly factory in Queens. She told Tom that she and her fellow ex-con workers put together things like brushes and pails made from bright colored plastic fabricated and exported by a company in China somewhere.

Two years passed without official incident.

But along the way Tom experienced a whole raft of unofficial trouble. He was tasked by cell-block kingpin Billy Biggs to bring in drugs in order for Billy to put out the word that other inmates had to stop abusing and beating him. The only way he could achieve this goal was to ask Patricia to get one of her friends, who was still using, to smuggle a sachet of Oxycontin pills into him.

Carellia Thorn, a light-skinned Black woman, took the job and visited Tom under the pretext that she was a distant cousin. For the past year the guards had been allowing Tom open-desk visiting privileges due to his good record. To his surprise they put him at a station in the far corner where there was a modicum of privacy. Usually only the wealthier prisoners got that seat when their girlfriends or wives visited.

Carellia was large but not fat, what his mother called big-boned. Her face was beautiful and sensual, and she had a smile that actually made the twenty-four-year-old convict's heart skip.

"Hi, baby," she said when they were alone. "Patricia says hi too."

"That's a pretty dress," Tom answered. The one-piece frock was peacock blue with serious décolletage.

"You like it?" she asked through a conspiratorial grin.

"A lot."

"I paid the visitin' manager to give us this desk because I wanted to be able to give you what I got without some stick-up-his-ass guard tryin' to mess with us."

With those words on her red, red lips she stood and walked around the wooden desk to where Tom sat. She handed him a package of ochre paper tightly bound with yards of Scotch tape. He took the bundle, looking up at the woman, trying to remember how to breathe and talk at the same time.

Leaning down Carellia kissed Tom's lips, running her tongue around them lightly.

"When's the last time?" she asked.

"Huh?"

"The last time you had a woman."

"Never yet," he said.

"You think you might be ready for me to sit on your lap?"

On that day, September 17, 1992, Tom Exit lost his virginity, was arrested in prison, and, ultimately, earned another eleven years of jail time. He found out later that Carellia had a brother in Rikers and that he started getting preferential treatment after his sister's visit to Tom and Tom's subsequent arrest for receiving contraband.

Maybe she set me up, Tom reasoned, but he couldn't help but feel grateful to the first woman that had ever loved him for real.

Tom stabbed Billy Biggs four days after the three-day trial that increased the length of his captivity by more than a decade. Billy had his men beat him three days in a row for failing to bring in the drugs.

The day of the attempted murder Tom had been talking to a new con named Jeff Fartheran. Jeff was white and had done many stints in New York state prisons as well as elsewhere.

"They give you two black eyes, huh, brotherman?" Jeff said. He and Tom were loitering in the recreation room waiting for a turn at the Ping-Pong table.

"They say they gonna beat on me every day until I finally die," Tom mourned.

Fartheran was of that select species of convict who believed in justice. He never complained about being arrested or convicted, sent to prison, or even taking a beating if he deserved it. But Jeff could not brook an attack on a man when that man had done nothing wrong.

After Tom explained his circumstances Jeff shook his hand, passing the young prisoner a shard of sharpened metal that had a cardboard haft bound to it with dark green nylon twine.

Tom left Jeff, going out into the yard where he saw Billy and ran at him. It wasn't until sometime later he realized that the exceptionally short blade was meant for slashing and not stabbing. Tom knifed the cell-block boss thirty-two times without inflicting any serious damage when he could have cut Biggs's throat with a single swipe.

In the end he was happy that he hadn't killed Billy. He didn't think of himself as a killer. He didn't think of himself as a convict either but there he was.

This trial lasted longer. They kept Tom in a cell inside the courthouse in Brooklyn. There he glanced through picture magazines and started drawing mob scenes populated by dozens of stick-figure men. By the fifth week he had been found guilty. The last trial date was to be held on Friday of the seventh week. He wasn't really worried about the sentence, figuring that Billy and his friends would kill him long before he had any possibility of parole.

That Friday morning, he was mildly surprised to see a man instead of the public defender, Charlotte Hampstead, sitting at the defense table. He shuffled up to the white man because he was chained, hand to foot.

"Art Cohen," the new lawyer said, patting Tom's shoulder. He wore a herringbone jacket, loud yellow pants, and a black shirt decorated by intersecting silvery white-line circles. He also sported an extraordinarily bushy mustache.

"Tom," Tom said. "Tom Exit."

"That's an odd name. I never heard it before."

"My great-great-great-great-grandfather exscaped in the Underground Railroad and took the name Exit because that's what he did from slavery."

"Well, we're gonna try and get you on that train, my friend."

"What happened to Charlotte?" Tom asked.

"She had a heavy load and I've been following your case. Now that they found you guilty I thought I might try something. You game?"

"Uh. Okay . . . I guess."

The court was called to order and the judge, Vivian Mars, entered.

"Mr. Cohen," she said as she lowered into her chair, "what has you slumming with us today?"

"Justice is deserved by everyone, Your Honor."

"Justice is about to sentence your client."

"I understand that, Judge. My client has been found guilty, but I believe that before he is sentenced I should bring a few extenuating circumstances to your attention."

"The trial is over, Art," Vivian Mars said.

"We do not dispute the guilty verdict but only wish to tell a brief story about how Tom Exit came to be here."

"How long will this story take?"

"Twelve minutes from start to finish. I timed it while trimming my mustache this morning."

"Go on then."

Art Cohen told about Tom's first arrest and conviction following up with the later convictions that now had him teetering on the brink of a life sentence.

"Tom Exit is standing before you today for no reason other than the fact that he believed a woman was being assaulted by two men," Cohen concluded. "Those detectives manhandling the woman were in plain clothes. His mother presented documents provided by a social worker that explained the young man's actions, but the judge refused to allow them."

"I can feel the passion, Mr. Cohen," the judge said, "but Mr. Exit received fair trials in each incidence."

The sound of Mars's voice was somewhat sad, Tom thought.

"Not exactly," the flashy lawyer replied. "Because of the evidence that was suppressed Mr. Exit has never been given the proper psychological testing. The rush to judgment in every trial never took into account the prisoner's inability to deal with the world—untreated."

So, on a rainy day in April, Tom Exit was transferred from the Brooklyn courthouse to a minimum-security hospital where people suspected or convicted of crimes were examined, tested, and found either crazy or sane.

The facility was called Lorraine, just the name with no other adjective or appellation. It had four floors, a small, mazelike flower garden, good food with plastic cutlery, and real lighting—not that fluorescent bullshit they used in prison.

The second floor was for testing, interviews, group therapy, and one-on-one psychological analysis. The third floor contained the barracks where the women stayed in the corridor that went to the right while the men occupied the opposite side. The fourth floor was one big recreation room where the patients sat and spoke and sometimes smoked on a fairly large outside deck attached to the rec area.

It was on the first afternoon on that very deck where Tom met Calhoun Dieterman. Calhoun was a biracial man born of a Black soldier and a white German man in Frankfurt. Calhoun and Tom

hit it off right away because Art Cohen had given Tom three packs
of unfiltered cigarettes before putting his client on the prison bus
to Lorraine.

"Use these like you would money," Art had told Tom and Tom
gave a pack to Calhoun when he asked for a cigarette.

"But if you waitin' for judgment on attempted murder then why
they send you to minimum security?" the German-American asked
his friend after the first group therapy meeting they both attended.

"My lawyer," Tom said. "He told how I attacked the head of a
gang but it was because him and his friends beat me almost every
day. He had infirmary records and the judge took pity on me."

"You lucky to have a lawyer like that. You rich or sumpin'?"

"Naw. It was just a lucky break, I guess."

A few weeks later Tom and Calhoun were in the flower garden
looking into one of the therapist's windows because Calhoun knew
that on Tuesdays at four forty-five in the afternoon Milla Thymeman
visited with her therapist Morton Rawls. The doctor and patient
never took off their clothes, but they were vigorous in their athletics
and now and then let slip the sight of a nipple or erect penis.

Only Calhoun knew about this regular assignation, and he'd
never told anyone other than Tom. The young men watched for a
few minutes and then Tom began to rub himself. Calhoun joined
in and soon they were both balls-out masturbating. That didn't
last long and so the two wandered away from the high rosebushes
where they could see without being seen.

"How come they got you in here?" Tom asked Calhoun when
they were sitting on a heavy cast-iron bench which was painted pink
and bolted to the concrete path that wound through the gardens.

"They think that there's a, a what they call a chemical imbalance
in my brain that gets in the way of me being able to say no."

"You can't say no and that's why you in jail?"

"If my brain is tuned to that radio station and somebody ask me
to help them move a bed, suck somebody dick, or rob some store
I say, yeah."

"Even if you don't wanna do what they ask you?"

"I cain't explain it," Calhoun said. "They cain't neither, not really,
but when you got a MD and a PhD and things like that people got
to listen 'cause they know that they don't know."

"So nobody knows what's wrong with you?" Tom Exit asked his new friend.

"You ever think about Detroit?" Calhoun replied. He was well-known for changing the subject mid-conversation. That was one of the things Tom liked about him.

"Not really. I mean I know it's a city or maybe a state but probably not a state because I know all them. But anyway, I don't know nobody from there."

"Well," Calhoun said. "In Detroit, down on Tyler Street in Forest Park there's a, there's a real old buildin' called Miller's Mine—"

"Like a gold mine?"

"Like a diggin' in the ground kinda mine."

"Oh," Tom said, nodding his head though he didn't really understand.

"You got any talents?" Calhoun asked.

"What do you mean?"

"Can you do anything useful that most other people can't do?"

"Like what?"

"My buddy, Sharkie, used to have a girlfriend who had a brother and he lived at the mine. Sharkie told me that there was a guy there called Gary Goodman," Calhoun said. "He forty-something and built like a brick shithouse. Gary stand behind the front door of the mine. He so strong that nobody, not even a professional football player, could push past him."

"What if that somebody got a gun or a knife?" Tom asked Calhoun. It was a common question on Rikers when discussing superior strength, martial arts, or a big brain.

"Penta," Calhoun responded. "Penta Lively. Half-Mexican, half-Black chick from Texas could shoot any gun or throw any blade an' hit the target just like she was reachin' out across to you with her fingertip. Her father was a hunter an' taught her everything he knew."

Tom thought that these were indeed good talents, especially if used together. Then he thought that he didn't have anything like that in his *bag of tricks.*

Tom's uncle, George Finez, would always ask his nephew, "What you got in your bag of tricks today, TE?"

Tom managed to most often have a pebble or some other found object in his back pocket to show Uncle George because if he had anything he would receive a quarter.

Calhoun was still talking but Tom had been distracted by the thought of his favorite uncle, who died of diabetes when Tom was almost fifteen.

". . . and so if you use that door and can remember the name Miller's Mine on Tyler Street in Detroit you might just be able to do it," Calhoun was saying.

"Huh?" Tom said.

Calhoun grinned because he knew that Tom wasn't listening. He knew and he was playing with him. Tom always thought that Calhoun had been a good friend.

"Hey, you two," the guard, Hardy Moore, called from one of the aisles of roses.

That call meant it was time to leave the garden and go in for dinner.

The dining room was large and usually pretty calm. Most of the eighty-two inmate/residents were medicated because of their possible conditions; and most of these were nonviolent offenders. Tom was one of the rare exceptions. His doctor, Ferral Ericson, a psychiatrist from Denmark, was interested in his initial retention scores and wanted him free from chemical intervention until his testing could be completed.

Tom and Calhoun were sitting at opposite ends, and on opposite sides of the long dining table. It was a men's table and calm. A few of the patients babbled to themselves. Felix Todd was whispering jokes to no one then laughing quietly at them. Meat loaf, mashed potatoes, and wax beans were served and a window was open. Tom could feel the breeze on the back of his neck.

. . . *there's a door behind the dark red rosebush like these ones here,* Tom remembered Calhoun saying. He knew with recollecting that phrase that sooner or later he could put together every word Calhoun had said.

Thinking of his friend Tom looked up and saw it coming.

Big Bo Thigman from East St. Louis was walking with purpose toward their table. Bo's fists were clenched and his eyes set on Calhoun. Bo was big and brick colored and bald. His last name, Thigman, Tom thought, was something like his strong thick arms. When Tom told Calhoun what he thought about Bo's name and strength Calhoun began to call Bo "Thickman" as a kind of joke.

Bo, whose mental illness was a bad temper, was not amused.

Tom could see that the big man from East St. Louis intended to hurt his friend the same way Tom meant to hurt Billy Biggs. That day stayed in Tom's mind for the rest of his life because it was the only time he experienced slow motion like in the movies. He put his left hand on Mills Tormé's right shoulder and pushed up until he was standing in the middle of the table. Then he ran to the opposite end just as Bo Thigman grabbed Calhoun's head with both hands. Tom leaped and, slipping on a mashed potatoes and gravy plate, went flying through the air at Bo. He heard, or thought he heard, Calhoun's neck breaking just as he grabbed Bo by the left arm, pulling him away from the table and down to the floor.

The fight continued there but the security guards were already on them and so pulled Big Bo off of Tom.

By that time Calhoun was already dead.

2.

Calhoun's death stayed on Tom's mind like the crucifix, he thought, that was always in his paternal grandmother's, Ruth's, thoughts.

"Jesus loved us so much that he died for us," Ruth would say. "I remember that every day."

"And what was in your mind when you jumped up on the table and started running?" Ferral Ericson, the forty-seven-year-old Scandinavian psychiatrist, asked. She had brown-and-gray hair with a face that Tom thought of as *sharp*.

"Um . . ." Tom said. "I, uh, was moving real slow."

"I don't understand what you mean," the doctor primed.

Outside the window there was a hummingbird darting from flower to flower. Tom loved birds, especially hummingbirds. Mrs. Crandel in tenth-grade remedial English had said that those birds were a *Met For*, something like that, hummingbirds and somehow that meant he wanted to be free like his ex-slave many-times-great grandsire that came up with his family name.

"It was like I was in a dream one time and this giant was chasing me and I was running but I couldn't get nowhere."

"Like slow motion on television?" Ericson suggested.

"Yeah," Tom said. He was listening to the doctor, but he was thinking about something that he couldn't remember about the fast-winged bird.

"You felt that you couldn't get to your friend in time to save him," Ericson interpreted.

Turning to her Tom replied, "It's like that hummingbird. She's faster than anything but sometimes she's just stuck in place."

"You loved your friend," she said.

In prison you never said that you loved anybody but Jesus or your mother; that was more or less a hard-and-fast rule. Tom had been raped and forced to do other things dozens of times, but no one ever told him they loved him.

They hurt him, they spit on him, they beat him like a dog, but no one ever loved him, no one except for maybe . . .

"What do you think about that little bird?" Ericson said.

"That she loves red roses and that they like her too."

Dr. Ericson advised the guards at Lorraine that Tom was not a threat and he could be released from lockdown.

The next afternoon he went to the dark red rosebush and, when nobody else was looking, he climbed in behind it, coming to find the old, corroded copper door that Calhoun promised was there.

"If you make it through that door you could be free," Calhoun had said when Tom was thinking about his uncle. "And if you're free you could go to Detroit and find Miller's Mine. I'm gonna do that one day. You better believe it too."

Tom didn't want to leave Lorraine, but Calhoun was his friend and he seemed to be telling him to run away for him; to run like he couldn't do on that table.

"Dr. Jericho," Tom said. He'd asked for a meeting with the director of Lorraine two weeks before.

"Mr. Exit," George Jericho acknowledged. "Please have a seat."

It was a big office with dark brown bookcases and hundreds of books. Tom liked books. He couldn't read hardly at all but some of the best times in his life were spent listening to books being read out loud.

"How have you been?" Jericho asked.

Sunlight from the large window seemed to be spilling across the director's desk. The shadows of windblown leaves made the green blotter look like a flowing stream.

"C-can I stay here, Doctor?" Tom asked.

"I don't know what you mean exactly."

"This is like the best place I've ever been in my life. When I was a kid in school the other kids all picked on me. And when I left school and got jobs I always got fired. Then in prison people did awful things and my mother hardly ever came and I'd always be in trouble even if I was just protectin' myself."

Jericho's skin was nearly paper white. He had a bald head and kind eyes behind rectangular-lensed glasses.

"No one ever showed you kindness," the director said.

"Only my uncle George Finez but he died," Tom said. "And, and, and . . ."

"And what?"

"There was a Patricia Neil. I saved her from the cops and, and she said that she was my friend forever. Mine. But I'm in jail and she isn't, and Lorraine is the best place I ever known."

"And so you want to stay here at Lorraine?" the doctor-director asked.

"Uh-huh. I'm really sorry about Calhoun gettin' killed and I feel bad that I couldn't save him. But instead of sending me to court and more prison you figured out that I was tryin' to do the right thing and didn't punish me."

A gentle smile on his lips the director said, "So you want to stay because it feels like a place you can live in harmony."

"I think so."

Peering through the glistening lenses Dr. Jericho smiled and looked sad at the same time.

"Part of the problem," Jericho said, "is that this place so fits your mood that it's hard to find that moment where you lose control. When you jumped up on the table to try and save your friend that was an example of your response to stimuli, but no one would call trying to save a life aberrant."

"So you're gonna send me back to prison?" Tom Exit asked.

"Most probably. But Dr. Ericson and others feel that you have an innate ability to decipher information that forms your responses in a way you cannot control. It will take at least another five months of study to come to an understanding of this process."

"Most probably." Tom repeated the phrase as if it were a life sentence handed down from the court.

After his meeting with Dr. Jericho Tom visited the corroded copper door every chance he got. He took an awl from the leather-working workshop and used it to excavate around the lock. He enjoyed this work and did it diligently all the while thinking of his friend Calhoun.

"And so what did your uncle George say again?" Ferral Ericson asked Tom. It was a brilliant Saturday and most of the patients were off to nearby Lake Amedne for what they called the Lorraine Spring Picnic.

"He, um," Tom said. "He, um, said that this bright shiny green bug called the, called the cicada takes seventeen years or maybe thirteen sometimes to turn from a nip, a nip-m to a insect. They been around forty-seven million years and mostly live under the ground. Uncle George really liked bugs an' he liked to read about 'em."

"How long ago did he tell you about the cicada?"

"It was on July seventeen when I was stayin' with him an' his girlfriend Melba in St. George on Staten Island. I remember because it was funny that he was livin' in a place that had his name."

"And how old were you then?"

"I was, was seven. That was the year my mother and father broke up and she went home to her mother because she was so sad."

The Scandinavian psychiatrist spent the next few minutes reading a document while Tom stared out the window at the dark red rosebush that hid the old copper door.

"What you readin', Dr. Ericson?" Tom asked when looking at the rosebush began to make him nervous.

The woman looked up at Tom with soft, faded brown eyes.

"Your talent for verbal and mental retention is truly amazing," she said, a sense of awe in her voice. "In the past four weeks you have told me nineteen stories about things you learned, your family, and your experiences. Every description has been specific and when I ask you about them days later you remember it all word for word."

"Uh-huh. Does that mean that there's somethin' wrong with me?" Tom asked hopefully.

"Just the opposite," Ericson said. "Your mind is like a computer, taking data in and storing it perfectly. And what's more you don't remember this information until three to fourteen days after hearing it. It's like you have a built-in buffer that filters what you know before cataloging it."

"Mama used to ask me where things was that maybe she lost and I always knew. She used to say I was like a fortune-teller only I wasn't because I couldn't see the future."

"Your mind is truly amazing," the doctor said. "I've never seen anything like it."

"But I'm not sick?" Tom asked. "I still have to go back to Rikers?"

"We have to follow the rules as they exist," Ferral said. "And though your ability is extraordinary it cannot be classified as a disorder."

"But couldn't you just say that it is? You know, that the way I think makes me do things I don't know about or sumpin'?"

"No, Mr. Exit," she said. "No. Whenever we recommend that a patient be institutionalized the state demands corroboration."

"Huh?"

"They make you see other doctors to get their opinion."

"So you would get in trouble?"

"Yes, but the real problem is that you would be sent back into prison anyway."

Something like a red fog rose up in Tom's mind. He remembered then that the same mist appeared up when he beat the nurse-intern Bernard Walters and when he stabbed Billy Biggs. Tom felt lost and afraid at that moment. He remembered the years of being beaten and abused and made fun of by guards and prisoners. Even worse than those moments of pain and humiliation were the sounds in the night of men crying and hurting, screaming and begging. He was angry but there was no one to hit or stab. Dr. Ericson felt as bad as he did. And, like she said, she couldn't help it that his *talent for verbal and mental retention* wasn't a sickness.

Those few seconds in time, when the red fog mixed in with a memory of words, Tom felt something he'd never experienced before. He had a problem and the answer was in his mind. He knew how to maybe keep from going back to prison. He remembered what his good friend Calhoun Dieterman was saying about the copper door, the mine in Detroit, and having, having . . .

"So my remembering things is a talent?" he asked the doctor.

"Yes," she said, "and something much, much more."

"You know what they gonna do to me if I go back to prison," Tom said. "Right?"

After a moment hesitating Ferral said, "Yes."

"And that's wrong, right?"

"Yes, it is."

"So if I didn't go then it would be better than if I did," Tom Exit concluded.

"Yes. But why are you saying all this?"

"Can you give me a pass to make a telephone call, Dr. Ericson?"

3.

Sixteen days after a phone call to the Bronx, somewhere between 1:00 and 2:00 A.M., early on that Wednesday morning, Tom Exit slipped out of the third-floor window of the men's dormitory and shimmied down the ivy vines, slipping and sliding until he finally fell to the lawn below. From there he went to the dark red rose-bush and finished the excavation of the locking mechanism securing the copper door. He pulled on the door grasping the hole where the lock had been and pulled with all his might. At first the portal did not budge. This was not part of Tom's plan. The door was supposed to open; that's what Calhoun had said. There was an odd animal sound in the air. It took Tom a minute before he realized that the sound was his own whimpering from the fear of failure, the dread of being sent back to prison. At that moment the red mist rose in his mind and he pulled as hard as he could for what felt like a very long time.

When the ancient hinges of the copper door gave they whined and groaned, and a loud popping sound came from the breaking hinges.

"Who's there?" shouted Delmont Trextin, the nighttime guard at Lorraine.

Tom heard the late-night sentinel's fast footsteps coming toward the red bush and copper door. He slipped through the narrow space to the outside. There he found that he was on a steep hill dense with bushes.

He loped down the incline, allowing the thick barrier of vines and branches to keep him from falling.

"Stop!" Delmont Trextin cried from somewhere above.

"I hear him down this way!" another man, whose voice Tom did not recognize, called out.

Tom ran faster, pressed harder against the wall of leaves and branches. Now and again he saw bright lights flashing through the foliage behind him. Other voices sounded. They were getting closer.

Then Tom broke through the thick hedges and went flying down the slope. He tumbled and fell down the hill that led up to Lorraine. His right ankle hurt and his hands stung from where dirt caked in them but he didn't care about the pain. Rising to his feet at the bottom of the hill he fell because his right foot couldn't support him. So then he crawled toward where he thought the road might be.

"He's down there!" a voice cried from up above. "We got him!"

Tom wanted to cry but he held back the tears in hopes that all was not lost.

"Tom!" she cried. "Tom!"

A moment later he felt her arms encircle him. He smelled the mild sweetness of the perfume she wore when she visited him in jail.

"Patricia," he gulped.

"Come on, baby," she said. "My car is just down here."

For the rest of his life Tom Exit remembered the acceleration of Patricia Neil's used Ford as he watched the electric torches of four guards, felt the agony of his swelling ankle, and the joy in his heart of finally being free.

"What did you say, baby?" Patricia Neil asked him as they turned onto the throughway going east.

"I will die before I go back there. I will die before that."

4.

Patricia brought Tom a change of clothes and old brown shoes that were a little tight, especially on his swollen right foot. She took him to a little motel outside of Syracuse. There he bathed and then luxuriated on one of the two single beds.

The emergency room doctor treated his cut hands, broken ankle, and the abrasions from the branches and thorns on his skin. Patricia explained to the admitting nurse that they had gone camping but then heard a growling they thought had to be a bear and ran down the hill.

"Tom went first," she explained to the medical receptionist, "and so he cleared a path for me."

He was lying in his bed half-asleep and happy that he was free for the first time in so long. Then he felt a weight next to him and hands—one on his chest and the other groping around between his legs.

"Does that feel good?" Patricia whispered.

"Uh-huh."

"When was your last time?"

"With your friend Carellia."

Patricia's grip on Tom's penis tightened and he moaned.

"Are you mad at Carry?" she asked.

"N-n-no."

"But why not? She tricked you."

"I, um, I, um, I . . . that was my first time so in a way I kinda, kinda loved her."

Patricia started pulling both softly and quickly on Tom's erection. She pressed her lips next to his ear and whispered, "This feel good?"

"Uh-huh, yeah, uh-huh . . ."

"I'ma do it till almost and then I'm gonna stop and then I'ma do it again and again until you can't hold back."

"How, how come?"

"Because when you finally can't stand no more you'll relax and sleep good."

Halfway across the northern border of Ohio Patricia asked Tom, "So you don't hate Carellia because she fucked you?"

"I'm really shy around girls. I mean I really like the way they look and smell and smile and stuff. I like how nice they are but that makes me all the more scared."

"You scared of a girl?" Patricia said.

"How come you helped me get outta Lorraine?" Tom asked, using Calhoun's technique of changing the subject.

"You saved my ass from them cops," she said. "You been in prison for years because'a me. First because you stopped them cops from searchin' me and then because Carellia did you like she did."

"That was so great last night," Tom Exit said.

"It was like you hadn't come in a month'a Sundays."

"Does that mean you're my girlfriend now?"

"Uh-uh, baby. We just friends. I'ma let you off wherever it is you wanna be in Detroit and then I'm goin' back to the Bronx. You know my old man, Nathaniel, 'spects me back day after tomorrow."

"Was he mad that you came to help me?"

"I didn't tell him," she said. "That wasn't none'a his business."

"But what did he say when I called?"

"I told him that you needed some money in your canteen account, and I owed you that for savin' me."

"And what he say . . . ?"

"Stop askin' me questions, Tom," Patricia Neil commanded. "I'm here, baby. That's all you have to know."

5.

After crossing the Michigan border, they passed through Monroe and Dearborn, finally entering Detroit. It was a city of freeways and shattered streets; people that walked with a kind of dignity that convicts only pretended to in prison. There were a lot of Black and brown people and to Tom it seemed like another time like when in a television show people go through some kind of *energy door* that puts them in the past. He smiled at the thought of having slipped into yesterday.

"Nobody could find me if I wasn't even there no more."

"What did you say?" Patricia Neil, his best friend ever, asked.

"Nuthin'," Tom said for fear of breaking the spell.

"It's like a war zone," Patricia said when they finally made their way into the Forest Park neighborhood.

Whole blocks had been demolished and people moved around furtively behind rubble and into houses that looked as if they were soon to be gone.

"You think there's soldiers?" Tom asked, looking fearfully out of the passenger's side window.

"The soldiers done come and gone, looks like," Patricia said. "You sure you want me to leave you here?"

They were stopped at a traffic light that was turned green but there were no cars behind them. Both sides of the road had once been rows of small houses that were now just remnants of concrete foundations, stagnant ponds filling open cellars. Sapling trees and man-high wild weeds had taken ownership of the fertile devastation.

From behind the beginnings of a neighborhood forest a tall man emerged. He was walking straight for their car.

"We better get outta here," Patricia said. But before she could step on the gas the man reached the road.

He was tall and jet black, maybe forty and strong from a life lived by his body alone. He had dreads, a straggly beard and wore only a loincloth that had once been white.

"Oh my God," Patricia uttered.

Tom noticed that her nostrils flared.

The man walked up to the passenger's side window. A wild smell assailed Tom's nose. It wasn't a bad odor but different than any scent he'd experienced coming from a man.

"Do you know where Miller's Mine is?" Tom asked. These were the only words he had.

"On Tyler Street."

Both Tom and the wild man seemed surprised by the exchange, as if words were a step down on the evolutionary ladder, unworthy of the grace that they had attained.

"We don't know where that is," Patricia said.

"Just keep on goin' the way that you goin' and you'll be there. It's a blue house on the corner and then you turn right for three."

"Three houses?" Tom asked.

The wild man nodded and then asked, "She yours?"

"She's my best friend."

At that the tall Black man leaned down and peered through Tom's window at Patricia.

"If you at Miller's I'll see you one day soon," he said. It came across like a promise. Patricia actually gasped.

"That man looked like a god come straight outta Africa," Patricia said when they were pulling up to the curb in front of their ramshackle destination.

"This is it," Tom said.

Miller's Mine was a big rambling building constructed solely from weathered wood that the paint had peeled from long ago. It was four stories and defied economic description. It might have been a mansion or apartments, an early-twentieth-century factory

of some sort or maybe even a hotel. But now its shattered windows
and broken doors, a roof that had half blown off, transformed the
structure into the skeleton of a creature both extinct and nameless.

"How can you tell this is the right place?" Patricia asked.

"Calhoun described it. I wasn't listenin' at the time but after a
while I remembered what he said. We go through the front door
and walk all the way to the back. Then there's a basement door
and steps that aren't very steady. You have to hold on to the rails
but then, when you get three levels down, there's a wall that was
painted blue maybe ten years ago. You knock on that wall and
shout out, 'Miller's Mine,' while you do it and sooner or later
somebody will answer."

"This is crazy," Patricia said. "I'm not goin'."

"Okay." Tom opened his door, more sure than he had ever been
that he was doing the right thing.

"Tommy," Patricia Neil whined.

"What?"

"Nathaniel don't know I'm here. I didn't tell'im I was leavin' so
I cain't go back there."

"But you said you were gonna leave me here."

"I was. But I'm scared. I thought I could go stay with Carellia in
DC but Nate knows her and he's hella jealous."

"But why? Why would you take such a big chance if you were
gonna get in so much trouble?" Tom didn't intend for his question to be mean, but Patricia winced and looked like she was
about to cry.

"Because when you were on trial I watched you and you seemed
all right. You helped me and you still just sat there . . . ready to go
where you had to for what you did. You're my best friend."

"But not your boyfriend?"

"Uh-uh. No. Never."

The subbasement was lit by maybe a dozen sixty-watt bulbs placed
at no place in particular. The blue door was really just a wall.
There were oil-stained planks, thick pine pillars, and a few holes
that opened onto darkness. Tom banged his fist on the wall and
yelled out, "Miller's Mine."

"We should go back," Patricia said. "You know I almost fell
through those steps."

"Miller's Mine!" Tom yelled and then he kicked the wall.

"There ain't nobody there, Tommy."

"There's got to be. Calhoun said so."

"Maybe he was wrong."

"He was right about the rosebush and the door. He was right about the name. The naked man knew where it was. We here, Patricia. They got to be too."

"What the fuck you want!" a man shouted.

The voice came from behind them.

Patricia turned quickly, shoving a hand into her bright yellow calfskin purse.

Tom turned, twisting his ankles together, and fell to the dusty, debris-strewn floor of the subbasement. When he looked up he saw a huge man of burnished skin, swollen with muscle and expressive of rage. A few steps behind him stood a petite, raspberry brown young woman holding a long slender knife by the tip of its blade.

"That hand better come out empty, bitch," the woman said. "'Cause if I see even a tissue with it you gonna have this here blade in yo' th'oat."

Tom scrambled to his feet.

"Gary Goodman and Penta Lively, right?" he said.

The angry man's face took on a stunned expression.

"And what's your name, Stumblefoot?" Penta asked, keeping her eyes on Patricia.

"I'm Tom. Tom Exit. My great-great-great-great-grandfather was a slave who excaped on the Underground Railroad and named hisself Exit because that's what he did from slavery."

The muscleman smiled slightly.

"What you doin' way down here, Stumblefoot Exit?" he asked.

Tom managed to stand up straight and tell everything from the time he fought with the police over Patricia to his escape from Lorraine.

". . . I wanted to stay there but they had to send me back to prison," Tom said toward the end of his dialogue, "so I came here because my friend Calhoun said so."

What surprised Tom was that the sentinels of Miller's Mine listened to his whole story without complaint or derision. Usually people got upset with his long tales filled with details that meant nothing—to them.

"Where is this Calhoun?" Goodman asked.

"He got killed by a dude name of Big Bo Thigman. Big Bo was okay, but he couldn't take a joke."

"We lost our comedian," Penta said. She was wearing a rainbow-colored dress that only came down over the middle of her powerful thighs. "Simtek was arrested for shoplifting, and they got him on an old assault and battery charge."

"Why you here?" Gary Goodman asked.

"I wanna live here," Tom said. "Calhoun said that you might take me in."

"We never heard of no comedian name of Calhoun," Penta said. She took a step forward and it seemed to Tom that her eyes were the color of the kind of rainbow that appears in oil slicks. It wasn't until weeks later that he learned she wore rainbow-colored contact lenses.

"He told me that the only people they let in Miller's Mine had to have a talent that they could use down here. He said that he bet that I had what you wanted and that I should come ask."

"Did he tell you what we do with people who don't have what we need?"

"That you kill 'em and th'ow 'em in a lime pit under a lake they call Green Acres."

"What!" Patricia exlaimed. She turned to run but Gary, moving deceptively fast, caught her by the arm.

"Mothafuckah, let me go! Fuck you! Fuck you!"

Tom felt bad that his friend was so upset. He wasn't worried, just sad that she was so scared.

The Blue Door Guardians took Tom and Patricia down a long tunnel that led deeper and deeper into the soil beneath Detroit. For the first half hour or so Patricia shouted and screamed and tried to pull away. But after that she allowed them to drag her along.

There were electric lights here and there in the long tunnel. In places the passway bulged out to accommodate living quarters. They went by jury-rigged homes made from metal and bamboo, plastic containers, and boxes from all kinds of materials. There was even a home that looked like a castle fabricated from discarded car and truck tires. It was here that their journey came to an end.

"Go on in," Penta said. "Lamarelle in there with her seer— Blind Bob."

"This is crazy," Patricia said but she followed Tom beyond the pillars of tires.

There was no door to the used tire castle. It was a maze of pillars stacked as far as twelve feet high. Gary and Penta followed Tom and Patricia until they came to a large empty space where a beautiful woman of maybe fifty years sat behind a desk fashioned from the dashboard of an old American car. She had blond hair, fair skin, and wore a coral-colored T-shirt. When Tom and Patricia entered the largish space, she smiled.

"Hello. I am Lamarelle."

"Do you run this place?" Patricia asked. "Because you know I'm not even supposed to be here. I just gave Tom a ride and I got to be goin'."

Lamarelle studied Patricia for maybe ten seconds, then turned her attention to Tom.

"You seek refuge?" she asked.

"I want to live here," Tom said. "My friend told me I did before he died."

"And what is this friend's name?"

"Calhoun Dieterman."

"I don't know that name."

"But he told me to come here. He was planning to come himself but then he got killed."

"You realize that we are a secret place," Lamarelle said. "That we cannot let you out of here unless you become a part of us."

"So you gonna kill us?" Patricia cried.

"Bob," Lamarelle called.

From behind a double pillar of deep-tread tires came a man of maybe thirty years who wore a ruby-colored sarong and a silk, a soiled blue T-shirt, and an emerald-hued turban. A blind man in comfortable surroundings, he moved with confidence.

"Come forward, Tom Exit," Lamarelle offered kindly. "You can use that stack of tires to sit upon."

Tom sat staring into the cornflower blue eyes of Lamarelle. Blind Bob sat between them.

"Do you have a talent useful for Miller's Mine?" the woman asked.

"If you tell me something, anything—I will remember it starting about fifteen days or so after I hear it. It doesn't matter what was said, I don't have to understand but I will remember exactly. And I never forget."

"What about what you've read?" Lamarelle asked.

"Maybe if I could read I would remember but I don't read too good and so that don't work too well."

A moment passed then Lamarelle said, "Bob?"

The blind man held his palms up and shrugged.

"Who is that guy?" Patricia asked.

"Be quiet, woman," Penta said.

"No," Lamarelle told the markswoman. Then to Patricia, "In most situations Bob can tell when a lie has been told. He says that there's a pulse in every word a person says and in that pulse is the barometer of truth."

"Is he ever wrong?" Tom asked. "'Cause you know I'm nervous but I'm not lyin'.".

"He can't read you at all," Lamarelle said with a sad smile on her lips. "You confuse him."

"Then why don't you just ask 'im yourself?" Patricia said. "Why don't you just ask Tom?"

Lamarelle laughed and then stood up from the dashboard desk. Her coral T-shirt came down to the tops of her thighs and Tom could tell that she was pregnant. The bewilderment showed on the escaped convict's face.

"You think I'm too old to bear a child?" Lamarelle asked.

"Um."

"I have come to term twenty-one times in my life. All of those pregnancies have resulted in either twins or triplets—all except one."

"That's crazy," Patricia said.

"It is my talent," Lamarelle corrected. "Everyone here in Miller's Mine has something to offer; a talent that they were either born with or that they have learned."

"Do you know what the babies in your belly can do?" Patricia asked, unable to keep the sneer from her mouth.

Lamarelle laughed again and then said, "They will be educated by the people of the mine. They will be of us."

"Why havin' babies is a talent?" Tom asked.

"Twins and triplets often have unexplainable connections. They know each other better than most people can know one another.

This knowledge, this connection, makes them treasures amid the devastation of our world.

"This is our mission—to create a place of wonder built upon the bones and minds, the souls and the magic that make us as rich as any millionaire or president, as powerful as any queen or army."

"Are you the leader here?" Tom asked.

"No. We have no single leader. There is the council of fourteen and the general elections."

For a moment there Lamarelle and Blind Bob, Gary and Penta, Tom and leery Patricia remained silent in the car tire palace.

"Tell me the history of the United States of America," the pregnant not-leader of Miller's Mine asked of Tom.

The request entered Exit's mind like a living thing, a fish or burrowing insect, a lightbulb illuminating some forgotten memory, memories. First came his second-grade teacher, Mrs. Reynolds, making all the kids learn the states in alphabetical order and the capitals of each state. Mr. Garner in eighth-grade civics told about the structure of Congress, the Supreme Court, and the president who oversaw what he called the executive branch. There were dozens of teachers, relatives, TV shows, and radio programs—all of which held part of the answer to Lamarelle's request.

Tom was no longer underground, no longer in a room full of friends and strangers. He couldn't smell the rubber of the tires or see the motes of dust dancing in the electrical light.

For maybe a quarter of an hour the young man who had been abandoned by the schools, the government, the legal system, his own mother, and most everyone except for Patricia—who would never be his girlfriend—for that quarter of an hour he felt an ecstasy of organization, bringing every thought about the United States and its history into alignment.

When finally everything felt more or less in order he began to speak.

"To understand the history of the New World," he said, parroting Miss Chin, his eleventh-grade history teacher, "you must go all the way back to when Asia and North America were closer than they are now and the ocean between them froze sometimes and the Asians came and discovered a place that no human had ever seen before . . ."

He spoke for hours. During that time people wandered in and

took up seats where they could listen to the lecture of a lifetime of study that Tom had never been aware of. The Louisiana Purchase and the Dred Scott case, Thomas Jefferson and his slaves, slaves and their masters, the Civil War, and the War of 1812.

As more and more people came into the palace they began to move the tire-pillars aside so that they could all fit. After a while there were nearly a hundred people from the ages of maybe five to ninety. Some came and listened for a while and then left to be replaced by others. Some stayed the whole time, rapt in the tales where Tom changed his tone of voice to the teacher, announcer, or relative that related that part of the history.

He was in the middle of talking about the Harlem Renaissance when Lamarelle said, "I think that is probably enough for right now, Tom Exit."

The interruption manifested itself as a headache above Tom's eyes. There was so much more that wanted to get out.

"Excuse me," somebody said. It was a man. A white man.

"Uh-huh?" Tom replied. He looked out over the audience, amazed at the number of people there.

"You said that the Chinese discovered America, but they taught me in school that it was Christopher Columbus and my daddy was a eye-talian and he told me that it was true."

The speaker wore drab clothing and was missing a few teeth. He might have been thirty years old or sixty; Tom couldn't tell. But he recognized the anger in the man's voice.

"I don't know," Tom said.

"You don't know what?" the man asked, his voice rising on the tide of anger.

"I can only say what I remember. I don't know if it's all true. All I know is what I heard, word for word. The only thing I can tell you is that somebody told me and now I'm tellin' you."

"What good is that?"

"I don't know," Tom said again.

"I have a question," another man said. A deep brown man. He was tall and wore a fancy off-white suit with a navy shirt and a perfectly knotted yellow-and-red tie. There seemed to be a flesh-covered horn, maybe nine inches long, protruding from the questioner's forehead.

"Okay," Tom replied, a little put off by the diabolical appearance of the strange man.

"My name is X and I have earned my place among the Chosen of Miller's Mine because of my particular affinity for evil."

"Uh-huh," Tom said, thinking that it would not take him fifteen days to remember the words this man had to say.

"You're a fountain of information," the horned man allowed. "But there's no way of telling what is truth or what is not. Your trove of knowledge is actually just a repository of misinformation."

"Um," Tom said. "I, uh, don't know what you're sayin'."

"I'm saying that we can't trust you and so you and your girlfriend should be sent to Green Acres."

"Listen, Dick Head," Patricia said. "Maybe you think you all special 'cause you got that bone implant but Tommy didn't come here to tell you a history class. He said what he said and maybe it was true and maybe it wasn't. But that's not what's important."

"No?" X asked, his smile revealing teeth most of which had been festooned with a bright jewel.

"No," Patricia replied. "History we could argue about. We could look it up. We could think about it. But what if Tommy was in a courtroom and the judge said this and the prosecutor said that? What if some witness said sumpin' that nobody remembered but Tommy? Wouldn't you be glad if he remembered the one thing you needed to know? And what if there was some kinda contract or sumpin' he could remember. You know a insurance policy only need one thing wrong for them to turn you down."

"But your friend can't even read," X sneered.

"Cain't you read, Dick Head? All Tommy need is to hear sumpin' once and he know it forever."

The crowd murmured and X frowned.

6.

Miller's Mine was a series of subterranean tunnels that traveled for miles under the city of Detroit. When Tom Exit and Patricia Neil joined what the citizens of Miller's Mine called *the Sovereignty* there was a population of 857 citizens. Of these, 642 were adults or adolescents accepted because of their talents. There were lawyers and cat burglars, therapists and lie detectors, killers and soldiers, seducers and those who could change their voices and appearance so as to fool almost anyone. Miller's Mine had doctors and dentists, undertakers, tacticians, dancers, performers, jugglers, what they called a master librarian, and even a jail. There once was a comedian but he had been captured in the *Upper World.*

Over time the leadership of the Sovereignty had purchased and otherwise acquired houses all over the city. The underground tunnels connected these places so that it would always be easy to escape the nets of The Man.

Tom was accepted because he could attend trials, public speeches, classes, and even hang out around the cops when they were after some member of the Sovereignty. All he had to do was hear something spoken once and he never forgot—after two weeks. They accepted Patricia because she was one of the few people ever to out-talk the Devil, X.

"Why you even have a man like that down here?" Patricia asked Lamarelle a few days after she and Tom moved in.

"Evil is a part of life," the Great Mother replied. "If we don't know evil we are bound to be defeated by it."

The naked man that Tom and Patricia met on the way to Miller's Mine was also a member of the Sovereignty. His name was Survivor and he would be their last hope if The System ever got the upper hand. Patricia and Survivor married in the way of the mine and Tom cried for weeks. He still did his job, attending trials and public hearings, talking to librarians and community college teachers. He even learned how to read, after a fashion. But Tom was heartbroken for days and months and years over the loss of Patricia. He refused to talk to her or respond to Survivor. When the council of fourteen ordered him to settle his issues with his friend and her lover Tom replied, "Take me to Green Acres or shut the fuck up."

One night, a few months after Great Mother Lamarelle had delivered quadruplets, she and Tom were drinking spirits late at night in her tire palace. In the Upper World there had been instigated an investigation that Tommy and a young woman nicknamed Loga had discovered using his preponderance of knowledge and her ability to make sense of even the most abstract input. Loga and Exit came up with monthly reports identifying the Enemy and its likely moves.

"Dr. Hands told me that I'll never be pregnant again," Lamarelle was saying as she poured the golden-colored liquor that was unique to the Sovereignty into Tom's mug.

"How many kids you had?"

"Sixty-four that survived."

"You almost as bad as Genghis Khan."

"Are you ready for love, my friend?" Lamarelle asked.

"What do you mean?" the ex-con, honey-ant of knowledge asked.

"Patricia."

"I can't talk about that," Tom said. He shifted on his stack of tires as if maybe he was going to get up and walk away.

Lamarelle put a hand on Tom's wrist and said, "We all die. And the only way to survive death is to forgive and feel and admit love into your heart."

Holding back his tears Tom said, "Patricia was the first ever in my life who was there for me, who stood up for me. I love her. I love her. And she out with Survivor with his big dick and strong arms. It hurts me all the way through my whole life because I know I'm not good enough to be with the woman I love."

"But she's your friend," the Great Mother argued.

"That's not enough."

"I've had twenty-four broods from twenty men," Lamarelle said. "I liked all of them. But the man closest to me is Blind Bob. He reads my heart. He knows my soul."

"But does he want your body along with your heart?" Tom asked.

"Probably, yes."

"Then," Tom said, "if you understood him you would know the pain he suffers every time you call his name."

"But we all have a duty," the Great Mother said. "Our lives are owed to the future."

"Maybe," Tom allowed. "But for a guy like I am love only comes around once."

Three weeks later the Detroit police invaded the Sovereignty. Sixteen citizens were killed. One hundred and forty-eight were arrested. But 1,107 escaped into the properties bought by the Central Committee of the Sovereignty.

Now aboveground these foreign citizens began to make a political society that could one day control the out-of-control city of Detroit.

*

Years passed.

Romulus Exodus, né Tom Exit, personal secretary of Laverne Mamman, sat at his post in her city council office on a Thursday when Patricia Neil appeared.

"Tom Exit!" she exclaimed.

"Not Exit anymore," he said.

"I miss you so much, baby," she said sadly.

Tom Exit heard her, understood what she was saying, believed that her words were true. He thought about his dead father and absentee mother, about prison and the ninety-four times he was raped. He imagined Patricia coming to see him every week when she was on heroin and then once a month when she was clean. He thought about the seven years underground with the Citizens of the Sovereignty and then the invasion of the Detroit PD.

He thought about Loga, now called Mary Smart, and their children, Marcus and Stellar.

"You saved me and then you left me," Tom Exit said. "Can't we just leave it at that?"

Patricia waited a moment before rising.

"Can't you forgive me, Tommy?"

"There's nothing to forgive," he said. "You haven't done anything wrong."

"Then why can't we be friends?"

"Because," Tom said and then paused. "Because I hurt before you came to see me in prison and the pain came back after you were gone."

"Then you'll never be free," she said.

"No," he said. "Probably not."

Valley of the Moon

FROM *Electric Literature*

MY SISTER IS in town and wants to meet. I pick Suite 100 for its wide selection of French varietals and its convenient location on the B55 People Mover. The People Mover pulls up late as usual. The seats are filled, the aisles blocked with crutches, broken sacks of clothing, and for the first time, a dog.

It's a big dog, with a big craggy head resting like a boulder of teeth on the mat. How it got past the bus driver, I have no idea. The girl holding on to him is not blind but seems to have achieved a dazzling chemical distance from the rest of our fellow passengers. Despite her painful-looking dreads, she leans against the window, bewitched by the starless purple sky and the bright palaces of commerce that line Dimond Boulevard.

I sit down next to her, just to be closer to the dog. He is the mottled color of tortoiseshell. A strand of frothy drool dangles from his lower lip. The girl nods off and a few stops later, rests her head on my shoulder. She smells of poop and woodsmoke and sticky raspberry brandy. I breathe through my mouth and try to straighten up a little, to keep her head from lolling back and whiplashing her awake.

Her eyelids flutter. The whites are ragged with broken red.

Fred Meyer's slides by. Then Alaskan Reindeer Sausage Factory. Las Margaritas with its thatched roof and neon FAJITAS! FAJITAS! sign. The girl smiles faintly through an opioid-flavored dream. The dog pants on my ankles. I sneak a pet on his head. A gust of diesel heat blows down the aisle. Then a silver gum wrapper.

October is a snowless month in Anchorage, but colder than anyone ever expects. People use the People Mover as a floating motel
until service ends at 9 P.M., which I did not know until I lost my
license for a wet and reckless the previous summer. This was a lucky
turn of events, Dad says, considering the current proclivity of local
judiciaries to declare cases such as mine as DUIs with mandated
jail time. A wet and reckless in 2014 is just not what it was back in
the day, when guys used to cruise down Northern Lights Boulevard
with a twelve-pack in their cab, tossing beers to promising young
ladies at stoplights.

Most of the luck, however, was fabricated by his rabidly diligent
lawyers. I don't mind not having a car, not really. There is something almost cozy about being driven where you need to go, with
no other responsibility except to hold up a girl's head and push
the button to get off. I would not mind staying here. It is almost
tempting to. I'm a little afraid of my sister. At the old shut-down
Borders I look in my purse, but there is no money—I'm not allowed
money—only Mom's Amex. I stick it in the girl's pocket. Maybe
she will find it and use it to buy herself dinner. And a bag of kibble.

Suite 100 is located in a boxy, low-rise complex next to a vision
clinic and a podiatrist practice. The windows are tinted, and the
entrance is a hallway lined with rent-a-plants and a framed listing
of professional tenants. I click past all this—pleased as always by
the official sound of my heels on the tile—and pull open the door.
Other than the missing treasure chest and the receptionist's desk,
the decor of the wine bar still looks like the dentist office it formerly
was: a muted assortment of chairs and tables, inoffensive lighting.
A few men wait at the bar peering into voluminous glasses of caber-
net, as though an ancient *Highlights* crossword might surface from
the depths.

On a hook by the hostess hangs a key attached to an awkward hunk
of driftwood—presumably meant to keep you from misplacing it
on the journey to the restroom. The hostess is missing and the tables mostly are empty, save for a few women with tasteful sunsets of
eye shadow over each eye. They sit by the fireplace, bronzed in the
clingy light. At least one is familiar to me: High school? Cotillion?
Girl Scouts? Katie? Kirsten? Carleen? There is something familiar
about her spray-on tan, her charm bracelet, her hesitant way of
crossing her legs.

The most reassuring part of dropping out of the Anchorage elite is that you no longer have to remember who is who or the last time you forgot it. You can just smile and nod slightly, as if you are on your way to pick up your free bouquet of flowers on the other side of the room. This is my method, and tonight is easier than most. I am swaddled, head to heels, in creamy beige cashmere, stolen from my stepmother's latest Neiman Marcus mail-order shipment.

Jamie waves me over. She has taken an expansive leather booth for six or more all for herself. She does this everywhere we meet, but this time she has a reason. She is pregnant, indisputably so, overflowing onto the table.

"Don't get up," I say and slide in next to her. She smells of cocoa butter and the faintest whiff of morning sickness. I can't help it; I reach for her stomach. It is so warm, so firm. As if on command, a dense lump of baby heaves up under her skin, the size and shape of a tiny head. I follow it with my hand and meet my sister's hand and when all three of us are stacked up like this—me, Jamie, baby—the whole world seems to go quiet, beautiful, glazed with the kind of understanding we used to have, back when we could look at each other and know, without a word or a peek into each other's cupped fingers, that we had both chosen identical butterscotch candies from the bowl on the bank lady's desk.

"You are amazing," I say. "You're going to be a mom."

"I'm already a mom," says Jamie, which is true but slightly painful. Her three-year-old daughter, Jude, lives with her and her wife, Flora, in Portland, Oregon. I have never met them or seen their blue bungalow covered in wild sea roses, except on Instagram. Jamie refuses to bring her family up to Anchorage and I can't leave Mom by herself more than a few hours.

We let go hands, and Jamie begins to cry. Her tears are loose, silent, runny. They go on for a while. She doesn't even rub them off with her napkin. According to my memory, which is not always the most reliable, Jamie doesn't cry in front of other people. She also doesn't eat pineapple, sleep on her stomach, or talk to Mom, except in the presence of Dad. And even then, she won't look at her.

"I can come back," says the waitress. She is older than us, with a faint white scar down her cheek that I like to think is from a tabby cat who did not mean to scratch her, but that is so clean, so precise on its edges it implies only a knife. My sister and I had a babysitter

with a similar scar on her face. Her name was Fern. When I think
of Fern, I think of Mom. When I think of Mom, I worry that she is
trying to do something ambitious. Like trying to make popcorn on
the stove instead of the microwave. We have an agreement about
this, but it's not as if I'm exactly stringent about rules.

"A bottle of Stag's Leap. Nineteen ninety-seven," says my sister,
still crying. "The Cask Twenty-three."

The waitress glances at her baby bump. "We have tests in the
restroom. Free of charge." This is the most recent idea of a local
city councilman, who retrofitted the tampon machines in local bars
to dispense two-minute pregnancy sticks. A record-setting number
of babies are born in our state with fetal alcohol syndrome. Drunk
women are supposed to go into a stall, pee, and if a plus sign pops
up, stop drinking.

There are potent mysteries in this logic. Such as: what women
do when panicked. I am not the genius in our family—Dad and
Jamie vie for that—but I do have a terrible feeling that if you were
to graph the number of Jäger shots against the number of positive
pee sticks on the bathroom floor, you might end up with a data set
of rapidly escalating birth defects.

"The wine is for her," my sister says, pointing at me. "I'm not
drinking."

I look at her—again, confused. My sister never lets me drink,
and besides, my license has a Do-Not-Serve line through it. One of
the unavoidable downsides of a wet and reckless.

Over by the fireplace: laughter, more laughter. The waitress
glances at the Sunsets, as I name the group with the eye shadow.
The woman next to the woman whose name I can't remember
mouths silently to the waitress: *crab cakes.* Then holds up her empty
glass. *Merlot.*

"Anything else?" says the waitress to my sister.

"Just the bottle." She blows her nose. "And why the fuck not?
A dozen oysters."

A few things for the record that might explain how the night un-
folds: The first one took place long ago, when our mother did not
drink except at parties and left the house regularly for groceries
and trips to stores and offices and other grown-up places. Even
then, however, she pulled Jamie and I from school for "snuggle
days," during which we never changed out of nightgowns and read

picture books in bed. *The Velveteen Rabbit* mostly. Or *Sylvester and the Magic Pebble.*

Mom was a loving, wonderful parent, even when she started disappearing in the afternoons. She hired a girl named Fern to babysit us. Fern was nineteen and soft in a plump, bewildered way as if she expected you to throw a can of soda at her. She had the scar, plus braces and limp, feathery hair that smelled of hot oil treatments—a ritual she completed each week with a magical little vial she heated in the microwave.

That summer, Fern also had a boyfriend named Buck, who worked at the strip mall carnival in the back lot of Fred Meyer's. The strip mall carnival had been on our radar for most of our lives. Out it sprang each July—suddenly there on the asphalt like a little toothpick city against the mass of the mountains, each teetering, aging ride pierced with tatters of falling screams.

Of course, we were dying to go. Dying! Fern wouldn't let us. We fought her and crushed her and hopped in the back of Buck's eagle-hooded car for an afternoon of all-free rides and all-free games, the last of which was when Buck tried to take me into a Porta Potti and show me how to wipe his dick. I was seven. Jamie was thirteen. Jamie banged on the door, yelling she was going to puke on his boots, she was going to call the troopers. When he opened up, she grabbed my hand and ran with me to the popcorn cart, where we hid until we heard Fern calling for us.

"Guys?" she said in her helpless voice. "Come on, you guys. I'm going to tell your mom on you."

She didn't tell. We didn't either. Instead, Jamie made Fern make us sloppy joes every night for dinner and give us home perms in the guest bathroom. By the end of the summer, Buck was arrested for aggravated assault and rape. His victim was a sixty-five-year-old Native lady walking home from a picnic. Six months later, when Fern tried to steal Mom's Mikimoto pearls to pay for Buck's bail and bungled the effort, Mom fired her, then arranged a job for her as a receptionist at our father's office. Then paid for computer classes so Dad wouldn't fire her either.

"Imagine," Mom told us. "Being so alone in this world." She smiled as if a sad, old-fashioned song had just come on the radio and only she could hear it.

At the time, Dad may have applauded her efforts. No one in our family was ever denied the opportunity to self-improve. Like most people in Alaska, we had come from dirt and sorry circumstance, as he described it. Even our house was constantly being gutted and redone, with all new carpet or crown molding. He still lives there with our stepmother, though even I can hardly recognize it under the stonework and marble and acres of fastidiously painted white decking that, in the winter when Diamond Lake freezes, makes it look like a cruise ship doing a deep final dive into the Arctic Sea.

A shiny flotsam of airplanes and speedboats and snow machines washes up by the dock, depending on the season. The old family Beaver changes from skis to floats and back to skis. It is an enormous plane painted the same electric green as the tractor Dad drove as a boy growing up on a dirt-floor farm in Minnesota. He bought it to fly Jamie and me out to the wilderness to fish and hunt and not turn into spoiled lake kids. To reinforce the message, he drew up homemade contracts we both had to sign: I will go to college, learn to fly, shoot a caribou, and vote in every election. Signed, Jamie (age eleven) and Becca (age six).

The order in which we were to accomplish all this was at our discretion.

Dad is an orthopedic surgeon, but only when he's not starting corporations and shell companies in the Caribbean. He brought the first MRI to Anchorage and developed what many in the town call a medical monopoly, which includes various surgery robots and DNA centrifuges and other then-visionary diagnostic devices. He housed them in a for-profit clinic, where the majority of patients proceeded to pay their bills using an in-state subsidiary of a larger out-of-state HMO on whose board he silently serves. Some of this success was accomplished while he was sober—but not much.

Or so I've heard. I am too young to remember the details of parties that neighbors and various strangers bring up, still dumbfounded and nostalgic about the night in the backyard with Danny Bob: the time Danny Bob sculpted a king salmon out of ice using an electric turkey carving knife, the time he drew a drill bit for ACL reconstruction on a cocktail napkin that would go on to be patented and render all other models obsolete, the time he shot his compound bow off the roof of the house and hit a watermelon in a canoe floating in the middle of Diamond Lake.

Then there was the glacier bear, about which these people always say, "Did Danny Bob ever get that blue bear back?"

Mom has the bear, as of a week ago. Dad showed up at the door and gave it to her. She was so happy to see him and made a huge, sloppy fuss about my putting it in the living room, by the window. She asked him to stay for dinner, which at our house means take-out Siam Cuisine, a handful of Klonopin, and a vodka-blueberry smoothie. He was very kind about declining and very kind about the rotting piles of newspapers, which Mom stacks up and uses to cut out paper snowflakes. They are very worried-looking snowflakes. And there are a lot of them.

Dad picked one up and looked at me through intricate, shaky slits. Then said in a tender voice, which took me by surprise, "It wasn't all shit and shenanigans, sweetheart. At the end of the day, we managed to end up with you."

I stood there, letting all the little quiet bubbles of happiness fizz through me, but also wishing in a secret, terrible way that Jamie had been there to hear him say this.

I'm still not sure how memory works. Sometimes I can remember the silky rush of Mom's dress as she walked by and the bright electric bits that sparkled off her, between the pantyhose and fabric. I can remember looking at Jamie to see if she had seen these magical fireworks and confirming by the bright brown gasp in her eyes that she had. I can remember sitting on Dad's lap as he flew us in the Beaver, and his pointing to the sky ahead and telling me to pick a cloud, any cloud—and my believing, at this time, that they were his to give.

No one can ever understand the particulars of another person's loneliness, but it still seems so confusing that it was Dad's best friend that Mom fell for. Jamie says this happened the summer with Buck and the carnival, which explains why Mom was never around. She was across the lake at Will Bartlett's "getting her rocks off," as Jamie describes it.

According to Jamie—and Jamie is the only person who will tell me about what happened—everything came out at Dad's annual Christmas-in-July party. I do not remember everyone leaving or Dad banging Mom's head over and over against the edge of the mahogany credenza or Mom dragging herself and me and Jamie through the kitchen and down into the crawl space to hide. I do remember the smell, though. Most of the newish houses on Diamond Lake are built on stilts in case of flooding. Once you

have spent a few hours squatting in dank salmon-smelling clay,
your mother's hand over your mouth to keep you quiet, you can't
walk across a living room—even one lined in glossy white Italian
stone—without feeling at least somewhat disconcerted about what
lurks underneath.

A few days later, Mom loaded up Dad's cream-colored Coupe De-
Ville and drove us down the unpaved Alcan to British Columbia.
Two thousand two hundred miles of potholes and radio static
and great lush Canadian trees rushed by, as Jamie and I lay in
the back seat—bickering and a little afraid. Mom refused to wear
sunglasses and walked right into whatever little roadside store we
happened upon with her bashed-in eyes like two burned-out light-
bulbs in the center of her face.

Mom is a delicate, overly patient woman who speaks as if she is
reading a good-night book while asking you to take out the garbage
or go see if a man is hiding in the bushes at the end of the drive,
her voice rising up at the end of every sentence the way kindergarten teachers' do when they're about to turn the page. Not once
has she ever yelled at us. But there was a flinty, fearsome resolve
she displayed during those two long weeks that I have never forgotten and never seen since. She had a plan, and the plan was not
what we expected from a woman who had never been outside of
Alaska, except for a honeymoon to Hawaii and the tiny factory
town in Ohio where she had been raised.

The plan, she told us at the steering wheel, was Montreal. They
spoke French there, she said. She had always wanted to learn
French. It was the language of diplomacy. And art. And culture.
Jamie, to my surprise, was all for it. She wanted to see a ballet.
A real one with toe shoes. Like in the movies.

We spent six hours in the suburbs of Montreal, before Mom
turned the Coupe DeVille around and drove us straight back to
Alaska. My sister was the one who walked into our house and
found it stripped empty, save for Dad's blue bear. Everything we
had owned was gone and so were most of the walls and appliances.
Upstairs, she found our soon-to-be stepmother—Fern—with some
tile and wallpaper catalogues.

I was asleep in the car, but I can picture it from what Jamie later
described in lavish detail. Fern's disco shorts. Her bangle bracelets.
Her plastic slip-on heels. She had dropped the weight and gotten

highlights and now spoke in an airy tone, with which she still addressed me as a bunny. For example: "You poor bunny, sit down and let me get you a glass of Evian."

Meanwhile, our mother was having a nervous breakdown in the driveway, from which she was never to fully recover. I say all of this only because this is where my memory fizzles out and I feel terrible for Jamie and need to recognize some of the hardships she endured. It was Jamie who drove Mom to the hospital and forced Dad to buy the crappy rancher next door for the three of us to live in after Mom was released. It was Jamie who made Dad sign a homemade contract that somehow held up in court, stipulating that he pay for a working vehicle for Mom, plus heat and electric, as well as any living expenses Mom might incur as long she provided itemized receipts.

Jamie was fifteen by then. Nobody knew it but me, but she still had the ballet tickets. She hid them in her jewelry box. Under the lining in the back of the top compartment. Les Grands Ballets. Orchestre. L33, M33, S36.

Even now, I wonder which one of us would have had to sit alone.

As it stands, Mom and I still live in that rancher. Jamie moved out a few weeks after we got settled and, without a word to either of us, moved in with Dad and Fern. For the next few years, she was either running around in a bikini with Fern across all that new white decking or racing down to the dock to jump in the Beaver with Dad and whatever captain of industry he was flying out to the wilderness to fish and cut another deal by the campfire. There were no parties. But sometimes Fern or Dad invited me over to dinner, where a chef named Ernesta made all the food—sushi hand rolls mostly. Afterward, Jamie took me upstairs to her room and told me all the old stories, over and over, plus new ones: how Fern had spent sixty thousand dollars on an opal necklace, how she drank pineapple juice to make her twat taste better, how she didn't let Dad near any booze and he went along with it, because it turned out, "Dad was a total fucking pushover" when it came to women.

The whole time, Jamie was brushing her hair and throwing clothes at me to try on—sweaters and sequins and leg warmers. "You should move in," she said. "We could share a room."

I went home to Mom. Those were the years when we were reading all the James Herriot novels about his veterinary practice in the English countryside. Or playing Boggle. Mom only drank the little bottles of vodka then, and only three or four at a sitting. She just didn't like to leave the house very much. And it wasn't that hard for me to buy what we needed or just sneak over and take it out of Dad and Fern's cabinets.

Meanwhile, Jamie got her degree at MIT paid for and her pilot's license. Then her PhD in biomedical engineering. She shot a big-horn sheep with Dad in Arizona and got her nose touched up with Fern in Argentina. On a random research trip to Portland, she fell in love with a kindergarten teacher named Flora. She stayed there and invented a smart-foam pad you insert in the bottoms of running shoes, which reduces your chance of knee injury by 40 percent. Despite the offers from Adidas and Nike, she produced the insert herself and it is now sold around the world, in every pharmacy and big box store on the planet. Ten percent of her profits, she donates to abused women shelters.

As soon as the oysters arrive, Jamie wipes her face, leans over and tells me that my snuggle days with Mom are over. I don't know what she's talking about exactly, but the oysters look like what oysters always look like—hunks of dead lung on a shell.

I look at the water glass, the little bubble of fabric where the tablecloth has bunched up. The wine is not here. Where is the wine? Jamie gives me a patronizing smile. "Miss," she says to the waitress. "My sister needs her bottle. Right now."

Off the waitress whisks, as people so often do around her, suddenly electrified with the desire to serve. "Have an oyster," says Jamie. "They're a delicacy."

"I need to check on Mom," I say but don't leave.

"Look," she says. "You're in trouble. Do you understand that yet?"

The idea has occurred to me. I am not the best with email or voice mail or mail-mail or meter readers or people that come to the door and ring the bell.

"I've been telling you this day would come," says Jamie. "Dad and Fern are overextended. He's aging and made some risky moves that didn't pan out. She's spending the way she always has and won't listen. Last year, I offered to take over Mom's mortgage, plus both your expenses. But the more I thought about it . . ." Her voice slows, silkens. "I just feel that the situation isn't healthy. Not for you. Or Mom."

She stops. She looks at the oysters but doesn't eat one. She loves oysters. For a minute, I think she's trying to prove to me how disciplined she is—unlike my slovenly, wet, and reckless self—then I remember that pregnant people can't eat shellfish.

"And so," she says, "I came to a decision. I will continue to pay for the house. I will get Mom a professional caretaker. Under the condition that you move out—and get a job. "

I eat an oyster. I eat another one. They taste like what oysters taste like: chilled death. I eat another. I wonder what Mom would do, but I know what she would do, make a vodka-blueberry smoothie and forget to put the top on the blender and tell me I'm her "magical baby girl" for cleaning the splatter off the ceiling.

Taking care of Mom, as much as I love her, is a lot of work.

Down in Portland, Jamie's life is one long farmers' market, with her and Flora and Jude running around in matching sneakers and licking Popsicles. They throw sticks for their golden retriever. They grow kale in their backyard. I see it all on the Instragram, when Flora posts the pictures.

What this makes me hope is that one day all this happiness will make Jamie happy. Last year, she tried to start proceedings to put Mom in some kind of facility. I didn't know that a social worker could deem you unfit for wanting to stay in your own home, cut snowflakes, and drink vodka-blueberry smoothies, but as it turns out, if you are an agoraphobic alcoholic with a caretaker who occasionally takes your antianxiety meds and one night drives into a Papa John's pizzeria, the state can mandate certain at-home visits. It has been six months since Mom and I finally got rid of Miss Caroline and her preprinted self-care checklists.

I look down at my hands. They are shaking. "Where is Flora?" I say. "Why didn't Flora come?"

"She's busy transitioning Jude into a toddler bed."

I swallow the last of my oysters. The wine comes. The poor waitress doesn't even know how to present it and improvises with a few flourishes and some clumsy drama involving a napkin. Due to the vintage, it has to breathe in a carafe for twenty minutes, during which I watch the dense velvety liquid behind the swoop of glass—along with the reflection of my stunned, stupefied face. "I thought Dad and you don't talk anymore," I finally say.

"We don't. We negotiate."

"I know how to negotiate," I say.

"Great. I'm open. We're at the table. What do you want?"
This takes me a minute. I want so many things. "A dog?" I say.
"Go get one," says Jamie. "You're not really the fuck-up in this
situation. You'll see. Once we get you away from Mom and her
more-helpless-than-thou power trip." On she goes: Mom is the
problem. Mom let the world run over her and dragged me under
with her. When was the last time I showered the shit off her when
she messed herself? Last night? Tonight?

Though this last situation happens more regularly than I'd
prefer, it's not as if Mom does it on purpose. She always cries. She
always tells me to just go ahead and leave her like Jamie did.

The only thing I know how to do when my sister is talking like
this is to go into the little home movie I have in my mind of her
cutting oranges on a beach. So much of my memories are gone
but not this one: Jamie has a little knife. Dad is downriver fishing.
Mom is lying on a blanket reading a book. Jamie takes the slice of
orange and peels off all the white stringy yuck and feeds it to me—
with the tips of her fingers. "You be the baby eagle," she says. "And
I'll be the eagle."

Even then, I thought, I want to be the eagle. But at the time,
I thought the game was only going to last for the afternoon. And
besides, she wanted to be the eagle so bad.

The Cab, of course, is not ready. I sit up all the same and pour
myself a glass—that first sip glittering through me like melted
ruby slippers. I take it with me when I leave the table. Jamie is still
talking. I may be passive, as she says. And self-harming, as she says.
And willfully loving to those who cannot love, as she says.

But I am not beyond self-defense.

Over at the bar, the men perk up—aware all too quickly that a
woman in her late twenties is headed their way, clutching booze.
They are useless to me, unrelated to Jamie and what might upset
her. I swerve over to the Sunsets. As I suspected, I do actually know
them.

"Becca," says the one I noticed when I entered. She smells like
every scented candle in the world. The whole delicious gamut:
toasted almond to Zanzibar.

"I meant to come over earlier." I gesture vaguely, as if sweeping
aside the pesky crumbs of time. We clink glasses. A name sizzles
through me, as sometimes happens: Kirsten. Kristen. I mumble
out some version of the two.

And her friends? Stacey, Michelle, and Dina. Which, like Mark, John, and Dave are really all the same name. All four are plastered on wine by the glass—a purchasing habit that incenses Jamie. Not just because it costs double, but because women have to stop lying to themselves about their desire to get drunk and just order a bottle.

"So you're still in town," says Kristen.

"Only when I'm tipsy," I say.

She laughs.

I laugh.

"I heard that," she says, in a kind voice. "Is there anything I can do?"

It is true that my arrest—but not the settlement with Papa John's—made the papers. But something else lumps in the back of my mind, a crude and reptilian understanding that makes more sense as soon as Kristen looks over at Jamie.

Jamie looks down at the oysters. Because—of course as I must have known without really knowing—they were sweethearts way back when, hanging out upstairs on her white canopy bed in Dad's all-white house, supposedly studying for a Mathtastic match.

Kristen raises her glass. Jamie nods and saunters over—as only she can do while eight months pregnant. "Are you hitting on my baby sister?" she says. Cool as a mountain stream.

"I heard you were in town," say Kristen. "Jerry and I wanted to have you over." She looks at me. "We'd love to have to you too. I mean it's silly, you and me living so close by and us not getting together."

I nod, listen, weep internally for her as she continues: Jerry and her live across the lake from me and Mom. Jerry and her have two girls. Jerry and her have a chocolate Lab. Jerry loves double espressos with foam. Jerry is doing so well at Exxon. In public relations.

"Wow," says Jamie. "Public relations."

Luckily, one of the drunk, lonely guys at the bar comes over. "Hey, ladies," he says, thickly. "Calamari?" He is holding a half-finished basket. I am so anxious for Kristen, for being so obviously still hung up on my sister, so anxious about whether or not my sister is about to do something cruel or kind or terrible to her. Or to me. Or worse, cheat on sweet, absent Flora back at home transitioning their toddler into a toddler bed, that I grab hold of a calamari and pop it in my mouth.

All five glossily highlighted female heads turn toward me—

horrified. I have accepted something from Drunk and Lonely and because of that the odds are that Drunk and Lonely will now think that he and I are destined to leave the wine bar together. I try to spit the piece out. But it is too late. Drunk and Lonely has friends—a table full of them—they cheer him.

"Thatta girl," says Drunk and Lonely. He puts his arm around me. He gives me a nice big squeeze, heavy on the shoulder.

I look at my sister. She looks away.

"Excuse me," says Stacey. "Not to be rude, but my husband is in the state legislature."

"We're all just getting along," he says. "We're eating some seafood." He sniffs my glass. "We're having a nice glass of old-vine Cab."

Everybody knows—with all the fear and familiarity of women in a bar alone in Alaska—where this is going. Drunk and Lonely's friends start moving over to our table so they can try to meet all of us and we can all just get along.

The waitress shows up to try and help. "Is everybody comfortable?" she says to our table, glancing at our neighbors. "How about a crème brûlée on the house? Five spoons?"

"One more bottle of whatever she's drinking," says the guy, and lets his finger brush across my nipple.

"Are you sure?" says the waitress. "It's quite pricey."

"I can cover it."

"It's two seventy-five."

He smiles, recovers. "Why not?" he says. "Worth the investment."

It is time to leave. And it is time not to make a scene. We all laugh. Then Michelle and Dina go off to pee and never come back. A few minutes pass, during which Stacey orders a round of shots and pretends to get a call on her cell——then she goes out in the hall to pick it up. We all toss back our shots, whereupon Kristen recognizes an old friend who is really a random busboy who walks her out. I eat another calamari. And another.

Jamie looks a little bewildered now that we are alone with the guy. And his table of friends. I am not exactly sure what to do about her. She needs to get up on her swollen feet and find some excuse to leave. Except that maybe she has been in Portland for a little too long and forgotten about the sexual assault situation in our hometown, which clocks in as the second highest in the nation—and not in a roofied and raped kind of way, a bash-the-girl-and-drag-her into-the-woods-behind-the-strip-mall kind of way.

"Please," I say to her. "If you're going to puke, don't do it on my cashmere."

"Oh," she says. "Right! I'm morning sick." And lumbers out of there.

"I think—" I say.

"If you're going to run off," says Drunk and Lonely. "Run off. You don't have to be so mean about it." His face is hurt, puzzled.

"I'm not mean," I say. "Do you think I'm mean?"

"Yes," he says—in a voice so thick with hate, you can feel the spit beneath it.

I get up.

He gets up.

"Hang on, buddy," says the bartender. "Let's settle up for that bottle before we rush out."

We have about three minutes to make a plan. None of the Sunsets drove. As it turns out, Stacey's husband really is a state legislator and drops the three of them off on Fridays and picks them up at midnight. Jamie took a taxi from the hotel; her rental car won't be dropped off until tomorrow morning. "It's not even nine o'clock," says Michelle. "We should go back in and enjoy our evening."

"We could go downtown," says Kristen, looking at Jamie. "The Captain Cook is open." The Captain Cook is a bar. And a hotel. With the obvious hotel rooms upstairs.

"Can't somebody call us a taxi?" says Jamie.

I am feeling a little anxious. So are Stacey, Michelle, and Dina by the looks of how they are scanning the parking lot—which is dark and full of landscaping bushes and too far from an intersection and if Drunk and Lonely and his band of merry friends shows up, it's going to get tense and ugly quite fast. "We can always take the People Mover," I say.

Laughter all around. Understandable. There are about four People Movers in the whole city. And in their world, who doesn't own a car?

"I love the bus," says Jamie, suddenly. "Why not?" The Sunsets giddy up, her and Kristen bringing up the rear. It goes without saying my sister was student government president and general king of school and that everybody saw her on the cover of *Wired*.

The bus lunges up. It's empty. Save for the driver and the dog. The dog is tied to the last seat and has managed to slink underneath it, leaving only his whippet tail exposed. This is maybe why the driver has not noticed him. Either that or the driver is too afraid of getting bit. I sit next to the poor guy and try to hide him with my legs.

Dina, Stacey, Michelle come down the aisle.

"A doggie!" says Dina.

I put a finger over my mouth.

"Got it," she says and winks.

There is a whine of machinery. The driver is lowering the handicap ramp for Jamie, who apparently looks too pregnant to mount the steps. Kristen helps her down the aisle to our seats, which is when my sister whips open her maternity jacket and pulls out the carafe of Cab.

"Party bus," says Michelle.

Around the wine goes. Around it goes again.

Kristen turns it down. "I guess you know about Jerry," she says, but mostly to Jamie. The other Sunsets circle around. Hugs. Toasts. Jerry is selfish. Jerry is a fucker. Jerry is having an affair with a woman who runs a natural food store. She is ten years older than Kristen, which should make it better but only makes it more humiliating.

"Well," says Jamie. "My wife kicked me out of the house last week."

We all swivel our heads, even the dog.

Jamie waddles over, takes a glug off the carafe. It happens so quickly, it's almost as if she forgot she is pregnant. Then she takes another glug. Then she starts to cry. Loudly. "She says I stifle her. She says I'm overbearing."

"I just don't know," says Stacey, the wife of the state legislator, "if I'm okay with this."

"You guys are so—so American," I say—me, whose one trip out of the country was our six-hour stay in Montreal. "It's perfectly fine for a pregnant woman to have wine."

They all look at me.

"It's red," I say, "an antioxidant."

"I'm out of here," says Stacey. She waves at the driver as if he is the chauffeur. And with a small, exquisite smile he ignores her. She sits back down, punches into her phone for a taxi and there is nothing but fluorescent, rattled silence until the next stop. The door heaves open, Stacey flounces toward it, Michelle and Dina follow. Then Dina hurries back. She kneels down in front of me and hands me a card. Darn Yarns, it says.

Her store, apparently.

"If you need a job," she says, "call me. My mom always told me how your mom made her all that caribou stew when she got cancer."

I must look confused. She brushes the bangs out of my face and says, "I was in seventh grade. You were still pretty much of a baby."

"Of course," says Jamie, "love on my sister. Like everybody else."

There is so much I could say to this, but why bother? My sister is a jerk. My sister is a bag of toxic vagina. The bus lurches off. Kristen and Jamie start whispering. And I lean on the window making breath fog on the glass, until the empty carafe rolls down the aisle and hits the fare counter. The bus pulls over. The driver leans down and toes the carafe. "Off," he says. "Use the back exit and don't try to pretend you're passed out."

The dog looks at me. I don't have a knife and I don't know knots, I tell him with my eyes. My sister strides in and undoes the rope with the assurance of a person who has tied up a lot of turbo floatplanes and speedboats in her life. "Well," she says. "You got what you wanted at least."

She hands him over. He looks up at me. He has a quizzical, un-cooperative look to him. This is not the dog I wanted. I wanted a golden retriever or one of those fluffy, pillow-sized dogs that sleep in your lap while you watch TV until three in the morning, Mom rambling beside you about a totally unrelated episode from *Falcon Crest* circa 1989. But that is my problem, isn't it? I didn't ask for what I wanted. Because I don't know what I want—except not to leave Mom alone or do anything Jamie wants me to do—and so I asked in the general category of what I thought I could get.

The doors fold open and we step into the night. It is foggy. Something in the trees smells like lighter fluid and swamp. A park service sign looms by a parking bollard.

"Holy fuck," says Jamie.

"Oh," I say. "This is perfect."

"Valley of the Moon!" says Kristen, with an awe that endears her to me for the rest of our lives. Valley of the Moon being a playground that every kindergarten teacher in town takes her class to on field trips, which for me transcended even the joy of visiting the downtown art museum (where we got to carve a bar of Ivory soap into a Native sculpture of a guy in a kayak) or the mile-long walk to a Quik Stop (where we all got a free pack of Twizzlers).

I can almost taste the tipsy, wrecked half-planet made of metal bars you can climb up to reign as Lord of the Universe. Or the creaky spinning wheel where you lie down—your friends running, gathering speed, jumping on at the last minute, the sky whizzing by in a puffy, peaceful vomit of clouds.

Best of all is the rocket-ship slide, which requires you to climb a rusty ladder so high up you want to climb back down but can't— not with everyone watching—then force yourself to dive into the dark of the endless metal tunnel, at the end of which a series of painful screws erupt from the metal, followed by a pile-on of kids that try to block your high-speed exit with their bodies.

And yet, when Jamie, Kristen, and I break out of the trees that shelter the entrance, we find that everything has been replaced. There is still a planet, a spinning wheel, and a rocket-ship slide. But they are the plastic versions of the old equipment—all with the soft, molded feel of crayons. The moonlight makes them glow a little. Dully.

A fresh round of gloppy fog rolls in from the trees. "I can't believe it," says Kristen. "We used to get high here in high school." "I'm doing the rocket ship," says Jamie.

"Are you sure that's a good idea?" says Kristen. "With your size?"

"I'm fine. Pregnant women can go down a slide." Up Jamie goes, slowly on the plastic steps, as if accentuating the loss of our rusty ladder. Kristen jumps around in the grass, doing spritely dance moves. A leap. A twist. A split.

"Didn't you used to be a ballerina?" I say.

"I wish," she says. "Gymnast."

Jamie is now sitting at the top of the slide. She waves. Kristen cartwheels through the grass. Handspring. Round off. She waves to the crowd, accepts an invisible medal.

"Becca?" says Jamie.

"I'm not going down," I say. "This is Fern's cashmere I'm wearing. I may need to sell it."

"No," she says. "It's just—can you come a little closer?"

I come over. I look up. She has her hands gripped on either side of the guardrails. "I'm—" she says. "It's pretty high up here." I remember, in a dim, possibly erroneous way, she is afraid of heights. "Just come back down the steps," I say. "You have a baby inside you."

"I know," she says.

"I can't catch you. I have the dog. And you're too big."

"I know you can't—"

"Then come down—"

"It'll make me feel better," she says. "If you're there, at the bottom. Just in case." Up at the top of the not-so-high slide, her face is clenched, pale, needy looking even.

This is a story she will later tell us both, I realize. Her story will be funny and self-lacerating and so horrifically precise about our love and fury for each other—that whole diseased seesaw we both dare the other to get off of. At the end, Jamie will have either shot out of the slide, landing on me and the dog and knocking us both over in the mud. Or whizzed off the end, when I stepped back from it, allowing her and her unborn child to land on her fragile, forty-four-year-old tailbone.

There is another story, though. I have almost told it to her every day of my life but haven't, even now I am unsure as to why.

Back in Montreal, at the hotel Mom checked us into, we had to leave the Coupe DeVille in a parking lot in the basement and go to the theater on a train that ran underground. It was called a metro. *Metro,* I remember saying to myself. *Metro.*

We went down some stairs and through a metal bar that spun around. Then we stood on a long cement platform, with a bunch of other people. Some of them were kids. My sister and Mom stood together, Jamie hanging on Mom's shoulder. This was how Jamie was back then. Always trying to get Mom's attention. Always playing with her necklace or the mole on her chin as if it were a little brown diamond, always the first to find her keys when she lost them, the first to say you're the best mom in the world.

I was younger, slower, dumb to the race we were in. Most of time I was dawdling off in a corner, unintentionally forgotten. A few feet down from my spot by the column, a woman with long dark hair and two shopping bags waited beside me. Both bags were made of brown paper and filled with what looked like little balls of tissue paper, as if she were moving and had decided to pack up all her glasses and fancy, breakable things and take them with her.

On the top of the bag closest to me, a sliver of shiny red showed through a gap in the tissue. Everything in me longed to reach in and touch it. If only to know if it was a Valentine as I suspected. Or a bit of chocolate foil. Or something else, something mysterious and Canadian.

The cement under my feet began to rumble. The woman moved closer to the yellow line. I had never been on a subway or a train. I moved closer too. She moved another step closer. Me too. Our toes were right on the edge, which is how you got on a subway, I thought. You want to be the first one. You had to be right next to the train to get on.

The headlights roared in.

When I looked back, Mom had her hands over Jamie's face and Jamie was screaming and everyone was screaming. Except for Mom. She was staring at me. Her eyes were huge green bruise holes. When she came over, she walked dreamily, slowly, as if underwater. I didn't know where her purse was and I don't think she knew where it was either or where the Kleenex were inside it, but all the pieces of tissue paper from the woman's bag were floating by us. Mom plucked one from the air and wiped the blood and sticky other stuff off my cheeks.

Then we went back up the long dark stairs and back to the hotel and got back in the car and drove straight back home. Mom saying the whole time we were all okay. We would figure it out. We would put me in a hot bath and go to school and do our homework. Jamie was crying. "I can't believe you," she said. "I can't believe you're taking us back. Not to him." She chanted this over and over all through the vast plains, the lakes, the forests, the cities, the gas stations, the truck stops—that whole endless foreign country speeding by us in the windows.

I was in the back seat, pulling little threads off the edge of my jeans. Mom kept pulling over and shaking me by my shoulders saying, "Are you all right? Are you hungry? Do you want a hot chocolate? We can stop for hot chocolate if you want." I was fine. I was tired. I leaned against Jamie, who had just begun not to talk to Mom or to talk to her as if she were a ghost with bad breath.

I was seven years old. I knew nothing, except that I was not upset the way Mom and Jamie were upset and never would be.

They had seen the part on the platform that I didn't see or didn't remember. And I had seen what they were too busy and far away to see—how peaceful the woman looked, how happy even as a train thundered in and she jumped into the lights with both her bags, the bags exploding into hot white flowers of tissue and shattered glass, as if we might be at the ballet already where Mom and Jamie had told me beautiful, tiny ladies leapt into the air while snow fell and music played, and we all clapped to be polite and show them that we recognized how hard they had worked, how strong they were, how much we wanted them to stay in the air above us and never come down. Bravo, I was told to say. Even if I never got the chance to say it.

33 Clues into the Disappearance of My Sister

FROM *Ellery Queen Mystery Magazine*

1.

Silky white fabric, bodiless. Pool of silk, in languid-liquidy folds on the floor where (the viewer/voyeur avidly assumes) she'd shrugged her naked body out of the shift, let it fall slithering like a snake, but a sheerly white, purely white, camelia white silky snake falling past her hips, her thighs, and to the carpeted floor in a hiss.

Though bodiless, boneless, smelling faintly, fragrantly of a (female) body.

2.

Is this a clue? The flimsy white silk Dior "slip dress" belonging to my sister M. discovered on the floor of her bedroom subsequent to her disappearance on April 11, 1991.

Or is the article of clothing of little significance, purely chance, irrelevant and accidental, *not* a clue?

3.

(In a later time in history, certainly in the twenty-first century, M.'s silky white slip dress would have been examined for DNA; particularly the scummy clue called *semen*. But in 1991 in small-town, upstate Aurora-on-Cayuga, New York, forensic science was little known, and so the chic silk dress with the spaghetti straps, neatly hung on a hanger in M.'s closet, by me, the protective younger sister, has awaited M.'s return all these years undefiled.)

4.

(Though yes, possibly the silk dress on the floor of M.'s bedroom was a "clue"—if we'd known if the dress had been purchased by M. herself during her three-year sojourn in New York City or if it was a gift from a lover and if so, which lover.)

(Also, a clue in that it had been dropped in haste, or negligently, by M., who was ordinarily so fastidious she would never have allowed an article of clothing to fall to the floor and not retrieve it immediately, hanging it in a closet, or folding and putting it neatly into a drawer. For Marguerite Fulmer was *cool, calm, control.* A self-styled sculptor: one who *shapes* but is not *shaped.*)

(Letting clothes fall onto the floor of her room, accumulating over days, weeks, refusing to allow the housekeeper into her room is more characteristic of M.'s "difficult" younger sister G. but since G. had not ever gone missing from Aurora-on-Cayuga no one gives a damn about the condition of G.'s room.)

5.

Double mirror. The means by which I saw my sister on the morning of the day she was to "disappear" from our lives: that is, the means by which I happened to see M.'s reflection in a mirror for (in fact) I did not see Marguerite herself, only her reflection.

It is imprecise, if common, to say that the (reflected) image is the person; but, in this instance, the reflection of M. was but a reflection of the (unknowable, inscrutable) M., in fact *the reflection of a reflection.*

The door to M.'s room was not latched properly and had come open, very likely as a consequence of a draft in the second-floor corridor; for the old house was drafty, and wind from Lake Cayuga was relentless, even in April bearing a wintry chill.

M.'s room was (in fact) a suite of three high-ceilinged adjoining rooms running along the eastern side of the house and overlooking, at a distance of about one hundred feet, the choppy waves of Lake Cayuga, the largest of the "scenic" Finger Lakes.

Passing by M.'s room on my way downstairs, surprised that the door eased open as if of its own volition, for usually M.'s door was shut firmly against unwanted intrusions and cheery morning greetings, I could not resist glancing inside, and so happened to see, in the vertical mirror attached to the inside of my sister's closet door, which was also partially open, about six feet away, the reflection of M. on the farther side of the room, facing her bureau mirror; so that, wholly unpremeditatedly, in the suddenness of the moment, my eyes took in, without accessing, scarcely registering, my sister's wraithlike face in the bureau mirror reflected in the mirror on the closet door—that is, an image *double mirrored.*

All of this, vertiginously recalled (now) twenty-two years later as one might recall a dream of utter mystery which, in the intervening years, has not lightened in mystery but deepened.

(Possibly, in the periphery of my eye I "saw" the Dior dress on the floor. But such "seeing" was not conscious at the time and if it seems conscious in retrospect, that is the mind playing its mischievous and perverse tricks upon itself.)

What I do remember clearly: my (beautiful) (doomed) sister standing with her back to me on the farther side of the room as she was brushing her long straight silvery-blond hair, reflected in the vertical mirror upon which my eyes fixed in a sort of startled fascination even as the thought came to me *No—this is forbidden!*— gazing with dread upon my sister as if I were, not an adult woman in her mid-twenties, a woman with a definite, one might say *indelibly* formed personality, but a pubescent child; for years in awe of the (aloof, elegant) sister six years older than I.

Peering through a doorway into the interior of another's life: the apprehension that we will glimpse the other, the sister, in a state of unwanted intimacy, nakedness.

Was M. naked, standing before the bureau mirror reflected in the closet mirror? The pale straight back, perfectly shaped waist, hips, thighs, legs.

Shadowy vertebrae, slender wrists, ankles.

(Of course) in reporting this (fleeting/involuntary) glance into M.'s room to detectives I would say that I didn't remember exactly what M. was wearing, probably just her usual dressing gown.

*

No doubt she'd showered, shampooed her hair as (I had reason to think) she did several times a week (in contrast to me, the younger sister, who often didn't trouble to shampoo her hair for weeks), and was now brushing it in swift punishing strokes causing hairs to crackle with static electricity.

Yes, I'd noticed *that*. A *frisson* of static electricity, that caused the hairs on my arms to rise in sympathy.

Strange how M. was oblivious of me. *Oblivious of what was rushing at her from the future on wide-spread dark-feathered wings.*

This phenomenon of the "double mirror" is both of *little consequence, purely accidental* in the exigency of the moment, and *essential*. For, though the fleetingly aligned mirrors were necessary in order that, for the final time, I would see my sister, the *double mirror* was the only means by which I could have seen her, since the door would have blocked my view of her in front of the bureau as I made my way along the second-floor corridor to the front staircase with its worn maroon plush carpeting, as distinct from the narrower, thinly carpeted back stairs of the massive old seven-bedroom, five-bathroom English Tudor on Cayuga Avenue; at the same time it should be acknowledged that these mirrors, precisely because they were so accidentally aligned, and so fleetingly, may have suggested, to me, a premonitory aura of the unreal, the unsubstantiated, even the phantasmagoric, to what was but an ordinary domestic scene: a resident of the house passing by the doorway of an older sister on her way downstairs to breakfast at about 7:20 A.M. at the outset of what should have been just one in a sequence of mostly unremarked, ordinary days in April 1991.

Which leaves the matter ambiguous: Was the *double mirror* the means by which I "saw" into a profound and inexplicable mystery, or was the *double mirror* the profound and inexplicable mystery itself?

6.

Missing person. It would be claimed that M. "stepped off the face of the earth"—"vanished into thin air"—"disappeared without a trace."

Was this true? *Is* it?

For no one is truly *missing*. Everyone is *somewhere* though we may not know where.

Even the dead—their remains. *Somewhere.*

This is a fact: M. is *somewhere.* Every hour of every day I grind my teeth in dismay, despair, resentment, fury. *My sister is not "missing"— my sister is SOMEWHERE.*

In hiding, maybe. Or in disguise. Just to spite us. To spite *me.*

Or maybe (as some say) she is no longer living—still she has got to be SOMEWHERE.

If only the slender bones, a swath of the pale silvery-blond hair that fell past her shoulders.

The remains of the perfect teeth, maybe. That final grimace looking like triumph.

7.

Early spring. In upstate New York spring is slow to emerge out of winter as a steaming breath out of a cavernous mouth.

Exactly when M. left the house is not known. *I* did not see her leave nor did Father. Our housekeeper Lena did not see her. Presumably after 7:20 A.M. Possibly as late as 8:30 A.M. For it was M.'s routine to walk/hike to the college and it was rare that she arrived there, if she was going there at all, after 9 A.M.

It was a thinly overcast morning. A Thursday: the very epitome of a *nothing-day.*

Dripping icicles from the eaves of our house, ice-toothed sludge underfoot, northern sides of yews serrated with frost slow to melt. Is this what M. noticed, or was M. thinking of something very different?

Was M. thinking *guiltily* of something very different?

Aurora-on-Cayuga is built on a half-dozen hills overlooking a lake and so it is always at the whim of the "lake effect"—rapidly shifting weather, piercing sun through clouds, a possibility of spitting rain.

This seems to be definite: M. was wearing her ankle-high mahogany-dark Ferragamo leather boots with a low but distinctive heel. Her footprints led through the tall yews behind our house in the direction of the narrow asphalt road that within a half-mile bifurcated the steeply hilly "historic" campus of Aurora College for Women, founded 1878: a cluster of austere old redbrick buildings with grim weatherworn facades, South Hall, Minor Hall, Wells

Hall, Fulmer Hall adjoining the newly built Cayuga Arts School where M. was artist-in-residence and taught a "master class" in sculpting.

M.'s boot-prints, leading from the rear door of our house through the trampled grass of our back lawn stretching for an acre then passing out of our property and into the no-man's-land of winter-damaged deciduous trees and underbrush that belonged to Cayuga County, soon lost amid myriad footprints and animal tracks on the path winding through the woods.

If we'd known. If we'd realized she would never return. Photographing the Ferragamo prints. Determining if the prints continued on the farther side of Wells Road or if by that time they had vanished, which could only mean that someone (unknown) had stopped for M. on the road, forced her into his vehicle or (perhaps) M. had climbed into the vehicle of her own volition calling softly to the driver, "Here I am."

8.

Last seen. How many times asked: When did you see your sister last? And what did you say to each other?

And very carefully I would explain that I'd seen my sister at about 7:20 A.M. on the morning of her "disappearance" but we had not exchanged words.

I had seen *her;* she had not seen *me.*

And the fools would persist asking when had I spoken with my sister last, and what had she said. And I would make every effort to remember, and to answer sincerely.

Saying *Marguerite did not say anything to me that would indicate that she was unhappy or anxious or worried.* Not saying *We did not have that kind of relationship! We were not sisters who confided in each other, you are very naive to assume so.*

Nor did I tell them that I'd seen, not my sister, but the reflection of my sister in the *double mirror.*

And not M.'s face, not clearly. For M.'s face was framed in the bureau mirror, a blurred face, as if partially erased. Scarcely recognizable, if I hadn't known it was her. The beauty, and the blemishes in the beauty.

For mirrors double distances and make of the familiar, strangeness.

9.

Revenge. There is a famous/notorious work of art, a drawing by
Willem de Kooning "erased" by Robert Rauschenberg in 1953. You
could say that the lesser artist revenges himself upon the greater
artist by erasing his work. A playful sort of vandalism that might be
mistaken for whimsy.

For what other revenge can the lesser artist achieve, than erasing
work by the greater artist?

I was not an artist. M. had no fear of me erasing her work.

I *was* a poet. But my poems were secrets scribbled in code for
mice scrambling in my desk drawers to peruse.

The spell M. cast upon all who knew her: our parents most of all.

Her beauty, that was unjust. For all beauty is unjust. Her kindness, her softness of heart, her (apparent) love for *me*. Or, affection
for me.

As if I were, not a rival of M.'s, no one to take seriously, the
awkward younger sister, a slightly unkempt sheepdog, burly, bum-
bling, bulgey-damp-eyed, with a big moist nose, pink tongue panting,
quickly out of breath from the stairs.

Indeed it was said that M. had moved back home from New York
City for my sake after Mother's death.

Among the relatives, in particular our callow catty girl-cousins, it
has been said that my sister returned to Aurora to "save" me when
(it seemed) I was *suicidal.*

(Which is absurd: I do not "believe" in suicide any more than,
for instance, Father would believe in suicide which, to him, as to
his Teutonic-warrior *Volkmar* ancestors, would be *giving God-damned
solace to the enemy.*)

Why I hated M., if I'd hated her which (I am sure) I did not.

For *why* would I hate my sister who took pity on me, when she
took notice of me, when she had time for me. *Why* hate my sister
who was (said to be) the only person who cared for me enough
to care for me, for Christ's sake. After Mother's death which was a
misty-crappy-smelly-bog time inaccessible to (my) memory.

Fun times! Overseeing the vacuuming, cleaning, scouring,
airing-out of my pigsty-room from which poor despairing Lena
had been banished for a full year, and Father himself, the Zeus of
our household, had not the courage or fortitude to enter.

Pressing on me her fancy French lavender soap, a "bribe" for me to shower more often.

Plaiting my thick "obstinate" hair, as she'd called it. A promise of a birthday excursion to Niagara Falls—"just the two of us, Gigi . . ."

Gigi!—M.'s secret name for me, that no one knew.

Gigi!—a sensation rises in me like delirium, the impulse is to shout, laugh wildly, scream, and it is hateful, so many years later when such folly should be laid to rest. Someone should shove dirt into my mouth, to quiet me.

Is it possible, though not very *likely*, that my sister had passed on to me the expensive designer boots she'd purchased in New York City and in her (typical) carelessness allowed to become weatherworn, corroded by wet?—a cruel joke since Gigi couldn't possibly have jammed her (size 10) feet into the elegant (size 7) boots.

(For it was like M. to insist upon expensive things, high-quality merchandise from the very best stores, though soon afterward she was negligent with such possessions out of indifference or embarrassment, and gave them away, or set them out at the curb with the trash as if to say—*You see, I am not vain. Good riddance!*)

Yes but *maybe* there is a diabolical scenario in which the calculating Gigi, wielding the boots in question, ingeniously managed to create boot-tracks leading from the rear of our house into the no-man's-land where the tracks became "lost"—though not on the morning of April 11, 1991, probably.

Possibly the previous night, and undetected.

So many *maybes*. Yet (this is the tantalizing promise of clues!) one of these *maybes* however improbable and implausible is the Truth.

Miss Fulmer, can you think of anyone who might wish to harm your sister? Any enemies of your sister? Any men involved with your sister?

No, no, and *no*.

10.

Jealousy. Is there any revenge, except jealousy is the flame that ignites it?

Of the men who'd loved M., each had hoped to "possess" her.

(I have put quotation marks around this word to indicate that yes, I think it's a silly word. I think it's a silly wish. But I understand that the wish to "possess" is a wish of many men confounded by a woman who eludes them.)

There was D., there was W., there was Y., and there was N. And, yes—(though he'd seemed to have dropped out of M.'s life years before)—there was S.

Each of them men with whom M. had been (possibly) involved. (Possibly) sexually involved. In Aurora, in New York City, and in Ithaca over a period of years.

I would not name these names. *I* would not lower myself by repeating crude and prurient gossip.

In fact, I did not know the men's names—not their full names. Others in the family, our callow cousins, scattered friends, and former high-school classmates of M.'s not above repeating gossip under the guise of aiding the police in their (slovenly, futile) investigation that would replicate, over the next decade, the paths through the woods hopelessly crosshatched with the footprints of strangers and even the hoofprints of white-tailed deer, these persons would name the names of the "men in M.'s life" who would then duly be interviewed by police as *persons of interest*.

Malicious delight in such *naming of names*. Revenge on M. for having, at one time at least, excited masculine interest, desire; and revenge on the *persons of interest* for having had such desire.

To these five names the wide sprawling net of the (ongoing) police investigation would add, in time, many more names. For a police investigation into an "unsolved" crime will have no boundaries and, in theory, will have no end.

No end to a police investigation means no mercy.

No end to a police investigation means sorrow yielding to anger, and anger yielding to sorrow.

Of the *persons of interest* there would be no singular *suspect*.

The consensus had emerged, he'd picked her up on Wells Road. Whoever it was, who'd carried M. from us.

Forced her into his vehicle—possibly into the trunk. Tied her, gagged her, hauled her away still alive, to an uncertain fate.

Unless: On Wells Road she'd stepped into the vehicle as planned. Breathless and yearning and having brought with her virtually no personal possessions and (probably) less than one hundred dollars in cash in her wallet, judging by the most recent withdrawal from M.'s savings account at the Bank of Cayuga which had been less than five hundred dollars and had not in fact been recent.

In which case, who was driving the vehicle? And where was the vehicle driven, after Wells Road?

Jealousy! I was not *jealous* of the (alleged) men in M.'s life because I was not jealous of M. A younger sister can't plausibly be jealous of an older accomplished beautiful sister, she can only be in awe of such a sister, grateful for attention from the Princess, fleeting smiles, words of approval now and then tossed like gold coins from a pocket.

Were you and your sister close? Did you become closer after your mother's death?

Did your sister confide in you?

No, no, and *never.*

11.

"April 11, 1991." An ax splitting your skull in two.

The time *before* an event that changes your life, the time *after* an event that changes your life.

For no one could have predicted that April 11, 1991, would be transformed into "April 11, 1991," indelibly imprinted upon the memories of all who'd known my sister.

Who could have predicted, a day of no significance transformed into a day of great significance.

Certainly not M., who'd marked the day in pencil on her calendar, 2 P.M. (class), 4:30 P.M. (committee meeting). And the following day, dentist's appointment at 9 A.M.

Following week, more of the same: routine appointments, nothing of significance one might decode as a *clue.*

Unless the calendar for April was carefully planned. To deceive with very ordinariness.

On most weekdays it was M.'s custom to arrive early in the morning at the Arts School to work in her studio undisturbed until late morning and so when M. failed to arrive by noon her (apparent) absence began to be noted though not (yet) particularly remarked upon, until 2 P.M. when students arrived for the "master" sculpting class, M.'s absence now acknowledged and calls to M.'s phone unanswered; queries began to be made—*Have you seen Marguerite today? Have you spoken with Marguerite today?*

You have to imagine: The name "Marguerite" is spoken in a certain tone. Admiring, not accusatory. *Mar-guer-ite:* the full, melodic name, not a vulgar rush of syllables.

Surprise that M. wasn't there, hadn't left any messages. No Post-it on the door of her office.

But not (yet) alarm, no actual concern that M. might have met with a mishap, might be ill, derailed by an emergency, in any sort of distress except among those who'd known M. since her high-school years in Aurora when "something mysterious" had happened to her, details of which were obscure.

Very possibly, there was a "family crisis"—for it was known, not generally, but by some, that M.'s younger sister G. had "some sort of history . . ."

What kind of history? Mental—? . . . hospitalized? In Buffalo?

Only cautiously were such possibilities mentioned for indeed M. was a *very private person* who did not speak casually of her family life unlike most of her artist-colleagues who joked openly and cruelly of their difficult/comical families presented for the ribald consumption of others like comic strips on a bulletin board.

Very private too about the men in her life. Not clear if indeed there was a man in M.'s life at the time of her disappearance.

Unless the silky Dior slip dress was a clue: not "fragrant" as I've said but "smelly" with the unmistakable smell of a man . . .

But no one will know: discreetly I would pick up the wisp of a dress, light as lingerie, and hang it on a hanger, and place it (inconspicuously) at the very rear of M.'s closet, where no prying detectives were likely to find it.

For though I did not approve of M.'s (possible, probable) sexually promiscuous life, kept entirely secret from me, I did care, very much, about the *good name* of our family which dates back to the time of the earliest settlers in this part of New York State: 1789.

Through the afternoon of April 11 calls began to come to M.'s private line at our house which rang only in M.'s room, and which Lena did not answer, by M.'s request; these were calls from M.'s colleagues and friends at the Arts School, wondering where she was.

Messages were left. In all, eight messages from "concerned" friends (which were never to be heard by M.).

(And where was I during this time, I would be asked by detectives, happy to inform the fools that I was *at work,* where would they think?—a steady stream of customers at the Mills Street Post Office, plus my two coworkers at the counter, and our supervisor, all could and did testify to my *whereabouts* that day.)

(So ridiculous! *Whereabouts, alibis—clues.* Cliches of the police investigation banal and threadbare as a worn old carpet over which, nonetheless, one has to trudge, eyes straight ahead in a pose of lockjaw-deadpan innocence.)

After I'd returned home from work (at approximately 5:35 P.M.) (for I too walked to my place of work and back, in all a distance of a mile and a half; unlike M., I did not have the use of a motor vehicle as I did not have a license to drive such a vehicle granted by the State of New York to some while withheld arbitrarily from others) I heard the phone ringing in M.'s room which was down the hall from my room. Several calls, or the same caller calling repeatedly, which was annoying to me, for after a long day at the post office waiting on idiots with poorly taped packages to send parcel post my nerves are easily jangled, so I demanded of Lena that she provide me with a key to M.'s room—(yes, M. so distrusted her family, she kept the door to her room locked like a schoolgirl with something disgraceful to hide)—and dared to enter M.'s quarters and answered M.'s phone in a voice making no effort to be polite: "Yes? Hello? If you're looking for who I think you are, sorry, she isn't here."

It seemed to me, this sudden concern for M. was exaggerated, the alarm in the silly woman's voice seemed to me ridiculous, and I may have said so, in my blunt no-bullshit way, and silly Sally or whatever her name was was shocked, and said, stammering: "But— where *is* Marguerite? Are you the sister? Aren't you worried? This is not like Marguerite . . ."

"And how do you know what my sister is 'like'?"—I couldn't resist, the caller was no one I knew and I doubted that M. knew, either. Hysterical like a hen with its head cut off if the decapitated head could chitter and chatter. "She could be in Timbuktu by now, what's it to *you?*"

Hanging up then, laughing. And a few minutes later the phone rang again, and again I answered it: "Sorree wrong number. Good-*byee.*"

Giving my voice a sort of Chinese inflection. Had to laugh.

For they were *all so silly.* When there was no cause for alarm, *not an emergency situation at all.*

Shut and locked the door to M.'s room. So that, when M. returned home, she would have no reason to think that anyone had violated her precious privacy.

By this time busybodies from the college had begun to call my father, informing him that Marguerite hadn't come to the college that day, she'd missed appointments "which wasn't like Marguerite" and so they were wondering if she was home, and if she was all right; and Father sent Lena to check M.'s room which was (of course) empty, and Father went himself to check the garage where M.'s pale yellow Volvo was parked, beside his stately black Lincoln sedan: still, nothing out of the ordinary since M. rarely drove to the college a mile away, preferring to walk even in inhospitable weather.

Yes it was true, M. sometimes walked, hiked in the hilly countryside, or along stretches of Lake Cayuga where the shore was open, not fenced off by private landowners.

Preferring to walk alone. Though a few times in recent years, she'd invited me to join her.

Awkward and annoying, how M. would stride ahead as if forgetting me then stop abruptly, and wait for me to catch up panting and perspiring.

Not rolling her eyes—oh, no! Never.

Wondering then why I declined to join her. As if she had no idea!

There was Father peering near-sightedly at me over his bifocals. Encountering me on the stairway landing where I was staring out the window at curious-shaped clouds blown overhead like a ragged flotilla of sailing ships, my mind utterly blank.

At this time of day, Father was usually in his office at the rear of the house conferring by phone with investment advisors in New York City, directing stocks to be purchased, stocks to be sold, with the vehemence of a warrior doling out rewards and punishments. From childhood we'd known not to interrupt Father at such times—(as if we'd had any reason to interrupt him!)—but here suddenly was Father looking disoriented like one who has lost his way, agitated, distracted (fortunately not noticing how I guiltily hid what was in my hand, some trivial item from M.'s room, a small piece of inexpensive jewelry M. would never miss, unless it was a [used] tube of Midnight Rose lipstick, essentially of no use to me who would no more smear makeup on my face than I would smear putty on my face with a trowel and rub clown spots of rouge on my "chubby" cheeks) asking if I remembered having seen Marguerite at any time that day and through a beating of blood in my ears I didn't hear this question, and Father repeated the question, and a scream surprised us both erupting from my lips:

No! I *had not* seen M., not since that morning, why was everyone always asking me about her!

Soon then, relatives began to call. In Aurora-on-Cayuga, population 1,768, news spreads rapidly.

Where is Marguerite? Have you heard from Marguerite? Have you seen anyone who has seen Marguerite?

Scarcely was M. missing eight hours, already word was out that *something must have happened to M., this is not like M.*

Yes, it was ridiculous! Only I seemed to know.

Father insisted upon answering these calls. Not even allowing Lena to pick up the phone.

Fatherly voice of "command." Loud voice of a man who is accustomed to being listened to. Loud voice of one who is hard of hearing. Though relatives were calling to ask about M., Father fired back questions at them like an irascible ping-pong player firing back shots.

Any news of his daughter? Had Marguerite called any of them? Had Marguerite gone out of town, without telling them? Marguerite had friends over in Ithaca—was Marguerite (maybe) in Ithaca?

(But if so, why was Marguerite's car in the garage?)

(This would be cited as proof that M. hadn't gone away of her own accord—the Volvo in the garage! As if that proved anything.)

Father insisted upon driving through the village in the stately black Lincoln slow along Main Street past darkened storefronts (property owned by Father, in fact), slow along Church Street past the darkened cemetery out of which weatherworn tombstones glowed with the eerie luminosity of radioactive teeth taunting our foolish and futile quest. Sharp uphill onto the Aurora College campus, stark redbrick buildings lonely as frigates riding the crest of an inland sea. Bell tower, chapel. Dull tolling of the hour 9 P.M. and the white clock face illuminated like the very face of idiocy devoid of human expression.

She hadn't wanted to return to Aurora-on-Cayuga. Her return was "temporary."

Nervy and condescending that she'd come home from New York City for *me.* Maybe she'd been jealous of *me.*

It was after Mother's death. Which (I guess: I don't remember clearly) I'd taken pretty hard.

Though I had not loved Mother—not *much*.

But then I don't love anyone—*much*.

M. had accepted the position as artist-in-residence at the college with the understanding that her salary would be channeled into a fund for scholarships. But in utmost secrecy, for M. did not wish to be known as any sort of "philanthropist," she did not want her artist-colleagues (some of whom were older than she) to feel uneasy in her presence.

Of course, they were inferior to Marguerite Fulmer. And made to know it. Any one of them might have wished her harm.

Our family had long been prominent in Aurora. Father's father and grandfather had been trustees of the women's college, as Father was now; they were a family of bankers, investors, real-estate developers, philanthropists. To M.'s embarrassment, one of the older and more dignified redbrick buildings on the campus was Fulmer Hall.

Mother too had been "from a good family"—of course! Never doubt.

A family in which, it would be revealed, women had a predilection for a certain sort of cancer. And a predilection for dying of this cancer.

The specificity of which, I think, I do not care to disclose.

I wondered if Father was thinking such somber thoughts. If Father dared think of the loss of Mother, which had torn our not-so-substantial household in two.

Frowning and sternly glaring driving slow along curving campus roads pausing to stare into the darkness between buildings and into shadows that, when exposed by headlights, were flat and banal as the interior of a cardboard box.

Beside Father in the passenger's seat of the Lincoln sedan I sat with my fists between my knees gripped tight to keep from shifting and twitching for I am restless at such times not daring to speak aloud what clamors to be said—*Do you really think Marguerite is skulking in the shadows here, Father? Do you really think you will find her here?*

If the Princess does not want to be found, the Princess will not be found.

Sighting a lone female figure on a walkway outside the college library Father braked the car to a stop and fumbled to lower the window—"Marguerite? Is that you?"

His voice cracked. I'd have wanted to laugh but realized suddenly that Father was truly upset.

Fortunately, the girl didn't hear. Hurrying past us clutching her books to her chest without a backward glance.

12.

Damned day (cont'd). By 10 P.M. that night a light rain had begun to fall. I stood by an upstairs window gazing out into the night thinking *She will get wet now, and cold! Now, Princess will come meekly home like a dog with its tail between its legs.*

Still, by 11 P.M. M. had not returned home, nor had she called to explain where she was; nor had anyone called on her behalf.

Was I beginning to be frightened, yes I was beginning to be frightened because a great wave of dirty water was rushing at us though our house is on a hill above the town and *I do not like upset.*

I do not like upset (unless it is an upset that I have caused myself). I do not like a violation of the household routine. I believe that there is nothing so upsetting as a violation of the household routine. I am on duty behind the counter at the Mills Street post office for eight hours five days a week and when I am not at my post at the Post Office I am safe and quiet in my room in my father's house where I do not like a violation of our domestic routine like supper postponed for hours, kept in a warm oven by Lena and tasteless as last week's leftovers, and above all I do not like the damned telephone jingling and jangling and no calls ever for *me,* always for *her.*

It was clear, no one would sleep that night in our house. Nine hours is required for me to sleep if I am to be clear-minded and suffused with energy in the morning to face eight hours upright and "customer-friendly" at the post office but there was not the slightest care for me, not that this was surprising, of course it was not.

At last Father called 911. Others had encouraged him, excitable relatives who lived a block away on Cayuga Avenue, and even Lena, wringing her hands with worry over my sister, so Father made the call, hesitant in his speech, faltering, uncertain, revealed as a man on the brink of being *old.*

Yes, an emergency!—"I have reason to think that my daughter Marguerite is in grave danger."

Telling the (two, uniformed) police officers who arrived at our house that something must have happened to M., she'd been missing all day, hadn't appeared at the college as she was expected, *it was not like his daughter to behave so irresponsibly*. Should have known that something was wrong, he hadn't seen M. at breakfast that morning. (As if the three of us routinely had breakfast together! Sometimes we did, but only by chance. Since Mother's illness and death our mealtimes were not formal affairs. Often, Marguerite skipped breakfast altogether. Or, if she had breakfast, it was at the college, in the cafeteria. My breakfast is my own business. I might have Cheerios with banana and milk at the house, and a second, larger breakfast at the diner across from the post office—scrambled eggs and bacon, rye toast and grape jelly. Father might have just black coffee and oatmeal prepared by Lena, as late as 11 A.M. on one of his dark-mood mornings.)

Not like my daughter to behave irresponsibly was several times repeated as if this statement were profound in itself and would impress the police officers as it seemed to impress Father.

Of the policemen, one of them was distinctly younger than the other. To my disgust I recognized the callow porcine face of a boy who'd gone to my high school now grown beefy, swarthy-jawed, blinking and squinting at the high-ceilinged interior of the English Tudor on Cayuga Avenue where otherwise he'd never have been invited to set foot like any of his ilk.

And staring at me startled. As if he did not, yet did, recognize me but dared not acknowledge me as I scorned to acknowledge him.

For I have changed much since high-school days, I think.

Both my face and my body. Where once I was weak now I am sturdy as a turnip.

Where once I was vulnerable to fools and bullies now I am impervious as a mollusk that, when you peer at it, all you see is a fine-ridged shell and not a bit of pink exposed flesh.

The elder policeman spoke with ponderous slowness like a hippopotamus summoning speech. *Maybe your daughter is away for the night Mr. Fulmer but will return in the morning, we see that lots of times. Doesn't mean that she's a runaway.*

Runaway! So ridiculous, I burst into derisive laughter.

Both policemen stared at me astonished. Father stared at me, disapproving.

The elder policeman asked me what was so funny and I told the fool point-blank that my sister Marguerite wasn't a teenager, she was thirty years old, artist-in-residence at Aurora College and an accomplished sculptor, hardly a *runaway*.

Father laid a hand on my arm to calm me, for I was laughing hard, and then I was coughing, and both policemen were staring at me at too close quarters.

Such fools!—I gave up on them, left the room heavy-footed on the stairs and slammed the door to my own room.

Thinking—*Now they will search M.'s room. Now they will search the entire house.*

Attic to basement. Three floors. In the "new" basement, which is finished, and in the "old" basement where no one ever treads which has an earthen floor smelling of rancid damp and rot.

But no: they did not search M.'s room that night, still less the entire house.

This day! This day! This damned day.

So very long, at one end you could not see the beginning in a hazelike mist rising on the lake and drifting inland. Someone with good intentions had switched on all the lights in the house and the house was ablaze like a Hallowe'en pumpkin announcing to all of Aurora that something had happened at 188 Cayuga Avenue: But what?

And all of this M.'s fault, calling such attention to herself, always the center of attention, *I hated her and would never forgive her.*

13.

The Search. Rarely in the history of Aurora and its rural surroundings had adults been reported missing; more commonly, teenaged girls who vanished from their homes were labeled *runaways*. Rarely had there been serious crimes here: a single homicide in eighty years, which would have been labeled *domestic violence* in contemporary times.

No kidnappings, no abductions—if rapes, sexual assaults, beatings, these were not reported to police, consequently were not on the record.

The most common crime in Aurora and surroundings in the

1960s was (teenaged) vandalism: graffiti, mailbox bashing, dumped trash, and fires in fields on Hallowe'en.

And so now in April 1991, confronted with the mysterious disappearance of a local *heiress* the four-man Aurora Police Department required assistance from the Cayuga County Sheriff's Department.

Twenty-four hours is generally considered by law-enforcement agencies too short a period of time for an adult to be declared officially missing but circumstances, and Father's insistence, as well as Father's social position in Aurora, suggested that Marguerite Fulmer's disappearance had to be taken seriously. Local media was alerted, TV and radio bulletins were broadcast striving for a tone somewhere between excitable-alarmed and dignified-restrained. Astonishing to turn on the TV and see M.'s face gazing out at us above the caption *Aurora woman reported missing overnight by family.*

On the morning of April 12 search parties were organized to look for my sister, now acknowledged to have been missing for twenty-four hours. Law-enforcement officers, volunteer firemen of Cayuga County, high-school students released from classes for the occasion, strapping young female athletes from Aurora College, citizen-volunteers from the community. Later in the day, Cornell University students who'd heard the news bulletins about the *missing woman* for whose sake a $50,000 reward was being offered by her family made the hour's journey around the lake from Ithaca in a caravan of vehicles.

Father had wished to offer $100,000 but had been discouraged by detectives who worried that so high a sum would attract too much attention which would be *counter-productive.*

Already police were receiving calls of "sightings"—"suspicious persons"—in places they should not have been. TV and radio stations were beginning to receive calls, which would escalate alarmingly in subsequent days.

Each lead, we were assured by police, would be followed. One of myriad lies in a succession of lies stretching through the decade to come, and beyond.

It was determined, by Lena and me, that no suitcases of M.'s seemed to be missing from her closet. None of her clothes seemed to be missing. (But how would we know? M. had clothes she hadn't worn in years, stored in several closets. Of course, Lena would not murmur an opinion that contradicted any of mine!) She'd taken just the hemp-woven shoulder bag she used routinely, not one of her more expensive leather bags, containing her (Prada) wallet and other personal items.

By midday of April 12 there had been no credit-card activity on her account. No withdrawal from her savings account at the Bank of Cayuga.

There was never to be any "activity" on M.'s accounts. Whether this was good news, not-so-good news, or neutral, was a matter of speculation.

Yes! I intended to join one of the search parties: the girl-athletes at Aurora College.

Except I'd slept very poorly that night. My legs were strangely leaden, a dull pain throbbed behind my eyes. Barely could I make my way downstairs. I had no appetite for breakfast, to Lena's distress; for Lena knew how lightheaded I might be, if I went without breakfast. She had to steady me as I tried to jam my feet (in woolen socks) into (rubber) boots, panting and cursing. But by the time I hiked over to Aurora College the search party had set off without me, there was no reasonable hope of my catching up.

Could have wept with frustration, disappointment! Girl-athletes hiking through fields, united in the common cause of looking for my sister, and I was not among them . . .

Other search parties did not interest me. Fulmer relatives— cousins, nieces, nephews—tramping through fields with a hope of seeing themselves on TV news that night—particularly did not interest me.

Seemed like forever passing out flyers and posters in town. Of course I was anxious but the main feeling was boredom. People gaping at me, asking damn-fool questions. *Are you her sister? When did you see her last? How did she seem?*

Public-library bulletin boards, community center, post office. Had to laugh, seeing *Marguerite Fulmer* side by side with *FBI Most Wanted.*

Weird to see M.'s face everywhere in Aurora and below it the headline MISSING: MARGUERITE FULMER.

It seemed cruel, M. was smiling in the photograph. Looking happy, confident. No idea what was coming for her.

A very good reason never to smile when your picture is being taken, yes?

The shiny little arrow-shaped scar in M.'s left cheek just below her left eye did not show in the photograph. Though I stared and stared, and brought the poster into the light where I could see better, I could not detect it.

14.

Heiress. The first (local) media headlines were *Missing Aurora Woman*, by the next day altered to *Missing Aurora Heiress* to be promulgated through New York State, syndicated by the Associated Press, and by April 17, 1991, find its way into the magisterial *New York Times*.

And once M. was identified as a *missing heiress*, she would never again be identified as merely as *missing woman;* nor would much be said about her career as a *sculptress.*

Indeed, very little would be made of M.'s art, which was "abstract"—"nonrepresentational"—think elegant Kandinsky, Brâncuşi, Moore and not the more popular feminists Marisol, Bourgeois, Kähler; no figurative work, no outrageous images which the media could present to suggest that there might be some connection between the *sculptress* and her fate as *missing.*

Yes, it was a shame! An insult.

Reducing a woman artist to *heiress.* When nothing in M.'s life had interested her less than her identity as an *heiress.* And nothing in her life interested her more than her identity as an *artist.*

15.

Abduction. Eventually it would seem most likely that *abduction* was the (probable) explanation for M.'s disappearance.

That is, a consensus of police, journalists, local authorities, family, relatives, residents of Aurora, and, in time, assorted amateur *aficionados* of (unsolved) mysteries, some of them very ignorant, annoying, and offensive persons, indeed.

In the crazed days immediately following M.'s disappearance, when "sightings" of my sister were being reported through the

Finger Lakes region in New York State and beyond, and Aurora police officers were stationed round-the-clock at 188 Cayuga Avenue to protect our beleaguered house from unwanted visitors (unauthorized journalists, TV crews, volunteers, and vigilantes of all kinds), *kidnapping* had (also) been a possibility.

Of course, considering the social prominence of the *missing woman/heiress*, kidnapping would have been plausible.

Through Cayuga County the name "Fulmer" evoked wealth, stature, privilege.

(Exaggerated, of course! As everything is exaggerated in small-town America.)

Detectives had advised Father to alert them immediately if kidnappers contacted him, not to attempt to negotiate with anyone, and certainly not to pay anyone any ransom, to which Father agreed, for Father was, as he liked to boast, "no fool"; yet, I am sure that if kidnappers had called him, if M. had spoken with Father on the phone pleading for her life, in a heartbeat Father would have capitulated.

But no kidnappers contacted Father. No ransom was (ever) demanded.

The phone rang maddeningly often in those days, for detectives told us that we should keep the phone on the hook and answer it; yet, it was never *the* call.

Each ring of the phone, a leap of the heart; each disappointing call, a sinking of the heart.

And so, barring kidnapping, increasingly it looked as if M. had been *abducted*.

In this case there would never be a call but (cruelly) a proliferation of days of awaiting the call never to come for, if *abduction,* as police allowed us to know, it was likely that M. was no longer living and it was likely that her whereabouts would never be known; most abductions of young women, girls, children end in death, sexual mutilation, hideous death; many/most bodies of such victims are never found though there is the (rare) possibility that the murderer will one day confess to a prison cellmate (for instance) or in the final days of his life suddenly pleading for mercy from God.

Contemplating these possibilities Father drank Scotch whiskey solemnly shaking his head.

"Not at all. No. We will see Marguerite again. *I have a feeling.*"

16.

Legal Rules & Procedures Defining Missing Persons (New York State)

23.0 A missing person is one who is reported "missing" from a residence and is:
a. under 18, or
b. 18 or over, and:
  1. mentally or physically affected to the extent that hospitalization may be required, or
  2. a possible victim of amnesia, drowning, or similar mishap, or
  3. has indicated an intention of committing suicide, or
  4. absent without any evident reason under circumstances indicating involuntary disappearance

23.1 The term "missing person" shall not include a person:
a. for whom warrants have been issued
b. wanted for commission of a crime
c. 18 or older, who voluntarily leaves home for domestic, financial, or similar reasons
d. fitting the designation "voluntary absentee"

17.

The Wallet. The "Clue." Though soaked with rain, battered and muddy, the black leather wallet wasn't old or worn. No cash remained in it, no credit cards or identification, the wallet flat, sadly inconsequential except for the designer's label—*Prada.*

Found by the side of a country road eight miles east of Aurora, nearly a month after M. had (evidently) disappeared, by a bicyclist who'd seen it lying "in plain view" like trash tossed from a passing vehicle.

Weeks had passed, there had been no activity on M.'s credit card. Father was arranging to shut down all her accounts.

Was the battered wallet M.'s? It was true, M. had had a *Prada* wallet, purchased in New York City years ago. As M. had owned other designer items, including the silky white Dior dress, purchased in New York City in those (three) years she'd lived there.

Everyone in the family was convinced that the battered wallet was M.'s. Even those persons who'd never glimpsed M.'s wallet or had the slightest idea of what a wallet of M.'s might look like were convinced—*This had to be her wallet!*

And if it was M.'s wallet this was proof that M. had been forcibly abducted from Aurora and had not left Aurora of her own volition, thus defined as a "voluntary absentee" and not a "missing person."

Except G., the younger sister, was not one of these gullible persons.

Knowing at a glance that the wallet found so conveniently by the roadside was not my sister's wallet.

But—isn't this "evidence"? A "clue"?

Too obviously "evidence"—a "clue." Too obvious to be true.

In exasperation they asked me why I would say such a thing, obviously the wallet was M.'s, for God's sake how many *Prada* wallets would there be in Cayuga County!—especially wallets discarded by the roadside shortly after M. had gone missing.

Because I have my reasons. Because I am not such a fool, to take at face value a wallet that has been, or might have been, *planted*.

Tossed by the roadside, in a visible place. *Not* tossed, inconveniently, in tall weeds, or in a ditch, or into Lake Cayuga.

Tossed by the roadside by M. herself, like trash. As she was tossing away her Aurora life like trash with no more concern for those (of us) who loved her as for those (of us) who disapproved of her.

Exasperation with G. soon turned to dislike, fury. But this was nothing new: no one in the family, in either Father's or Mother's branch of the family, had ever liked me.

And why?—because I am not pretty-pretty like the Princess. And because I tell the truth.

Never. I will never. Never change my mind, that was not my sister's God-damned Prada wallet.

18.

Clues? As you are beginning to see, *clues* abound in any case of a mysterious disappearance.

But so many, and so variegated, there is a *chaos of clues* and not a *story*.

For instance, the lost/found Prada wallet. Which seemed to

some observers to mean one thing, and to others to mean just the opposite.

For instance, on M.'s March 1991 calendar, a notation (in pencil) which no one would think of any significance except me: knowing what "MAM: 10 AM" meant.

Also, M.'s astrological sign: Aries. (M.'s birthday was March 23.) In contrast to my sign: Leo. (Birthday August 18.)

Believers in astrology can make of these birth dates what they will. The human brain strains to comprehend what is incomprehensible. If you fuss and fume enough, you can draw a conclusion or two from the fact that M. was born on March 23, and/or that I was born on August 18, and that Aries and Leo interact in certain fixed ways, but *there is no logic to the births, and there is no relationship between our births:* astrology is a long-discredited, utterly worthless pseudoscience.

Yet, outrageously, an Aurora resident who called herself an *astrological psychic voyager* took it upon herself to draw an extensive astrological chart based on my sister's birth date and the date of her disappearance; shameless hocus-pocus leading to the conclusion that Marguerite Fulmer *never left Aurora but is here (still).*

First, this shameless publicity-seeker (dyed red hair like Little Orphan Annie, Peter Pan collar, and ballerina flats) tried to meet with Father and me, and was rebuffed; next, she went to Aurora police where she was, I'm told, humored as a local eccentric, but finally rebuffed; next, she dared to knock on the door of our Fulmer relatives, some of whom were stupid enough to have invited her inside, to hear her mad prattling . . .

One of our cousins called me, to report. (Oh, I know: Bernice called me *to torment me.*)

Quickly I interrupted: "Just—stop. This is nonsense, and you know it. Marguerite did not believe in 'signs'—Father and I do not believe in 'signs.' Astrology is sheer superstition. 'Psychics' are charlatans. I am going to hang up now."

"But Georgene, wait! This Letitia person says that she can 'see'—"

"She *cannot see.* She *cannot dare to intrude in Marguerite's life.* If she persists, tell her that I will kill her."

"Georgene, what are you saying? You will *kill*—?"

"I will sue her. I said—*sue.* And I am hanging up now, this ridiculous conversation has gone on long enough."

19.

The End of the Beginning. One of the persons of interest to be interviewed by police was W.—"Walter."

Of the men who'd loved M., Walter was the only one I had ever set eyes on, several years before M.'s disappearance.

Showing up (uninvited) one day at our house anxious and apologetic hoping to speak with Father (whom he'd never met) about why so abruptly M. had stopped wanting to see him, and had departed for New York City without saying goodbye—as if Father would have any idea what M.'s motives were! Or any patience, discussing them.

But Father took pity on this Walter, unexpectedly. Invited the distraught young man into his office instead of sending him away as I'd have expected. Listened to him sympathetically. Embarrassed that his daughter seemed to have behaved so capriciously with a man who (it appeared) loved her very much.

This Walter, I didn't know. Not personally. Later it would turn out that he was a research biologist at Cornell, whom M. had met through mutual acquaintances; a "highly promising" postdoc from Harvard who'd been seeing M. for several months, but whom M. had never gotten around to introducing to her family.

Daring to eavesdrop outside Father's office. My heart beating hard.

Did I feel sorry for "Walter"?—I did not.

Would-be lover of my sister. Would-be husband. Weak-willed, to fall under the (trite, predictable) sex-spell of the Princess.

Through the closed door of Father's office, Walter's despairing young voice spoke earnestly, pleadingly.

Asking Father if he knew, if he had any idea, why M. had stopped seeing him? Wouldn't answer his calls?

Why she'd never spoken of Walter to us? Why she'd never invited him to the house?

How shocked Father must have been, to meet "Walter"—about whom he knew nothing.

Of course, I knew nothing of Walter, either. M. had never confided in *me*.

For forty minutes the men spoke together, in grave tones, in Father's office. This was amazing to me for two reasons: the first, that Father seemed to be tolerating the aggrieved young man, instead of ridiculing him; the second, that Father should speak to a stranger for so long on any subject when, I was sure, he'd never spoken to me for forty minutes at a time about anything; scarcely, indeed, for more than four minutes at a time.

For what is there to *say*, when so much must be left *unsaid?*

And how bitter it was to me, that two men should, for forty minutes, or four, so gravely discuss the whims of my sister's heart; sickening to me, the fury-knowledge that never, but never will any men discuss *me*.

Wanting to laugh loudly and rudely so that this insipid Walter would hear me. So that both men would hear me.

Fool fool fool—what did you expect?

Until at last the conversation ended. The door to Father's office opened, Father saw the unhappy young man to the front door.

From the landing I observed them in the foyer below. It was not like Father, in my experience of him, to be so *kindly* with a fool, whether a "highly promising" research scientist or otherwise; it was not like Father to be so friendly toward a stranger with a sexual interest in his daughter.

Stammered words lifted to me on the landing above: "I hope I can see you again, Mr. Fulmer . . ."

And Father's terse reply: "Well. We will see, son."

Son! That odd, unexpected word, like a nudge in (my) ribs.

Father extended his hand for a brusque handshake. The visit was over.

On the front walk Walter checked his bearings. Disoriented, hesitant like one who has forgotten where he is, or why.

Glancing back at the house, at the second-floor windows, with a look of such grief, such yearning, it was clear to any observer that the poor fool half-expected M. to be watching him from above.

But no: no one was watching from the second-floor windows.

No one was going to wave to him from the second-floor windows.

Walter's car, a battered-looking Ford, was parked at the curb at the end of our long pebbled driveway. And how fitting for Walter, a bearish young man, slope-shouldered, with a large head, kindly if baffled eyes, not handsome, though not bad-looking. *Not Cary Grant, Clark Gable but Fred MacMurray: stolid.*

And there suddenly I materialized as if by magic, slightly panting from my run (from the side door of the house) along the driveway beneath tall oaks and yews to the strip of bright green grass at the curb.

Half my face a smile, half my face a sneer.

"Want my advice, Walter? Forget her."

Walter. The casual sound of his name, uttered by a stranger, had to be astonishing to him.

"First point: she doesn't deserve you."

I am the one who deserves you.

"Second point: she treats everyone like this. So don't feel singled out."

I too have been spurned by her.

I too will have revenge.

A flush rose into Walter's face. Taken by surprise by this *chance encounter.*

For a delirious moment it looked to me—(as I stood smiling hard/not daring to breathe)—as if Walter would relax suddenly and laugh at my words, laugh at *me.* For it was a scene in a romantic comedy of the sort I (usually) scorned, in fact did not watch on late-night TV.

We would begin speaking together, laughing together, like old friends, or at least old acquaintances knowing ourselves linked by a common wound.

"Are you Marguerite's sister?"

"I am numerous things, of which 'Marguerite's sister' is but one, and not the crucial one."

Truly, Walter appeared to be entranced by me! Just stared.

"Is it—Georgia? Georgene?"

"'G.' is sufficient."

"Well, hello—'G.'"

But it was a goodbye, not a hello. Clever repartee turns pathetic as used confetti when it fails to ignite.

What I'd hoped would be the beginning of a (thoroughly unexpected, delightful) romance turned out to be the end. The end of the *beginning,* to be precise.

For already W. was opening the door to his car, slipping awkwardly inside. Embarrassed to be confronted with me in this way knowing that I knew what he'd have preferred no one knew, the humiliation, shock, shame of being rejected by a woman he believed he loved; and *no,* this was not a link between us that would define us or even survive these fleeting minutes as W. fumbled to start the car, avoiding my bright gleaming eyes while trying to be polite, nodding, smiling, eager to escape.

In this way breaking off the *chance encounter* that in a romantic comedy on late-night classic-film TV would have had a very different ending.

Driving away, back around the lake to Ithaca, not a backward glance.

And the younger sister G. left behind at the curb staring/glaring after the departing vehicle.

Telling herself she isn't surprised. No!

But still, she is furious. Heavy-jawed, impassive-faced as a crude Inuit carving in soapstone.

I am the one who deserves you. Fool! You will see.

20.

The hideous thing. Inside the cellar wall there had come often a frantic scratching. Through the wintry spring of 1991 and reaching a crescendo in April.

Near-inaudible at first like a faint radio station and then louder by degrees until in my room two floors above I lay awake long nights unable to not hear it, through the walls I heard it, through the furnace vent I heard it, barefoot on the hardwood floor I felt vibrations, a continuous thrumming-shuddering that determined the rhythm of my heartbeat, became the heartbeat in my mouth, loathsome, unspeakable; and soon then, high-pitched cries through the floorboards that tore at my nerves like wires strung unbearably tight.

The hideous thing, the creature, its panicked scrambling claws, filthy matted fur and maddened eyes, almost I could see the eyes in the perpetual twilight of my room with a single lamp burning (for even at my age I retained a childish fear of the dark), smell the stink of the creature's terror which was like the scent of fresh blood in my nostrils, and would not let me sleep. And so in the night making my way down the back stairs barefoot and trembling and along the (lightless) corridor past the shut door of the housekeeper's room to the cellar door at the rear of the old house in silence unerring like a sleepwalker and with the audacity and recklessness of the sleepwalker who understands that, so long as the trance of sleep is upon her, she cannot be harmed, she is suffused with great and terrible powers, and how fortunate it was, the door to Lena's room was shut, in her bed Lena slept oblivious of the angel of death passing so closely by her, for if the housekeeper had surprised me, if the foolish old woman had attempted to deter me, what might have happened to Lena, what might have come crashing down on Lena's head, crushing her skull I could not have prevented, whispering *Thank you God, thank you God for sparing Lena* as, descending the cellar stairs, no need of switching on the bare lightbulb overhead, for *the hideous thing in the wall,* the creature, its scrambling claws, high-pitched unbearable cries, could not elude me, a shovel in my hands, one of those old, heavy iron shovels with wooden handles worn smooth by the effort of generations, and with this shovel I struck at the creature, slamming the flat side of the shovel against its head again, again, and again until its cries ceased, it convulsed a final time and released foul-smelling liquids and was still.

On my knees on the earthen floor, tears creasing my cheeks, I had not wept like this in years, in silence my lips moved—*Thank you God.*

Then, in a corner of the earthen-floored cellar, with the bloody shovel digging a shallow grave in which to hide the broken bleeding *thing.*

21.

"Voluntary absentee." As I would not concede that the Prada wallet found (so conveniently) by the roadside soon after my sister's disappearance had to be my sister's wallet so I would not wholeheartedly concede, as so many others did, that M. had to have been abducted.

There came to be a quarrel among the Fulmers for the predominant thought was—

We must not say anything to suggest that M. is anything other than a victim of an abduction, we must present a united front against the world. And so G. became a pariah in the family. For with my rude mouth I would say—*Bullshit.*

Which has always been my way. *She* admired me for it—saying those things aloud, and loudly, that no one else would say (including M.).

But why, they demanded, would Marguerite leave home in such

a way? She might have left openly, as she'd left for New York City a few years before; she might have simply moved out of the house to live elsewhere in Aurora, or in Ithaca; no one would have stopped her, certainly, though her father would have been unhappy with such a move, so soon (he would have said) after M.'s mother had "passed away."

Why make of herself a "voluntary absentee," as the law called it. Why cause so much trouble for her family, and for law enforcement?

Father was particularly disgusted with me. (Though I was, indeed I am, Father's only daughter remaining now in Aurora.)

Why would your sister act so recklessly, so selfishly, of course she wouldn't have, why do you say such cruel stupid stubborn things, of course how like *you*.

So they disliked me, even more than they'd previously disliked me.

Accusing me of being provocative, perverse. Insulting the (precious) memory of my sister.

Hoping that my sister will never return home.

Which made me laugh in their faces as I have always laughed in their faces.

She's alive! She's in hiding, and alive! You are fools to be grieving her!

Not a victim of abduction but a "voluntary absentee" and alive— somewhere.

22.

The Story of the Scar. Never was the story told to me and yet I knew it by heart. I knew it as if it had been my own story. I knew it from M.'s silence which was an angry silence. I knew it from the shiny little scar in M.'s face that winked and squinted if you looked at it too long like a furtive eye. I knew it because it *had not* happened to me. I knew it because no man had ever followed me in the early dusk after school when I was seventeen years old on my way to my piano lesson and no man had ever come up swiftly behind me and struck me so hard with his fist against the back of my head I fell without a cry, only a faint whimper of something like surprise— *Oh why* . . . And no man had ever dragged me along the ground by my ankles on my stomach, on my face scraping raw against filthy concrete and helpless to scream though not far away was a busy thoroughfare, traffic hurtling past like thunder; and no man had ever cursed me, and put his hands on me in a rage, and tore at my clothing, and afterward there were leaves and twigs in my hair and dirt stuffed into my mouth to gag me and a bleeding face like a Hallowe'en mask. *None of this had ever happened to me and yet I knew. I was not a beautiful girl of seventeen and I would never be a beautiful girl of seventeen and yet I knew, I rejoiced in what I knew because beauty deserves to be punished because beauty is selfish. Because beauty should be dragged by its ankles and its face scraped raw. Because beauty is not a child with a wrong-sized "bite" that had to be surgically corrected and beauty is not a mouth too crowded with teeth for the lips to close or a forehead low like an orangutan's or coarse curly hair and a nose shiny as a bugle or eyes that appear mismatched or "crossed" though they are staring straight at you seething in contempt.*

23.

Not Really, Seriously Assaulted. This had been a time before Mother died. A time so long ago G. was but a young child, ten years old.

This time long-ago when my sister returned home after dark crying, disheveled and her face bleeding, by which time Mother was in an agitated state for Marguerite had failed to appear at her piano teacher's house and the piano teacher called our home to ask where she was, if she was coming, lessons had to be canceled forty-eight hours ahead of time or the usual fee was expected, and so Mother was annoyed but also frightened, her first impulse was to scold, shocked to see what a sight M. was with torn and filthy clothing, and her hair matted, and her face bleeding, quickly Mother pulled M. out of my sight where I was gaping and gawking for (of course) I'd been waiting for Marguerite to come, home peering out a window into the rain dusk; Mother pulled Marguerite into a downstairs bathroom and locked the door, ran cold water with which to rinse M.'s bleeding face, telling M. to please stop crying, not to become hysterical, not to disturb Father (who was home, and in his office at the rear of the house), and not to call attention to herself, what on earth had she done to herself Mother demanded; and M. said that a man had "hurt" her—a man had "put his hands on her" and "dragged her" along the ground— and told her he would "hurt her worse" if she told anyone; and he would hurt her family too. She had not seen his face clearly but he was an "adult man"—"a big man"—"a white man"—he had seemed angry with her as if he knew her or (maybe) he knew Father; (maybe) he'd been watching her, waiting for her crossing the park to the piano teacher's house; and Mother cried, what a thing to say!—of course this person didn't know Father, that was ridiculous, how would Father know such riffraff, M. should never make an accusation like that again. And Mother washed M.'s face tenderly. And Mother gave M. one of her pale pink lozenge-pills to "calm her nerves"; and Mother ran a hot bath for M., in her own bathroom upstairs with the claw-footed tub, and examined M. without her clothes so far as M. would allow her for M. was crying, wincing, pushing Mother's hands away, still agitated and upset despite the lozenge-pill.

After M. soaked in hot water for a half-hour she became drowsy, and ceased whimpering, and Mother helped her climb out of the deep claw-footed tub, dried her tenderly in one of Mother's enormous thick bath towels, and put a bandage over the bleeding wound in M.'s face, took some time to brush briars and dirt out of her damp hair; led her like a young child to lie down on Mother's bed with a quilt over her admonishing her to *try to sleep.*

All of this, or much of this, Mother relayed to Father. What a lot of fuss! This *bad thing* that had happened to their beautiful daughter.

All this I knew, don't ask how. Nothing happened or happens in our household that *I do not know. For I do.*

Should they take M. to a doctor?—should they call the police?

Or—should they spare M. the further upset, by *keeping it quiet.*

At this time Father had an office in Aurora, upstairs over one of his Main Street properties. Through the weekdays, sometimes until Saturday noon, Father was at work. What the exact nature of Father's work was, we did not know, for Father was mysterious laying his forefinger against his nose saying *Money begets money, in the right hands.* He summoned one of his most trusted attorneys, a close friend from college days at Cornell, he and the attorney and Mother discussed the situation at length for it was "not an easy call"—as Father said: for, as Mother said, M. had not been *really, seriously assaulted*—(by which was meant: M. had not been *raped*)—so far as Mother could see; and by M.'s account, the man had been interrupted by someone or something, or had changed his mind, releasing her and running away, leaving her limp and unresisting on the walkway, now on her back, part-naked, arms and legs helplessly outflung and her breathing so short, she could not call out for help.

In this way deciding to *keep the matter to themselves.*

To spare M. To protect M. Nothing in the newspaper!—Father was determined.

Protecting their (beautiful) (honor-roll) daughter. Protecting the family name.

For one thing—the "main thing": as the attorney explained—M. had been "roughed up" but had not been "raped."

"Rape" has but one legal meaning and, it seemed, the man had not "raped" M., he had not even "molested" M. with his fingers, or so Mother claimed.

Yes, he had "done things" to her, that was clear. He had said "terrible things" to her—and he had "threatened her."

But lacking witnesses it would be difficult to prove (exactly) what he'd done.

And M. had not wanted to be taken to a doctor. Excitable, and upset, stammering *No no no.*

Admitting that she hadn't seen her attacker's face. It would be impossible to identify him. And the humiliation, and the shame, and "people talking" at her school, that would be like a stain on clothing, a permanent stain, worse than an actual scar.

For M. was one of the popular girls at Aurora High School. Pretty, popular, a class officer, active in many clubs, expected to be admitted to an excellent college. Not Aurora College where her mother had gone, and several of her relatives, but Cornell perhaps, or Vassar, or Amherst.

M. acknowledged that she had not been seriously injured. M. acknowledged, she had not been *really, badly hurt*—by which M. meant, without saying the actual, ugly word, she had not been *raped.*

Just beaten, and dragged along the pavement, and her face scraped raw, and her teeth bloodied. Disgusting things he'd said to her, she would wish she could kill him, murder him. If she'd had a knife. If she'd had a knife and the courage to use it.

But—*it hadn't been the very worst. No.*

Over a period of days, the issue was decided. Quietly they'd talked to M.

The younger sister G. had not been told. Not a word!
Yet, the younger sister G. knew. All.
To be a (greedy, voracious) younger sister is to know all.
Aurora Police were not called. No appointment was made to
bring M. to our family doctor. No report of an "assault" was ever
made. No record, the last thing you want in a small town is anything
like a *record*, a *reputation* Father's attorney did not have to explain
to Father and Mother nor to M. herself, M. was an intelligent girl,
she understood.
   *Worse scars than a near-invisible shiny scar on her face that looked,
close up, in a certain sort of light, like a teardrop.*

24.

Passing. At Cornell M. would pledge Kappa Kappa Gamma, one of
the preeminent sororities on campus.
   Why?—She'd laughed, saying, just to see if I could do it. If I could
pass for a Kappa.
   *A teardrop scar is easily disguised by makeup, all sorority girls wear
makeup, most commonplace disguise of all.*

25.

At the piano. After the assault in the park which (officially) had
not occurred when M. was a junior in high school, M. refused to
return to piano lessons. Refused to return to the brownstone facing
the park where, on the ground-floor, garden level her piano teacher
had met with her each Thursday after school.
   Refused to begin lessons elsewhere saying she'd come to hate
the very sound of a piano, the distinctive sharp smell of a piano, she
threw out her lesson books but Mother retrieved them from the
trash, brushed them off and gave them to me and for a few months
at the age of ten I took piano lessons, not with M.'s teacher (who
was the best piano teacher in town) but with an instructor at my
grade school, practicing my lessons when M. wasn't in the house
for M. could not bear to hear my stumbling efforts at the keyboard; but soon it became clear that M.'s younger sister G. had no

talent for piano, no talent for music, she could not "count beats"—could not hear when she struck a wrong note—flat, sharp; and so at the piano often I would drum the keys with my fists; at the Steinway spinet which had originally been the property of great-great-grandparents of M.'s and mine which had a cherrywood veneer and smelled of a certain kind of furniture polish that roused me to rage drumming with my fists at the black keys in particular which vexed me until some of them became stuck and did not play as they had for my sister M. and so one day Mother came up silently behind me and seized my fists to stop their drumming, closed the keyboard, and brought my piano lessons to an abrupt end with a single word uttered in disgust—*Enough.*

And soon then, the Steinway spinet was locked. And ever after, the Steinway spinet was avoided, in a corner of the living room. To this day, no doubt badly out of tune, its formerly beautiful cherrywood dried and warped, mice nesting in its frayed strings and a patina of dust covering its surface, the piano has remained locked and silent and protected from the brutal assaults of a malevolent child's fists.

26.

The haunting. Soon after M. left us it began to happen. When I was alone. On a street in town. On my way to the grocery. The drugstore. The Mills Street Post Office.

Glancing up squinting and seeing—*her.*

M., just turning a corner. M., crossing an intersection, back to me. M., reflected in a store window staring contemptuously at me.

Strangely, I did not ever see M. with another person: always, M. was *alone.*

Nor did I see M. in a vehicle, either driving or as a passenger.

Of course, these sightings of M. were not really *of M.* Rather, strangers who resembled my sister; or, in some cases, didn't really resemble M. much at all, when I recovered enough from my shock to look closely at them.

Often too, in months to come when I began walking (alone) on Wells Road, and on the hilly campus of the women's college, and in the old Aurora cemetery (in which the earliest Fulmers were buried beneath weatherworn tombstones tilted in the soil, thin as playing cards) on gusty days in particular I would see, or imagine that I saw, M. at a little distance from me, but usually with her back to me, or in profile; most frequently, inside the post office, where I was trapped behind the counter like a pig herded to slaughter, in the late afternoon just before closing there came the door pushed open with unusual force as if blown by the wind, a blurred presence entering, the visceral shock of seeing past the bland pie-face of a customer at the counter—*her face* . . .

"Ma'am, are you all right?"—the pie-face called sharply to me seeing that I seemed to be fainting, could not remain upright falling, grabbing blindly at something to break my fall, hold myself up, whimpering in fright as heavily I fell to the not-clean linoleum floor behind the counter clutching at sheets of "forever" stamps crumpled in a sweaty fist.

27.

"Farewell Note."

> *Dear Father,*
>
> *Please forgive me.*
>
> *I will explain my selfish behavior one day.*
>
> *Your daughter,*
>
> *Marguerite*

This laconic note, hand-printed, in blue ink, I took the liberty of composing on a sheet of white construction paper belonging to M., on the day following the afternoon when I fell in a dead faint behind the counter at the post office and was revived only by a (busybody) coworker kneeling beside me pressing paper towels soaked in lukewarm water against my burning face; and urged to leave as soon as I could walk unassisted, though twenty-five more minutes remained of my workday.

Imagined as a therapeutic undertaking, to alleviate Father's anxiety, which was exacerbating my own.

(For Father too had begun to speak of "seeing" M. in town, at a

distance; always with a feeling of shock and disbelief that did not
subside for hours afterward.)

Hours of practice were required for me to master just M.'s signature, the only part of the note I dared to write in her hand.

Block-printing was something that M. might have done, in fact.
In mimicry of an "artistic" font.

Selfish was not chosen lightly but with much care and precision.
For virtually everything in M.'s life was, indeed, *selfish*.

Later, rereading the note for the dozenth time, I decided to add
a date beneath the signature—11 April 1991—using the French
way of dating, as it was M.'s way, one of her affectations.

In this way hoping to allay Father's fears: that Father would
cease grieving for M., obsessing over M., accept the fact that M.
was gone (voluntarily) from Aurora, and *get on with his life*.

Yes, and turn his fatherly attentions to *me*, his (other) daughter.

"No. Better not."

So my better angel advised me. Though the note was, in my
opinion, a masterpiece of brevity, and though I agonized for days
over "discovering" it amid M.'s papers in her room, I decided finally
not to bring it to Father after all.

Not because it was a forged document but rather that it might
be exposed as a *forged document* by police suspicious of my finding
it belatedly among M.'s things; if the letter was addressed to Father,
why wasn't it left for Father to find?—they were likely to ask. And
perhaps it was a giveaway, that I'd signed only M.'s name, and did
not attempt to mimic her handwriting for the rest of the note.

"Absolutely no! *Not*."

Father might have been relieved to think that M. had not been
abducted and murdered but still, Father would have been upset,
and would have notified the Aurora police; in turn, the Aurora
police would have brought in a forensic handwriting expert to determine if this note had really been written by M. Though I was
fairly confident in my ability to deceive the experts, I was not one
hundred percent confident, and could not risk being caught. And
so I ripped up the very note I'd labored over for hours reasoning,
like Falstaff, that discretion is the better part of valor.

Did not dare risk. Foolish risk. Unnecessary risk.

"Forging a note"—the fools would naturally suspect me *of having
something to do with M.'s disappearance.*

28.

"Disappearing." It's a basic human right! For all I know, it's protected by the U.S. Constitution.

So I have argued. So, in advancing the possibility, if not the probability, that my sister Marguerite disappeared of her own volition, as a "voluntary absentee," I annoyed and offended quite a few Aurora residents who preferred to think of her as a *victim of abduction.*

But M. did not like to think of herself as a *victim.* Pride, vanity, integrity, "feminism"—all these mitigate against *victim.*

As I, though I have plenty of reasons to complain of mistreatment, misunderstandings, and indiscriminate discrimination, do not think of myself as a *victim,* thank you.

In the history of the United States an untold number of persons have disappeared: no doubt, millions.

Like M. they leave for work one morning, a seemingly ordinary morning, and are *never seen again.* They go on brief journeys but never reach their destinations. They drive away in their own vehicles, or board buses, trains, airplanes. They walk, hike in remote places. They leave for a rendezvous with a friend—and never show up. They step out the back door to breathe the night air—the house has been so confining! They call out to a spouse that they are making a drive to the drugstore and will be right back; but they are never *right back.*

If they withdraw money from a bank, it's clear that they are voluntarily "disappeared." But many do not, as they do not pack suitcases, prepare for a trip. They don't take a change of clothes, a toothbrush. Like M., they leave no farewell note, they give no "sign."

According to statistics, more than six hundred thousand Americans disappear each year, of which ninety thousand are never found; of those found, approximately one-half return of their own volition, and one-half are located by police.

Of those voluntarily missing, who then return, a considerable number are emotionally unstable. "I just wanted to see if someone would ask if I was okay when I returned"—a woman who'd gone missing for several weeks told police.

One fact struck me: of those who return voluntarily, ninety-seven percent return within two weeks.

Perusing the news, I discovered that, during the week that M. disappeared from Aurora, residents of Lake George, Cheektowaga, and White Plains (all New York State) also disappeared, and did not return: a pattern? Sheer coincidence?

The resident of Lake George took out a small family boat with an outboard motor to fish on the lake alone, near dusk, and in the morning the boat was found by New York State rangers empty and drifting . . . In Cheektowaga, a suburb of Buffalo, a woman several years older than M., wife, mother of two young children, disappeared in her Ford station wagon having said she was going grocery shopping . . . And in White Plains, a distance of 250 miles from Aurora, a man in his mid sixties, a recent widower, disappeared from his home apparently on foot, leaving his house unlocked, the radio in the kitchen tuned to a popular local station, dishes soaking in the sink . . .

How eagerly the brain seeks to *make sense* of these cases. To unify them, somehow. To relate them to M. somehow.

Each case of a missing person, fascinating in itself. Those cases in which the missing persons were located, or showed up, with perfectly banal reasons or excuses, were of no interest at all, like the persons themselves, intriguing only because they were *missing*.

So I came to see how my (beautiful) (doomed) sister was but a figure in a pattern, not singular; how each year a certain number of Americans *must disappear,* to make up the statistics.

Could there be a year when *no one at all* disappears? Why was this not likely? Improbable? But not impossible?

When M. had been gone for several weeks, and "sightings" of her began to subside, and we heard less frequently from the (blundering, incompetent) police, I went to the Cayuga County Public Library and spent hours researching *missing persons,* including the infamous Judge Joseph Crater who'd vanished, allegedly, after having stepped into a taxi on West 45th Street, Manhattan, on August 6, 1930. But the circumstances of Judge Crater's disappearance were very different from those of my sister's disappearance for, as it turned out, Crater had been involved in various political schemes, and was soon to be exposed as corrupt in the press; and he'd left a touching note for his wife: *Am very weary. Love, Joe.*

Judge Crater was never found, as we know. Nor did anyone ever unearth a single clue to his disappearance.

Similarly, Jimmy Hoffa. Like Crater, a man involved with criminals, no doubt executed and his remains hidden—a different sort of mystery.

But the other sort, that remains baffling because inexplicable: a fifty-year-old man in Seabury, Oregon, disappears on his way to work; his car is found on the shoulder of a freeway, abandoned: keys on the floor, doors locked. A forty-six-year-old woman in Larchmont, New York, a middle-school principal, disappears over a weekend; a forty-nine-year-old insurance salesman in Evanston, Illinois. Fascinating, at least initially. The cases are excitedly reported and there is a flurry of media interest, sometimes rewards are offered, sometimes "suspects" are questioned, but weeks, months, and years pass . . .

Sometimes, of course, they *are* found: that is, their corpses.

Or, they are discovered alive, hundreds of miles away, living under different names, with forged documents and Social Security numbers. But I am not concerned with these people: I am concerned with those who'd disappeared permanently.

Like Marguerite, who never returned to us after twenty-two years, and has never been located.

29.

Aftermath. Of course, there came to be rumors. Preposterous, laughable.

Such as: M. was "pregnant"—M. was "involved in drugs"—M. had "eloped" with a man whose identity was so shameful, she could not acknowledge it publicly.

Such as: M. "committed suicide" by weighing herself down with rocks, wading out into the lake, and drowning one hundred feet from our house in Lake Cayuga.

(At least, this ridiculous rumor could be investigated: The Cayuga County sheriff's department arranged for a diver to search the lake behind our house, to a distance of several hundred feet; a rocky shoreline, an uneven lake bottom, at its deepest fifteen feet, with much seaweed and debris from construction sites close to shore. Skeletal remains of creatures were indeed discovered amid the muck but—*no human remains.*)

As for "eloping"—how was it possible, when no man appeared to be missing; at least, no man known in Aurora and vicinity?

No one reported missing at the time M. disappeared, so far as police knew?

Yet, we had to endure the humiliation, the ignominy, the (nuisance) calls and letters, the *innuendo* that accompanies a "disappearance."

Months, eventually years—

> INVESTIGATION INTO MISSING AURORA
> HEIRESS STALLED
> POLICE CONCEDE "NO LEADS"

And—

> FAMILY OF AURORA HEIRESS MISSING
> SINCE APRIL 1991 "STILL HOPEFUL"

If only. If only we (Father and I) knew, is M. dead, and should we mourn; or is M. in hiding, and should we erase her from our memories?

30.

If my daughter is living, no fee is too great to pay to find her. And if my daughter is not living, no fee is too great to find her poor remains and give them a proper burial.

So Father spoke solemnly, publicly. But to no avail.

After twelve desperate weeks, frustrated by the lack of progress in the police investigation, without my knowledge or approval Father hired a private investigator from Buffalo to search for her.

This "P.I." was a suave smooth-talker like Richard Widmark in a *noir* film of the 1940s who did little more, indeed less, than the police had done while racking up a shocking expense account over several months which Father would refuse to pay in its entirety. Whether his name was "Leo Drummard" (as his New York State private investigator's license declared) or whether the name was a *noir* fabrication I did not know but I did not trust this person whom Father had hired in desperation, through a business associate's referral—that is, bringing into our private life an utter stranger and allowing this stranger to search M.'s room, even to photograph her things, under the (mistaken) impression that "nothing had been removed" from M.'s rooms since the day of her departure.

(Of course, as I had protected my sister against even the possibility of scandal by hiding away, at the rear of her closet, the silky Dior slip dress, that may, or may not, have been soiled with a stain of some lurid sort, so too I had busied myself, before Aurora police returned to search her things on the morning of April 12, taking away a drawer of M.'s personal correspondence and her 1991 desk calendar with its diary-like notations including, for March 31, the scribbled "MAM: 10 AM" [which I knew to be "mammogram: 10 A.M."—an appointment at a radiology clinic in Ithaca], and disposing of these far from our house, in a Dumpster behind a slovenly 7-Eleven store. By the time busybody "Leo Drummard" came on the scene not a thing remained in M.'s room that might have been interpreted, or misinterpreted, as a "clue" to her disappearance.)

"Well, Mr. Drummard," I said, my voice as heavy with sarcasm as my eyebrows were thick, dark, and heavy, nearly meeting at the bridge of my noise, "—did you find anything 'of interest' in my sister's room?" and Mr. Drummard glared at me and said, "Miss Fulmer, I think you know the answer to that question, don't you," and I said, almost demurely, resisting the impulse to laugh in the fool's face, "Why yes, Mr. Drummard, I believe that I do."

However, when Drummard requested permission to search our entire house, attic to cellar, I overruled Father by saying, vehemently: "No, sir. You will not."

"But—how am I to investigate your sister's disappearance if . . ."

"You can be sure, Mr. Drummard, that my sister is *not in this house*. If you'd done your homework you would know that my sister's wallet was discovered on a country road and the consensus among professionals is that she was *abducted by force*. (Or is *by force* assumed in the word *abduction?*) She is likely somewhere far away from here. Hardly in this house. What my father and I expect from you is to complete the *woefully incomplete police investigation* and find her."

At which Drummard glared at me with fury. Male indignation, impotence, fury.

But he dared not utter an impudent syllable since Father was present, and Father was his employer.

"Miss Fulmer, that is exactly what I intend to do."

Pushing a fedora onto his blunt bullet-head, like a "P.I." in a *noir* film. Taking his leave of us by shaking Father's hand gravely but only just nodding brusquely to me, fat face flushed.

From a window I observed Drummard stiff-striding out our front walk, to his vehicle parked at the curb.

Silly man!—as if he could threaten *me*.

This would be the last, as it was the first, face-to-face exchange I had with the "P.I." from Buffalo, who would disappoint Father and me as the police would disappoint us, but from this shady personality we would be informed of much that police detectives never troubled to report to us: that there had been, at the time of M.'s disappearance, and afterward, numerous female victims of amnesia, women of M.'s approximate age, scattered across North America, who were never identified; women who had (seemingly) "disappeared" from their lives and turned up elsewhere, in places they did not recognize, victims of assault; possibly, victims of abductions whose abductors had decided not to murder but to free them.

So many!—amnesiac victims, female, who might have been M., but were not; whose pictures, faxed by Drummard to us, were of strangers.

Of course, some of these women *resembled M.* Not so blond as M., not so beautiful as M., not so refined-looking as M., but *resembling* M. as if they might be distant cousins.

More upsetting than these were (unidentified) female corpses, discovered in remote rural areas, as in vacant lots in cities and towns; in parks, in forests, by roadsides; in shallow graves, and in landfills; women and girls of all ages, most of them described as "poor"—"mentally ill"—"suspected prostitutes." A few weeks after M.'s disappearance the naked body of a woman of M.'s approximate age was discovered in Alcott, New York, on a littered beach of Lake Ontario; so badly decomposed that identification could be made only through an examination of dental work, which required a week's time before Father and I were notified that the remains were not M.'s . . . *Such grisly relief! To be grateful that someone else's daughter and sister has died, not your own.*

Through the effort of Drummard to assure us that he was working very hard, and justified in charging Father an outrageous sum, we became aware of a nightmare of female victims discovered in abandoned houses, in ravines and lakes, hidden beneath piles of debris, bodies so burnt that nothing remained but a few charred bones, teeth; floating in the Mohawk River at Troy, in a campsite in the Adirondacks, at the outskirts of the village of Lake Skaneateles, the most "scenic" of the Finger Lakes less than an hour's drive from Lake Cayuga. There was the figure of pathos "Jane Doe"—a disarticulated skeleton discovered buried in the earthen floor of a dairy barn near Middleport, believed to have belonged to a girl of about fifteen, who might have died a decade before; another "Jane Doe," a woman of about forty, garroted, bizarrely preserved in a storage locker, wrapped in airtight plastic, in Syracuse.

And these were just *unidentified female bodies* found in upstate New York within a narrow span of time.

In this way I learned of the notorious "Highway of Tears"—a 450-mile rural stretch of Highway 16 between Prince George and Prince Rupert, British Columbia, Canada—where the bodies of dozens of women, most of them aboriginal, have been found between 1970 and the present; and of equally notorious I-35 running north-south through Oklahoma and Texas where for decades the bodies of numerous women and girls, many of them never identified, have been dumped by the wayside. *The earth is bloody with the bodies of raped, murdered, cast-aside women and girls.*

Though none of these turned out to be M., nor could have been M., yet I began to lie awake in my bed thinking of them, strangers, yet sisters (of a kind); never before had I seriously thought of other women as *sisters,* for it was enough (it was more than enough!) to have my own older *sister.*

Thinking *So many! How has God allowed so many.*

Thinking how, if things had been just slightly otherwise, M.'s corpse could be among them. *Or my own.*

31.

The stoic. Over the years Father has become a stoic. Now in his early eighties he still walks ramrod-straight, his white hair is thick and tufted, and his eyebrows have grown gnarled over melancholy pouched eyes. His skin is relatively unlined, for a man of his age, but appears to have thinned, and bleeds easily; his forearms and the backs of his hands are often bruised for he must take prescription medicines that "thin" his blood in the hope of preventing strokes.

He has ceased publicly lamenting the loss of Marguerite, as he has ceased complaining bitterly of the "shoddy" police investigation into her disappearance, that was allowed to *go cold* so soon; nor does he condescend to speak of the "private investigator" from Buffalo who failed so utterly. He has given up his office on Main Street but continues to involve himself with philanthropic work and with his financial investments, sometimes with good results, I gather, and sometimes with not such good results, depending upon the vicissitudes of the market, to which he is cheerfully indifferent—indeed, *stoic.*

Of the Fulmer family estate, I have only the dimmest sense. I know that, following the advice of his money managers, Father has "divested" certain stocks and real-estate properties; it is my sense that his holdings have diminished somewhat, but we never discuss such matters. I understand that Father has established a trust to assure my financial well-being, if and when I find myself living alone in this house; there is said to be an equivalent trust established for Marguerite, should she ever return to claim it.

(Yes, relatives shake their heads over what they perceive to be Father's stubborn optimism, not realizing that it is simply a stoic's way of *hedging his bets.*)

In recent years Father has, surprisingly, resumed the habit of church-going, interrupted for decades after Mother's untimely death; he has become a "pillar" of our Anglican church, a familiar presence amid the company of Fulmer relatives he has grown to tolerate, and whom I avoid. Not often but sometimes, if I am in a perverse mood, I accompany Father on Sunday mornings for it can be gratifying to snub nosy relatives and neighbors; in the Fulmer family pew Father sits in silence, in melancholy repose, an unopened hymnal on his lap.

Once, at the conclusion of a particularly tedious service, Father glanced about us blinking as if uncertain of his surroundings, and murmured in my ear: "Remind me, please—Why did your sister marry outside the church? *Did* she 'marry outside the church'?"

Somewhat stricken by this query I could only stammer: "I— I can't speak for Marguerite, Father. No one can."

Surely it is progress of a kind that Father so rarely speaks of M. even on her birthday, or on the anniversary of her disappearance, but I know that he is thinking of her as his eyes soften with regret, sorrow.

At which time I reach out to squeeze his cool, thin hand, with its bruised skin, which responds with an absent-minded sort of paternal affection, and a startled glance at me—"Oh! Hello!"— as if, for the moment, he has forgotten who I am.

32.

Confession. Here is an unexpected surprise. In March 2013 a sixty-nine-year-old inmate serving a life sentence without parole at the Clinton Correctional Facility in Dannemora, New York, suddenly broke down and confessed to the Catholic chaplain that he'd killed a number of women in upstate New York in the years 1982–1994, of which one, New York State detectives had reason to believe, was *Marguerite Fulmer.*

Desperate to be forgiven for his sins, and said to be suffering symptoms of syphilitic dementia, this person, whom I will call "Gordo" (his fatuous name resembles this fatuous name), confessed to abducting, raping, and murdering "women and girls" in the Finger Lakes region of New York State as well as other parts of the state (Albany, Rome, Troy, Lake George, Rochester, and Buffalo); "Gordo" had been a suspect in two of these cases but had been prosecuted and found guilty for just one, the abduction, rape, and murder of an Albany woman in 1995.

Shown photographs of (possible, likely) female victims "Gordo" had identified my sister M. "unhesitatingly," according to detectives, saying, "That's one of them"; though when questioned closely he was vague about the circumstances of when and where he'd found her, where he'd taken her, and how he had disposed of her body; at first claiming to have abducted her from a parking lot in a city—maybe Rome, maybe Albany. Later, "Gordo" changed his account claiming that he'd confused M. with another "blond-haired" woman, claiming he'd abducted M. from a "country road" and left her body in a lake weighted down with rocks.

Not a big lake. One of those—what d'you call them—little lakes . . .

Asked if it was Lake Cayuga "Gordo" frowned as if he'd never heard the name before, then nodded vigorously.

Kai-yoo-gah. Yah.

Asked why he'd killed these women whom (evidently) he had not known "Gordo" explained earnestly *It's the only way to get them to pay attention to you.*

In all, this degenerate claimed to have stalked, abducted, raped, and murdered eleven women and girls—that he could remember. The prison chaplain was convinced that he was telling the truth but detectives were skeptical. It's common in cases like this (evidently) that a serial killer will exaggerate the number of his victims. He may be boasting, bragging to his listeners/hoping to impress them as well as "baring his soul." He might have killed some of the women but not all of them; he might be appropriating murders committed by a cellmate or a buddy; he might be misremembering. Clearly "Gordo's" brain was deteriorating, his memory corroding. He grew excitable remembering isolated (and lurid) details of the killings but not which woman was which, or where.

He insisted yes, he'd killed them all. He spoke in a wistful cracked voice. He wept "like a sniveling baby." He was said to have lost a great deal of weight as if (possibly) he had some other illness like cancer. He was talking fast, stammering and coughing—"desperately anxious" to confess his sins before it was too late.

So many of them, I killed them all. When I could, I buried them in water.

All this was disgusting to me, to be told. But fortunately the detective (a stranger to me) spoke with me and not with Father who I'd said wasn't available to come to the phone right now.

I am temperamentally equipped to deal with such a preposterous development in the *cold case* as a hippo is equipped, with its thick rubbery skin, to deal with pestiferous insects.

I explained to the detective that Father's health is surprisingly stable for a man of his age but still, Father is *not young.* Things can change rapidly in the elderly if there is a trauma, a shock. I was determined to protect Father from any shock.

And so I said firmly: Unless this individual can lead police to an actual body, and unless there is forensic evidence linking that body to my sister Marguerite *definitively,* I have no intention of informing my father, or even of listening much longer to this drivel; for if (syphilitic, demented) "Gordo" has not said anything specific enough that might be said to *prove* that he was my sister's murderer it is clearly all a ruse, and a waste of my time.

There was a startled pause. Relatives of murder victims are more tractable and credulous, on the whole, than I, perhaps; no doubt, they are grateful for the most meager crumbs tossed at them by overpaid, underachieving "professionals" in law enforcement, and it would never occur to them to doubt what nonsense they are told, let alone articulate their doubt so clearly over the phone as I have done.

And then the detective said: "Fair enough, Miss Fulmer. You are correct, there is no way, at the present time, for us to know if this man is telling the truth about your sister being one of his victims."

I hung up the phone. Hand trembling with indignation and fury.

For: I know that "Gordo" *is not* telling the truth, indeed this is *drivel.*

33.

The dawn: the summons. Awakened by a tapping against the window near my head—hail, icy rain. Jolted awake in this twilit hour before dawn in late March 2013 in despair of falling back to sleep.

Flurries of snow, a sudden blizzard on the very eve of April! Not unknown in upstate New York but a rude surprise nonetheless.

Waking I feel a sensation of floating—bodiless—like "atoms in the void"—then—the sudden coalescing of the self, the soul; the world slams back at me like a door shutting in my face.

I, I, I am G. I am who-this-is. I am no other.

Fierce wind, light swirling snow, a maelstrom of snow. The old house rocks in the wind like a galleon on the high seas. Lights flicker like fibrillating hearts—if the electricity goes out we will freeze!

By 8 A.M. snow is falling less heavily. The sky is clearing in rough patches, a hard cobalt blue that would freeze your tongue if you were foolish enough to press your tongue against it.

At a high window I can see out into a sculpted sea of flawless white untouched by human or animal tracks.

And then I see her: my sister Marguerite, in dark clothing somber and still against the white snow. Beneath one of the yews in the back lawn as if she has been there, very still, patient, waiting for a long time.

My first impulse is to step back quickly before M. sees me. But of course M. sees me.

So many times I have "seen" M. in the past twenty-two years, this is not such a shock, really. But this time M. does not turn away aloof and disdainful but continues to gaze at me, lifting her eyes to my window where (I realize) I am not hidden but revealed.

My heart has begun to pound rapidly. I would like to call to Father, or to Lena, but my throat is tight, I cannot speak. My fear is so great, it is a kind of peace, like a tidal wave washing over me— *Now, it has happened. I have waited so many years.*

Hastily I throw on clothes: bulky down jacket, trousers. Jam my feet into boots. Not M.'s boots, *my boots*—that fit my large solid feet in woolen socks.

My hands are trembling badly. I fumble with the doorknob.

I am outside, at the rear of the house. It is windy, surprisingly cold. Dry powdery snow blowing against my face as if to suffocate.

Pleading with M.: I am not young like you, I am forty-seven years old. My joints are arthritic. My legs have become flaccid, my ankles are thick, swollen. In this cold wind my eyes leak tears.

Sternly Marguerite watches me. The little teardrop scar on her left cheek glitters in the sun. *Come with me, it's time.*

There is the promise that I will be strong enough. I will not be tested beyond my strength.

Marguerite turns slowly to lead me through the frost-stiffened grasses. I am given to understand that *my life* is something fragile and living between us like the flame of a candle.

Oxygen rushes to my brain making me giddy. I am elated, excited: for at last I know where Marguerite *is*. Foolish to think, M. could be "buried" anywhere.

I feel a thrill of satisfaction, that I alone of all the world am granted this knowledge, withheld from others.

Whatever happened, it was no one's *fault*. And now it is clear: Marguerite is *buried nowhere*. Not water, and not earth.

You silly Gigi! Come take my hand.

Making our way through the overgrown backyard. Everywhere are fallen tree branches like amputated limbs. A juniper tree, split by lightning this past winter, or the winter before, has never been pruned but allowed to split further, partly sprawling on the ground now like a girl who is bowed down, hair spread before her.

My boots sink inches deep in the hard-crusted snow—I am not nearly so graceful as M.

Tracks in the snow, small tracks, birds, animals. Deer—you can see the sharp hooves. And where are Marguerite's tracks?—I don't see them.

But I can see Marguerite clearly. It is crucial to follow her, never losing sight of her slender dark figure gliding light as shadow.

In the years since M. vanished from our lives Cayuga Avenue has lost its prestige. Neighboring houses have been sold, rezoned, and divided into apartments. Fulmer relatives have quietly moved away, I am not sure where. For they never invite us.

Father and I live alone in the big old house, I've forgotten— Lena died several years ago. We are looking into her replacement.

In the house, we live in just a few rooms. M.'s room is untouched, awaiting her return.

Rarely do I step inside M.'s room for I have memorized it entirely. The mirror on the back of the closet door, which is now kept closed. If I position myself correctly I can see, through this mirror, the mirror on the bureau; but the mirror on the bureau reflects nothing any longer: an emptiness.

In the closets M.'s beautiful clothes are intact, I suppose. Except for moth holes in woolen things. Camel's-hair coat, cashmere sweaters. Perhaps mice have built little nests on the shelves. Open a closet door, it will look as if M.'s expensive shoes have been cavorting together on the floor.

No, I didn't know: what the March 1991 mammogram said. *If* the mammogram said anything out of the ordinary.

How would *I know?*—M. did not confide in G.

Not a *clue,* I don't think. Though (possibly) among M.'s things which I'd hurriedly thrown out were subsequent documents, printouts of medical tests, not unlike Mother's myriad tests, no way to know this, pointless to speculate, too late now and already too late then.

Come on, Gigi! Forget that.

You know, it's time.

At the top of the incline M. has paused, waiting for me. Without my knowing we'd crossed over into the no-man's-land owned by the township but not maintained. Here are shattered trees, underbrush, litter. Shocking to see, near Wells Road, that people have been using this land as a *dump.* What sort of slovenly citizens toss out broken toilets, filthy mattresses, wrecked bicycles, ravaged tires?—I am sorry that M. has to see this.

Perhaps for this reason M. leads me on an alternate path, away from the dump and through a stand of tall ravaged oaks and yews, where snow is deeper, no one is likely to intrude.

Oh, my lungs ache! I am feeling how delicious it would be, to lie down in the fresh snow. To make a little nest for myself beneath yew limbs heavy with snow like wings.

Such loneliness, I am feeling now. I have not realized until now.

As M. walks resolutely ahead. I am frantic not to lose her. For I am so, so lonely.

I have been unwell, my blood pressure is high, my eardrums feel as if they might burst. *I am not what people think. Only you know, dear sister forgive me.*

Why does M. walk so swiftly, knowing that I can barely keep up! Wanting M. to take my hand. She'd hugged me, when we were girls. *Why are you crying, silly Gigi!*

Slip-sliding in the icy snow. If I fall on this hill, my leg will twist beneath me. If I fall heavily, something will crack in my rib cage. I will lie very still, I will make a little nest for myself in the snow, the freezing wind will blow over me, sparing me. Bones creaking about me like the ribs of an old seafaring ship and the anger seeping out of my heart that beats slower, slower.

Slow-dawning sun, a cold blue eye opening overhead with excruciating precision.

The Invitation

FROM *Mystery Tribune*

BRITTANY PLANS TO SPEND the summer interning at *The Globe*. Between junior and senior year at Boston College's School of Journalism, students can sign up for an unpaid summer of experience on one of the area papers. First come first served. She knows she's lucky to get *The Globe*. But the day before she is due to begin, everything changes. An old romantic interest she hasn't heard from in more than a year calls and, after the minimal "how've you been?" and "yeah, I know what you mean," asks if she wants to spend a month with him in Barcelona. "I'm paying," he adds, before she has a chance to say no.

She puts a name to the face. Brock is someone in whom she once had more than a passing interest. Now she brings up the good things rather than the bad and thinks what the hell.

She says yes.

Brittany puts down the phone, astonished at how quickly she's assured Brock it sounds perfect. She'll have to invent something she can tell *The Globe*'s newsroom editor. She was so eager during their interview. No matter, she thinks now. Another journalism student will be glad to get my spot. She'll take the train to New York and be ready to leave with him in a week. A trip to Barcelona suddenly seems meant to be. Brittany stops packing only long enough to get online and google Gaudi, the Sagrada Familia, and the Gothic Quarter. A series of romantic-looking villages along the Catalunya coast beckon from her iPad screen.

Having taken a cab from Penn Station to Brock's fourth-floor Greenwich Village apartment, Brittany is out of breath from hauling both her suitcases up the narrow stairs. She is further flustered when a woman wearing one of Brock's shirts buttoned wrong and nothing below mid-thigh opens the door. The two women look at each other in embarrassed confusion. Brittany can hear her former lover's voice from the bedroom: "Who's there, honey?"

The other woman, awkwardly introduced as Penny, quickly changes into her own clothes, and leaves without saying goodbye. Brittany can't remember if a soundtrack accompanies her retreat. Now Brock is doing a bad job of explaining Penny's presence— something about wrapping things up and last goodbyes and thinking she'd said she was arriving this afternoon—as he urges Brittany to sit at the Formica-topped kitchen table and brews her a cup of her favorite piñon coffee. See, he remembers. After each garbled utterance, he turns to her with those earnest eyes she recalls once made her forgive him almost anything, waiting for the absolution he's been used to since prep school quarterback fame.

"Anyway, you're here." That boyish grin. Yes, Brittany thinks, I am.

The intoxicating scent of the small white fruit of a desert tree roasted to perfection soothes Brittany's hurt pride and banishes her doubts. She told *The Globe* an out-of-town aunt had been taken ill and said goodbye to her Boston friends after excitedly revealing her sudden invitation. Returning in defeat would be harder than ignoring Brock's bad timing and telling him he could go off to Europe without her.

That night Brittany thinks she can still smell Penny on Brock's sheets. She might have played hard to get for a day or two, but boyfriend habits die hard. Instead, she mimics her old responses to his romantic overtures, fakes orgasm as she did when they briefly lived together, and does her best to convince him it's all good. The afternoon she returns for the trip, he proudly flashes the Iberia tickets at her, pointing out that he splurged so they could fly Business Class. Brock was always one to speak in dollar signs.

Brock's offer is enticing. But an internship at *The Globe* isn't something to be taken lightly. Brittany feels tempted, but says no.

Her first day on the job, the newsroom editor tells them he's glad to have such a promising group of interns. He asks each of them if they have any special interests or fields of expertise. "Write about what you know," he says. "It may sound like a cliché, but believe me, it's the best advice anyone will ever give you."

Brittany can't think of an answer that might set her apart from the other bright young students, all women and all but one wearing uniform tan slacks and starched white shirts. The one from Idaho is in an outdated denim jumper over a pale pink blouse.

Theater? Gardening? Brittany surprises herself, then, by saying something about the crime beat, how her father was a cop and took her with him to the precinct on Saturdays when she was a child. She'd always been interested in what he did. The newsroom editor looks at her quizzically, then says she should feel free. The other three interns look at her with a mixture of jealousy and mild resentment, for beating them to something more interesting than fashion or summer socials.

Over the preceding months a stalker or peeping tom plagues Cambridge in the area around Harvard Square. A freshman in one of the women's dorms is the first to report catching sight of a guy looking in her first-floor window when she's undressing one night. Upon seeing him, she immediately draws her curtains but can still glimpse his silhouette. She says he lingered. Black or white? She can't be sure. But with a paunch. A few weeks later it's a middle-aged housewife who reports she was followed home. She manages to enter her house and lock her door before he can force his way in. When she looks out the window he's gone. No, she hadn't noticed any distinguishing features.

The woman who was raped while jogging around Fresh Pond early one morning in May also has a hard time providing the police with a physical description of her attacker. She felt more than saw him, thinks he might be Italian or from somewhere in the Middle East. Dark. Shadowy. A strong smell of garlic. She can't be sure of his build. She says she feels like she left her body during the ordeal, must have been concentrating on making it out alive. Several other rapes that happen within a two-month period might well have been committed by the same guy. None of the victims mentions anything as unique as a birthmark, a tattoo, or unusual piece of clothing.

These are separate events. No news story suggests a connection. But so many events so close together and in such a short period of time? Brittany has a hunch. As a child she remembers her father telling her that hunches are important. "Ignore them and you may be sorry," he said, as if he knew his daughter would be solving her own crimes one day.

And so, Brittany's summer job begins with an aura of possibility. She visits her father's precinct, where a couple of the guys who remember him give her access to files, photographs, evidence. They get a kick out of helping Joe's baby girl. Not that they expect her to be able to come up with anything useful.

Brittany reads interminable police reports, stares at disturbing images of bruised thighs and enlargements of desperate finger-nails concealing possible clues. She covers her dining room wall with pictures she hopes might suggest a pattern. She links some of the items with red linen thread she finds in the sideboard drawer. She can't remember when or why she bought it. The wall looks like something straight out of one of those TV crime shows in which the alcoholic or bipolar detective defies his superior who's suspended him for flouting the rules, and he solves the crime. Brittany sees only a random display of clippings, each concealing a story she can't decipher.

The newsroom editor isn't demanding. Let these young women get the feel of a big city newspaper, he thinks. That's enough. If none of them produces an article all summer, at least he won't have to waste time rewriting bad copy. He isn't being paid to turn amateurs into professionals; this is all extracurricular. No one babysat him when he started.

Brittany puts down the phone, surprised that she said yes so quickly.

From that moment on, she thinks of little but Barcelona. A place she's never been. During the few days at Brock's before they de-part, she easily falls back into her old habit of making do with a less than ideal situation. When she isn't acquiescing to her ex-lover's frequent demands for sex, she passes the time watching the Rick Steves's Barcelona and Catalunya video she downloads from YouTube or thumbing through the Fodor's on Brock's bedside ta-ble. He's highlighted entire pages with yellow magic marker. She's never been with a man she doesn't feel she has to make excuses for—even to herself. Her father, for all his old-boy reputation on the force, was a big kid her mother managed until he'd died suddenly of a burst aorta at the age of fifty-seven. Brittany has no greater expectations of her own relationships.

By the time they're settled into their Business Class seats on the transatlantic flight, Penny is no longer a memory. Brittany doesn't have to work at convincing herself she'll have a great summer. The Bloody Mary's the flight attendant deposits on their tray tables go a long way toward sustaining her anticipatory mood.

Maybe she'll be sorry later, but Brittany says no.

It's Lynda with a y, the intern from a small Idaho farming community, who sends Brittany in a direction she hasn't thought of before. Her quiet colleague finishes a predictably effusive note about Boston's big Flower and Garden Show at the city's Seaport World Trade Center. The piece is filled with superlatives about the spectacular color of a particular rose and the velvety petals of another. Their editor praises her efforts and publishes it in the next day's home and garden section.

Brittany notices that he leans in a little too close when pointing out a few places where Lynda might have shortened her sentences. She thinks the Idaho transplant seems uncomfortable. Perhaps that's why she invites her over after work that afternoon: "Do you like Chinese?" she asks. "I can pick some up on my way home. Here's my address. It's not far from here."

Brittany thinks Lynda seems grateful for the invitation. Maybe she doesn't yet have many friends in the city. She arrives with a modest Merlot and a bouquet of spring flowers that look like she picked them herself. What to Brittany is a spontaneous invitation, provoked by the embarrassing sight of an overeager boss, is obviously more than that to Lynda. She must be lonely, Brittany tells herself.

Over vegetable spring rolls and stir-fried tofu with rice—she'd forgotten to ask if Lynda is a vegetarian—the two women talk about the office atmosphere but avoid sharing confidences about their boss. Brittany asks Lynda a few polite questions about her family and why she chose Boston College. She tries to interest herself in Lynda's answers. It's her guest who stands up and approaches the wall with its map of clippings, photos, thumbtacks, and red thread.

"I heard you're looking at these attacks," Lynda says. "What makes you think they're connected?"

"I don't know. Just a hunch. Anyway, it doesn't hurt to explore all angles. The police haven't solved any of these crimes and women are afraid. We seem to have all summer with no real pressure to produce. I thought I'd follow my instincts." Brittany pushes one of the two fortune cookies across the table and breaks the other in half, extracting its tiny hidden strip of paper and holding it at arm's length. Her reading glasses are in the kitchen.

"You'll be hungry again in one hour," she reads out loud. Both women laugh. No Eastern wisdom, this fortune is meant to be humorous. Brittany wonders who writes these predictions and how much they get paid. Despite her disbelief in such portents, she thinks of the leftover pieces of cheesecake she has in her refrigerator. If they're hungry again in an hour, she can always bring them out.

Lynda hasn't broken her fortune cookie. She doesn't seem interested in the message it holds. She is staring at Brittany's evidence wall, obviously absorbed in what it has to say. "What makes you draw a connection between the Fresh Pond rapist and the stalker outside the Harvard student's window?" she asks. "Is it the dates?"

"Maybe. He must have been frustrated when she drew her curtains. And then the attack at the pond is just two days later."

"I've always wondered what motivates stalkers, rapists, men who are compelled to attack women." Lynda might have been talking to herself; her tone is even, almost emotionless.

Brittany doesn't respond right away. She wonders why she only really thinks about the physical evidence and not the more motivational aspects of these crimes. Maybe because they are just the extreme edge of how most men see women, she thinks, rapists simply being those who take their sense of conquest to unacceptable, criminal, levels.

But Lynda is talking again, still thinking out loud: "Riggio's isn't far from Fresh Pond. I've eaten there. Delicious food, but I've only gone with my sister when she came to town, never with a man. It's like they cook every dish with so much garlic. You smell of it for days."

Brittany makes a mental note to check out Riggio's.

She knows she's accepted Brock's invitation without giving it much thought. Sometimes you just have to take risks, she tells herself now.

They hop in a cab from Barcelona-El Prat to their hotel in the city center. Brittany wonders out loud if it wouldn't have been cheaper to use RENFE, the train that leaves every half hour and only takes twenty-five minutes, but the dismissal on Brock's face tells her he doesn't think in terms of saving money. The more expensive, the better. He's reserved a room he's several times described as luxurious at a place called Majestic Residence. "It has everything," he tells her, proudly, as if he built it himself. Brittany decides not to question any more of his choices. After all, this is his invitation. She will try to relax and accept the gift on his terms.

The next couple of weeks is a whirlwind of sightseeing and restaurants that advertise diverse continental menus. Brittany favors long slow walks on which they might get deliciously lost and then found, discovering hidden treasures crying to be explored. She wants to eat at small family places where they can savor such local dishes as cannelloni stuffed with stewed beef or some of the tapas for which the region is famous.

Brock insists on their not getting tired. He anticipates all-night sex every night. Brittany bears up under his unimaginative performance, trying to show an acceptable level of emotion. He's clearly still the beloved quarterback, at least in his own eyes. Each morning after breakfast at the hotel, he rushes them into a waiting taxi and they head for the destination of his choice. He checks off museums and churches like a birdwatcher making his way through a master list of species.

The day they take the tour to Montserrat, the famous monastery an hour outside the city, Brock seems to have memorized its combination of Romanesque, Gothic, and Renaissance features. He spouts all sorts of details about the Benedictine order and its devotion to the Virgin of Montserrat. Brittany enjoys the mountain air but doesn't love the hodge-podge architecture or the way the square blocks interrupt the natural beauty of the rocky cliffs behind them. Brock talks nonstop all the way back to their hotel. He seems intent on transmitting his excitement to Brittany, or maybe just sparking in her some appreciation of his vast knowledge.

They've been in Barcelona for three weeks. Brock always finds something new in the guidebook for them to see. Brittany longs to walk aimlessly in the fascinating city, eat in restaurants unlisted in Fodor's, strike up conversations with anyone who speaks English or is willing to put up with her limited high school Spanish. Brock always has a better plan. Eventually Brittany surprises him by announcing she feels like staying at the hotel. She needs some time to herself. He should go out. She doesn't mind, will find something to keep her busy. He looks at her in disbelief but finally has no alternative but to give in.

Brittany spends much of that day talking to one of the hotel maids. The woman, whose name is Gabriela, speaks some Spanish and even a little English she's picked up from guests over the years. Brittany asks her about her family. They are from a small village called Taüll in the Boí Valley. Brittany looks it up in her guidebook and sees photographs of old stone buildings nestled against a backdrop of mountains, some of which remain snow-capped most of the year. "Three and a half hours each way," Gabriela responds to Brittany's question. Seven hours round trip! Brittany tries to imagine the energy that must take.

Gabriela has eleven brothers and sisters. She is one of the oldest. Her own husband left her, and her three children stay with her widowed mother while she sleeps at a hostel in the city during the week. She only sees them a few hours on Sunday when she gets up early to make the long bus trip home and returns as late at night as she can so as to be ready for work again Monday morning.

Brittany rejoins Brock for dinner that evening. He talks without stopping about his day—a monument to local victims of the Spanish Civil War and a museum he's sure she will be sorry to have missed. He says he just happened to spend time with the museum's director, who was impressed by how much he knows, and they made plans to see one another again. "You'll love him," he tells Brittany, assuming she'll want to meet him too. She listens attentively, then tries to share her conversation with Gabriela. Brock makes a pretense of listening, scanning the menu as he does. She stops, waits for him to give her his full attention. "What's the matter," he demands, a bit grumpily she thinks, "I can listen and read at the same time. One of the hotel maids, you say?"

Brittany thinks about Brock's invitation from time to time but is glad she turned him down.

It is Lynda's comment that a few days later sends Brittany to Riggio's. She tells the owner she's working as a summer intern for *The Globe,* visiting area restaurants, interviewing the staff. She doesn't exactly say she's writing for the food section but leaves that impression. He tells her he has seven working there, including the kitchen help, bartender, hostess, and the two waiters who attend the small dining room. He doesn't object to her talking to them as long as it doesn't interfere with their jobs.

Brittany has lunch at the restaurant a couple of times. She asks to be seated at different tables and manages to strike up friendly conversations with both waiters. She just wants to get a sense of who they are. Such impressions go a long way. The following week she shows up for a late dinner, hoping to be one of the last guests when the place closes. The chef comes out to inquire about how she enjoyed her meal, and she's equally friendly with him, even flirts a bit. They talk for almost ten minutes.

It takes her several more maneuvers, though, before she can figure out where each of them was on the date and at the time of the attack on the Fresh Pond jogger. When she's gotten responses from everyone but the chef, she decides to ask him outright. Despite her best efforts, she blows her cover and is forced to beat a hasty retreat. Now it's time to check out each alibi, see if they all pan out.

As often happens when someone follows a good lead, the perpetrator begins to slip up. Riggio's bartender claims he was at work on the morning in question, but Brittany knows the restaurant doesn't open until eleven. The jogger's rape took place much earlier, just past first light. And then, the bartender often comes in an hour or so later than the rest of the staff. Not many diners order more than a beer or wine with lunch, and Brittany has observed that the waiters themselves handle drinks that don't have to be mixed.

Brittany convinces one of her father's old buddies at the precinct to run the man's name. It turns out the bartender is a registered sex offender. He exposed himself some years back in Hartford. Brittany thought Connecticut and Massachusetts would share such records, but for whatever reason the guy had no trouble getting the job at Riggio's. The sex-offender piece gets the sergeant's attention. When they bring the bartender in for questioning, they get a DNA swab. It matches the DNA in the jogger's rape kit. The bartender confesses, though he claims he has nothing to do with the other crimes linked by red thread on Brittany's dining-room wall.

The day Brittany's story is published, the newsroom editor opens a bottle of champagne. Paper cups all around. Brittany credits Lynda in her article. Lynda says she shouldn't have, it was only a chance comment after all. After reading the story she looks at Brittany: "You'll be hungry again in an hour," she says laughing.

Hmmm, Brittany thinks, she's got a sense of humor. This might be the beginning of a real friendship.

It was an easy decision taking Brock up on his offer of such an exotic-sounding trip. It isn't like this sort of invitation comes along every day.

But the rest of their time in Barcelona is awkward at best. Brittany begins making excuses when Brock comes onto her each night. They spend their last two days in the city separately. He manages to check off the final two monuments on his to-do list and meet with his museum-director acquaintance. She accepts an invitation from Gabriela to visit her village. They invite Brock but he isn't interested.

It's at the old stone farmhouse where Brittany finally has a chance to taste the famous calçotada, those long spring onions grown during Catalunya's winters, cooked in the ashes of an open fire and then wrapped in paper and served alongside a bowl of romesco sauce. Gabriela's mother says something to her daughter and nudges her to translate for their guest. "She wants you to know that the red-pepper sauce should have nuts," Gabriela tells Brittany in her halting Spanish. "She's sorry she didn't have any." Brittany looks at the older woman gratefully. "Tell her it's the best meal I've had," she replies, surprised that her eyes are unexpectedly wet.

On the flight home Brittany thinks of all the things she liked about this Barcelona adventure. She's been to many wonderful places, gotten a glimpse of another culture, had experiences she'll always remember. She buries what the trip cost her in sexual favors and humiliation.

She wonders what interning at *The Globe* would have been like.

The Blood-Red Leaves
of Autumn

FROM *Mystery, Crime, and Mayhem*

TWO KIDS FOUND the body lashed to a silver maple. They'd snuck into the tree farm on a dare, two preteen boys playing grab-ass among the blackberry brambles and creeping vines that grew at the base of the trees while the starfield rotated endlessly overhead.

Station B-31861 didn't have a coroner or a detective or even an official cop, just one doctor and a skeleton crew of security officers. The security officers spent their time dealing with petty theft and malicious mischief and breaking up the occasional fistfight. Even highly educated botanists and engineers got bored after enough time stuck in space tending the station's living archives devoted to plants of the North American continent. They played practical jokes on each other, got drunk on the twenty-second-century version of the same moonshine their ancestors had brewed, and screwed each other. Eventually some of them had kids who were even more bored than their parents.

Kids hadn't been part of the original plan for Station B-31861, but human beings rarely stuck to the plan. If they had, Station B-31861 and all its sister stations wouldn't still be orbiting Earth, waiting decade after long decade for the world's politicians and mega-corporations and religious zealots to agree on exactly how to reverse centuries of abuse to the planet's fragile ecology so that the plants and animals in the living archives and the people who tended them could return home.

If the ecological disasters could even be reversed. Wallace Beckett was head of security. He didn't know the science. He just had faith that someday it would all work out.

He crouched next to what was left of the body, trying to ignore the stench coming off the remains. The dead woman had been there a while. Her wrists had been tied together and yanked up over her head, then fastened to the silver maple's trunk. The thin synthetic twine used to bind her wrists and her torso to the tree had sunk into the wood as the tree grew, the bark overlapping the twine in places.

Even a layman knew it took a while for a tree to do something like that.

"Know who she is? Or was?"

The question came from the station's director, Lyzette Golden. She was the only true administrator on the station, and the only other person in the farm with Beckett. The division heads were part-time administrators. Their primary functions remained scientific. Station directors like Golden oversaw supply runs, scheduled crew rotations, and arranged VIP tours, all with the assistance of a lone human clerk. An AI could probably do the job just as well, but Golden put a human face on B-31861 at all the official functions sponsored by the global consortium that owned B-31861 and all her sister stations.

Beckett didn't technically report to Golden. The consortium oversaw all security personnel on the stations. In theory that kept Beckett and his crew independent from any directives Golden might want to impose that would hinder his job, but the consortium was headquartered on Earth. Golden might not have any direct authority over him, but Beckett had always tried to treat her with the kind of respect her title deserved.

"I was about to ask you the same question," he said. He'd pinged the division head in charge of the tree farm to see if the man knew who the dead woman was, but so far he hadn't responded.

The tree farm, like all the farms on Station B-31861, was a pest-free environment. That meant no maggots, no beetles, no creepy crawlies to feast on the dead woman's flesh. What was left of her was a decomposed mess. The stench overwhelmed the rich loamy scent of healthy growing things. If the body had been left in one of the farms where food for the station was grown—farms that actually required a human presence on a regular basis—the smell alone would have alerted crew to the body long ago. The tree farm required far less human attention.

Those two kids would be having nightmares for weeks. He knew he would.

Golden leaned closer to the body. She'd put on a thin environmental suit, probably to keep out the smell. Wallace hadn't. He'd smeared ointment beneath his nose that kept out most odors he encountered in his job, like vomit, but the ointment wasn't designed to handle something like this.

"No identifying marks on her clothes that I can see," Golden said. "I sent for the doctor to see if we can get a DNA match."

Not to mention cause of death. The remains of her head didn't look bashed in, and there were no obvious burn marks that could have been made by tools the engineers used for station maintenance on what was left of the rest of her. That was the limit of what Beckett could tell just from looking at the body.

He was out of his depth, and he knew it. Golden probably did too. Security officers weren't trained to investigate murders, and that was clearly what had happened here. The dead woman hadn't tied herself to the tree.

"Anyone miss a shuttle in the last few weeks?" he asked.

Station B-31861 had a crew complement of over a thousand, most of whom tended the more labor-intensive of the hundred farms contained in the rotating rings arrayed around the station's central core. No one had reported any missing crewmembers. Reports like that were routed to security.

It was possible that a crewmember who was rotating off the station could have missed their shuttle back to Earth. Golden tracked the comings and goings as new crew came on board to replace crewmembers who'd decided not to renew their yearly contracts, although her clerk probably handled most of it. If Golden routinely sluffed off too many of her responsibilities onto her clerk, slipups could happen. Overworked people made mistakes.

"No one missed a shuttle," Golden said. "I checked on the way here. If she's one of the crew, someone's been logging reports and doing assignments she should have been covering. No pings from the system."

Reviewing crew logs wasn't part of Golden's job. The system only notified her if scheduled logs weren't updated. If the division heads didn't take care of the problem themselves, it fell to Golden to remind the errant crewmember that failure to perform their assigned tasks had far greater consequences for the future of the planet than simply forgetting to watch grass grow.

"You said 'if' she's crew," Beckett said. "What else could she be?"

He couldn't remember the last time the station had any visiting VIPs. The farms on the B stations just weren't a big enough draw for celebrities and billionaires who could not only afford to pay their way into space for themselves and their entourage but also pay a hefty fee to the consortium for the privilege of getting a personal tour.

The A stations were the ones that got all the attention. Billionaires didn't have a problem spending the kind of money necessary to tour a station where they could see elephants and rhinos and buffalo and a million other species preserved in the habitats on the A stations.

Golden straightened up and stretched her back. "Some people have been here a very, very long time," she said without looking him in the eye. "They've learned how to keep their dirty little unauthorized secrets."

"Unauthorized" was admin-speak for anything not in the original plans for operation of the stations. Brewing alcohol on farmland was unauthorized. Gambling was unauthorized. Bribing shuttle pilots to hide contraband substances in supply runs was unauthorized.

Children were unauthorized.

Beckett couldn't suppress his astonishment. What she was implying seemed more impossible than a crewmember who'd failed to show up for a scheduled shuttle ride back to Earth.

"You think she's . . . what, someone's hidden child?" he said.

Was such a thing possible? Children might be unauthorized, but they were still registered in the system.

The leaves on the creeping vines that ran along the ground had begun to turn red. Long ago the botanists in charge of designing the farms had determined the plants they housed would have a better chance of surviving in space if their environment mimicked Earth's seasons as much as possible. The air in the farm felt crisp, the climate-controlled humidity sharp against Beckett's skin, but that wasn't what sent chills down his spine.

Autumn in space. It shouldn't be possible, but it was. Beckett lived every day with things that would have seemed impossible two hundred or even one hundred years ago. B-31861 had been in existence for generations. The trees in this farm were mature, the blackberry brambles thick and overgrown.

Beckett couldn't rule out the possibility that the dead woman was someone's unregistered child. Food wasn't rationed. The station grew more than enough food to support the crew, and the water processing system supported the farms and the crew with ease. Crew movements weren't tracked beyond an ancient key-card system that allowed authorized crewmembers access to the restricted areas in the station, which was pretty much everywhere except recreational facilities and dining areas. Hacking the key-cards apparently wasn't all that difficult. The two preteens had managed it.

"We won't know who she was until the doctor gives us a report," Golden said, "but don't discount the possibility." She gave him a hard stare through the thin skin of her environmental suit. "One thing I do know is someone killed this poor woman. That some-one might still be on this station, or they might have rotated out by now. I don't want a killer on my station, Wallace. Am I making myself clear?"

"Yes, sir," he said.

She didn't have to tell him that—technically she didn't have the authority to tell him that—but the fact that she had made him re-alize she must be making a record. Environmental suits had video and audio recording capabilities, and the tree farm didn't have audio or video surveillance equipment. Beckett had been making his own photographic record of the scene, but hers would be far more complete.

She hadn't put the suit on just to avoid the stench. She was cover-ing her ass. If that was the case, she'd taken a big risk giving him as much information as she had.

Just what was going on here? And what, exactly, did she know that she wasn't telling him?

"Cause of death was a broken neck."

Emilia Sopa sat in a chair next to the blessedly empty exam table. Whatever she'd done with the body, at least Beckett didn't have to look at it.

Dr. Sopa was currently the only doctor on the station. The station's other physician had rotated out only six months into a twelve-month contract. He'd forfeited the hefty bonus he would have been paid at the end of a normal rotation just to get the hell off the station. Not everyone was cut out for life in space.

Emilia Sopa had been on the station nearly thirty years, far longer than Beckett's eight. Unlike her departed colleague, she was apparently content with a life that consisted of treating minor injuries, performing the occasional routine surgical procedure, and delivering babies. Any crewmember who developed a serious medical condition was immediately released from their contract and shipped back to Earth.

"What else can you tell me?" Beckett asked.

"She was dead before she was tied to that tree." Sopa called up a screen and squinted at the readout. "The long bones in her arms and legs showed signs of past trauma." She glanced at him. "Never treated in this office."

"Trauma? You mean broken?"

"I mean trauma. Evidence of scoring by sharp objects in multiple places."

She closed the screen with an abrupt movement of one hand and leaned back in her chair, her face impassive, but Beckett could see the anger in her dark eyes. She was furious and trying to contain it.

"This woman was systematically abused over a period of time," she said. "Repeatedly stabbed with an object sharp enough to damage her bones without breaking them. Wounds like that should have been attended to by a physician. They weren't. I ran her DNA. She was never treated by any medical personnel on this station."

Beckett's stomach roiled, but Sopa wasn't finished.

"She was put on display after she was dead." Sopa's dark eyes practically blazed with the force of her anger. "Whoever killed her could have buried her. There's certainly enough soil in the farms on this station to bury a body—hell, the undergrowth in that particular farm would have hidden the body even if she wasn't buried—but they tied her to that damn tree instead and left her there. Abusing her for years wasn't enough."

Beckett swallowed hard against the bile he could feel building at the back of his throat. Sopa had removed the body from the tree farm, and she'd not only noticed something he hadn't, she'd reached a conclusion he hadn't thought of. He told himself it was because he hadn't known the woman was dead before she'd been tied to that tree, but it didn't help.

He had to clear his throat before he felt like he could trust his voice. "How long has she been dead?"

This time Sopa didn't consult her notes. He had a feeling she hadn't needed to before, that she'd only called up the screen to give herself time to try to control her emotions.

"I can't give you time of death," she said, "but given the decomposition, I'd say two to three months. I'll have to review the farm's hydration records, temperature variations. Consult with the botanists who work that farm to determine how long it would take for that tree to grow enough bark to cover the bonds. At this point, I'm not sure I want to do that."

Beckett almost asked her why, but then he got it.

The dead woman's body had been left on display in the tree farm for a purpose. The only people who would have seen it—who would have gotten whatever message the killer had meant to send—were the botanists assigned to work there.

Beckett didn't know how often the botanists actually accessed the farm itself, but he was going to find out.

"You said you ran her DNA," he said. "Did you get an I.D.?"

Just because she'd never been treated in the medical office didn't mean her DNA wouldn't be on record with the station.

"No match," Sopa said. "And before you ask, I ran her DNA against current crew and those who rotated out within the last five years. I didn't have to run it against visitors. The station had none during that time period."

"Why five years?"

"This woman was in her early twenties at the time of death," she said. "The station doesn't accept crewmembers under eighteen years of age, and children below eighteen aren't allowed to tour the station, so there was no need to check any earlier tours."

New crewmembers weren't allowed to bring children with them. The only children living on the station were those who'd been born here.

The sick feeling in Beckett's stomach was eating his guts alive. He had to know if Golden was right, if the dead woman had been a crewmember's child.

"Run her DNA against current crew and those who rotated out within the last twenty-five years," he told Sopa.

"Twenty-five years? I told you—" she began, but Beckett cut her off.

"This time you're not going to be looking for her," he said. "You'll be looking for her parents."

Kenneth McGwire, Division Head for the crew of botanists assigned to work the tree farm, blustered into Beckett's office an hour after Beckett left Dr. Sopa to her DNA research on the dead woman's parentage.

Like all the offices on B-31861, Beckett's office had just enough room for a comfortable chair that automatically adjusted to the contours of his body, a desk that held controls for the holo-screens that floated over the desk's surface, and a single visitor chair. Only in Beckett's case, he'd removed the standard visitor chair and replaced it with a reclining lounger.

Space for crew on the station was limited. Most crew quarters housed more than one person. Only a few division heads or people who'd had children got quarters of their own. Beckett's eight years on the station didn't qualify him for his own quarters.

While he'd liked most of the security crew he'd shared living space with, more and more often these days he needed time to himself. The reclining lounger gave him a private place to sleep.

He'd added a few other touches to the office to make it feel more like a home, like the holo-screens he'd placed on the walls. Currently two of those screens displayed images of Earth as seen from the station. A third displayed a forest scene complete with clear blue sky, mature pines and healthy aspens, and a gurgling brook of clear water.

The holo must have been taken more than a century ago. He'd found the image in the station's computer database under the file name "Hope." Beckett supposed the name came from what the scientists on the living archives hoped to achieve one day—a return to the natural beauty of the Earth of the past.

Beckett preferred to think of the image as "Belief." Hope was ephemeral, something that could easily be dashed. Belief let him think that the years he'd devoted to this station in support of a common goal hadn't been wasted.

McGwire shot a look at the reclining chair, but he didn't sit in it. "What the hell's the idea of locking my crew out of the farm?" he said.

McGwire was one of those wiry little men who thought belligerence made up for a lack of height, and rudeness was an adequate substitute for respect. Attitudes like that didn't work for Beckett. He deliberately ignored McGwire and kept scrolling through the information on his screen.

"I asked you a question," McGwire said.

"And I pinged you earlier." Beckett minimized the screen without shutting it off. "You chose not to reply. Mind telling me why?"

McGwire had started to lean toward Beckett, but now he shifted his weight backward. "I was in the middle of a process that couldn't be interrupted."

"A process." Beckett kept his expression impassive.

"You didn't answer my question," McGwire said. "What the hell is so important—"

"Let me show you something," Beckett said, cutting McGwire off before the man could really work up a good head of steam.

Beckett touched a control on his desk. The image on the holoscreen to McGwire's right changed from the image of Earth as seen from space to an image of the dead woman tied to the silver maple in McGwire's tree farm.

McGwire's face had started to flush with anger, but when he looked at the dead woman, the color leeched away and his skin turned gray. He made a choking sound deep in his throat.

"I pinged you to ask if you know who this woman is," Beckett said calmly, "and why her body was left in your farm."

McGwire rubbed the back of one hand across his mouth. "That's my . . . ?" He closed his eyes. "You say you found her in my farm?"

"She's been there for some time," Beckett said. "You want to tell me why no one noticed her until today?"

He didn't add that two kids had found her. McGwire didn't need to know that kids had managed to hack keycards to the farm. Beckett planned on handling that little problem himself. It just wasn't a high priority right now.

McGwire gave his head a little shake, like he was trying to reboot his brain. When he looked away from the screen toward Beckett, his eyes were haunted. "I've never seen anything like that before in my life. I need a . . ." He cleared his throat and started again. "What did you ask me?"

"Why your systems didn't find her. Why none of your crew discovered her before she looked like that." Beckett jabbed a finger at the holo-screen.

McGwire closed his eyes for a long moment. "That's a mature section of the farm," he said, eyes still closed. "It's basically a forest. It doesn't require a lot of attention. Light, heat, moisture, that's it. That's all the systems keep tabs on." He opened his eyes. It looked like he was making an effort to keep his gaze on Beckett and away from the holo-screen. "We cut back the vines once they go dormant, process the material for mulch, but we won't hit that section for a couple more weeks."

If the woman had been placed on display for a reason, the killer must have known the crew's schedule. And that meant the killer hadn't expected her to be found just yet. They'd deliberately put her body in a place where no one would see—or smell—her until McGwire's crew went in to trim the vines.

So why was McGwire complaining about his crew being locked out of the farm?

Instead of asking directly, Beckett decided to take a different approach. "The farm's a crime scene. I'll have to keep it shut down for the next few days, maybe as long as a week. Will that be a problem for your crew?"

McGwire's eyes flickered away from Beckett's face. "We have processes," he said.

"Processes?" Beckett asked. "Like the one you were stuck in when I pinged you earlier?"

"Experiments," McGwire said, biting off the word. Now that his initial shock was over, some of his earlier belligerence was coming back. "We call them processes in my division."

Beckett nodded. "And you need to access the farm for those processes?"

"Part of it."

"Tell me what part, and I'll see what I can do."

McGwire's nostrils flared. He was clearly a man who wasn't used to having his authority questioned, but he called up a portable screen that displayed a map of the farm. A small section close to the access door the preteens had used was outlined in red. It didn't include the silver maple where the dead body had been found, but it was damn close. Close enough for whoever was conducting the experiments to notice her?

"Who's doing the experiments?" Beckett asked.

"I am." McGwire closed the map. "With the assistance of one of my crew."

Had the body been put on display for McGwire? He wasn't the killer. His reaction to the image of the body had been genuine. People couldn't fake shock like that.

"I need to finish my own process of the scene," Beckett said, "then you can have access."

"How long will that take? These things can't wait."

Beckett leaned back, the contours of his chair reshaping themselves to the change in his position. He planned to walk not only the scene, but the entire section of the farm where McGwire wanted access.

"I'll need the name of the crewmember who'll be assisting you, along with the names of the crew you've assigned to cut back the vines in that section," Beckett said.

McGwire's eyes narrowed. "You don't think one of my crew . . ."

"I'm investigating a crime," Beckett said, "involving a farm your crew has access to. At this point, I believe the term is 'person of interest.' The sooner you get me those names, the sooner you can have access."

McGwire glared at him, but he left without saying another word.

Only after he was gone did Beckett realize McGwire hadn't answered the most important question of all.

Did he know who the dead woman was?

And if he did, did that mean he knew who'd killed her?

It took McGwire nearly an hour to send the names of his crew to Beckett. The delay made Beckett wonder if McGwire had made any last-minute adjustments to his crew assignments.

Beckett had already looked up all of McGwire's six-person crew. No married couples, no registered partners, and no registered children among them. McGwire had been on the station nineteen years, scrabbling his way up the promotion ladder until he'd been appointed division head twelve years ago after the previous division head rotated out. The remainder of his crew had been on the station anywhere from two to twelve years, with nothing remarkable in their records.

Most of the botanists who spent the kind of time on the station that McGwire had switched farms over the years as a way of combating boredom. Not McGwire. He'd stayed with the tree farm for his entire career. He probably thought of the farm as his own private woodland preserve. No wonder he'd been so pissed off when Beckett locked him out.

Beckett had been walking the scene in the tree farm when he'd received the information from McGwire. He'd entered by the same access door the preteen boys had used, but he still had to hike a good ten minutes to get to the silver maple.

When he'd first been assigned to the station, he'd tried to memorize all the pertinent facts about each of the farms, but there was just too much information. Each of the farms was over twenty-five square kilometers, complete with hillocks and dips and trails and thousands of varieties of plants.

The rotation of the rings provided the farms with as close to Earth normal gravity as possible. Overhead lighting was programmed to deliver the optimum sunlight equivalent, and hydration systems provided a combination of ground water and mist in the air, all calculated to nurture whatever plants grew in each farm.

Dr. Sopa might have been right about there being more than enough dirt on the station to bury a body, but the task would have been difficult, if not downright impossible, in this section of the tree farm. The vines caught his feet and the blackberry brambles scratched his hands and arms as he made his way to the silver maple. The ground was covered with fallen leaves, and when he tried to dig at the dirt with the toe of one boot, he dug through more leaves than dirt.

The first time he'd been here, he'd been too intent on the body—on the pure shock of it—to fully take in the scene itself. This particular silver maple was set apart from the others in the little grove. It looked like an afterthought, shorter than the other trees, like something that wasn't planned but merely happened, and the botanists had left it alone.

Was that part of the message? A death that wasn't planned? Or had it been the life that wasn't planned?

Sopa said the woman was dead when she was bound to the tree. Had she been killed here? He'd taken images of the crime scene, but he hadn't been looking for signs of a struggle. And even if there'd been a struggle, would signs of it still be here after two or three months? The vines and brambles were living, growing things.

He toed the ground again, disturbing some of the red leaves that had fallen from the vines. He was frustrated with himself, with his lack of training for a situation like this. The woman, whoever she'd been, deserved better than she was getting from him.

A ping sounded in his right ear. He was getting a call from Dr. Sopa.

"What do you have for me?" he asked.

Her image didn't appear as a little hologram floating in front of him. The call was voice only, unusual for official communications.

"Come see me," she said. "But not in my office." She gave him the location of one of the dining rooms in an inner hub of the station. "Twenty minutes," she said. "I won't wait for you if you're late." Then she signed off.

It had taken Beckett ten minutes to hike into the farm. He'd just barely make it if he left right away.

Leaves had stuck to the toe of his boot. He didn't want to track leaves all over the station. He bent over to brush the leaves off, and that was when he saw a glint of white beneath the red leaves on the ground.

He slipped a clear glove over his hand before he dug through the leaves to retrieve the object, taking images as he went. He already knew what he'd found, but he held the object up anyway, making sure he took images of all sides.

It was a broken keycard, cracked down the middle and caked with bits of leaves and dirt.

And the chip that made it work, that would have identified the owner of the card, was missing.

The designers of the stations realized that crew stuck in space for extended periods of time would need places to blow off steam. Not simply exercise rooms with equipment that worked well in the less than Earth normal gravity of the inner rings where the crewmembers lived, but places where the crew could gather and eat together, drink together, or watch entertainment vids together.

The public dining room Dr. Sopa had chosen for a meeting place was in one of the station's smaller recreational areas. The menu was limited to sandwiches and salads, the drinks to a variety of coffees and teas, and the tables were industrial-grade white plastic bolted to the floor. The chairs were not quite as comfortable as

Beckett's office chair, but they could be adjusted to allow crew-members to sit at varying heights and distances from the table.

Sopa was already sitting at a two-person table near the rear of the dining room when he got there. She had a mug of something hot and steamy on the table in front of her, and her hands were wrapped around the lidded container.

"Do I have time to grab something?" Beckett asked. He hadn't had a meal since breakfast, and it was nearing the end of his normal day. Not that anything had been normal on this day.

She looked up at him, and he was startled by the haunted look in her dark eyes. "You won't want anything. I'm not sure I'm ever going to eat here again."

Beckett had intended to at least get a mug of his favorite tea, an oolong blend usually only in stock for a short period of time after the station received a shipment of supplies from Earth. The last shuttle had been two weeks ago, and the tea was due to run out any day now. Instead, he sat down in the chair across from Sopa.

"What the hell did you find out?" he asked.

She glanced over her shoulder as if to double-check that no one was within earshot. The dining room was nearly deserted, with only the crewmember who processed the food orders standing behind a half-wall at the front of the dining room and two other crew, both botanists from one of the food-growing farms, sitting at a table near the front. A soft instrumental piece was playing over speakers embedded in the steel gray walls.

The music, together with the fact that the dining room, like the crew quarters, had no video or audio recording devices, gave the crew a sense of privacy, something that was missing from nearly every other part of the station. Especially for the crew who shared their quarters with another crewmember.

Apparently satisfied that no one could overhear them, Sopa turned back to Beckett. "You asked me to run our victim's DNA again for a very specific reason," she said. "I'm not going to say what that is, nor am I going to tell you that I deleted our prior conversation from the station's records."

She was speaking so quietly Beckett could hardly hear her, but he heard enough. His eyebrows shot up and he leaned back in his chair. He felt like she'd slapped him.

Deleting station records wasn't officially possible. He should know. Part of the training for his job had included training on the station's computerized data storage systems, which were extensive, ridiculously redundant, and—according to the designers of the systems—hack proof.

The living archive project was too important to the future of the planet to risk a loss of data. Keeping the farms thriving in space was only part of the project. Most of the work done by the botanists had to do with developing hardier versions of the plants in the farms so that they could thrive on a planet that had become hostile to them.

Apparently Sopa had been on the station long enough to figure out how to delete recordings made in her office. Like their conversation about the dead woman and his request that Sopa look for the woman's parents. There would be no record of their conversation in the dining room, only the fact that they'd both been there at the same time.

If Sopa had figured out how to alter the station's official records, other people on the station could too. Beckett worked among some of the most brilliant minds the consortium could find and convince to spend what might be a significant part of their lives isolated in space.

What else had been deleted from the station's records? Was there even a way to find out? The possibilities made Beckett's blood run cold. If Sopa could alter the records in medical, could the botanists alter the records of their experiments? That didn't make sense, but another reason to alter records did.

In all his years on the station, the only crimes reported to security were petty crimes or heated arguments that had escalated into fistfights. What if those weren't the only crimes committed on the station? What if records of other, more serious crimes, had simply been deleted from the system?

What if someone else had been murdered and all evidence of that murder had simply been erased, the victim reduced to compost or buried deep within the dirt in one of the other farms? Like one of the farms where food was grown for the station?

All of a sudden, he understood Sopa's comment about whether he'd ever want to eat again.

"I will tell you that once you know how to delete a thing," she said, "you also know how to spot when a thing has been deleted."

She glanced down at her mug. "I won't tell you that I've learned how to be more careful than most."

She was holding onto her mug so tightly that her knuckles had turned white. The rich aroma of coffee rose with the steam from the opening in the mug's lid. He wondered if her hands were as cold as they looked.

"Data isn't stored in just one place," she said. "When something's deleted, all references to it have to be deleted or the data's still there. If you know where to look."

Beckett thought about all those ridiculously redundant data-keeping systems he'd learned about and mostly ignored, trusting the process to work as it had been designed. His job was security, but in all his years on the station, he'd been focused on the physical safety of the crew. He'd only been doing half his job.

"What the hell did you find?" he asked her again, thinking of Golden's comment about crew who'd been here so long that they knew how to keep their dirty little unauthorized secrets.

Sopa swallowed hard enough that he saw her throat move. "A pattern," she said. "A decades-long pattern. Something that's been going on right under our noses, sight unseen, until someone lashed it to a tree and we discovered it first."

She looked up at him. Her eyes were still haunted, but he saw a hint of the anger she'd had back in her office.

"Take a look at the shuttle manifests," she said. "Cargo weight. Fuel consumption. Station-to-station supply runs."

"What am I looking for?" he asked. If he could even find what she'd found. His training on the station's data-keeping systems had been nearly a decade ago.

Instead of answering him, she got up from the table, and he thought their meeting was over. Then she looked down at him, and he thought she looked older than she had just a few hours ago. Older and incredibly tired.

"All these brilliant minds," she said. "I believed in what they're doing, what we're all doing up here. That was why I stayed, but I've had enough. I thought my colleague was an idiot for taking an early out, and now I'm going to do the same thing. I'm taking the next shuttle and getting the hell out of here."

She left the dining room without another word.

Beckett stared after her for a long moment, then he walked up to the crewmember in charge of the food. He wasn't hungry, but he was going to be working late trying to find whatever had frightened Sopa so badly that she wouldn't tell him even in this place where no one could overhear their conversation. Frightened her so badly that she was fleeing the only home she'd known for nearly thirty years. He doubted he would ever see her again.

At least she'd told him enough to give him a place to start.

If he could make the systems work the way she had. He had to, or somebody who'd worked on this station was going to get away with murder.

After two hours spent in his office peering at manifests and fuel consumption logs for station-to-station supply runs, Beckett had managed to give himself a tension headache, but he was no closer to discovering what had frightened Sopa.

The broken keycard he'd found in the tree farm was a dead end. The card belonged to one of the parents of the preteens who'd broken into the farm. Once the kids had discovered the body and realized what kind of trouble they were in, they'd broken the identity chip out of the card, covered the card with leaves and loose dirt, and thrown the chip as far away from the body as they could.

He'd thought the keycard was an important clue. It wasn't. If he couldn't figure out what Sopa had found, that would mean he'd wasted time running down another dead end. If that happened, there was a strong possibility he'd never find out who'd murdered the dead woman, much less find out who she'd been.

Sopa had specifically mentioned station-to-station supply runs. He'd never had a reason to get involved with those shuttles. The supply runs had been instituted long before Beckett had taken the job as head of security for B-31861 as a means to combat a unique—and unexpected—problem.

Thanks to the efforts of the B stations' botanists to improve the hardiness of the plants in the farms, the vegetable farms produced far more than necessary to feed the stations' crew. The A stations had a similar mandate—improve the hardiness of the animals in their living archives. Those efforts were successful enough that the A stations' habitats began to suffer from overpopulation.

Someone in the consortium got a brilliant idea. Instead of incurring the expense to ship freeze-dried vegetables from Earth to

the A stations and preserved meats from Earth to the B stations
to fill in the gaps between what the stations produced for themselves and what the crew needed to keep themselves healthy and
happy, why not have the stations ship their overflow to each other?
Station-to-station shuttles were cheaper to run thanks to lower fuel
consumption, which meant the shuttles could run more often.

Problem solved.

Which was why Beckett's turkey sandwich was made with real
turkey, and why the crewmembers on the nearby A station had
fresh tomatoes and lettuce for their sandwiches.

He put his plate with the remains of his turkey sandwich on his
desk and pinched the bridge of his nose. It would help if he knew
what leaps of logic Sopa had made. Cargo weight, she'd said. Fuel
consumption. On station-to-station shuttles. What did that add
up to?

She had to have uncovered something else first. He'd asked her
to check DNA for the parents of the murdered woman, and somehow she'd ended up checking station-to-station shuttles.

B-31861's trading partner was A-27430. It was the closest A station, which made for the shortest shuttle run. The manifests and
fuel consumption records were available to Beckett as head of
security. Golden was in charge of monitoring the shuttle runs, but
the logs of those runs had all been approved by her assistant.

Her overworked assistant.

Overworked people made mistakes.

Beckett leaned toward his screens. This time he put up the logs
for the last year side by side. On average, the shuttles between the
stations ran every week. Looking at them this way, he saw something he'd missed before.

Every so often, the data for fuel consumption and cargo weight
was identical from one shuttle originating on A-27430 to another
shuttle originating on A-27430, right down to the decimal point.

That couldn't be a coincidence. He hadn't noticed the dupli-
cate data until he'd pulled up the records side by side. He doubted
Golden's assistant would have noticed at all before she simply
marked them as approved.

Shuttle data was automatically entered into the station's database by the systems on the shuttle. That data was disseminated to
a wide variety of places—fuel storage, food storage, meal prepara-
tion, and even the systems that tracked the proper mix of gases in

the station's air. If someone had erased the actual data by substituting a copy of old data in its place, had they tracked and erased the data from all those various places?

Sopa had talked about deleted records. Had she found the actual records for the shuttles originating on A-27430? And then followed that data until she found something that truly terrified her?

Beckett spent the next three hours diving through the overly redundant data storage systems on the station until he found a small part of what Sopa must have found.

"Son of a bitch," he muttered to himself.

The cargo weight of a station-to-station shuttle originating on A-27430 three months ago had been 52 kilos heavier than the altered log reported.

Fifty-two kilos. The weight of someone like the young woman who'd been killed and left tied to a silver maple in McGwire's farm for him to discover.

McGwire's status as a division head and his seniority on the station afforded him private quarters. It was the middle of the station's night when Beckett knocked on McGwire's door, but the man opened his door only a few seconds later. He was still dressed in the same clothes he'd been wearing when he blustered into Beckett's office, only now his belligerence was gone.

"I was wondering how long it would take you to put it together," McGwire said. "You surprised me. I thought I had at least another day or two."

He backed away from the door, and Beckett stepped inside.

McGwire's quarters weren't large. Most of the station was devoted to the farms, the labs, and the machinery that kept the stations going decade after decade. Crew quarters were a place to sleep, to shower, maybe have a private communication with any friends or family left behind on Earth or on the other stations.

Communications weren't monitored—private was private—but the station's systems did keep track of the fact that communications had taken place. After Beckett had discovered the weight discrepancy in the shuttle, he'd checked both McGwire's communications data and data concerning the process McGwire had scheduled himself to perform in the farm.

The crewmember McGwire'd said would be assisting him with the process had been added to the schedule after McGwire had left Beckett's office. That must have been part of the reason for McGwire's delay in relaying that information to Beckett.

The other reason for the delay was a communication McGwire'd had with one of the station-to-station shuttle pilots who lived on A-27430.

An open suitcase, half filled with clothes and other personal items, sat on McGwire's bunk. He was leaving too, just like Sopa.

"The dead woman was left as a message for you," Beckett said.

McGwire didn't argue the point. Instead he dropped down on the bed next to his suitcase like his legs had given out on him. "I didn't kill her."

Beckett already knew that. She'd been killed on A-27430 and shipped to B-31861 like so much dead meat. The logs listed live weight (the pilots) and dead weight (the cargo) as different entries. But she'd been a human being.

"If you didn't kill her, why was she—"

"Because I wouldn't cooperate!"

McGwire's bluster returned so suddenly that Beckett took an involuntary step backward. Beckett had clipped a stunner on his uniform belt before he'd left his office, and his hand dropped instinctively to the stunner's handle.

"The farm's my fucking farm and I wasn't going to pollute it with their failures." McGwire ran his fingers through his hair. "They knew my schedule. Knew I had processes I needed to conduct at the turn of the season. Knew I'd find her and I'd have no choice but to bury her if I didn't want to implicate myself in what they've been doing. 'Get your hands dirty,' he actually said to me."

He slumped forward, fingers laced at the back of his neck. "They're cocky little bastards over there," he said. "Think they're hot shit because they get all the VIP attention. If those VIPs only knew what was really happening in those labs. 'It'll be easier for you the next time,' he said, like I had to just bend over and take it."

The next time. What the hell was actually going on?

"Make me believe you didn't have anything to do with this," Beckett said. "Make me understand."

Without looking up, McGwire started talking. Beckett made sure he captured every word on his own personal recording device, not on the station's system. He didn't want this recording to disappear.

"You know our mandate," McGwire said. "Engineer stronger

plants, make them able to thrive on Earth as it is, not as we hope it will be someday. Good old genetic engineering. They have the same mandate on the A stations."

Beckett knew that, but he kept his mouth shut. He didn't want to interrupt McGwire now that the man was talking.

"What most of us don't know is there's a special division on A-27430," McGwire said. "I didn't, not until I made division head. They have the same mandate, only they're trying to improve people. Good old genetic engineering." McGwire's voice hitched. It sounded like a sob.

Beckett's hands felt like ice. McGwire was telling him that A-27430 was not only experimenting with genetic engineering on *people* but doing it as a mandate from the consortium.

"Clones?" he asked.

"No," McGwire said. "In vitro. They shuttle in volunteers who're assigned somewhere where they're not noticed, young women who need the money, and pay them big bonuses to keep their mouths shut."

McGwire rubbed a hand across his mouth, then he looked at Beckett with eyes as haunted as Sopa's had been.

"You're not a scientist," he said, "so you might not realize the number of failures it takes to get even a partial success. Fail with a plant, you mulch the failure and grow another one. Fail with a person? If you're lucky, it's a miscarriage. If you're not, and the failure doesn't appear until after the baby's born or . . . after it grows . . ."

He trailed off, glancing away like he couldn't meet Beckett's gaze. Maybe he couldn't stand the look of disgust, of horror, that Beckett couldn't quite keep off his face.

"They need some way to get rid of the bodies," McGwire said. "The habitat systems on the A stations would record the decomp and send bots to remove the dead animal. Can't have bots finding a dead kid instead of a dead racoon or baby bear. Can't shoot a dead kid out an airlock and have the station's monitoring systems pick it up as space debris. Sure as hell can't recycle the body with animal by-products. The recyclers pick up human DNA, and they can't ship the body back to Earth on a shuttle with crewmembers who have no idea what's going on. So they send their failures here for burial in farms that don't need a lot of attention."

"Like yours," Beckett said.

"Never mine!" McGwire glared at him. "I never allowed that."

Which explained why McGwire had never transferred to another farm. His farm was the only one he knew was clean.

"Tell me about the dead woman," Beckett said.

McGwire shuddered visibly. "She had no pain receptors, that's what he said. They tested her repeatedly."

By stabbing her, among other things. Beckett didn't want to hear what else they'd done to her, but he didn't want McGwire to stop talking.

"At first they thought it was a good thing, but there was something wrong with her brain," McGwire said. "The older she got, the more they couldn't control her. I guess it's hard to run a secret division if the secrets keep trying to escape."

So they'd killed her, or she'd broken her neck trying to get away. Then they'd used her to try to get McGwire to cooperate.

"I'm going to have to report this," Beckett said.

McGwire snorted. "To who? Your bosses? Think it through. These people have a mandate. Where do you think that comes from?"

Beckett felt the blood leave his face. He hadn't thought it through. He was just as screwed as Sopa and McGwire. And probably as screwed as Golden, who'd felt it necessary to make a recording to cover her ass when she told him to make sure the killer wasn't on her station.

McGwire stood up and snapped his suitcase shut. "My suggestion to you," he said, "is to bug out. Just leave. Now that you know what really goes on here, this place will eat your soul if you don't."

Beckett knew this day had already eaten his soul, no matter what he decided to do next.

Beckett lasted another week.

The day after he'd confronted McGwire, Beckett went to Golden's office to give her an update. He told her that the body had been too degraded to find any useable evidence, and with Sopa gone, he had no hope of getting any additional forensics. It was only a partial lie.

"What about the killer?" she'd asked.

"I found no evidence to indicate this death was anything other than a one-time incident," he said, another lie. "I'm still investigating."

"My assistant will give you all the support you require," she said, a dismissal if he'd ever heard one.

He had no doubt that the official record of their meeting would be deleted, just as he had no doubt she'd made her own private recording of what had been said. He had.

He went through the motions of looking for a missing crew-member who should have caught a shuttle but hadn't, but his heart wasn't in it. He slept poorly, ate poorly, and even turned off the holo-screens on his office wall.

He'd thought briefly about playing the hero. The consortium was the most powerful global entity on Earth, but people needed to know its mandates were killing innocent children. He had no proof of that, but he did have a dead woman.

Or he thought he did.

When he tried to track down what Sopa had done with the dead woman's remains, he discovered that her body was missing. Sopa's autopsy report had been deleted from the station's records.

Whoever had done that got their instructions directly from the consortium, which meant they'd have no qualms dispatching Beckett if he became a problem. They'd bury his body in one of the farms, then alter the station's records to make it look like he'd returned to Earth.

If they killed Beckett, they'd probably kill the two preteens who'd discovered the body. He couldn't do anything for the dead woman, but he could save those two boys.

He still believed the primary work being done on the stations was important to the future of the planet. Was human genetic ex-perimentation moral? His job had always been simply to enforce laws as they existed. That had been his moral compass, but now that compass was broken. A broken man couldn't do the job he was expected to do.

Before he caught the shuttle that would take him back to Earth, Beckett visited the tree farm one last time. The vines were rapidly shedding their leaves now, and the maple's leaves had taken on a blood-red tinge of their own.

Beckett's worst fear was that the consortium had only mandated genetic experimentation on people because they believed Earth wasn't redeemable. Maybe the squabbling among politicians and mega-corporations and religious zealots had gone on too long, and Earth was past the tipping point.

Or maybe the mandate was a *just in case,* worst-case scenario. He had no way of knowing. He didn't know science.

He picked up one of the fallen leaves and tucked it in his pocket. He still had faith in the basic purpose of the stations. The plants and animals in these living archives deserved to be preserved and cared for. Even if Earth would never again be a place where they could thrive.

He patted his pocket then turned to make the ten-minute hike out of the farm.

It all boiled down to hope for the future. He was surprised that his was still intact.

Maybe hope wasn't so ephemeral after all.

The Ticks Will Eat You Whole

FROM *Cowboy Jamboree*

HE COUNTED EIGHT, no, nine, no, *ten* fucking deer ticks on his khakis long after this death march through the woods stopped being a good idea. Never was a good idea for Gavin, but for his wife, Tilly, and his mother-in-law, it was a necessary death march.

A literal death march.

Tilly tromped about twenty steps ahead of him on the grown over path, following faint tire ruts, carrying her dad's ashes in a wooden box.

When his wife told him they were going to spread some of her dad's ashes, Gavin thought it would be something, like, dignified. Churchy, even though her parents had stopped going to their Catholic church decades ago. Tilly had never shown any interest.

But still, *dignified.*

Gavin wore khakis he hadn't worn since losing his job during the pandemic. Blue denim dress shirt. Some slip-on tan leather loafers he'd bought for his own grandma's funeral nine years ago. Should've known something was wrong when Tilly put on some cargo shorts, her mud-caked Keens, and one of his flannel shirts over a T-shirt she'd bought in Greece ten years before. It said *Greece* in script, but written across a drawing of the Roman colosseum.

This was their sixth stop of the day. *Sixth.*

1. Father-in-law's parents' graves
2. his cousin's grave
3. a spot in the woods he just liked for some reason

4. another spot in a different set of woods that required climbing over a barbed-wire fence
5. behind his parents' barn
6. and now, even more itchy, buggy, stinky woods.

Sweat through, worn slap out, itchy, his shoes wet and squishy, ticks climbing his body like Orcs scaling the walls in *Lord of the Rings*. Tilly and her mom had swung back and forth all day between pissed off at each other to weepy and hugging.

Tilly was short, with short brown hair, easy to mistake for a junior high boy, which it seemed like she wanted. She wore less make-up as every year passed, thirteen years of marriage. She loved being out in the woods, and had worked in a State Park before they met. He called her "Nature Girl" and hated to admit he was kind of turned on by her not shaving anything anymore—armpits, legs, cooch.

Bad day for sex fantasies. Part of him wanted to push her up against a tree and rip her shorts down. The rest of him felt like the ticks would eat him whole, the bushes were all poison and the bare tree branches might put his eye out.

Farther up ahead of Tilly, making quick work of the trail like a deer or a bear, was his mother-in-law. Gavin called her Pauline, her real name, but everyone else in the family called her "Nookie" for whatever the fuck reason, at least one they never told Gavin.

Not even Tilly, short for Matilda, could explain it, but Gavin knowing "Nookie" sixteen years now explained a lot of why anyone would saddle their kid with a name like "Matilda" because she'd been saddled with a name like "Nookie."

Pauline was seventy-one, but not little old lady seventy-one. More like Patti Smith seventy-one. Thin as a rail. She wore her usual dirty jeans and hiking sandals, one of her husband's XXL mechanic's shirt with the sleeves cut off so you could see her black bra and translucent skin. Gavin was pretty sure she still snorted cocaine, ate some pot brownies from time to time. She usually walked with a cane for her bad hip, but out here she was feeling no pain, pointing out spots to spread more ashes.

"Here, he liked to hunt here because he could see three ways down these paths, see?"

"Chuck loved these plum trees. Leave some by the plum trees."

"We were going to build our first house here, before Chuck got that job in Fargo. Shame no one ever did. I had hoped someone would. It'd be such a nice home."

For hermits, Gavin thought.

Like she knew what he was thinking, Tilly gave him *the eye.* She did as her mother said, sifted some of her dad from the plastic bag in the box. None of them thought to bring a measuring cup.

The grass and leaves under his loafers were wet this far out, and he didn't know why. No rain, no water nearby. Just a sudden everything being wet. Smelled like piss too. Like deer shit and deer piss and cat piss, probably the meth lab they passed—*had* to be a goddamn meth lab. Gavin could've sworn he'd seen a face peek out of the rusted-out Airstream welded to a U-Haul.

Bout, what, eight, nine minutes ago?

They'd passed his father-in-law's auto graveyard. This was his parents' land, passed down to him when they both passed away. He'd grown up in these woods, and any time he got a new car or truck, he would drive the old one out here to the graveyard, park it among the trees.

Gavin asked Chuck one time, "You ever going to do anything with them?"

The old man looked at Gavin like he was an idiot.

Looked at Gavin like he was an idiot most of the time, though.

Pauline had spotted the Airstream and U-Haul and said, "What is that? What is going on there? I don't remember those, no, I don't at all."

Gavin shushed her.

When they'd pulled into the drive at the old house earlier, there was a car there—brown Malibu. No license plate. A bumper sticker saying, "Tread on Me. I've Got Fangs."

Tilly said, "I didn't think anyone was staying here."

"Some of your cousins, now and then, if they need a place. No big deal." Pauline climbed out of the car and walked to the front door. Knocked hard and loud. Knocked harder and louder. Stood around, then peeked into the front window. Gavin hung back near the car, the door like a shield for him if the shooting started. He searched the second-floor windows for signs of life, or afterlife, *shiver.*

No one answered, so Pauline said, "Alright, let's do it."

Tilly asked, "Do you want to drive?"

But she was already headed for the field, the rutted path leading to the tree line, shouting behind her, "It's not all that far."

Lying bitch.

Don't take it wrong. Pauline had never been anything but lovely to Gavin. Made him non-pot brownies every time he visited. Kept real Coca-Cola in the fridge just in case, since she nor Chuck drank it. Made Tilly jealous. Where were *her* brownies? Where were *her* fizzy drinks?

But then Chuck died—COVID made worse by COPD—and they moved her to their suburb outside of Minneapolis, four hours away from the woods. They helped her buy a new house, but she hated it. *Hated* it. The town, the house, *hate hate hate.*

She bought a German Shepherd with diarrhea. He shat all over the house. Tilly was the one who had to go clean up. Calls all hours of the day, asking for help with one thing or another, or offering to pick something up at the store, or worried the dog might die.

Also, she bitched about how her dead husband had been spoiled by his mother, then by herself, but it was still somehow his fault for letting it happen. Just a selfish, spoiled, son-of-a-bitch who quit his cushy corporate lodge job to work on semi-trucks instead. He didn't mind getting dirty, but god forbid you leave one of his *thousands* of tools out of place. His pork chops had to be seasoned just right. Exactly right. If not he wouldn't eat it, and would instead grab a box of Milk Duds or a couple Cherry Bings for "dinner."

When Tilly hung up after a call with her mom anymore, her cheeks were bright red. "She never even asks how I'm doing. Just goes right into it."

Gavin whipped his head around. Swore he heard twigs snapping and echoing behind him. He caught up with Tilly. "Where the *fuck*—"

"Not now. You should've stayed at the car."

"We should've driven."

"Enough. This is already hard enough as is."

"I told you I'd be here for you."

"Then be nice."

Pauline shouted back to them, "Right around this corner. Right here."

Tilly said, "Buck up," and then went to catch up with her mom. Gavin stayed put. He was done. Another glance down at his pants—six, seven, eight more ticks. The ones he could *see*. He swore they were crawling under his pants, up the skin of his legs, heading for his balls, his ass crack, and he wouldn't find them until they'd bloated three times their size on his blood, trading it for a lifetime of Lyme.

Another twig snap.

He didn't flinch, didn't whip his head around this time. The monster stalking him—*Bear? Wolf? Deer?*—wanted him to know it was there.

Gavin slipped his hands into his khaki pockets. He shambled in a little circle, looking up at the trees. Oaks or maples or birch, he couldn't tell trees apart. Pine, he knew. Pine was easy. And sticky. He brought his chin down, his eyes down, and standing a few yards away, there was this guy.

This guy.

Younger than Gavin by a decade. Untied Nikes, baggy jeans, a band of boxer-briefs, and a white-stained-yellow T-shirt, tight. A white kid with shaggy hair, almost like one of the Ramones, but Gavin bet this kid wouldn't knew who that was. Trucker hat with *I like it dirty* on the front.

Gavin nodded. "Hey."

Dude nodded back. "Alright?"

"Yeah, just fine."

"What's going on here?"

Gavin's first impulse was to say *None of your goddamned business,* but we're talking a *really* short impulse. "Oh, just. Spreading some ashes." He pointed up the trail. "My wife, my mother-in-law. My father-in-law died from COVID. Did you know him? Chuck Oakley?"

Why not just give him your social security number too, Gav?

"That's pretty gross."

"You think?"

"Spreading dead guys out here? Not telling people."

"He grew up here, back at the house." Another point. "In these woods. Used to be his land."

A new cough a little too close for comfort. Gavin flicked his eyes. The other one had been standing there all along, just behind a tree off to the right. Closer than Dirty Hat. Camo pants and scuffed-to-hell work boots. A puffy vest over a tight bare chest. No eyebrows. Too many piercings—lip, nose, both ears, eyebrow, chin. Mr. Clean dome. He held his right hand straight down, out of sight behind his leg.

Gavin thought, *If you don't think it, it's not there.*

Like telling someone "Don't think about an elephant."

The first thing you do, right?

So yeah, Mr. Clean had a gun.

"Used to be?"

Gavin blinked. "Maybe still is. They sold the land next door, though."

"Maybe."

He glanced back over his shoulder. Tilly and her mom were almost out of sight. Out of hearing range, for sure. The one time he wished Chuck was still alive, still here, because he was a gun nut. He always carried a Glock, even to Fleet Farm or Home Depot. He had a heavy-as-fuck gun safe they couldn't take along to Pauline's new house, so they had to take all the guns one by one, carry them in the trunk, and hide them in a closet until she'd bought a new safe for them all.

"He left you a .45," Pauline told him. "He'd had it for thirty years."

Gavin had told her to keep it in the safe. He wasn't ready to risk having that in his home. Why did she need to keep them all? They were worth a lot of money. They were just going to rust in the safe.

Yeah, the one time he wished Chuck was there, paranoid as shit, bulge on his hip, even if it would make Gavin feel like a little man, he was instead scattered on the leaves of a plum tree.

Gavin said, "That's it."

Dirty Hat crossed his arms. "That's it, then?"

"Pretty sure. I just follow along. Do as I'm told."

Mr. Clean cleared his throat. "Thought I heard the old lady say something about an Airstream?"

His voice was a gargle, causing Gavin to raise his hands waist high like every gangster in every black-and-white film when the cops catch up to them. Every muscle in Mr. Clean's neck pulsed, word by word. Could've drank some Drano when he was a kid.

"Sure, back with the old cars? Back there? You guys see it?"

"The old cars?"

"Chuck's old cars? Pauline said she hadn't seen the Airstream before. I told her it might have been some cousins or something left it there."

Go ahead and give them Pauline's PIN numbers too, why don't you?

"Some cousins." Dirty Hat winked at Mr. Clean. "I hear you."

Gavin thumbed over his shoulder. "I've got to catch up with them. One last spread and we're done."

"What's the last one?"

"I don't know. Another hunting spot? So many."

He lifted his hand, sort of, kind of, a little wave. Jesus. Sent a burning embarrassment through him. The meth cookers had the gun. They were the "cool kids." Gavin was the nerd who did their homework.

He turned his back on DH and Mr. C to show them he was tough—turning his back on a *meth cooker with a gun,* the thought muscled its way in front of some others. *He's not a high school football star, idiot.*

Too late. He started down the trail, peeked over his shoulder, and caught the tail end of their convo. Not the words, but the nods and "Hm"s and "Yeah, yeah." They started down the trail after Gavin. Not fast or anything. Moseying. DH's hands in his pockets, and Mr. Clean bopping the pistol off his hip. Dirty Hat whistled to a tune Gavin didn't know.

The urge in his gut was *run, fucker, run.* But *run, fucker, run* might get him shot. Playing it cool might still get him shot, but maybe he could distract the goons so Tilly and her mom could get away or hide.

Hard to imagine dying for someone. He thought he could, when it came down to it, but it was goddamned hard to imagine. It would have to be a frantic moment, Gavin fighting for the gun, shouting at Tilly and Pauline to vamoose, when the gun goes bang—right in his midsection—and he goes down slowly, his light fading, off to the big sleep.

But that's only in movies.

The reality, more likely: Gavin on his knees, begging them to leave him alive. Every muscle flinching and cramping because he could see it coming. Any second now.

Gavin's mouth was bone dry.

He said, "Going my way?"

Dirty Hat caught up with him. "We only thought it right to pay our respects."

Mr. Clean, on his other side. "Mad respect. That's hardcore, coming out here like this."

"Important to her. To them."

"Yeah, almost forgot." Dirty Hat flung an arm around Gavin's shoulder, the crook on the back of his neck, and hugged him closer. "Tell me about your wife, Gavin. Tell me all the details."

"Details?" Slow on the pick-up.

"Like, blonde, brunette, red? Tall? Short?"

"Short, pretty short."

"What's that like?"

"What's what like?"

"Riding a short girl," Mr. Clean said. "Can you hold her up steady? Bounce her on your dick?" Already starting to laugh before getting it out. DH too.

"Dude said she was short, not a *child*, man. C'mon, how much does she weigh?"

Gavin tried to twist out of DH's hug, but the guy yanked him back. Jesus, the smell. Ammonia, skunk, awful breath, and some sort of fruity cologne.

"Listen, guys, this is kind of private."

"It's guy talk, is all. Ain't nothing to it." Another laugh. A giggle? Can you call a meth cooker a giggler?

"I mean the ashes. The spreading. I don't think my mother-in-law wants anyone else—"

"See, that's too bad." Mr. Clean shook his head, scratched his armpit with the front sight of his pistol. "You know us, right? You know that camper back there is ours. But we don't know you. I mean, all of you."

"We're going to make our introductions, explain a couple of things, then I swear, you'll be rid of us forever."

"And ever."

The idea of dying, *really dying*, had never crossed Gavin's mind quite this way. Murdered. Watching Tilly murdered, or her watching him. "Fuck."

"Now you're catching on."

"We've got people waiting on us. Our, yeah, our kids. My wife's friends."

Grasping at straws, because for the life of him, Gavin couldn't think of anyone waiting on them right then. Most of the people in their lives might not miss them for a few days or more, mostly work friends or Tilly's cousins. Nobody else waiting by the phone.

Sad, man. Sad.

"Everybody's got someone waiting." Mr. Clean looked oily. Maybe it was just a sheen of sweat, but it looked oily. He had had deer ticks crawling all over his abs, his chest. A few had latched on and were already inflating with blood. It made Gavin gag. He tried not to. It was a reflex. The ticks, the slick skin, the smell of these guys, the gun.

"Look, I'm not going to tell anyone." He got out in front of these guys and turned to them. Hands out again. Surrender palms. "You've got nothing to worry about. I don't care what you're doing."

Dirty Hat sighed. He took off his hat and wiped his arm across his forehead. "That's all well and good, but if we let you go, let your family go, without at least a warning, and them son-a-bitches, you know, Sheriffs, they'll show up a few days after and we're caught with our cocks in our hands, you get it?"

"Please, please, I'm serious." His hands doing most of the work. "My wife, her mom, they don't even know you're here. I won't tell them. It'll just be me who knows, and I've got nothing to say to anybody."

Mr. Clean grinned. "Aw, you'll tell them. It's too good a story not to tell them."

"I swear."

"We already heard the old bitch about the trailer. Do you think she's going to let it go?"

Dirty Hat put his hat back on, snugged it, and stepped up to Gavin. He grabbed both shoulders, gave him a twist, turning him toward the trail again.

"Keep walking."

"Wait, wait."

Dirty Hat's momentum, plus his hand on the middle of Gavin's back, kept them going. If Gavin would try to slow down, he'd trip. "I'll tell her I checked it out, it's why I'm so far back. Tell her it's empty, rusted through the bottom. I'll tell her to leave it with the rest of the cars."

Quiet for a minute, except their feet squishing leaves into the mud.

Gavin said, "I've got to pee."

They laughed. "You'll pee soon enough."

"Why you got to do this? What are you getting out of it?"

Mr. Clean shrugged. "Get to fuck your wife's ass. She won't like it. I will."

"That's . . . no, man, that's . . . please."

How do they do it? The heroes. The cops. The firemen. Even Chuck with his Glock ready at all times, the good guy with a gun. How do they stay tough in the face of this bullshit?

"What? What's that? You say that's what?"

"Don't do that."

"Do what? Fuck your wife's ass? Or my buddy over here going to choke your mother-in-law with his big white snake?"

"Jesus, stop it. Don't do any of that. Jesus. This is . . . fuck. Please, please."

Mr. Clean stopped dead in his tracks and turned to Gavin, chest to chest. "Where's the fun in that? Can you tell me? Before you turned up, we were going to cook up a batch and make *bank*, alright? But now we get to fuck some pussy and spill some blood and still make bank. I'd say that's a pretty good day above the ground."

Every day is a good day above the ground, is what Chuck would've told them.

"Hold up." Mr. Clean brought the gun barrel up, brushed it underneath Gavin's chin. Made out like he was examining Gavin's neck. Then, "You got a little something, right . . ."

He slid the gun down Gavin's throat to the side of his neck, then flicked the skin with the front gunsight. "It was a tick. Got it."

Gavin took a heaving breath and felt his chest burn.

Dirty Hat went *hmph.* "Those things'll eat you whole if you're not careful. Give you Lyme's Disease."

"Please."

Gavin got down on one knee. Mr. Clean tried to stop him, drag him to his feet. But Gavin leaned out of the way, plopped his other knee into the mud. It was an awkward spread, Gavin wobbling back and forth. Hands still up and out.

"Please."

Mr. Clean looked over to Dirty Hat. "Mother fuck. I'm tired of him."

"Let's keep the noise down."

Gavin couldn't see Dirty Hat, but heard the sound of the hunting knife being pulled from its sheath. Steps coming up behind him. Gavin humped his shoulders and rolled his head on his neck.

"God, no, please, no."

Dirty Hat grabbed his hair and yanked his head back as Gavin squeezed a scream and let go of his bladder and then —

"Gavin!" A woman's voice. Tilly's voice.

Two fast and loud *pop pops* out in the brush.

The meth cookers hopped up like popcorn. Dirty Hat let go of Gavin and said, "Shit, shit shit!" His arms pulled in protecting his chest.

Mr. Clean let out a yelp and turned and started firing wildly into the trees. Gavin's ears felt like they might bleed. He covered them with his hands and flinched with each shot.

Two more shots, farther out.

Gavin was nearly deaf by then. He watched Dirty Hat crumple to the ground on his back. He watched Mr. Clean finish his magazine and try to run like there were wolves on his heels, but he stumbled, fell onto his face, then tried to crawl away.

Pauline and Tilly appeared from the trees. *Angels. Beautiful angels.* Pauline held a pistol in her hand. The boxy black frame he'd seen Chuck carry many times before. While Tilly ran for Gavin and dropped at his side—"Are you okay? Are you okay? Did they hurt you? Can you hear me."—Pauline calmly stepped over to Mr. Clean, still trying to crawl. He flipped onto his side and pawed the air between them with one hand.

"Hey, bitch, you're nothing bitch. Cheap shots, bitch."

Then she raised the Glock.

"Wait, wait, wait, wait." Mr. Clean was running out of breath. "Wait . . . oh, I feel bad, I feel real bad. Help me, please."

"No."

Pop.

Like so. That was it. Tilly took Gavin's cheeks in her hands and told him to focus, to know that it was going to be okay. But he was too busy watching Pauline, now working her way over to Dirty Hat. She stood over him, a foot on each side of his body, and watched for a long moment. She didn't bother pointing her gun at him. He was done for.

Gavin opened his mouth wide a few times, trying to clear the rest of the fuzz from his ears. "I'm alright. Baby, I love you. I'm alright, I'm okay, I'm alright."

She gripped his hands and he hers and then Pauline was standing over them, shoving her husband's pistol into her waistband at her back. She turned her head slowly, looking out into the murk. On patrol. What if there were others?

Pauline finally looked at Gavin and reached down a hand to help him up. He took it. "How are you feeling?"

He cleared his throat. Then again. Croaked out, "Good. Good. Yeah. Good."

He couldn't ask her *What are we going to do? When will we call the cops? Are we in trouble?*

Not *we*. Her. Was Pauline in trouble?

She grabbed him at the back of his neck. Kneaded. Looked in his eyes. "Do me a favor?"

He nodded.

"Don't tell anyone about this. Not ever. Not *EV-UR*. Do you understand?"

This was not the sweet old woman who baked him brownies. Not anymore.

"You got that. Tilly? Goes for you too."

She nodded. "I'll go get Dad." Back into the woods again.

Pauline looked around. Two dead. But no one out here noticed the gunfire. Not a single one. She turned back to Gavin. "Go get the car. Bring it back here."

"Walk all the way back?"

"You don't have much choice, do you?"

"What about Tilly?"

Pauline crossed her arms. "I need her help here. She knows what to do."

So many other questions, but Gavin didn't have the rights words, or the right order, and it sure as hell wasn't the right time.

He jangled the car keys in his wet khakis, reminding him they were soaked in his piss. His loafers were ruined. His pride snipped in two. But he started walking. Didn't look back, didn't look down, not even when he passed Mr. Clean's body, the face staring right at him.

By the time he'd gotten past Chuck's other favorite hunting spot, his car graveyard, and the meth cookers' Airstream, there was only one question left he was desperate to know the answer to: *What did she mean, Tilly knows what to do?*

The Obsession of Abel Tangier

FROM *Low Down Dirty Vote*

WILLA TANGIER BURIED her fourth husband a week before the local school board would decide the fate of the Black history curriculum in Caddo Parish schools. During the graveside service, her cousin Ethel complained that the weather was a goddam Louisiana cliché: the sun yellow as piss in a washed-out gray sky, the humidity boiling until the air was thick like molasses.

"You'd think he'd shut up so we can get out of this heat," Ethel said of the good Reverend Thurston, who was probably thinking that Abel Tangier was owed more than a hasty goodbye.

"If you're so miserable, maybe you should just hop in there with him," Willa said.

"Maybe I should," Ethel answered. "At least it'd be cooler."

Willa didn't pay her any mind. Ethel was the woman you called when you needed help washing your dead. She nursed the sick, and provided the down-and-out a bed and a hot meal when needed. Ethel was the kind of woman who'd sit at the bedside of your dying mother while you ran out to buy tampons, or anything else you might need to get on with the business of living. Only her mouth was unkind. It was the place she carried her bitterness. No, Willa didn't mind Ethel's words. It was Big Buddy, their fellow school board member, and the tiebreaking vote on what kind of history Byrd's Landing schools would teach that did her in.

Willa hadn't seen Big Buddy at the church or graveside services, but here he was now at the repast. He blew through her front door with his gleaming bald head and big personality, shaking hands with everyone he knew. His laughter quieted when he spied her and Ethel across the room. He became somber, shaking more hands, and chuckling respectfully as he made his way to them.

When he reached them he pressed Willa's hand, as if they weren't at the tail end of a pandemic, and said, "Feels like old times with the three of us together."

By old times he meant how they used to play when they were kids. He was just Buddy then. They ran Byrd's Landing streets from dawn to dusk, earning the nickname "the fearsome threesome." In high school Buddy joined the football team. That's when he became Big Buddy and went his own way.

"Abel was a wonderful history teacher in our schools for so many years," Big Buddy was now saying to Willa. "He helped a lot of kids. I hope that brings you some comfort."

"What would bring her comfort is a mask covering your big, cast-iron-skillet face," Ethel said.

He laughed, patted Ethel's bony shoulder, and squeezed hard.

"No matter what happens, you're going to still be Ethel, ain't you?" he said. "PhD or no. Retired principal or no. Still loud and ignorant as the day is long."

Ethel jerked away.

Willa watched the anger move across Ethel's face with greedy eyes. Willa wore her own kindness like a heavy cloak, rarely daring to take it off. She was known for not having a mean bone in her body. People said she was the kindest person they've ever met. Since Abel's death the label had started to wear thin. It was beginning to smother her.

"I may be all that, ignorant, whatever you say," Ethel said. "But at least I'm not a killer."

Buddy drew up to his full seven-foot height and stepped closer to Ethel. Ethel, who had wrangled high school students for twenty years at Liberty High, didn't take one step back. If not nose-to-nose she stood toe-to-toe with Big Buddy.

"What did you say?" he challenged.

"What, money make you deaf? Abel was on the phone with you when he stroked out. It's your fault he's dead."

"The man was obsessed," Buddy said. "He was pushing himself too hard."

Yes, obsessed, Willa agreed silently. Abel had gotten his blood up about May 13, 1985, the day Mayor Wilson Goode bombed a Black neighborhood in West Philly, or, as Abel put it, bombed his own people. What bothered Abel most was that he hadn't known that Goode dropped a satchel of C4 from a helicopter on the MOVE compound, an organization that Goode and the police hated. That decision killed eleven people, almost half of them children. Sixty homes burned to the ground.

Ethel was drunk, and meaner than ever, the night Abel was going on and on about it. She teased him, and asked for another margarita before saying, "Hurts your ego, don't it? You should know *all* the things, right? A history teacher in Byrd's Landing, Louisiana? Even something that happened on the other side of the country almost thirty-five years ago."

"The police in the United States bombed its own citizens in 1985. They burned children *alive*. Yes, *I* should have known this. *We* all should have known this!"

After that night Abel covered the walls of his study with the evidence—one group picture of MOVE members in their signature dreadlocks, with slight smiles that said *we want nothing from you, not your technology, not your meat, and maybe not even your Black solidarity.* Another photograph, just after the bomb dropped— flames of yellow, gold, and red backlighting the narrow row homes like a sunset. And yet another image of a naked boy of about thirteen in the back of a police car. Willa swore she could see smoke rising like mist from his burned skin. And more and more pictures of cruisers, police in riot gear, residents pointing, crying, and what looked like acres and acres of rubble.

"He got himself all worked up," Big Buddy said, pulling Willa back to the moment. "You not going to put that on me."

"Obsessed or not, he was trying to do right. What are you doing? Siding with the MAGA hats so they'll hire your sorry ass security company to protect their shit."

"He was trying to turn me into a sheep."

Willa thought that Ethel had gone too far. People were staring. They were at her husband's repast, for Lord's sake. And Willa couldn't believe that Big Buddy, the boy she had grown up with, the man she had known all of her life, the man Abel had known, would vote to wash away sins committed against his own people. There was still a chance he'd vote the right way. She couldn't let Ethel ruin that.

"Abel's dying wasn't Buddy's fault," Willa said. "He had high blood pressure, didn't take his pills on the regular."

She placed a hand on Big Buddy's forearm, and felt it relax under her touch. "Thank you for coming," she said in her best pleasant voice. "I'm sure all this emotion will be put to rest after the vote. Maybe we could all get dinner and talk about the old times."

Ethel started bringing a loaded Smith & Wesson .45 to every school board meeting after the death threats started. She'd put it in her purse before she left home and slip it into the place for her personal belongings at her spot on the dais. No telling when she would need to defend herself against those crazies, she told Willa.

The Friday following Abel's funeral, Willa sat in the big leather chair next to Ethel, who pointed under her desk, and said, "Just like the video on YouTube told me to do it, safety's off. Red, you're dead." She grinned at Willa. "In case you need it."

"Be serious, I can't see myself shooting anybody."

Ethel gave her a "suit-yourself" look and gazed at the crowd on the floor. Just like the last few board meetings, this one was full to bursting. All the extra folding chairs that had been brought in had asses in them. People who couldn't find empty seats lined the walls, some of them in MAGA hats and rigid with outrage, others leaning against the wall with their arms folded. A broken air conditioner added to the tension, the room was so hot that Willa felt like she was in a stew. Three ancient ceiling fans clunked overhead, doing nothing but add more noise to the strident voices below.

Someone went to the podium and yelled into the microphone, "Ethel Anderson, you Nazi lover!"

The board chair, an elderly woman in a tan suit and a brunette wig, pounded a gavel while shouting, "Order, order, order!"

"That's a new one," Ethel said dryly.

Willa squinted, sat up, and leaned closer to her microphone.

"Aren't you Lana Rayburn's son? I taught your mama in tenth grade. How she doing?" she said, hoping to shame him.

The man waited a beat before saying, "She's fine. Getting along real good. But we ain't talking about my mama now, we talking about what y'all wanting to do to our kids."

"We don't want to do anything to your kids except give them a good education," Ethel said. "What we don't want to do is raise a pack of idiots with heads full of cotton."

"Now, come on, Willa," Big Buddy said. "Ain't no cause for that kind of talk. We discussing this in an objective fashion."

"Ain't nothing objective about what we discussing here," Ethel said. "Especially when we talking about whitewashing history."

"Why you always got to bring race into it?" Big Buddy asked.

"And why don't you ever?" Ethel said. "As dark as you are, I'm sure you never got a pass from being Black."

"Can you please restore some order to this meeting?" Big Buddy shouted at the Chair, who was now shaking. "Even though we a small town, we don't have to behave like a backwater."

Willa watched them, not knowing what to say. Her mind had started running like a river in one direction since she buried Abel. All she kept thinking about was May 13, 1985. The helicopter overhead, the bomb dropping. And everybody seeming to forget it ever happened.

". . . on the other side of the country about a bunch of criminals," Big Buddy was saying. "Why we need to wallow in all that? It ain't got nothing to do with us."

"Because it's history," Ethel said. "The kids should know about it. Just like they should know about Tulsa and Houston and Chicago. And these fools want to shut it all down."

Willa wasn't paying attention to Big Buddy or Ethel. She kept thinking about all that fire that Goode let rage on. No water on that fire for hours.

"What's that, Willa?" Ethel asked.

Willa gave her a confused look. "What?"

"Sounds like you finally got something to say," Ethel said. "We listening."

"I didn't say anything."

"Yes, you did," Big Buddy said. "You said to let it burn."

Next thing Willa knew she was in her bright kitchen with a cup of chamomile tea in front of her. Another thing that had been happening since Abel died, grief ate holes into her realities. She'd be one place and not know how she'd got there, say something, and have to reach way back in her mind to find out what she meant. The only thing that felt real to her were the flames burning her alive.

"Looks like you got plenty of casseroles left. Probably need to throw them out, but one more day of eating on them won't kill you," Ethel said as she wiped down the counter.

Willa didn't answer, just gripped the warm cup and brought the tea up to her nose so she could breathe in its fragrance. She hadn't thought about food in days.

Ethel stopped wiping and came and sat at the table across from Willa.

"You're worrying the shit out of me, girl. Maybe we should check you for Alzheimer."

"I don't have Alzheimer."

"Then what's wrong with you? You were weird tonight."

"I just can't seem to get out of my dreams," Willa answered. "I keep seeing snatches in my mind, smelling that fire. It's like I was there."

"You mean that MOVE thing that had Abel in an uproar?"

"Looks like it has the entire town in an uproar. If Abel hadn't proposed that we have a May 13, 1985, day of remembrance in Byrd's Landing, we wouldn't be having these conversations."

Ethel scoffed. "We'd be having these conversations no matter what. This has been going on all over the country. Stupidity is contagious."

"But I have nightmares about it. I feel like I'm being burned alive in my dreams."

Ethel narrowed her eyes. "Where you been sleeping lately, Willa."

"In my bed, my room. Where do you think I've been sleeping?"

"I've told you that you should spend some time at my house," Ethel said. "But you stubborn."

"I don't want you worrying about me, Ethel."

"That's the problem. You don't want nobody worrying about nothing. You want to fix things for everybody else but won't do anything for yourself."

"Don't fuss. Please don't fuss," Willa said.

"And you don't speak up when people do wrong because you worried about their feelings. Been like that all your life."

"What do you mean?"

"Big Buddy. That man's a jackal and you still talk to him with sugar in your voice."

"He's our friend. We grew up with him, remember?"

"Well, he doesn't think like us, no matter how many times we went roller skating together. What kind of man tries to erase the history of his own people?"

"You're too hard on him. He's a human being. He'll come around."

When Ethel left Willa made her way to Abel's study. She slept there because it smelled like him. There was a lingering fragrance of his woody cologne, and the lemon drop candies he favored. She slept there with the memories of the bombing all around her—the flames and faces of those who suffered. She laid herself down on his worn leather couch so she could soak up the memories of him and hold on to the last thing he cared deeply about. But all she got were faint scents that would soon be gone, and the horrors of May 13, 1985, settling deep into her bones.

The next school board meeting was just like the last one. Ethel slipped the .45 in the desk at her seat on the dais. Willa sat next to her before looking past her to Buddy, who sat where the dais had started to curve. He waved at her, gave her a wink, and a big, wide-toothed smile. *He's looking at me,* she thought. *That means we have his vote.* With his tiebreaking vote, they could put this strife behind them and get on with the business of educating children. And she could get on with the business of grieving.

"You still think he's going to do the right thing?" Ethel whispered to her.

"Don't, Ethel."

The Chair, her wig slightly askew, gaveled the meeting to order. Reverend Thurston led the hall in prayer. Willa glanced around while most heads were bowed to see Ethel leaning back in her chair with her arms folded across her chest. At least the crowd was quiet, though, and patient a good long time while the reverend prayed for something even God may not be able to give them. Peace.

It wasn't the boy who had called Ethel a Nazi lover at the podium during the public comment period, but there were plenty of others using words like "lies" and "shaming." Some spoke in favor of letting the teachers teach, but they were quickly booed down. When Old Man Millet stood up, the audience and board members groaned. Ethel covered her face with her hands. Willa thought she heard a *Lord help us* behind her shut fingers. Old Man Millet owned three acres of sugarcane on the outskirts of town. He didn't pass the ninth grade but prided himself on finding out things for himself and wasting a lot of your time telling you about it.

"Come on," Big Buddy said amid the groans. "Y'all had your chance to speak, so let Mr. Millet have his."

And Mr. Millet was definitely going to have his chance. He hitched up his pants before laying some papers on the podium. He cleared his throat and wiped his nose with a red handkerchief before stuffing it back into his shirt pocket. When he reached for his reading glasses, someone said, "Come on, Old Man Millet. We ain't got all night."

The Chair slapped the gavel on the dais. Millet licked his thumb before turning to the papers.

"Now it seems to me that all this talk started when Abel Tangier wanted to have a day of remembrance down at the school for them MOVE people."

"That's not all we're talking about here, Old Man Millet," Ethel said. "We're talking about teaching our kids Black history in the schools."

Big Buddy sent her a warning look. "Be respectful," he said. "In this room, it's Mr. Millet."

"He wasn't Mr. Millet when your ass was stealing his cane to chew on."

Actually, all three of them used to steal Old Man Millet's sugarcane to chew on. But neither Willa nor Buddy corrected her.

"It's all right," Millet said. "Don't confront me none what you call me. But these MOVE folk y'all won't to defend up in here today, I just gotta say something."

"We aren't defending anybody, *Mr.* Millet," Ethel said.

"So you say, but what I'm saying is how all this foolish talk started. Abel Tangier, God rest his tired soul, wanted to have this MOVE day. And when kids' parents found out about it they rightfully put a stop to it."

"Let him speak," Buddy said before Ethel could interrupt him again.

Millet bounced on his heels and said, "I want to discuss why we making so much noise and causing so much community hate about these kinds of people."

"What kinds of people?" someone from the crowd spoke up.

Millet ignored them.

"Now these MOVE folk wasn't like any of the Black folk in this town. They didn't eat no meat, take care of their children, or love Jesus. Why, I read that they children were so hungry they ate outta the garbage. That and they parents spewed curse words and filth, saying mother-trucking this and mother-trucking that from a bull-horn that they had stuck up on top of the roof. That's what the bomb was aiming for. Drove the neighbors to distraction hearing all them filthy things."

"They used the bullhorn so they could raise awareness about the other MOVE members in jail for things they hadn't done," Willa said, surprised at the annoyance in her voice.

Millet kept talking as if he hadn't heard. "It was they own Black neighbors what complained."

"The neighbors didn't ask Wilson Goode to drop a bomb on their neighborhood, Mr. Millet," Ethel said.

"Them police must have had good reason," Millet answered.

"Because they killed a cop," Big Buddy said. "They murdered a cop before moving to Osage Street."

Willa looked at him in surprise.

"I can read too," Big Buddy said.

"See, that's a good reason, right?" Millet said, motioning to the board with a wrinkled hand. "Them's bad people."

"Let me ask you something, Mr. Millet," Ethel said, leaning over the dais. "How would you like the sheriff's department to burn you out of your house because your neighbor, not you, but your neighbor, was thought to have killed somebody."

"I'm just saying we shouldn't be tearing our town apart over them."

He sat down then, amid pats on the back and "amen, brother."

Willa, her voice in a whisper, said, "They set the place on fire and said let it burn, Mr. Millet. When members of MOVE tried to escape, they drove them back into the flames with gunshots. They killed children. Burned down an entire neighborhood. Doesn't that count for anything?"

"Willa," Big Buddy said.

She looked over at him and tried to catch his eye. But he turned away.

"Doesn't it, Buddy?" she asked.

He bowed his head and pretended to shuffle papers around.

"We ready for a vote?" Big Buddy asked the chair, his voice brisk. "Any more public comment?"

"Motherfucker," Ethel said under her breath.

Willa knew then that they had lost Big Buddy. Without his vote, there would be no talk of May 13, 1985, or any Black history curriculum in the schools that hadn't been sanitized beyond all meaning and belief. This man wasn't the boy she and Willa had run with during their younger years, played red light, green light from sunup to sundown on the streets of Byrd's Landing.

It barely registered that Ethel was standing, leaning over Willa, and jabbing her finger at Buddy, calling him a sellout. No, this man didn't resemble the boy who defended them on the playground, and who, in turn, was defended by them, especially by Ethel who knew how to play crazy to scare off a bully. *Red Rover, Red Rover,* Willa thought. *Send Buddy right over.* Except the Buddy they knew was gone.

The entire room was up in arms. Chairs fell over. A couple of young boys were climbing over the front two rows to get to the school board members on the dais. Old Man Millet yelled, "Hey, hey, hey!" The two off-duty cops who were supposed to be keeping things under control hadn't moved from their spots. The only threatening thing they did against the crowd was to take their billy clubs out.

Over it all Willa heard Ethel shrieking at Big Buddy, who was telling her to get ahold of herself. It was then the room exploded with a single gunshot. Silence, for the space of a single breath, and then chaos. People rushed for the door, or flattened their bodies against the floor.

Willa couldn't believe it. She knew the gun was dangerous, but didn't believe that Ethel had it in her to hurt anybody. Big Buddy clutched his chest while blood poured through his fingers. His eyes rolled back into his head.

Willa's own hands were stinging. Why were they stinging?

And then she felt Ethel's sweaty hands on her own, prying something from her, saying, "Come on, come on, Willa, put it down, give it to me." Ethel pressed Willa back into her seat. She bent down to smooth her hair.

It was the gentleness in Ethel's touch that helped Willa understand that she had stepped through another hole in reality. Ethel didn't shoot Big Buddy. It was her, Willa. She had snatched the gun when Ethel was arguing with Big Buddy and shot him. The woman who didn't have a mean bone in her body. She dropped her face into her hands and sobbed once.

"Hey, now don't you worry," Ethel said. "We're going to get through this. Not your fault. Besides, couldn't have happened to a better asshole."

How Hope Found Chauncey

FROM *South Central Noir*

HOPE FOUND CHAUNCEY in the oven where she thought he'd be. Maria ran by searching everywhere in that filthy house, but Hope saw that the oven door in the kitchen was open. She walked to it slowly, knowing if she saw the wrong thing she'd be broken. But there he was inside of that cavernous old oven in his baby blanket curled up sleeping, clutching emptiness. She gently lifted him up, determined not to wake him, but her infant brother woke with a scream. She cooed and sang to him until he rested his head on her shoulder and wearily returned to sleep.

She figured he'd exhausted himself and had no energy left to cry; that he had been crying for a long time in the dark, filthy house that her mother somehow still owned. It wasn't the first time Hope had found him there, though Rika said she'd never put him in the oven again for safekeeping, but Hope knew she was lying, and she returned daily to check on him. It was about dark outside, and almost black inside the house; Hope didn't want them to be there a minute longer than they had to be. She skipped over trash, avoiding all the madness and filth that had accumulated in what used to be her home.

"I found him," Hope said, just loud enough for Maria to hear.

"He's okay?"

"She put him in the oven again, but he's okay."

"We gotta go," Maria said, her voice edging on panic.

Hope nodded. Chauncey might wake screaming his head off and Rika could appear like she would do, straight out of nowhere, like a horror movie monster, and snatch him from her arms. Not this time, she'd never give him up.

"You think she has any formula?" Maria asked.

"Under the bed. She hides it there."

They burst into the bedroom, holding their breath because Rika never would take the time to throw away soiled diapers; instead, she just tossed them into what had become a mountain of shitty diapers; but the bedroom reeked of something worse than that.

"I don't want to put my hand under the bed," Maria said, shaking her head.

Hope understood. Anything could be under there, but when Rika had some extra money and sense enough to pay a basehead to gank formula for her, that's where she'd hide it from that same basehead who might steal it back. She'd get enough cans of formula for a month so the baby wouldn't go hungry even if she spent all the rest of her cash on rock. All she needed was water; she could find that from a neighbor's hose even if the water was off in her house like it was now.

"Hold him," Hope said, gently handing Chauncey over to Maria. Because Chauncey was blond with blue-green eyes and pale skin that contrasted against her dark skin and even Maria's light brown skin, Hope knew that some people said she stole herself a white baby because there was no way that baby could be her brother.

She squatted down, gripped the bedframe, and lifted the bed high off the floor. "I see it. And I see all kinds of shit."

"Can you get it? I don't want to put him down," Maria said.

Hope could tell Maria was even more scared of what kind of nastiness she might touch than she was. Hope pulled up, flipping the bed over. The cans were there like they were supposed to be, but she couldn't bring herself to reach for them. They saw Booty, the pit bull that Rika was supposed to love, lying there dead and so close to the formula that his rear paw rested on a can. She had no idea of why it had gone under the bed to die, but it made as much sense as anything else that had happened to them.

"Can we go? Just leave the cans. It's no good now."

Hope nodded; she needed to breathe, seemed as though the entire time they were inside of the house she hadn't taken a breath. Outside, the sun was just setting at the western end of the palm-lined, nearly deserted avenue, and Hope began to feel Maria's panic run through her, making it hard to think clearly.

Hope wanted to catch the bus to the Snooty Fox, but Maria never went along with that idea. It was a waste of time, but she still had to try to get Maria to go along.

"Come on. It's a short bus ride."

"No, it's too crazy."

Maria would hardly take the bus in the day, but night, hell no, she just wouldn't consider it. She'd developed a way of walking so fast that nobody could catch her unless they sprinted, and then she'd just run. If she ran, no one could stay with her. She ran the 400 and the 800 at Locke for that pervert track coach—before things really fell apart. Hope hated trying to hang with Maria, and carrying heavy-bottomed Chauncey made it twice as hard.

"Do you want me to hold him?" Maria asked, but Hope shook her head. She'd keep up while holding Chauncey; she had no choice.

Hope glanced at the house she was raised in, praying that it would be the last time she'd ever see it; words couldn't explain how much she hated it. Maria had gapped her; doing that run/walk thing. Hope wrapped Chauncey a little tighter in his favorite Dora baby blanket and worked hard to catch Maria. Maria did have a point about it being safer to run everywhere you go; by the time the Kitchen Crips kicking it by the liquor store noticed them, they had already blown past. If they tried to catch them, they'd realize it was hopeless, and even if the knuckleheads burned out in a car, Hope and Maria would just cross against traffic and go in the opposite direction. It worked, but it was so hard; Hope was already winded. The relief she felt when she saw the motel in the distance made the burning in her lungs go away.

The Snooty Fox Motor Inn wasn't really the kind of motel you'd stay in with a baby; it wasn't the kind of place you'd stay in with a family or by yourself. Purple—everything was shades of purple except for the shag carpet which was thick and white. The ceilings were mirrored and so was the bathroom. Neither one of them could figure out why anyone would want to see themselves on the toilet. First time Hope saw the mirrored ceiling above the toilet, she shrugged and said, "Freaks got to be freaky."

She had the key, so Maria waited by the door warily looking

about, ready to bolt. Soon as they entered the room and locked the door, Maria put a chair against the handle and they both collapsed on the bed with the baby between them. He was wide awake, bright eyes casting about, taking in all the purple and then, to Hope and Maria's delight, his own image above them on the ceiling. When he waved at himself they both laughed, then Hope's stomach churned when she realized that the night hadn't ended.

"We've got to go back out."

"Why?"

"We need formula."

Maria shrugged and slipped on her sandals. It never seemed to be over because it was never over until you were dead. Neither wanted to go anywhere, not when they could kick it in the motel room, watching cable TV, eating cold pizza, and not having to dodge fools or answer to anybody; but there was no way to consider doing that when Chauncey needed a bottle and they had nothing for him, except sugar water. They wrapped him up again in the Dora blanket, and again they were off at Maria's break-ass pace. In front of the yellowish glow of the Food 4 Less they parted ways; Hope headed for the interior of the store, picking up a bunch of bananas and diapers, all the time feeling eyes on her. Security there, an even-at-night-sunglass-wearing, grim-faced Latino with tattooed, bulging arms watched her with an ugly smile that was more a leer or a smirk. Once, a while ago, he'd said something in Spanish that she wasn't supposed to know. She knew it and it might have been worth six months in juvenile if she had let herself go and smashed him in the face with a jar of pickles, but she'd just shined him on. Those days of acting a fool were gone; everything she did now had to be cold-blooded serious. It was about Chauncey and it was about Maria and then herself. It was about getting the hell out of Dodge before things got worse, and though that was hard to imagine, she was sure that things *would* get worse.

She glanced at the checkout line and saw Maria conversating with Hector, the used-to-be gangster who now had a job and a wife and kid, but still wanted some of Maria. Hope returned the smile of the security guard scoping on her, and he grunted an acknowledgment. She approached him and stopped close enough to make him take a step backward.

"I need a ride home. You know someone who'd hook me up?"

She could see herself reflected in his sunglasses, her long braids hanging about her face, her pretty full lips, and the tightness of her button-up shirt.

"Where do you need to go?" he asked, looking down with a puzzled expression at Chauncey's bright blue eyes.

"Somewhere with you," she said, stepping even closer to him.

The alarm went off at the front of the store and the guard took off to see what was going on. Hope followed.

Maria stood in the path of the electric eye of the sliding doors. She held two cans of formula, the stuff they keep in locked cabinets, waiting for him to arrive.

"Puta!" the security guard shouted, and charged to catch her as she ran. Hope trailed, still clutching the diapers and fruit in one hand and in the other Chauncey, who seemed to sense that something was about to happen and was wary and quiet.

"Fuck you!" Maria shouted as the big-armed guard chased her into the parking lot. Hope set off the alarm too, but the bagger, a big Black footballer she knew from Locke, shrugged and didn't try to stop her.

Hope waited for the guard, waving his gun above his head, to get closer to Maria, and then she stepped quickly in the opposite direction. As she retreated, she heard the security guard lustily cursing Maria with a surprisingly high-pitched voice, daring her to return. Hope laughed as she hurried away, delighting Chauncey, who laughed along with her.

They arrived at the motel pretty much at the same time. Hope suspected Maria must have run backward the entire way as she sometimes did. She unlocked the door and they exploded inside.

"We can't go there for a while," Hope said.

Maria laughed. "That's what you said last month."

The baby had finally had enough excitement and began whining for a bottle. Hope walked to the bathroom and carefully rinsed the Donald Duck bottle. She should have gotten another bottle and nipples too, now that Chauncey had started gnawing through the nipples. She'd save the banana for morning; now at sixteen months, Chauncey wanted much more than formula. She looked at herself in the mirror as she mixed formula, two scoops and slightly warm water, and he was good. Chauncey didn't look like her; he had their mother's face, her straight hair and white skin. Hope had met her own dad a few times, a Black firefighter who used to like to kick it with her mother, but he got off drugs and left town and Hope's mom could never find him to make him pay child support, or so she said.

Chauncey's dad was white, she knew that, but Rika would never admit to who he was, like it was some kind of secret. Hope had some ideas; sometimes Rika would visit her old school, so she thought it might be a teacher. You couldn't put anything past a teacher, but maybe the father wasn't a total loser. Chauncey was handsome and playful and with the sweetest disposition; he hardly cried and was so smart. When he was really little, when he was hungry, he'd point to his mouth, and when he was tired, he'd cradle his head. When Rika brought him home from the hospital, she seemed to want to live a different life. She even went to church for a little bit, but that didn't last. Hope had seen her decline over time, going from trying to be a good mother to just not giving a fuck.

Rika would say, "I'm going out, watch Chauncey."

That would be it; she'd bail and leave Hope with a baby. So, there she was, sixteen and trying to take care of a two-month-old. It was the most overwhelming thing that Hope had ever experienced, and it changed her. She realized she could *do*. She could be the mother for her little brother, at least she would try, and that was more than Rika ever did. She was sure she could do a better job than anybody else.

"Hurry up with that bottle!" Maria shouted.

Hope returned. At the sight of her, Chauncey squirmed out of Maria's arms to reach for the bottle and couldn't get the nipple into his mouth fast enough.

"He's hungry, this one," Maria said with satisfaction.

"Yeah, he is."

"Think we should take him to school tomorrow?"

Hope sat on the edge of the bed, surprised to hear the word "school" slip from Maria's mouth. "Maybe we should go, see what's happening."

"Yeah, maybe . . ."

Hope didn't think much of the idea and thought that Maria must be tripping. They both knew the score, what it meant to go to school with Chauncey.

"You go, Maria. I'll stay here."

Maria paused before she said another word. She put her hand on Hope's arm.

"I don't care if you go. But you know I can't go up there. You know Rika will be looking."

"I know," said Maria. "You're doing your best for him. I just wanted to see what's going on."

Hope nodded. Seeing what was going on didn't just mean seeing how much classwork she had missed. Hardest thing about doing what they were doing was giving up on the life they had before, no matter that that life was shit for the both of them.

"I'm not going to go to Locke without you."

"You need to do what you need to do. I ain't stopping you."

Maria started to cry then, softly like it wasn't really happening. Hope knew that Maria had a sister, but something had happened between the two of them and they hadn't talked in a long time.

"Do you want to catch the bus to the beach?" Maria asked.

Maria always wanted to go to the beach, especially when things were going bad. Things weren't there yet, but one more night and they had to be out of the Snooty Fox Motor Inn. Hope knew they had to plan. They had options but not good ones. If Chauncey got sick, or if they just couldn't stand another night at Aunt Thelma's, they'd do what they had to do.

"Manny comes back Saturday. We need to be out of here before that."

Maria shrugged, though it was her that Manny fiended over. Hope knew that if it was *her* the asshole wanted, she sure as hell would be trying to make sure they were long gone before he got back.

"We'll see Aunt Thelma. She'll help us out, but we can do that Saturday. We'll go to the beach tomorrow."

Maria smiled lazily, closed her eyes. The baby finished the bottle and began drifting off. Hope slid out of bed and checked to see that the lock was on and that the chair was secure under the knob. She made sure the half-sized bat was where it was supposed to be, near the bed, and the raggedy cell phone, the last gift her mother had given her before she went crazy, was where it was supposed to be, in the diaper bag, alongside the rusty .38. The .38 was Maria's, but Hope doubted that it worked or even that it was loaded. She hated guns and didn't want anything to do with them, yet Maria insisted they keep it.

Hope reached into the ridiculously small pocket of her jeans where she had five twenties rolled tight inside of a straw. That money would never be spent unless things blew up and they had to get out of town fast. Getting out of town seemed more and more likely, since they had already used up most of the favors they had coming from the girls they were down with; they were left with Aunt Thelma and Manny the Perv. She wouldn't consider help from people she didn't know well ever since that social worker tried to take Chauncey away. Hope had called her because she thought she had no choice; Rika and her boyfriend at the time were squabbling in front of the house and it got to the point that Rika had pulled her duce-duce on him.

That's when Hope figured that she had to do something, so she unfolded that barely legible number for Child Protective Services she had saved to do the right thing, but the right thing turned out to be so wrong. The social worker arrived the next day, a small, dark-skinned Asian woman who listened quietly and took a lot of notes. Soon, it became clear that she knew all about Rika and that she already had a thick folder on her. Hope realized that the social worker wasn't going to take Rika away, just Chauncey. Hope changed course and threw out the incontestable fact that Rika was the best fucking mother in the world and that she'd made up the thing about Rika chasing her fool boyfriend in the street, trying to shoot him in the ass.

Rika had realized that Hope was on her side and came on strong with lies knowing that she was a fly's finger from losing Chauncey.

"Oh yeah, the house is messy because I been working long hours—I don't own a gun and I've never shot at anybody—I've been off drugs and living a healthy life." Rika continued lying her ass off with the best butter-couldn't-melt-in-her-mouth routine. Hope nodded with fake enthusiasm at all the right places. The social worker shrugged, realizing that she didn't have a case and left with a bitter look on her face. After the social worker cleared out, Rika charged Hope and brutally slapped her. Rika was a relentlessly neglectful parent, not a physically cruel one, and rarely hit Hope, but this time she looked murderous. "If I had time, I'd beat your ass good," she had said, and disappeared into the street. That was just the start of the times when it went from really bad to unbelievably fucked up.

Hope wanted to fall asleep; it just wasn't going to happen. What she needed more than anything was a chance to catch her breath; she didn't see how she could. She had to calm down, to rest, maybe even sleep, though she didn't like her dreams.

First headlight beams flooded the room, then steps, a key in the lock. The chair stopped the door from opening.

"Open up! Don't keep me out here!"

"Oh shit, he's here," Hope said, still whispering as though Chauncey could possibly sleep through all the shouting. He wailed and Maria put her hands on top of her head as though she were trying to keep it from flying off.

"Hey, I hear you. Open the door!"

Hope knew the voice though she didn't want to. Not him, not now.

"It's Manny, he's early," Hope said, fear and anger in her voice.

Maria turned on the light and reached for the diaper bag and held it close to her chest. Hope held Chauncey in one arm and with her free hand pushed the chair away and opened the door.

Manny stood there in the doorway, silhouetted by the ample off-street lighting radiating from the parking lot—lighted parking lots supposedly kept gangsters away like sunlight did vampires, though vampires didn't shoot the lights out.

Hope ignored him as she cooed to the baby, doing her best to calm him. For whatever reason he didn't close the door behind him. Hope couldn't bring herself to do it either. Somehow it closed itself.

With liquor stink all over him, Manny stumbled over to the bed, sat on the edge of it, and unlaced his boots. Suddenly this room with all the mirrors and purple everywhere looked like what it was: a place that pervs like Manny could get their freak on. He was a little man who walked with a cowboy swagger when he wasn't staggering, and who drove a SUV so big it had a ladder. Brown-skinned and weathered like he earned a living outdoors, he was a building inspector for the city of Los Angeles. The owners of the motels around the bedraggled central city, all Patels and Kupuys—South Asians trying to make a living on some of the worst streets of Los Angeles—knew Manny's kind, and comped him rooms to keep him smiling and happy as he had his way with underage girls.

"Where'd you find the boy?"

"He's my brother."

"Good, good. Didn't know you had a white mama."

"My mother's not white."

Manny grimaced like talking to Hope was too much work. He looked away from her and focused on Maria. "I finished my vacation early, just so I could get back here and spend time loving on you."

Maria looked stricken, and it didn't help when Manny reached into the bag and came out with a brown leather jacket with fringes like you see on girls who dance to ranchero music.

"I got this for you. Come over here and try it on."

Maria took one step and, like a dog snapping at a fly, he grabbed her wrist and pulled her down onto his lap.

"I . . . wait," Maria said, still clutching the diaper bag.

Manny didn't wait; he clamped one of his hands onto Maria's leg and squeezed it. He tried kissing her on the mouth, but she turned her head, and he caught her ear. It didn't seem to bother Manny that Maria cringed every time he touched her. Actually, he seemed more than comfortable with her discomfort. Hope, though, was losing her mind. Maria put up with Manny because she felt she had to—of all the bad shit she had to deal with he wasn't the worst—but she really didn't have to live like that anymore. They both swore that they'd never let that kind of shit happen to them again.

Maria held out the diaper bag for Hope to take.

"You could party with us, but the baby would probably yell his ass off."

"No, I don't party."

"You don't?" Manny said with a frown while massaging Maria's leg.

"No, I'm watching my brother. I don't have time to party."

"Oh well. Maybe you need to give us privacy. Take the kid into the bathroom or something."

Maria pleaded with her eyes for some kind of help as Hope walked away into the sanctuary of the bathroom. What was wrong with them? They should have seen this coming. Manny had done it before to Maria, but times had changed, or at least that's what they wanted to believe.

Hope sat on the toilet and rocked Chauncey asleep, glancing up at herself in the mirror and feeling disgusted as she listened to what was happening on the other side of the door, whispers that weren't whispers; the grunts of a drunken-ass old fool and the sounds of Maria protesting.

Soon as Chauncey was sleeping, she put him into the tub on top of a nest of bath towels, and then took the .38 out of the bag and looked it over. Would it work if she pulled the trigger? Unsure, but determined to make things different, she swung the door open and stepped into the other room.

Manny was on top of Maria, grinding his tattooed body into her, grunting mightily. Maria had her arms across her face to keep his nasty mouth from kissing her, and Manny was too into it to notice Hope kneeling down and rolling the bat from beneath the bed.

Hope thought about what she would do next. Should she shoot him or hit him? She had promised Maria that she'd get her back, just like Maria said she'd get hers. Hope stepped forward, lowered the gun, and lifted the bat high, then came down on the back of Manny's head; the sound was sick like a coconut cracking, but at least Manny stopped with the grunting.

Maria kicked him off of the bed and scrambled to her feet and stood there shaking. She still had on those tight-ass Levi's cutoffs that would take industrial scissors to remove.

"He was too drunk to get them off," Maria said.

"How is he?" Hope asked, unable to look at Manny twisted up in purple sheets.

Maria bent down next to him for a long moment, then straightened up. "He's breathing."

Hope sighed, "I guess that's good."

"Yeah, I think so."

Now that she knew he was alive, she squatted next to him and fished keys out of his pants that were crumpled around his ankles.

"What now?" Maria asked.

Hope stood up with Manny's wallet in hand and shrugged. "Visit my aunt. Figure it out."

Maria nodded.

Chauncey started to cry.

Hope hurried into the bathroom and lifted him from the tub into her arms. "We'll figure it out," she said, as they ran for the hulking SUV outside of the motel room.

Crime Scene

FROM *Malice in Dallas*

WHEN ADLER GOT BACK to his private dock, Melanie Phelps was sitting at the end, legs kicking in the air over the water. Her Stevie Ray Vaughan T-shirt and khaki shorts made her look like the kid she'd been when they first met, thirty years ago. Adler hadn't seen her in more than a year. He cut the engine and let the little boat drift in, tossing her a line. As she tied it off, he climbed up onto the planks beside her, carrying his pole and a small cooler.

"Catch much?" she asked, nodding at the cooler.

"This is for beer," Adler said. "These days I let the ones I catch go. Too much trouble cleaning them." In truth, he hadn't wet a line in months. When he went out on the lake he mostly just drifted, staring out over the water. "How's your father?"

Melanie shook her head. "No change. Wish I could say different."

Lamar Phelps had spent decades as the country's top criminal talent scout, hooking crooks up with jobs from coast to coast for a slice of the proceeds. When a stroke cut him down five years ago, Melanie took over the family business. Adler went to Denver once to see his old friend but found nothing of Lamar in the chair being wheeled from one sunny spot to another. Given the things Lamar knew that would be of interest to prosecutors, the fact that he was completely nonverbal was, Adler supposed, a blessing in disguise. It was one bitch of a disguise, though.

"I was going to grill a steak," he said. "You want one?"

"You cook now?"

"Beats the hell out of driving an hour and a half for a Big Mac."

He grilled on the cabin's back deck. Melanie sat at the picnic table. He tried to remember how old she was while she chatted, mostly gossip about people Adler had long forgotten or never knew. She had to be in her forties, but she didn't show it. There was maybe a whisper of gray, barely detectable, in the blond hair at her temples.

By the time he served the food she was lapsing into a silence to match his own. He'd seen it before. The spell of this place. When a V of geese came overhead, close enough to hear not just their honking but the velvet sound of their wings cutting the air, she looked at them with an open delight that took her right back to childhood.

She finally pushed her plate away. "I can't remember the last time I had a steak and baked potato."

"I'm a simple man," Adler said. "Gonna talk about why you're here?"

"A job," Melanie said. "But you knew that."

He opened another beer and waited.

"One target," she said. "Your cut is a hundred K, twenty now and the rest after."

"Something with that kind of number attached has to be hairy."

"There are some complications. The target is locally prominent, and the customer wants him to get it in a very public place at a very specific time."

"Hold the pickles, hold the lettuce," Adler said. "Special orders don't upset us." He waved a hand at her confused look. "Before your time. Give me the details."

"Ever been to Dallas?"

"Passed through a few times. Never worked there."

"All the better if nobody local can make you." Melanie took an eight by ten from her bag and slid it across the table. It showed a silver-haired man in an expensive suit, his arms crossed. Some kind of publicity shot.

"Alex Lersch," she said. "Sixty-four years old, net worth a couple hundred million. Never married, no known children."

"Gay?"

"Don't know. Could be he's just allergic to sharing the pile. He got his start in real estate and software, but he's so diversified now that you couldn't really say what he does. Active in local politics and charities, mostly leans left, which isn't easy in Texas these days. Has a reputation as shrewd but basically honest."

"Who'd he piss off?"

"Don't know," she said again. At Adler's look she raised a hand. "Honestly. This one came through deep back channels. The money's real, but I don't know who the client is."

"I'm hearing warning bells, kiddo."

"I get you, but show me the cop who can put out this kind of cash just on the chance of netting somebody."

"What about the time and place?"

"You're gonna love this. Dealey Plaza on November twenty-second."

He gave her a flat stare. "You drove one hell of a long way for a joke."

"No joke. Lersch is an assassination buff, an obsessive. He's supposed to have the largest private collection of Kennedy materials in the world. Funds an annual conference that's a mix of legitimate historians and tinfoil nutjobs. One of the activities is a visit to Dealey Plaza that he leads himself on the anniversary. That's where you're supposed to tag him."

"Somebody's got a sick sense of humor."

"If you've got the money, I think it just counts as an eccentric sense of humor. Anyway, there it is. You in or out?"

He gave Melanie the extra bedroom to spare her the two-hour drive to the nearest hotel. After she went to bed, he sat on the dock, under the stars. It was too late in the year for fireflies, but the woods and the water were buzzing with the constant small sounds of living creatures.

Adler had done a lot of jobs in fields of work where nobody writes a résumé. He started in explosives, blowing safes for crews on the West Coast, then learned to hack alarm systems. He hired on for a handful of kidnappings, which always seemed to go screwy. There had been some hijacking, some smuggling. Eventually word got around that he didn't mind eliminating people under the right circumstances, and Lamar started steering hits his way. By his count, Adler had done thirty-four. If he thought hard, he could remember all their names.

Lately he'd been remembering them a lot, drifting around on the lake. It was always easiest to assume they all deserved what was coming. It was starting to bother him that for some of them, he didn't know. He didn't know why somebody in their lives wanted the hammer dropped.

The money from this Dallas job would be nice, but he didn't need it. He took it because maybe this time he could know why. Even thinking the question was breaking some rules, but he was too old and tired to care. November 22 was almost a month off. The way Adler figured it, how he spent that time was up to him.

He was going to spend it figuring out why somebody wanted Alex Lersch dead.

Two weeks later Adler set foot in Dealey Plaza for the first time. The Rangers ball cap pulled low on his forehead and the heavy black sunglasses covering half his face would complicate facial recognition programs that might be running on any one of the dozens of security cameras on an average American city block. The Cowboys jersey and the camera around his neck marked him as a tourist. He'd barely crossed the street into the plaza when a tall Black man with a canvas bag slung over his shoulder offered him a "personal tour" for a hundred dollars. Adler got away by giving the man twenty bucks for a reproduction of the November 23, 1963, edition of the *New York Times*. He held it loosely at his side as he wandered, letting it ward off the other hustlers.

On a pleasant Saturday afternoon, with the anniversary approaching, there were plenty of tourists for the hustlers to prey on. Some were rolling through on buses, the rehearsed patter of the guides echoing through tinny loudspeakers, but many were just walking around. Adler drifted among them, occasionally snapping a picture. In part of his brain, he held a sketchy biography of this version of himself. *Midwest. Retired schoolteacher. Middle-grade science. Widowed?* Mostly, though, he focused on getting a feel for the setting, finding the lines of sight, the obvious entry and exit points, the less obvious maintenance and structural features.

It was an odd place. The plaza itself was just a rough triangle of patchy grass, with the base along Houston Street to the east and the point at the west, where the streets defining the two sides swept under railroad tracks. All the energy and interest was along the north edge, where the former Book Depository squatted at the corner of Houston and Elm, Oswald's window clearly marked. Two big white Xs in the middle of Elm showed the exact places where Kennedy had been hit.

In an hour and a half, Adler saw at least fifty people, most of them young men, stroll out into the road to take a selfie on an X, usually with the Oswald window in the frame behind them. They seemed oblivious to active traffic on the street, and he wondered how many got hit over the course of a year.

He heard at least twenty-five people, most of them slightly older men, looking back and forth from the window to an X and proclaiming it an easy shot. "He was right on top of him," they usually said.

He heard at least fifteen people, most of them middle-aged men, saying that their lawn back home was bigger than the grassy knoll.

They were inane, but they weren't wrong. The place had the aura of a backlot recreation, a three-quarter-scale model that didn't quite convince. It was the field of myth, the pressure point where the American century shattered. The most devastating rifle shot in history shouldn't be so short. The grassy knoll should at least be large enough for everyone mentioned in the conspiracy theories to stand on. If it wasn't for the sheer weight of the names, Dealey Plaza would look like what it was: a stunted, inconsequential green space tucked into an odd margin of a big city.

None of this mattered. He wasn't Lersch, trying to solve some riddle for the ages. He was a professional, here to do a job. He watched where the cops strolled and what they were looking at. He watched the traffic lights, timing them in his head. He walked five or six blocks in every direction, noting parking garages, bus stops, and buildings with multiple access points. He verified what he already knew: that from every corner of Dealey Plaza he had a clear, unimpeded view of the neon red shirt he'd hung in the window of his room on one of the upper floors of the big hotel a couple of blocks to the southwest.

Before coming to Dallas, Adler spent a week in another hotel in San Antonio, buying the things he would need at several different stores using credit cards under several different names. One of the things he bought was a laptop. At night in his room, he used it to read everything he could find about Alexander Malcolm Lersch—interviews, profiles, news stories, the last few years of the available records on his various businesses and charitable funds.

He found nothing that provided an obvious motive for the man's murder. Lersch had no living relatives. Upon his death, half his fortune would go into a trust for the "perpetual funding" of a

Center for the Study of Assassination and Political Violence at the University of Texas at Arlington, which would also be the recipient of his personal Kennedy collection. The other half would be distributed to various local charities focusing on voting rights and hunger. In his business dealings Lersch was aggressive, but not ruthless, leaving no ruined rivals to dream of revenge. Even reading between the lines, Adler saw no evidence of scandal. No mysterious payoffs to former employees. No trace of money laundering or obvious bribes. From all appearances, Lersch was an upstanding citizen. The only unusual thing about him was his hang-up about the Kennedy hit.

Ideally Adler would have shifted from research to surveillance once he was in Dallas, but keeping eyes on a multimillionaire around the clock wasn't a realistic proposition. He could hardly hang out in the reception area of Lersch's offices, which occupied several floors in a downtown skyscraper. Sitting in a coffee shop across from the entrance to the attached parking garage, he did verify something mentioned in almost every profile: despite his wealth, Lersch still drove his own car, arriving at the office at nine every morning and making it a firm practice to leave at five. He spoke in many interviews about the importance of maintaining a balance between work and the rest of life, and of resisting overwork on one hand and unnecessary luxury or indulgence on the other.

Adler was grateful that Lersch's notion of "unnecessary luxury" did not extend to buying some anonymous sedan or SUV. He drove a silver Rolls Royce that was easy to follow. For several days in a row Adler trailed him from the office just after five, hoping to be led to something that would give him a thread to pull. A mistress. An underground sex club. A poker room. Every night, though, Lersch drove straight to his estate in Highland Park. Adler's research told him that the place was worth in the neighborhood of ten million dollars, and that Lersch lived there alone. Here too, he couldn't just sit on the street and watch the place. In a neighborhood like that, the cops would have been on him in twenty minutes. He made several passes a night, though, and never saw any other cars go near the place or anything remotely suspicious.

Driving back to his hotel, Adler drummed his fingers on the wheel. He was starting to wonder if somebody had just pulled Lersch's name out of a hat, or if maybe this was some kind of elaborate sting. He was tempted to call Melanie to try to track the back channels she'd spoken of, but asking questions like that in the middle of a job would set off every alarm she had. Melanie was fond of him, but she would assume he was either going soft or had flipped on her. Either choice meant that she would be visiting another one of her subcontractors soon and sliding a picture of him across the table. Adler was on his own.

He briefly considered registering for Lersch's assassination conference before rejecting the idea as too conspicuous. The schedule was online, though. There was nothing for him in the scheduled sessions on bullet trajectories and Cuban diplomatic archives. On the night of the twenty-first, though, there was a three-hour formal banquet, with a keynote address by Lersch himself. "Living in the Echo of Gunfire: The Continuing Legacy of Assassination Studies."

Poetic, Adler thought.

Lersch's estate backed onto a creek that, two miles away, ran through the grounds of a country club. An hour before the banquet was scheduled to start, with dusk gathering, Adler parked in the employee lot of the club. He walked to the creek and began following it, sticking as close to the edge of the water as he could. Most of the creek's path through the whole area was still heavily wooded, and along much of the way he was completely out of sight of any structures. He stopped occasionally to check his exact position on his phone's GPS. There was heavy undergrowth in many places, and the wet ground made for slow progress, but in forty minutes he was at the low wall marking the back entrance to Lersch's property. Ten minutes after that he was at the patio door at the back of the house.

The security system had been installed by one of the big national firms. Several years back, keeping his skills up to date, Adler used one of his dummy identities to go through the firm's hiring and training programs. There had been some updates since then, of course, but people in the security business are every bit as inefficient as people everywhere else. They couldn't always be bothered to, for example, check their systems for legacy backdoors left by a previous generation of programmers.

He had the door open in twenty minutes. It took him another thirty to find the security system's central drive, disable the cameras, and wipe the last two hours they'd recorded.

*

The speech went well, Alex Lersch thought. Perhaps a little dry, but he hoped his sense of urgency came through. He had spoken at length of the coming establishment of the Center at UT-Arlington, urging his fellow enthusiasts to unite their scholarship and investigative powers around its banner. The time had come to set aside petty squabbles and ensure the security of future inquiries. Had he persuaded them? Time would tell.

Tomorrow would tell.

When he got home he went into the office, intending to make a few final notes before the tour in the morning. The sconce in the hallway cast a long canted column of light across the room as he crossed to the desk. He was reaching for the lamp, thinking that something seemed odd without being able to put his finger on what it was, when a calm voice came from behind him. "Don't turn around," it said. "And don't turn on the light. I have a gun."

The chair, Lersch thought. The chair that normally sat in the middle of the room had been missing. Pulled into some corner for this man's comfort, no doubt.

Lersch put his hands flat on the desk and waited.

Adler gave Lersch credit for not panicking. He seemed perfectly calm.

"There was a revolver in your upper right-hand desk drawer," Adler said. "There isn't now. Go behind the desk and turn the chair to face the wall and sit down."

Lersch did as he was told. "I don't suppose you'd believe me if I said there's not much here worth stealing," he said.

"No, but it doesn't matter. That's not what I'm here for."

"And what are you here for?"

Adler could just make out the curve of Lersch's head above the top of the chair. "You and I have an appointment tomorrow morning."

Lersch was slow to answer, the extra beat confirming what Adler already knew. "I have an appointment with a lot of people tomorrow morning," he said. "I'm leading a tour."

"Our appointment isn't about an old murder."

Rich people always have the quietest homes. Adler knew the air conditioning was running, but it didn't keep him from hearing Lersch's breath getting shallow as he answered. "I don't know what you mean."

"How long have you got, Lersch?"

The answer came with a touch of acid. "I guess that's up to the man holding a gun on me."

"I've seen your medicine cabinet. I'm no doctor, but I've had plenty of time to Google the stuff you're taking. It's not for lowering your cholesterol."

For a time, he thought Lersch wasn't going to answer.

"Two months," he finally said. "Probably a little less."

"You put the hit on yourself."

"I've spent my entire adult life studying assassination," Lersch said. "I knew the kind of people to get in touch with. The professionals."

"Very flattering," Adler said.

"But not very professional," Lersch said. "This is not what I paid for."

"I've been trying to figure out why anybody would want you dead," Adler said. "That's why I came here tonight. I wanted to know the reason."

Lersch made a noise in his throat. "I've bought many things and services in my life. I've never before had anyone demand to know why I wanted them." He made the noise again. "Not professional."

"I'll report myself to the union when this is over," Adler said.

"And now that you know? Does my motive meet your exacting standards? It's rather late for me to seek alternate arrangements."

"Now that I know? There's no reason you have to bleed out on dirty pavement, Lersch. I can do this right now. I can make it quick. Painless."

"*Not what I paid for.*" For a moment Adler thought Lersch was going to come out of the chair, but he brought himself under control. "Please. Follow the directions you were given. Tomorrow, at the plaza."

"Why?"

"Why, why, why. You're certainly consistent in your curiosity, Mr. Whoever You Are."

"You're not answering."

The outline of Lersch's head dipped, came back up.

"Because I want what they have," he said.

"They?"

"Kennedy. Oswald. Two paths crossed, and more than half a century later we don't fully understand why or how. You know what lasts, Mr. Killer? A mystery. A riddle. We'll talk about the two of them forever because there is no final piece to the puzzle. And me?" Lersch gave a low whistle. "One of the foremost experts on the assassination, cut down in exactly the same place by an unknown assailant for unknown reasons. There will be books about me. Podcasts. I'll be part of the story forever."

"Very pretty," Adler said. "Is it from your speech?"

"It's from my life."

It was Adler's turn to be quiet, for so long that Lersch finally stirred. "Did I put you to sleep?"

Adler stood up. "No, but you should go to bed yourself, Mr. Lersch. You've got a big day tomorrow. I'll leave the gun on your back patio."

A little over twelve hours later, a bus adorned with the logo of the conference made the tight turn onto Elm and parked at the curb directly in front of the former Book Depository. The plaza was already crowded with more people than Adler had seen there before. He was across the street watching, back in his tourist gear.

Lersch was the first person off the bus, followed by about two dozen men and women. He had a small megaphone with him, and he led the group along the sidewalk, gesturing at the street and occasionally the building. Adler couldn't hear the speech. What looked like a rather old-fashioned hearing aid in his right ear was playing the police radio band, at a volume high enough to drown out most of the noise around him.

Lersch led his group along Elm, taking them to the spot where Abraham Zapruder's 8mm camera caught the only footage of the assassination, then on to the grassy knoll. He was using the megaphone less and seemed to be getting drawn into conversations with one or two individuals at a time. Adler shifted from foot to foot, seeming to stare at his phone while actually keeping track of the group's progress. Finally, Lersch led the entire bunch across to Adler's side of Elm and started bringing them in the right direction. He was focused on the building now, gesturing at Oswald's window. When he was ten feet away, Adler dialed the first of two preprogrammed numbers on his cell phone.

Four blocks east, the burner cell he'd dialed triggered a device in the base of a sidewalk garbage can. Adler always enjoyed a chance to go back to his earliest specialty. Demolition. The explosion blew out most of the windows in the nearest office building.

Which happened to house the Internal Revenue Service.

Within twenty seconds the voices in Adler's right ear exploded into pandemonium. The handful of uniformed cops standing near the corner in anticipation of the day's crowds clawed at their shoulder radios and began moving, slowly at first, in the direction of the explosion. The sound had been loud enough to be heard in the plaza, but as something distant and confusing. People looked around, slowly registering that something odd was happening, more from the actions of the cops than from what they had heard.

Lersch was five feet away now. He was standing near the curb, facing Oswald's window, still pointing at something. Adler slid through the crowd until he was standing immediately behind the man, and then keyed the second number.

This package was inside the big rolling suitcase standing against the floor-to-ceiling window in his hotel room. He'd built this one to be as loud as possible and to pour out a huge volume of smoke without actually starting a fire. In all of the plaza, his was the only head that didn't turn at the enormous *bang* to see black fumes billowing from a shattered window on an upper floor of the hotel.

The screams were immediate, from every direction. People began running, some toward the hotel, others away. Alex Lersch didn't scream or run, though. As he spun on his heel at the sound of the explosion, his chest met Adler's knife, coming in the opposite direction. Lersch's eyes widened. Adler put his left arm around the man's neck and pulled him close, the further movement of the knife masked by their two bodies, to all appearances just two men clinging to each other in the terror of the moment.

Many people nearby had fallen, either in shock or simply tripping out of panic. Lersch did not seem out of place as Adler eased him to the ground, on his stomach. There was no longer a cop in sight. He joined a knot of people moving north, away from what seemed to be the burning hotel, listening to the frantic voices in his ear coordinating the response to what looked very much like an organized attack.

His car was parked in the lot of an aquarium, half a mile away. On his way there he ducked into the YMCA, where he'd left another set of clothes in a locker. He was changing when the voice in his ear started talking about a body in Dealey Plaza.

Ten minutes later he was on the interstate, heading home.

"Not exactly stealthy," Melanie said when she brought the rest of his money a few weeks afterward.

Winter was slow in coming. There was beginning to be a bite in the air, but it was comfortable to sit out on the deck in light jackets.

Perfect bourbon weather, Adler thought. He poured another finger into his glass. "Stealthy was never an option," he said. "Not with what the client wanted."

"I guess not. But Christ, Adler, there's a damn federal task force on this now."

"Task forces aren't cops, kiddo." Adler sipped, feeling the warmth slip through him. "Task forces are politicians and press conferences and fourteen different three-letter organizations fighting over jurisdiction."

"You sound like Dad."

"There are worse ways to sound."

Adler was four years old when Kennedy got shot. Too young to really understand what was happening, but the memory was there, a dark time when every adult he knew suddenly seemed very angry and very, very scared. It must have been like that for Lersch too. In that moment when Lersch turned into the blade and his eyes widened, Adler saw the little boy who would spend a lifetime trying to understand.

"There are kids today," he said, not realizing he was going to speak out loud until he did. "Someday somebody will ask them what's the first big news story they really remember being aware of, and they'll say the explosions in Dallas."

"And this is a good thing?"

"Damned if I know," Adler said. "The mystery endures."

Melanie would stay in the extra room again. In the morning he would make pancakes for her and tell her he was retiring. She would protest but not much. After she drove away, he would untie his little boat, push off into the cold water, and try to decide if knowing why made any difference at all.

Flight

FROM *Hayden's Ferry Review*

1983

YOKI SAYS WE SHOULD hide out in the church and I don't want to argue, so I agree. At first, we have it all to ourselves. We scrunch down low in a pew, so close together that Yoki's breathing tickles my cheek and my hateful boobs keep brushing her arm. We play thumb wars and talk in whispers about which Menudo singer we'd French kiss, and her hair smells like flowers, and it feels safe here in the cool forgiving shadows. Then the old ladies in granny head-scarves show up to light candles for the dead, and they shoot us dirty looks to let us know we don't belong. When Father O'Connor comes in, we figure we'll get in trouble but instead he slides his big bottom into the pew to talk to us. In religion class, he was always telling us stuff he thought we should know but never stuff we actually wanted to know, like when I asked why girls weren't good enough to be altar boys and he just patted me on my Afro. Since then, I've made a habit of asking questions about church things that don't make sense to me just to see if I can annoy him. So today I ask: How is some communion wine that looks just like what my mother buys at the liquor store every Friday night supposed to be blood that can save our souls on Sundays? Yoki shakes her head and whispers that I'm going to Hell, but Father just smiles like he always does.

"We're all sinners, Kumani," he says, and he spreads his fat fingers wide like jazz hands, which Sister Kelly taught us about in music class. "But the Lamb of God saves us by paying for the sins of the world with the shedding of His blood."

"In no way does that answer my question," I say, but Father just gets up and says it's time for us to go if we aren't there to pray.

It is deep summer in Washington Heights and a heatwave is kicking New York's ass, and I try to tell him that we have nowhere to go and nothing to do, and that it's so hot we'll probably die out there, but he just does that shrugging, smiling thing, and I can't see his eyes behind his square glasses because they're reflecting me. At the church doors he tells us to be good girls before he throws us out. So, we walk into the punishing heat, and I think about being a sinner, and about how the church is like your mother—always telling you you've done something bad, sometimes before you even have a chance to do it. Like you came into the world wrong.

We pass the corner bodega where the cashier guy is standing in the doorway looking like he's melting. I tell Yoki that when Father O'Connor starts talking about that Lamb of God stuff, I always see those weak fluffy sheep from that Looney Tunes cartoon in my head.

"You know, the ones that don't even run or cry out when that skinny wolf carries them off? Like, do they even have mouths?"

Yoki tells me again that I'm going to Hell but she giggles like the Pillsbury Doughboy, which she sorta looks like today in her new white pedal pushers and tank top. A bright white banana clip traps her long brown hair in a thick ponytail. There's a hole on top of one of my Skippies where my big toe pokes out, and I'm wearing my old terry cloth shorts and halter top again. I hate how the top makes my boobs look big, and I'll probably catch trouble for wearing it today, but I've outgrown all my summer clothes, and there's no extra money so I have to make do. Yoki still has her baby fat, and she's lucky because she hasn't really grown any boobs to worry about yet.

I've always liked making Yoki laugh, so I try again. I tell her that the other thing that bugs me is the end of the Bible when the dead lamb comes back like a zombie and gets revenge on the world as this lion-lamb animal after Judgment Day.

"Now what does that even look like?" I ask, and I try to sound like Eddie Murphy on that cassette tape we snuck and listened to in her room. "Lion head, lamb butt? Like, does it go 'Baa,' or does it roar? How you gonna be fierce *and* fluffy at the same time? And what good is being fierce if you're already dead?"

But Yoki doesn't laugh this time. She gets all serious and tells me I'm stupid because I don't understand that the lamb isn't real, it's just a symbol for Jesus, and I should stop making fun of those things. I tell her that she's stupid because she obviously doesn't know that in Old Testament times people literally stabbed two *real* lambs a day.

"Then they'd burn them up to send a smoke signal to God, so he'd know it was time to forgive them again for all the wrong shit they were always doing. Then they'd eat the meat, 'cus why waste food."

She stops and twists her mouth at me. Her round brown face is already sweat-shiny.

"You made all that up."

A cherry red Trans Am passes us slowly, woofers thumping. The old gross dude behind the wheel is eyeing us instead of the road, but we ignore him.

"Nope. Bloody baby sheep sacrificed for stuff they didn't even do," I make a cutting gesture across my neck. "So messed up."

She shakes her head like I'm a disappointment to her.

"You always see things in some crazy way."

I get quiet because I'm pretty tired of Yoki telling me I'm wrong when I'm not. I just think about things differently, which these days usually leads to a fight—like our last big fight which was all her fault. It was bad enough that she stole my idea and also did her final eighth grade presentation on that new lady astronaut Sally Ride. What happened after was worse.

It was hard to keep from rolling my eyes when she told our class that Sally Ride was "a hero whose historic flight shows girls how high they can go in the universe." When my turn came, I told our class that Sally Ride could never be a hero to girls like me.

"First," I told our class, "she's a white girl."

Everyone got real quiet then so I knew I had their attention. Second, I told them, she grew up with a mom *and* a dad.

"Most of you only got a mom at home, right? And Reuben, you only got your nana."

"Keep it moving," Mr. Woods said.

"Okay, okay," I said. I told them how she played tennis as a kid

and went to private school, and how when life's all smooth and
easy like that, making it into the space program isn't really such a
big deal, if you think about it.

"And that's why Sally Ride can never be my hero," I said, and I
looked right at Yoki. "Because if you can't even walk down a street
without something getting in your way, how are you supposed to
make it past the sky?"

I waited for applause but then Yoki had to go and betray me.
She burst out laughing.

"That makes no frigging sense," she said. "You trippin'!"

And then everyone was laughing.

But that's just how it's been lately—us always getting on each
other's nerves, her always thinking she's better than me. I've been
thinking that I might hang out with some different girls once we
get to high school in the fall, but this summer I'm stuck with Yoki.
We've been best friends since kindergarten at Our Lady of Perpetual Sorrows, and we know all of each other's secrets—like how
she puts toilet paper in her training bra, and how I only own three
pairs of underwear. But I've been keeping stuff from her lately,
like this thing I found the other day that I haven't told her about
because she keeps making me mad, and because it's special, and I
don't really have anything special that is just mine. After she tells
me I'm stupid and crazy about the lambs though, I decide to show
it to her. Just to prove that I do know about something that she
doesn't.

Launch
definition: To set in motion.

The man in the dented van is waiting for me.

The city streets are early morning hushed. Supermarket shopping is Saturday's chore. Ground beef, orange juice, milk. Winter's
bony fingers push past a thrift shop peacoat, and breath escapes in
tiny white puffs that rise like smoke to the sky. The shopping cart
rattles and squeaks along behind. Rattle and squeak.

I am nine.

The man in the van calls out. *Can you help me?* Nobody else is
around. *Me?*

He smiles and beckons with a big hand. *Yes.*

You.

As soon as I am close, his door swings open and all of him is there to see, fleshy, red, and bare. Breathing stops and my world breaks open and freezes with the sickening recognition of a trap.

I am too young to really understand, but even so, this feels familiar to something old and weary that crouches deep inside me; something passed to me by my mothers all the way back through time and blood. It knows that this is where it all always ends, and where it all begins.

The hunter's cold eyes consider me while the universe holds still. I am a frozen snared creature with a heart threatening to explode inside its small chest. Don't move, become invisible, and maybe it all goes away.

Then the door slams shut. The van drives away. The driver doesn't look back, and I don't understand whether this was mercy or magic. *Did I really disappear?* I only know that I feel wrong, and that I'll never tell anyone about this, because if I keep my mouth shut, it did not happen.

My secret is hidden inside the park. Yoki hates the park, which means I'll have to trick her into following me there. So, I pretend I'm headed nowhere in particular, but I know exactly where I'm going.

The thick hot air makes breathing feel like drowning, and it has that smell that seeps out of the sidewalk grates—subway sourness and sewers all mixed up. It is the smell of New York when there's been no rain, but it always seems worse in Washington Heights—like all of the bad smells in Manhattan blow uptown on the hot winds and get trapped here like the rest of us.

Father O'Connor once told me that Washington Heights used to be really nice, back when everyone was Irish. These days, Washington Heights belongs to people from the Dominican Republic, and it's all graffitied buildings and chicken-bone-littered streets. Most summer afternoons, the Mister Softee ice cream truck jingle mingles with the police sirens and Merengue music that spills from open apartment windows.

Only a few kids in the neighborhood are Black like me, and a lot of times I feel like I'm an outsider. Yoki is Dominican, and if I had my way, I would be too. I'd roll my Rs and have a fancy name like Lourdes Altagracia Consuela Aurelia Rojas instead of my stupid name, which my mama says means Destiny in Africa, although she has no idea exactly where.

Fort Tryon Park, where we hang out, used to be really nice too, Father O'Connor says. Rich people even built beautiful mansions inside it, long ago. Now homeless men spend all day drinking on the park's benches, and at night they sleep in caves where Father O'Connor said Revolutionary War musket balls were once found. It wasn't until talk started about some rapist running around in Fort Tryon that our moms started nagging us about staying out of the park. Yoki is freaked out by the rumor, but it's been going around for so long that it feels like a boogeyman story to me.

I finally see the park up ahead but by this time, Yoki is complaining about the heat and her new Jelly sandals hurting her feet.

"The park's gotta be cooler with all the trees," I say, casual-like, but Yoki turns her mouth down at me. She starts scratching the inside of her elbow where she often gets this rash. Sometimes she scratches so hard she starts to bleed.

"There's nothing to do in there."

"Like we got something better to do out here?"

She cuts her eyes at me. "You know my mom said I can't go in there."

I roll my eyes at her. "How she gonna find out?"

Yoki frowns again as she scratches.

"Come on. There's something I want to show you."

"What?"

"Just come and I'll show you."

Yoki looks at her Swatch and shakes her head. "Nah, I'm going home, I gotta be somewhere later."

I wonder if today is one of those days that Yoki's mom gets off early from her waitressing job. Sometimes she treats her to a movie matinee so they can sit in the nice air-conditioned theater and eat popcorn. My mom works late most nights at her second job cleaning offices. Sometimes she goes to her boyfriend's after, which means I don't hear her key in the lock until the next morning.

"What are you going to go do?"

"Nosy," Yoki says, which annoys me, but I think about being alone with nothing to do if she leaves, and now it starts to feel like I need her to come with me. I fish in my top and pull out a damp five-dollar bill I stole from my mother's purse. I wave it.

"I'll buy you a slice of pizza after."

Yoki eyes the money.

"Two."

I suck my teeth. If I have to buy her two slices that means I can only get one if I also want a Coke, which I do. But I really want to get inside the park.

"Fine. But why you always gotta be so greedy?" I push the bill back inside my top and start walking. "You could stand to eat a little less, you know."

Yoki remains where she is, frowning and scratching. The fat sun is sitting heavy on my head, and all I want to do is get beneath the park's trees.

"Well, come on," I yell. And finally, she follows me.

Payload

Synonyms: Weight, burden.
There is a natural tradeoff between the payload and the range of the aircraft.

Empty emerald beer bottles clutter the worn table, and darkness smothers the kitchen window. I was asleep when I was dragged from my bed.

I am eleven.

Mama sits across the table with her black marble eyes. She is scribbling on a drawing I made today. I drew myself with long beautiful hair, even though mine is really short and nappy, and I am standing on a brown ground that swallows my feet. I forgot to draw a sky. I wonder if Mama even looked at my drawing before she started ruining it.

She thrusts the paper out. She has drawn a long worm-like thing and a dark, angry oval. "*Let this,*" she stabs at the long thing and I flinch, "*come near this,*" now a stab at the oval thing, "*and you will end up being nothing like every girl around here.*" She hisses this like a cat does when it's scared.

Earlier today I got my first period. When I told Mama about the blood she looked at me like I'd done something wrong again.

The black marbles blink. "*Do you understand?*" Not a question. A threat.

I don't. But I nod.

Fort Tryon Park is huge, hilly, and wooded, and sometimes if you go in too far, it's hard to find the same way out.

Small chubby clouds lie like lazy lambs above us, and a fluttering starts somewhere inside me as we enter the park. I realize I'm not really sure I can find my way again to the thing I found. Well, actually, I didn't find it. Miguel Perez showed it to me.

We know Miguel Perez from the neighborhood. He's a skinny pale dude with this wimpy caterpillar mustache. He's also one of those guys who doesn't seem to do anything. He's nineteen but has no job and only hangs out with younger kids.

A few days earlier I'd been on my way to the bodega for some Funyuns when Miguel saw me and said, "Yo, Mani, wait up." I could tell he was looking at my boobs so I crossed my arms. He asked where I was going and I said nowhere, and he goes, "Come for a walk with me." I didn't have anything to do so I went.

He took me into a part of Fort Tryon that I'd never been to before; way inside, then up a dirt path I'd never noticed. The path kept curving uphill and soon it didn't even seem like a path anymore, it was mostly dirt and old brown leaves. It got darker the farther we walked. The trees were tall and close, and their branches were all twisted above my head. I thought we'd get lost, but Miguel seemed to know where he was going.

Finally, we got to this broken-down building hiding in the woods. There was nothing left but crumbling walls. It sat all alone near the edge of a cliff, and from where windows probably once were you could see the Hudson River way below, all brown and slow. There was garbage on the ground—old Hostess wrappers, green broken glass, someone's black undies. I could tell it was the kind of place that people used and then forgot, but I still thought it was pretty cool. Miguel said he didn't know what it had been, but I guessed it was one of those old mansions that Father O'Connor told me about. Being there made me feel like a little kid, like I'd found a hidden treasure. And for some crazy reason that got me thinking about Sally Ride, and this thing I'd read about her not knowing why she'd wanted to become an astronaut. But the same article also talked about how her parents would let her just run around on her own and explore when she was a kid. And as I was standing there in the broken-down mansion, I got a little jealous thinking about how she got told to go explore instead of being told to stay away from places; and how she probably was never told to go straight home after school, and to make sure that no one was following her before unlocking her apartment door. Because I could see how feeling free like that could make you want to go right on exploring and discovering all sorts of things, bigger things, and all of a sudden I wanted to know what else the park was hiding that I'd never seen.

I leaned over the edge of a crumbling wall to look down the cliff at the river. I could feel Miguel looking at me like he was hungry. Suddenly he grabbed my hand.

"How old you now?" he asked, and I said almost fourteen, and he nodded and licked his lips like boys do when they're trying to be sexy. Then he asked if I wanted to go out with him. He promised to take me to a movie downtown, like a real date. Before I could answer, he pushed me against the ruined wall and kissed me. I didn't want him to, but I didn't say anything. His mouth felt cold and wet and fuzzy, and up close he smelled like a Big Mac.

I tell Yoki all about Miguel as we make our way to the broken-down mansion. We pass some boys on a bench with a huge boombox, and when they start saying nasty stuff to us, like I knew they would, I keep quiet because I know if you do they usually leave you alone after a while. But Yoki is always shooting her mouth off like she doesn't know any better. She calls them "dogs" and that only makes them jump up and call us "bitches," which makes my insides tight and skittery. They follow us for a bit, yelling over their loud-ass radio, and I think about giving up and leaving the park, but I really want to get back to the broken-down mansion, and the weird thing is, I feel like the broken-down mansion is waiting for me too. Finally, they stop following us. I pick up a big stick.

"To protect us," I tell Yoki, mostly joking.

I talk about Miguel Perez all the way up the hill as the trees above steal away the sun and the sky. Yoki is quiet, and I figure she's having trouble keeping up because I can hear her breathing all heavy and wheezy behind me. But since she always has something to say about everything I realize that she's staying quiet on purpose. I look at her.

"What?"

"Nothing."

"Why you buggin' then?"

Yoki shrugs.

"He's nineteen, you know."

"So?"

"So that's gross."

I suck my teeth.

"You're just jealous."

"He only wants one thing from you." She sings this, like kids on the playground do when they're teasing. "Stop being so dumb."

A part of me knows she's right about Miguel. I mean, there's something cool about a nineteen-year-old liking you when you're only thirteen. But then I think about how my mother will kill me if she finds out, and about that Big-Mac kiss, and about how he'll probably try to feel me up at the movies, and I get this icky feeling. But I'm not going to tell Yoki that.

"Yeah well, stop being such a bitch," I say instead.

Yoki's eyes wrinkle up like she's going to cry, but just then this old man and his two Chihuahuas pass us. The dogs start yapping and the old man yells, "Cállate! Cállate!"

"Frigging rats," I say after they disappear down the path. We always call Chihuahuas "rats." It's our joke. We used to have a lot of those—things that made us laugh so hard I'd nearly pee my pants. But Yoki just keeps sulking.

"Lookit, don't be such a baby." I want to apologize and I don't. Mostly, I'm annoyed and thirsty. The trees above are closed up tight, but they aren't doing anything to keep us cool. The hot air is a huge heavy hand pressing me down.

I start walking. "You coming or not?"

She doesn't look at me.

"My feet hurt." She leans against a big rock and pulls off her new Jellies. She wiggles her toes and I can see red marks pressed into her flesh. "You said it wasn't far."

"It's not."

She rolls her eyes.

"How much more?"

The truth is I don't know. It feels like we're close. But I also have that fluttery feeling again that it's going to stay hidden from me this time. I tell the feeling to shut up.

"It's just up there." I point with the protection stick. "I promise."

G-Force

A force that causes a feeling of pressure pushing you backward, when you are moving very quickly forward.

Mama's eyes are ice and knives.

"*He was looking at you.*"

The man is gone now; he left the elevator on the second floor. I try to smother my breasts beneath my tightly wrapped arms. Maybe if I press hard enough they will push back into my body as easily as they seemed to sprout. I wonder how I'm responsible for what that man did to me with his eyes. I almost ask this aloud but my words die as Mama's angry eyes roam my body. And suddenly I see.

This is my fault.

And as I continue to grow and curve, I will feel this truth in the hands of the men who block my way and grab at me as I walk to school or the bodega. I will hear it beneath their calls: "*Ppsstt, ppsstt, ppsstt*" as they follow me. They call me the same way my father taught me to call a cat, long ago, before he stopped coming around.

I am twelve. Minutes ago, I was outside playing tag. This morning I put on my favorite tank top with the kissing teddies and it was just a shirt, not a traitorous thing. I promise myself that from now on I will only wear things that help me hide. I will remember to be invisible so that maybe I'll be forgiven.

There is a buzzing all around; summer insects hidden in the leaves, telling us that something else is alive in these woods. We are so deep inside the park that we don't see anyone after the old man with his Chihuahuas, except for a guy way up ahead on the path who is heading our way. But then he must realize he's going in the wrong direction because he turns around and disappears back around a bend.

Now we are talking about a stupid TV show we like. Two girls on it are headed to college, so that gets us talking about what we might do when we grow up.

"My mother says I'll make a good doctor," Yoki says. No one ever talks to me about things like that, so I don't know what to say. I think about how once, when I was little, I told my mother that I wanted to be a judge after seeing one on TV, and she covered me in kisses, so I kept saying it to get more kisses until finally she told me to shut up. I try now to imagine becoming something one day, and I can't see anything. But then Sally Ride's face appears in the nothingness. I remember how after she returned to Earth a few weeks ago, she told a TV interviewer that she'd never doubted herself or feared anything while growing up. When the reporter asked, "What do you think that means about you?" Sally Ride laughed and said she didn't know. Something about her answer had bugged me then, like a mosquito I can't find when I'm trying to sleep. But it's not until right now, when I can't think of what I might grow up to be someday, that I realize I'm angry. I'm angry about that *laugh*. Because how could she be as smart as she's supposed to be and not know what that means? Even I, thirteen-year-old Kumani from crappy Washington Heights, know what that means. It means everything.

"Lookit," I say to Yoki, "you can't just go and be a doctor because your mommy says so."

"Says who?"

I stop walking and point the protection stick at her and my words come so fast it's like I have to spit them out before they burn my mouth.

"Your mother doesn't know shit, Yoki. She didn't even finish high school. She's just a stupid fat waitress at some tacky diner, and she can barely speak English. She buys you all that fancy crap, and so you think you're better than everyone else but you're not. You're nothing but dumb and poor, and you're probably going to end up just like her."

Yoki's face closes up tight. She smacks the protection stick out of my hand and rolls her neck like an angry cobra. "Don't you talk about my mother! I can be whatever I want!"

"No! You can't!" And I want to explain how some things are already decided even though everyone tries to trick you into thinking that they aren't. I want to tell her that there are things that stop you before you even begin. But I just don't know how to make her understand.

So, I turn to walk again. She stays quiet and follows and I feel like I've won. After a couple of minutes, though, the angry thing in me collapses and I just feel heavy and sick. I know I'll have to confess to Father O'Connor about being mean to Yoki, but I don't know how to fix the awful things I've said, so I just talk again like nothing is wrong. I ask if she's heard about how high school nuns whack girls with rulers if their school skirts are too short to save them from going to Hell for being sluts.

"I'm going back," she says. I turn around, and I don't recognize her because of how she is looking at me. "I'm gonna go hang with Rosa Rodriquez. She invited me and a bunch of other girls over."

Her words hit me like a slap. Yoki and I have hated Rosa Ro-driquez ever since the fifth grade when she told everyone she saw me using food stamps at the supermarket. Understanding floods into the black hole spreading inside of me. Yoki's been keeping things from me too, and her face tells me that everything may finally be broken between us. But before I can say anything, we see that same man who disappeared behind the bend just a few minutes earlier. This time it's clear that he knows where he's going. He has a knife and he's coming for us.

It's a fat jaggedy switchblade like the one my mom thinks I don't know she keeps hidden in her purse. He's holding it in one hand and unbuckling his belt with his other.

I'm not afraid. I don't even feel like I'm there. If we stay quiet, my thoughts tell me, he won't even notice if we slip past him, and then we can still get to the broken-down mansion and everything will be okay.

So, I walk toward him because I know I'm invisible. Yoki's hand shoots out and yanks me back. Her fingers find mine and we stand side by side, so close that I can feel her trembling. That's when he speaks.

"Don't run 'cus I'll catch you," he says, all calm and quiet-like, as though everything that's going to happen has already happened.

It's funny how when that awful icy water floods your insides, some things get wiped out and others flash-freeze in place. Later, they will ask what he looked like, and I won't be able to say. Every man I pass on the street will be him. But his voice and those words will stay. All my life, they will be the doorway through which I will hurtle back to this very moment when everything slows down and stretches out and stops. Now I cannot move or breathe or blink. But if I could open my frozen mouth, I would tell him that he doesn't need to tell me not to run because the ground has swal-lowed my feet. And besides. This is where I was always supposed to be anyway.

"Run Kumani!" Yoki screams.

But he is too fast. He closes the space between us before she finishes my name, and it is Yoki he reaches first. He smashes into her, and her hand rips from mine, and she is falling to the ground, and he is on her. The knife slips out of sight as they fight in the hard dry dirt, and her breath is heavy and wheezy and his comes in grunts and growls, and she is struggling to rise, but he snatches her long ponytail and drags her back down, and I am frozen, I am not breathing, I am not here, but still, I understand in my bones that when he is done with her he will come for me and I *will* be here, waiting.

I see the fat switchblade on the ground. If I weren't frozen, I could stretch my foot out and almost touch it. Yoki's tank top rips as she twists and pulls out of his big hands and tries to scrabble away on her dirty knees.

It's not a decision or even a thought. From a deep place inside me, something that still breathes awakens and frees my feet.

I turn away and blast off.

Now there are only sounds: my heart beating all the way up in my ears and my feet slapping the dead leaves beneath them. There is the sound of Yoki and the man still struggling behind me, but as I run, those sounds grow fainter, and even though I know I'm leaving Yoki behind, I keep running, and a part of me believes that I can reach help and still save us both, and a part of me knows that I can't, and soon there is just my feet and my heart still so loud in my ears; nothing but those two sounds, heart and feet, heart and feet, beat, slap, beat, slap. Until the scream. And then the scream takes up all the space, it swallows all the other sounds, it reaches for God up in Sally Ride's territory but gets trapped in the branches above and holds there, bloating the air; I can't hear anything else, just Yoki's scream, and then, when it finally ends, the quiet, which is just as horrible and just as loud. My eyes are wet and blind, but I don't slow down and I don't turn around and I don't stop. I just do what Yoki told me I could do. I run.

I am thirteen. I run and the greedy ground tries its best, but it can't catch hold of me again. I run so fast that it feels as though my feet aren't even touching it. I am flying, up, above the dim path, soaring toward a slender sliver of blue sky I can now see through the dense trees. And then, when I can't take the terrible silence anymore, I finally open my own mouth wide and roar.

Love Interest

FROM *Small Odysseys*

WHEN PEOPLE FIND out I'm a private investigator they often make fun of me: *Oh, can I see your gun? You on a stakeout? Ever shoot anyone?*

See, my gun is a computer. I'm a digital forensics expert who spends his days digging up and decoding financial records. I know what the snarky attorneys here at the firm call me: Nerdlock Holmes. Double-oh-dweeb.

I work for a group of Southern California divorce lawyers. It's my job to figure out where Rich Guy has hidden his wealth from Trophy Wife. Or I *help* Rich Guy *hide* his wealth from Trophy Wife. Either way, it's all cyber stakeouts: phony trusts, offshore accounts, shell corporations. Every once in a while, I'll get called in to find Trophy Wife's deleted texts, or Rich Guy's naked selfies, but usually, by the time a divorce gets to my desk, no one cares about that stuff. It's all about the money.

It's not a sexy job, is what I'm saying.

At least until she came in.

It was after six on a Friday. Everyone was gone for the day. I had come back to the office to get my Dungeons & Dragons character sheet from my desk.

A single knuckle rapped on my door.

A tall, elegant woman stood in the doorway: gray-haired, model-thin, wearing a simple white dress, crop jacket, sunglasses. She was older than me, in her sixties, and yet still this was the most beautiful woman I'd ever seen.

She sat down. "Justin Orr?"

"Yes."

"I'm—"

"I know who you are," I said. I was a film buff, and I recognized her right off, even though she hadn't acted in anything in forty years. She'd come up as a teenager on the New York stage, a student of Uta Hagen's, and for a brief moment, was a favorite of 1970s auteurs like Kubrick and Altman. She performed alongside Brando and the young Pacino, great actors of her generation.

Then, in her late twenties, she simply quit. Pulled a Grace Kelly. Left to marry a wealthy older gentleman whose name you'd only recognize if you were familiar with the top donor line of LA museums.

I'll call her Ms. M.

Ms. M. had gotten my name from a friend, a woman whose husband we'd represented in a contentious three-comma divorce—three commas because that's what it took to write a billion dollars.

"It was a difficult case," I said.

Ms. M. pointed to my desktop computer. "She told me you used that thing to rob her blind."

"If two hundred million dollars is your idea of being robbed blind."

She shrugged with one shoulder. "You were doing your job," she said. "It's why I'm here."

"Divorce?"

She shook her head. "My husband died six years ago."

"I'm sorry."

She shrugged with the other shoulder. "Thank you." It was a good marriage, she said, a week shy of thirty-five years. Two children. Three grandchildren. Fourth on the way.

"Happy ending," I said. "And yet, you're here."

She looked around, chewed her lip. "This is confidential?"

"Always."

She reached into her purse. Handed me a single folded page. A printout of an email. From one "ArGyLe BoRfUs," every other letter in his fake name capitalized, like a ransom note.

"I am aware," the email began, "that Actress1953 is your password.

> I require 100% your attention. I have installed malware upon
> your computer and remote desktop protocol give me access
> to your Facebook videos and photographs and also email list.

> I have use these to create a deepfake video very believable
> portraying you in sex acts and will send this pornographic to
> all your contacts unless you send 8ooUS$ bitcoin.

It went on like this, in that tortured Spam-glish that must be
taught by a malfunctioning robot somewhere.

She nodded at the letter. I sensed her shame. Fear. "Can you
find him?"

I smiled. "There is no *him*. You understand that, right?"

"My daughter says they can do things like this now. Put famous
faces in porno movies."

It was sad, not just that she'd fallen for this, but that she thought
she was still famous. That someone would go to the trouble of
making fake porn with an actress who hadn't been in a movie in
forty years. "Yeah, they can do that," I said. "Deepfakes. But that's
not what this is. This is just a scam."

She pointed at the page. "But that really is my password."

Of course it was. Actress and birth year. "Look, hackers buy passwords," I said. "Doesn't mean anything. They can't get into your
accounts. It's just spam. A phishing scheme."

She cocked her head.

"You don't spend much time online, do you, Ms. M.?"

"Arthur hated computers," she said. "After he died, my daughter
set me up with email, Facebook, Instagram." A wistfulness crossed
her face. "Sometimes I feel like I wasn't made for this time. The
world makes no sense to me."

I could see that. She was from a more glamorous era, more
mysterious. It ended in her business when the studios began chasing blockbusters: sharks, space aliens, superheroes. The end of a
certain kind of film acting.

"Look, this is no big deal." I waved the email. "Spam is just computer junk mail. Phishing schemes to get passwords and credit card
numbers. They can't really put your face on porn. As long as you
didn't answer the email, you have nothing to worry about."

She pursed her lips.

"You answered the email—"

Another shrug.

"Tell me you didn't send bitcoin—"

"Of course not. I don't even know what that is." Her face red-
dened. "Look, I don't need a computer lesson, I just want you

to find him." She reached into her purse and emerged with her checkbook. "Please."

I didn't want her money. But I said yes.

I figured I'd let a little time pass and then tell her what I already knew, that there was no Argyle Borfus, that the email came from some hacking farm in Malaysia. Estonia. I'd pick a ring that had been broken up by Interpol and say, *See, no need to worry.*

Meantime, I'd get to see her—and play movie detective—once more. I'd give her a report about phishing schemes, set her at ease. Then she'd pull out that checkbook again, and I'd reach over, put my hand on those long, delicate fingers, and say, *No charge, doll.*

She'd squeeze my hand.

Just doing my job, I'd say.

I skipped D&D that night to look up her movies online. Her entire career consisted of just nine films released between 1974 and 1980, three of the parts so small there's nothing much to see. In one, she's the young widow Steve McQueen questions in a murder case, in another, the girlfriend of Elliott Gould's innocent brother, until Gould recognizes her as a dancer from a seedy club.

Gould: You really like my brother?

Ms. M.: I'd hoped to.

In these small parts, she radiates something rare. You watch to figure it out, but it's never quite the same. It doesn't feel like technique. It seems natural, reflexive, *real.* A pained look, a twitch around the mouth, a glance away and you think: *she really* felt *that.*

By her last four films, she'd graduated to the female lead, playing against the great actors of her time. You see why these auteurs fell for her. She's beautiful, yes, but beauty is common in film. It's more like she's an open nerve, not portraying emotion. Feeling it.

James Caan is getting dressed above her. She says dreamily from bed, *I love you,* with a slight quaver, then we cut to an exterior shot of Caan getting on his horse, while she watches from the porch. The scene is filmed over her shoulder, from behind, with her holding the hitching post he's just untied his horse from, so that her arm frames the long shot as he rides away. A lesser actor would remove her hand from the post, cover her face, pretend at tears, or drop her head. *Look: sadness!* Ms. M. does neither; her hand grips the post even tighter, for support, and a shiver goes through that arm to the goosebumps rising on her neck, a shudder as the wind blows a strand of hair, and you wonder, *How did she do that? Convey utter heartache without ever facing the camera?*

The more I watched, the more I wished I could actually help her, defend her honor, drag this Argyle Borfus to her house and beat him with the butt of a pistol until he apologized for scaring her.

I bought some weed from my neighbor and ordered two pizzas and spent the weekend watching and rewatching her movies until I found myself feverish, fantasizing our next meeting. I'd pull up to her white mansion in Beverly Hills. Climb out of my sports car (which I'd buy between now and then). She'd be her young self, and I'd be a real detective, laconic, tall, without these glasses.

I found Borfus, I'd say. Then I'd light a smoke. *He's dead.*

But . . . I didn't—

It was him or me, Ms. M. And it sure as hell wasn't gonna be me.

Mr. Orr—

Justin.

Okay. Justin.

Then I'd step on my cigarette and take her in my arms—

I knew I was being delusional. I knew she was a rich widow thirty years older than me. But this was something I'd never felt with someone my own age. Maybe we were the same, Ms. M. and me. Maybe neither of us belonged in this world.

I was still stoned when I woke up Monday morning on the couch, surrounded by pizza boxes, her last film frozen on the screen where I'd paused it.

Ms. M. didn't want to meet at her mansion in the hills. "My daughter is home this week. She can't know about any of this. No one can."

So much for my stoned fantasies. Well, at least I didn't have to find a 1968 Spitfire before Friday.

She wanted to meet at the Starbucks on Montana and Fifteenth in Santa Monica, near her Pilates studio. She was there when I arrived, in yoga pants and a long-sleeve workout shirt. I couldn't reconcile it, this glamorous genius wearing the banal uniform of every woman west of the 405.

She was sipping some kind of blended green herbal drink. Good thing I hadn't taken up smoking. I got coffee and sat across from her.

I handed her a file. I'd found the perfect ring to blame the phishing emails on—a hacker group busted in Helsinki: distant, dripping with Cold War intrigue, but not too scary. The actual ring was involved in stealing shopping points from people's accounts, but it had a bitcoin scam going too. I knew she'd buy it.

"Like I thought," I said, "there was no Argyle Borfus. It was three losers in a basement in Finland. Hacked a department store for emails and passwords. Maybe you filled out a card at Barneys—"

"Barneys closed its Beverly Hills store," she said.

"Then it was some other Rodeo Drive store," I said. "Point is, you were just one of a million random phishing emails they sent out."

As she turned the pages, sorrow passed over her face. I thought about her films, the rawness of her emotions. So open and guileless. It must have been what her husband saw too—a vulnerability that made her beauty almost unbearable. Empathy so powerful it reflected back on you, until you wanted to create for her a world that deserved such a person. To protect her, and comfort her, and yeah—do other things too.

I thought: *it* hurts *to look at you.*

"Cheer up," I said. "This is good news."

"But I sent Argyle Borfus a reply," she said.

"The hackers destroyed their emails and contacts," I lied, "to get rid of evidence before they were raided. Don't worry, your email will never surface. You're safe."

I stared at her hand, on the little table between us. This would be the time. Reach out. Touch her. Instead, I just said, "It's over, Ms. M. There's nothing to worry about."

"You don't get it." She began to cry. Then, just like in the movies, Ms. M. told me everything.

She loved being an actress, especially early on. In some ways, she liked the smaller parts best. "You're making something out of nothing," she said. "A gesture, a look. It's all being present and aware."

But once she started getting leads, she became disheartened. No matter how many lines she had, she couldn't seem to go beyond a few gestures and movements. These began to feel like tricks, and she felt herself stagnating.

Then, she realized the problem. These were films written by men, directed by men, starring men, about men solving crimes, reconciling with fathers, coming back from Vietnam. As brilliant as her directors and costars were—and they *were*—these weren't *her stories.* It wasn't *her journey.* She was the wife, the girlfriend, the love interest. The same in the beginning of the film as in the end.

"Those words, *love interest,* began to feel like shackles," she said. "I was just another thing for the hero to conquer, stakes to overcome. A motivation. A reflection of his desire."

I pictured James Caan riding off into the sunset. "A frame," I said.

"I may as well have been a dress and a pair of shoes sent over from wardrobe." Then, in 1979, she met Arthur at a party, and she fell in love. "I mean, what could I do? All I ever got to play was *in love.* Now the real thing was in front of me . . . how could I go on pretending?"

So she walked away. Fired her agent. Got married. Had children. Never went on another audition. "I told Arthur that I never regretted my decision. And I didn't. But did I sometimes *wonder?* Yes."

After Arthur died, she saw her life as two diverging paths— the one she'd taken, and the one she hadn't. It wasn't as if acting ended in 1979. What if she'd gone on to become Meryl Streep? Or Emma Thompson?

That's where Argyle Borfus came in. If he could use a computer to put her face on a porn actress screwing a mailman, surely he could use that technology to simulate a little bit of what might have been.

Of course. How had I missed it?

She'd written back to Borfus and offered him $5,000 to put her face in a movie she *hadn't* made.

"Can I ask, what movie?"

"No," she said. "That part's private."

"I work for you," I said.

"Look." She sighed. "*I made the right choice.* I know that. I don't question it for a moment. I love my life. My kids, my grandkids." She leaned forward. "But can't you sometimes wonder about the wrong choice too?" She sat back in her chair. Took a deep breath. "*Splash.*"

I stared. "The mermaid movie?"

"Yes." It was the last Hollywood call she ever got, in the early eighties, a producer checking to see if she had any interest, right before they cast Daryl Hannah to play against a young Tom Hanks. "I said no." Ms. M. laughed bitterly. "'That's okay,' the producer had said. 'You're probably too old anyway.'"

I left the Starbucks with that feeling I'd had earlier, the desire to make a world worthy of her.

Two weeks later, I called and set up another meeting.

Ms. M.'s daughter was back in Europe, so I drove to her house, which turned out to not be a mansion in the hills. She'd sold that house after Arthur died, put money aside for her kids, and donated the rest to charity. She lived now in a simple townhouse a few blocks from the Santa Monica Starbucks.

I rang the bell. She answered. Dressed for Pilates again. She made coffee, even though she didn't drink it herself.

I told her how I'd called some old college friends: a film editor, a CG tech, a colorist. How I'd provided them with photos and videos from her acting career and from the home movies she'd sent me. I told her deepfake technology was still pretty rough for doing a whole movie like *Splash*—the blinking, lip-synching, and skin tones would be distracting. But there were some things we could do.

"It's no work of genius." I opened my laptop. "Ready?"

She covered a smile with that long, elegant hand. "I'm not sure."

On the screen was the movie poster of *Splash:* Tom Hanks. Daryl Hannah with a fish tail. But now the mermaid had Ms. M.'s face.

She burst into laughter. "Oh, my," she said. She leaned forward and studied the screen closely. "Oh, my," she said again.

For the next two hours, we watched highlights of a forty-year career she never got to have. Movie posters, trailers, scenes, outtakes, even part of an interview on *Inside the Actors Studio*. Any place we could get something to match the material we had for her, parts in memorable films from 1980 to 2020.

On the couch next to me, she laughed. Gasped. Curled her legs under her like a kid. She had me stop and go back. She slapped my arm. "No!"

She was a lawyer, a queen, an environmental activist. She killed aliens and investigated murders and taught at Hogwarts. She won a half dozen Academy Awards and her movies made billions. And not once was she in a scene as a wife or a girlfriend. These were *her* stories.

When it was over, she was weeping. From joy or wistfulness, I didn't know. I suspected it was all the same.

I told her I could email her the file. "Oh, God, no," she said. "Destroy it. Please." She said she'd seen it, and that was enough.

I think, in the end, this was her true gift: the rare ability to see through fantasy. And now that she'd had one more little glimpse, she was ready to go back to the real.

At the door, she took my hand. "Thank you, Mr. Orr."

I looked down at our hands.

"Justin," I said.

"Justin," she said. "Thank you."

I started to walk away, but then I turned back. "Look, I'm sorry about Borfus. But it was either him or me. And it sure as hell wasn't going to be me."

She smiled. "You did what you had to do."

"Thanks, doll," I said. I winked and ground out a fake cigarette with my foot. Then I climbed into my Honda Accord and drove home.

Contributors' Notes

Other Distinguished Mystery and Suspense of 2022

Contributors' Notes

ASHLEY-RUTH M. BERNIER'S short fiction has appeared in *Ellery Queen Mystery Magazine, Black Cat Weekly,* Stone's Throw, and *The Caribbean Writer.* Originally from St. Thomas, U.S. Virgin Islands, she is an emerging writer of contemporary Caribbean mysteries, which include a novel-in-stories and full-length novels featuring St. Thomian food journalist Naomi Sinclair. Ashley-Ruth is the winner of the North Carolina Writers' Network's 2022 Jacobs/Jones African-American Literary Prize for Black writers and an active member of Sisters in Crime, Crime Writers of Color, the Short Mystery Fiction Society, Mystery Writers of America, and the North Carolina Writers' Network. Ashley-Ruth currently lives with her husband and four children in North Carolina, where she teaches first grade and finds very few things more valuable than uninterrupted writing time.

• My grandmother, who was an educator, historian, and proud bearer of Virgin Islands culture, passed away in 2018 and left me the gift of her extensive book collection. Her home library was a treasure trove she'd collected over her ninety-nine years, mostly dealing with Caribbean, African, and African American culture. She owned volumes upon volumes of books about Virgin Islands food, flora, traditions, building codes, politics, and historical events—books with names like *Herbs and Proverbs, Traditional Medicinal Plants of St. Croix, St. Thomas, and St. John,* and *The Food and Folklore of the Virgin Islands.* The books always felt lofty and untouchable when I was a kid, but when I dove into them after her passing, *something* happened. There's no doubt that digging deep into these books inspired the adventures of food journalist and sometimes-detective Naomi Sinclair. In my stories featuring Naomi, I've enjoyed using Virgin Islands food and culinary traditions as a vehicle for telling larger stories about *people* and all the complicated ingredients that lie within both.

"Ripen" is different from the other Naomi Sinclair stories, in that it focuses on native flowering plants and fruit trees—an interesting subject choice from an author who can't keep potted plants alive longer than a couple of weeks! The Flamboyant trees, hog plums, mangoes, and sea grapes included in this story are the backdrop and the fuel of every St. Thomas summer. The botanical theme was a fun way to explore Naomi and Mateo's blooming relationship as well as the rotten behavior of a slimy ex-senator. And . . . since my taste buds still haven't forgotten the misery of sampling a bite of "lizard food" on Neltjeberg Bay the summer I was nine, I figured that a bellyful of it was exactly the ending that Lucky deserved!

WILLIAM BOYLE is the author of *Gravesend, Death Don't Have No Mercy, Everything Is Broken, The Lonely Witness, A Friend Is a Gift You Give Yourself, City of Margins,* and *Shoot the Moonlight Out.*

• Maxim Jakubowski invited me to contribute to an anthology dedicated to the work of Cornell Woolrich. Since I most often write about the southern Brooklyn neighborhood where I grew up, I knew I wanted to tap into the way Woolrich wrote about New York City. I thought about his great, atmospheric story "New York Blues," collected in *Night & Fear.* I started with a title that riffed on that, "New York Blues Redux," which also felt like it could be a Lou Reed or Jim Carroll or Sonic Youth song. I've always appreciated Woolrich's penchant for writing about doomed romantics stuck in desperate situations and bleak settings. Since those are the same folks I'm drawn to writing about, the story came together quickly: a single hot night in southern Brooklyn in the summer of 1986, a crew of down-and-outers assembling at an end-of-world dive bar. I aimed to let Woolrich's influence seep in while also keeping it very much my own kind of thing.

S. A. COSBY is a bestselling, award-winning crime writer from Southeastern Virginia. His work has appeared in numerous collections, anthologies, and magazines. His books *Blacktop Wasteland* and *Razorblade Tears* have both won the Anthony, the Barry, and the Macavity Awards as well as the ITW Thriller Award for best hardcover novel. *Razorblade Tears* also won the Dashiell Hammett Prize for crime fiction and was a selection for Barack Obama's summer reading list. He resides in Gloucester, Virginia.

• "The Mayor of Dukes City" came about because I wanted to write a true hard-boiled mystery story, but I also wanted to talk about loss and how it stains our souls. So many of us lose someone and we feel helpless. I wanted to write a story that bested that helpless feeling. I think crime fiction does that better than any other genre.

JACQUELINE FREIMOR'S short stories have appeared in *Ellery Queen Mystery Magazine, Alfred Hitchcock's Mystery Magazine, Rock and a Hard Place Magazine, Vautrin, Black Cat Weekly,* and *Mystery Magazine,* among others, and in the anthologies *When a Stranger Comes to Town, The Best Mystery Stories of the Year: 2021,* and *The Best American Mystery and Suspense 2022.* Her novella "The Case of the Bogus Cinderellas" won the Wolfe Pack's 2022 Black Orchid Novella Award, which included publication in *Alfred Hitchcock's Mystery Magazine.* Links to Jacqueline's work can be found at jacquelinefreimor.com.

• The seeds of "Foreword" were planted in a world literature class I took as an undergraduate back in 1983, which introduced me to Vladimir Nabokov's *Pale Fire.* I loved it, not only for its use of an unreliable narrator—a technique I still love—but also for its unusual form. Unfortunately, the professor of the class subscribed to the Great Writers brand of literary criticism, which held that these men—they were almost always men—wrote Universal Truths that spilled directly from their brains to their (fountain) pens, unimpeded by the circumstances of their birth or by the mundane concerns of daily living. Imagine my surprise when years later I discovered that many of these writers' wives had provided all manner of helpful services to enable their husbands to write, up to and sometimes including the actual words themselves (I'm looking at you, F. Scott Fitzgerald).

I don't blame the writers, because what writer in her right mind would turn down the editorial, critical, marketing, gatekeeping, secretarial, and domestic services of a Véra Nabokov, if she made herself available? No, I blame the professors and critics who discounted these women as partners and writers in the first place. Hence my pomposterous (thanks for the word, Jane Young!) narrator, who has a lot to say about his favorite Great Writer but very little awareness of what he's telling us. I hope you have as much fun reading the story as I did writing it—even though my husband, daughter, and dog kept interrupting me.

An Edgar Award nominee for Best Short Story, JAMES A. HEARN writes in a variety of genres, including mystery, crime, science fiction, fantasy, and horror. His fiction has appeared in *Alfred Hitchcock's Mystery Magazine; Black Cat Mystery Magazine; Monsters, Movies & Mayhem;* and other venues. "Home Is the Hunter" originally appeared in *Mickey Finn: 21st Century Noir, Volume 3,* edited by Michael Bracken. James and his wife reside in Texas with a boisterous Labrador retriever who keeps life interesting.

• "Home Is the Hunter" was born from a recurring dream. I'm walking with my dad through the scrub brush of West Texas, along one of the innumerable trails crisscrossing 150 acres of family land. We called this property the Old House. The name stood both for the hunting cabin someone had built there and for the land where it was situated. It is home; I am at peace.

And I wake up and remember. Dad has been gone since 2007, the victim of a rare bone cancer that began in his skull and touched his brain. In the intervening years, the land passed out of the family and the Old House was destroyed by fire. They say you can't go home again, but sometimes, through writing, you can. In "Home Is the Hunter," Joe Easterbrook returns to his roots in the wilderness of West Virginia. When Joe sets foot on the land he loved, his emotions are my emotions. When he recalls hunting with his father, his memories are my memories. And when he rebuilds his father's hunting cabin, I'm holding the hammer.

This one's for you, Dad. We'll be together again one day, and we'll take that walk.

LADEE HUBBARD is the author of two novels: *The Talented Ribkins,* which received the 2017 Hurston/Wright Legacy Award for Debut Fiction and the 2018 Ernest J. Gaines Award for Literary Excellence, and *The Rib King. The Last Suspicious Holdout,* her collection of short stories, was published in 2022. She is a recipient of a Guggenheim Fellowship, the Berlin Prize, and a Radcliffe Institute Fellowship as well as fellowships from Hedgebrook, MacDowell, and the Sacatar Foundation, among other organizations. She currently lives in New Orleans.

• This story emerged from my interest in the twenty or so years that preceded Barack Obama's presidency, a time that was sometimes called the "post–civil rights" era. I wanted to write about what it was like to come of age in the wake of the enormous changes in society that had been brought about in the 1960s and 1970s as well as the enduring trauma of the spectacular violence that often accompanied those changes. "Flip Lady" became a point of entry into my exploration of these themes. It is the first story in my collection, *The Last Suspicious Holdout.*

A. J. JACONO is a writer, musician, and mountaineer based in New York. His work has previously appeared or is forthcoming in *Southeast Review, Upstreet, Lunch Ticket,* and *Cleaver,* among many other journals. He is the founder of *The Spotlong Review,* an online literary and arts journal, and he is the owner of Bibliotheque, a bookstore, café, and wine bar in New York. If you would like to learn more about A.J., you can visit his website: ajjacono.com.

• "When We Remembered Zion" was inspired by the very true, very frightening case of Peter Manfredonia. In 2020, Manfredonia, a student at the University of Connecticut, killed two men, one of whom was his childhood friend, Nicholas Eisele. After murdering Eisele, Manfredonia kidnapped Eisele's girlfriend and forced her to drive him to New Jersey. Five days following the initial murders, Manfredonia was captured in Hagerstown, Maryland, after a multistate manhunt.

One of my high school friends went to UConn and was acquaintances with Manfredonia. While the murders were unfolding and Manfredonia was driving across the country to avoid arrest, my friend was inundating me with minute-to-minute updates about how everyone on the UConn campus was reacting. I also received frightening facts about Manfredonia's mental state leading up to the murders. He'd allegedly been experiencing paranoia, insomnia, and hallucinations.

For better or worse, the story captivated me. Even a few weeks after it occurred, it was still stuck in my head. I felt a strange obligation to write about it. At first, I wanted to adhere as closely to the truth as possible and pen an almost journalistic piece about the murders and kidnapping, but the pages took on a life of their own. This story is the result.

ADAM MEYER is a screenwriter, novelist, and short story writer. His short fiction has been nominated for the Shamus and Derringer Awards, and appeared in *Chesapeake Crimes: Magic Is Murder; Groovy Gumshoes: Private Eyes in the Psychedelic Sixties; Mickey Finn: 21st Century Noir, Volume 3;* and many other anthologies. He's written more than a hundred hours of television, including TV movies, documentaries, and true-crime series for Lifetime, Discovery, A&E, National Geographic, and others. He is the author of the YA novel *The Last Domino* and recently finished a new novel. A native of New York City, he lives with his family in Virginia. Find out more at adammeyerwriter.com.

• I remember back in late 2012, watching in horror as reports came in about a shooting at an elementary school in Newtown, Connecticut. At the time, I had an infant daughter, and I couldn't stop thinking: *What if my kid had been there?* I began to imagine a situation like Newtown, only one where things might've turned out very differently, thanks to an unlikely hero named Mr. Filbert. Those musings became the first draft of "Mr. Filbert's Classroom." I liked the story but had no idea what to do with it. Years later, I saw a call for an anthology of crime stories with a magical element . . . and thought about old Mr. Filbert. I reworked his story from the ground up and was thrilled to have it accepted by the editors of *Magic Is Murder.* By the time "Mr. Filbert's Classroom" was published, my daughter—like the original seed of the story—was actually ten years old, an elementary school student herself. She's had many great teachers over the years, though none quite like Mr. Filbert.

SILVIA MORENO-GARCIA is the author of *Silver Nitrate, Mexican Gothic, Gods of Jade and Shadow,* and many other books. She has won the Locus and British Fantasy Awards for her work as a novelist and the World Fantasy Award for her work as an editor. Her crime novel about the political clash in 1970s Mexico City, *Velvet Was the Night,* was a finalist for the *Los Angeles*

Times Book Prize and the Macavity Award, and her Baja California coming-of-age novel mixed with noir, *Untamed Shore,* has recently been re-released.

• I wrote this story in December, inspired by the holiday festivities back in Mexico in the days of my grandmother that included the dressing of a Baby Jesus statue. I also had in mind a real criminal case from the 1950s. The case in question is known as the Case of the Castle of Purity or the Case of the House of the Planters (Casa de los Macetones). In brief, a man isolated his family for their entire lives in a large, dilapidated house in Mexico City. The man manufactured rat poison and kept his family imprisoned because he feared they would be corrupted by the world. Eventually, the children were set free, and the father went to jail. The idea of isolation and Christmas festivities collided, and eventually solidified, once I remembered details of the house where my great-aunts used to live.

WALTER MOSLEY is the author of sixty critically acclaimed books of fiction, nonfiction, memoir, and plays. His work has been translated into twenty-five languages. He is the winner of numerous awards, including an O. Henry Award, the Mystery Writers of America's Grand Master Award, a Grammy, several NAACP Image Awards, and PEN America's Lifetime Achievement Award. In 2020, he was named the recipient of the Robert Kirsch Award for lifetime achievement from the *Los Angeles Times* Festival of Books and was awarded the National Book Foundation Medal for Distinguished Contribution to American Letters. Born and raised in Los Angeles, Mosley now lives in Brooklyn and Los Angeles.

• "Not Exit" came to me one early, early morning when I was lamenting having to go into a TV writers' room. I felt trapped and I wanted to remember being a fiction writer. So, the title came from that feeling, and the story arose out of desiring a new, a different that I could run to.

LEIGH NEWMAN'S debut collection *Nobody Gets Out Alive* (Scribner, 2022) was long-listed for the National Book Award for Fiction. Her stories have appeared in *Harper's, The Paris Review, The Best American Short Stories, One Story, Tin House, Electric Literature, American Short Fiction,* and *Timothy McSweeney's Quarterly Concern.* Her memoir about growing up in Alaska, *Still Points North,* was a finalist for the National Book Critics Circle's John Leonard Prize. In 2020, she was awarded a Pushcart Prize and an American Society of Magazine Editors' National Magazine Award as well as *The Paris Review*'s Terry Southern Prize for "humor, wit, and sprezzatura." She lives with her two kids, two dogs, and one insouciant kitty cat.

• I never plan stories. I start with a first sentence and go. I know this story started because I was thinking about October, first snow falls in Alaska, and the color of sky at night during that period of time, which is a high dense purple. While thinking about the sky, I put Becca on the bus.

Somewhere on the route down the boulevard, I realized where we were going: Suite 100. And once we were there, I could talk about the whole gamut of aggression and fear two women can face just having a glass of wine in my hometown—birth control tests to Drunk and Lonelies—most of which I have experienced myself. The threat of the guys is what allowed me to move the women out of the bar and down to Valley of the Moon Park, another favorite place of mine in Anchorage, both for its name and its rocket-ship slide. I do like when stories have plot pressure, i.e., because this happens (drunk guys), now that happens (run). But there was another pressure, that of Becca and Jamie's past pushing against their present. I had set the past up at the wine bar in order to get to know them, so when I came to the end of the story and started to face the panic of *How do we end this? How?*, I went back and picked up the place in the mother's running away that I had originally skipped. Getting from the suicide to the ballet at the very end was a visual trick: The falling tissue paper took my mind to feathers in *Swan Lake*, which took me to ballerinas leaping across the stage. Leap to Leap. Mostly, that is how I write any story, letting circumstance, character, and visuals lead the way, inserting ideas and places where I can, as long as it feels natural. But I will say that this story, along with "Howl Palace," is my favorite in the collection. Becca breaks my heart every time.

JOYCE CAROL OATES is the author most recently of *Zero-Sum: Stories* (Knopf). She is teaching alternately at Princeton University, Rutgers, and NYU, and is the 2023 recipient of the fiction award of the Taobuk-Taormina International Book Festival. She has been awarded a *Los Angeles Times* Book Prize, the Jerusalem Prize, the National Book Award, several Bram Stoker Awards, and an International Thriller Writers Award for Best Short Story.

• Decades ago, when I was living in another part of the country, and my life was very different from the life I live now, I'd experimented with a story titled "The Lost Sister"—a narration by a woman whose older, far more accomplished sister has gone missing, and who is, as the reader soon deduces, bitterly jealous of this sister, yet deeply connected to her. The story intrigued me at the time with its possibilities for expansion, but I set it aside, and during the pandemic re-discovered it with a surge of excitement and enthusiasm since, in my much altered life now, living alone in a large house in rural-suburban New Jersey, during a lockdown, I felt that I could better comprehend the isolation and loneliness of the narrator, which is shielded from her consciousness by her wry, acerbic tone. Georgene— "Gigi"—is a broken, tragic figure whose bravado attitude allows her to imagine that she is in control of a narrative in which she has virtually no role at all—and is totally mistaken about the fate of her sister.

At about that time, a friend invited me to visit with him in Ithaca, New York, and we drove around Lake Cayuga to the old, stately, small-but-upscale village of Aurora, New York, the home of Wells College. As soon as I saw Aurora and walked about its glacier hills and the "historic" campus of Wells College, I knew that I had the perfect setting for "33 Clues into the Disappearance of My Sister." This story could not be set elsewhere.

MARGARET RANDALL is a poet, essayist, oral historian, translator, photographer, and social activist. She lived in Latin America for twenty-three years (in Mexico, Cuba, and Nicaragua). From 1962 to 1969, she and Mexican poet Sergio Mondragón coedited *El Corno Emplumado/The Plumed Horn,* a bilingual literary quarterly that published some of the best new work of the sixties. When she came home in 1984, the government ordered her deported because it found some of her writing to be "against the good order and happiness of the United States." With the support of many writers and others, she won her case, and her citizenship was restored in 1989. Randall's most recent poetry titles include *Against Atrocity, Out of Violence Into Poetry* (both from Wings Press), *Stormclouds Like Unkept Promises,* and *Vertigo of Risk* (both from Casa Urraca Press). *Che on My Mind* (a feminist poet's reminiscence of Che Guevara, published by Duke University Press), *Thinking About Thinking* (essays, from Casa Urraca), and *Artists in My Life* (New Village Press) are other recent titles. In 2020, Duke University Press published her memoir, *I Never Left Home: Poet, Feminist, Revolutionary;* a short story collection, *Lupe's Dream and Other Stories,* appeared from Wings Press in 2022; and coming in autumn 2023 will be *Luck* (essays) and *Home* (poems). Randall lives in Albuquerque with her partner (now wife) of more than thirty-six years, the painter Barbara Byers, and travels extensively to read, lecture, and teach.

• At eighty-six, I've published more than two hundred books of poetry, essays, oral history, and memoir. I'd rarely written a short story and never a successful novel. The experience of COVID-19 in 2020–2022 produced dramatic shifts in all our lives, and these shifts surfaced in my writing as well. Sometime during those two years I started writing stories, and I soon realized I had twenty-three. I stopped as suddenly as I'd started. What gives *Lupe's Dream and Other Stories* the cohesion of a collection is the fact that each of the stories bends time or space in some way. The prolonged isolation caused by the virus, added to the general disorientation in this era of severe climate change, disintegrating social contracts, and global uncertainty, created a space in which genre stretched to embrace an altered consciousness. "The Invitation" is one of my favorite stories in the book. Science fiction? Mystery? Time travel? Parallel universes? My stories don't seem to fit into any of these categories. Rather, I believe they respond to a consciousness of the magical realism that infused my life during the decades I lived in Latin America. Bringing that consciousness home to the desert landscape of the American Southwest at this particular moment in human history gave birth to stories such as "The Invitation."

ANNIE REED has been called a master short story writer. She's a multiple Derringer Award nominee, was awarded a literary fellowship for one of her speculative fiction stories, and has appeared in back-to-back issues of *The Mysterious Bookshop Presents the Best Mystery Stories of the Year* (for 2022 and 2023). Her stories appear regularly in *Pulphouse Fiction Magazine* and *Mystery, Crime, and Mayhem*. Her short fiction has also been selected for inclusion in English-language study materials for Japanese college entrance exams. Her latest novel is *Road of No Return*. She lives in Northern Nevada and can be found on the web at anniereed.wordpress.com.

• Sometimes the spark for a story comes from my own backyard. That was the case with "The Blood-Red Leaves of Autumn." Anyone who lives in my area knows that Virginia creeper is the kudzu of our little neck of the woods. The vine takes over almost everything, but at least it looks pretty in the fall when the leaves turn a deep blood red.

I'd been out hacking away at the vines along my back fence, trying to reclaim at least some of my yard, when I uncovered a juvenile silver maple tree that the birds—or the wind—had planted years ago. That spring, I'd splinted a halfway broken branch to the tree's trunk with a piece of rope, then promptly forgot about it. The splint worked and the branch grew strong, but the trunk of the tree had grown enough over the summer that bark covered most of the rope.

While I'd been slicing and dicing creeper vines, I was thinking about what type of story I wanted to write for *Mystery, Crime, and Mayhem*'s upcoming science fiction issue. That embedded piece of rope gave me the first scene in this story, and the Virginia creeper vines gave me the title. Now if only every bit of yard work could be as fruitful.

ANTHONY NEIL SMITH is the author of sixteen noir novels, including *Trooper Down, Slow Bear, Yellow Medicine, All the Young Warriors,* and *Worm.* He is a widely published short story writer in crime, literary, and bizarro fiction, with stories in *Cowboy Jamboree, Bellevue Literary Review, Exquisite Corpse, Reckon Review, Tough, Connecticut Review, ThugLit, Needle, Out of the Gutter,* and many more. His work was included on the Other Distinguished Mystery and Suspense list in *The Best American Mystery and Suspense 2001* and *2002.* He cofounded and edited the online noir journal *Plots with Guns* and was an editor with *Mississippi Review Web,* where he edited several special pulp noir issues. He currently lives in central Minnesota with his wife, three cats, and one purely evil dog, where he is a professor of English at Southwest Minnesota State University. He likes Mexican food, California wine, and Italian poliziotteschi flicks from the seventies.

• The seed of this story was a real walk through the woods with my wife and mother-in-law to help spread my father-in-law's ashes at different spots around the land he'd grown up on and loved. He'd passed away from COVID-19 during the early part of the pandemic, soon after he and my mother-in-law moved from "up north" to be near us in a larger town.

Having already visited several of his favorite places—around hunting grounds, near graves of long-passed relatives and cousins, by his parents' graves—we headed to the old homestead out in the woods. The farther we walked, the creepier it felt, and emotions were already pretty sharp by this time. I think it probably would have made for a nice creative nonfiction essay if I'd stopped there, but then we passed his old car graveyard and an abandoned camper. The "what if" gears started grinding, and I spent the rest of the day imagining everything that could go wrong. I'm a naturally nervous person in that regard, I guess, which is why I write about the things that scare me through noir.

FAYE SNOWDEN is the author of Southern Gothic mysteries with strong (and flawed) women characters. She has published short stories and poems in various anthologies and literary journals. *A Killing Rain* (Flame Tree, 2022), the second book in her noir mystery Killing series, was named by *CrimeReads* as one of the best Southern Gothic mysteries of 2022 and selected as a finalist for the 2022 Foreword INDIES Book of the Year Award in the thriller and suspense category. Faye works and writes from her home in Northern California while enjoying the company of her extremely rowdy and gorgeous grandchildren. Learn more about Faye at fayesnowden.com.

• I was invited to contribute a story to a themed charity anthology for combating voter suppression. I wanted to write a story about how politicians assume that African Americans vote as a monolith, and how national political campaigns rarely consider the nuances of lived experiences and the interests of local communities. At the same time, I was learning about the 1985 MOVE bombing in Philadelphia, where the mayor authorized the bombing of an entire neighborhood. The story was born from thinking about how the bombing has all but disappeared from history, and how local school boards are limiting what we teach about the racial atrocities that have occurred in this country.

JERVEY TERVALON was born in New Orleans and was raised in the Jefferson Park neighborhood in Los Angeles. When he was a student at Foshay Junior High, he sold a poem to Scholastic's *Scope* magazine and got the writing bug. He studied literature and writing with Marvin Mudrick at the College of Creative Studies at UC Santa Barbara. Later, he studied with Oakley Hall and Thomas Keneally at UC Irvine. He was on the board of

PEN American Center and he was a Shanghai Writers' Association fellow. He started LitFest Pasadena, the second largest literary festival in California, with the Light Bringer Project and Jonathan Gold.

• The piece is based on two female students of mine at Locke High School who approached me after class and said they wanted to say goodbye because they were running away with the baby brother of one of the two girls because her mom kept putting him in the oven so that she could get high. I thought they were joking or exaggerating, but I never saw them again. I couldn't stop thinking about them and eventually I couldn't stop writing about them.

JOSEPH S. WALKER lives in Indiana and teaches college literature and composition courses. His short fiction has appeared in *Alfred Hitchcock's Mystery Magazine, Ellery Queen Mystery Magazine, The Saturday Evening Post, Mystery Weekly, Tough,* and a number of other magazines and anthologies. He has been nominated for the Edgar and Derringer Awards and has won the Bill Crider Prize for Short Fiction. He also won the Al Blanchard Award in 2019 and 2021.

• I've worked from home as an online teacher since 2004. It has advantages, but one significant drawback is a pronounced lack of social contact. That's one of the reasons I was excited to attend my first Bouchercon in Dallas in 2019. I had only published a few short stories at that point, but I felt warmly welcomed by the mystery writing community. I met some of my heroes, made a number of new friends, learned a lot, and in general had a great time.

The conference hotel was a short walk from Dealey Plaza, and one morning I went over to have a look at the most infamous crime scene in America. Despite all the movies and pictures I'd seen, the place was nothing like I expected; it's a smaller space than my imagination had conjured, an odd little corner of urban geography that would be completely unremarkable without the weight of history hanging over it. The book depository loomed, much closer than I had expected, over the X on the street marking the spot where Kennedy was hit. I immediately wanted to write a story set there, to try to capture something of the eeriness I felt. "Crime Scene" was the result.

I left Dallas intending to go to every future Bouchercon I could manage. I didn't know that the next two would be reduced to online experiences or that limited social contact was about to become a big problem for everybody. I wrote a good number of stories during our long-enforced isolation, but because of its origins, I'll always think of "Crime Scene" as my personal souvenir of that odd, disjointed time. I want to thank the North Dallas chapter of Sisters in Crime for giving the story a home in their anthology, and especially the book's editor, Barb Goffman, whose suggestions and comments made the piece much stronger. Barb, I owe you several large drinks at the next Bouchercon.

THAAI WALKER is a San Francisco writer and a former daily newspaper reporter for the San Jose *Mercury News,* the *San Francisco Chronicle,* and the *Oakland Tribune.* Her work has also appeared in *Ladies Home Journal, Oakland Magazine,* and The Imprint, an online source for juvenile justice and welfare news.

• As a reporter, I was greatly interested in stories that offered a chance to explore the backstory of a crime. "Flight," which originally appeared in *Hayden's Ferry Review,* is a coming-of-age tale at its core. But instead of journeying from innocence to knowledge, I wanted my young main character to enter the story already jaded by life circumstances and experiences that have robbed her of her voice, her sense of worth, and her ability to imagine a future. At thirteen, Kumani already believes her path in life is quite narrow. I was struck by the idea that childhood is often painted as a sacred, carefree time full of imagination, hopes, and dreams. But for some children, it is full of menace and peril, particularly those children who must navigate the darkness of family substance abuse, mental illness, poverty, and violence. In this story, Kumani is trying to survive these realities in general as well as a particular day that becomes increasingly threatening. I knew when I started writing "Flight" that Kumani and her childhood friend would become the victims of a terrible crime, but I was most curious about how Kumani arrived at that desolate spot in the woods on that day. I wanted to know all of the things that shaped her and led her to the perilous moment when she would face the choice of accepting a doomed destiny or escaping it. While the ending of "Flight" is full of betrayal, loss, and sacrifice, my hope is that readers also find transformation, optimism, and hope.

JESS WALTER is the author of ten books, most recently the 2022 story collection *The Angel of Rome and Other Stories* and the 2020 novel *The Cold Millions.* He won the 2005 Edgar Award for best novel for *Citizen Vince* and was a finalist for the 2006 National Book Award for *The Zero.* His 2012 novel *Beautiful Ruins* was a number-one *New York Times* bestseller, and his books have been published in thirty-four languages. His work has appeared three times in *The Best American Short Stories* as well as *The Best American Nonrequired Reading.* In 2022, he served as guest editor for *The Best American Mystery and Suspense.* He lives in his hometown, Spokane, Washington.

• "Love Interest" was written for *Small Odysseys,* an anthology celebrating the thirty-fifth anniversary of *Selected Shorts,* the long-running public radio show. I had hoped to channel old-time radio, to practically hear the heels clicking down the hallway. But since most detective work is now done on a computer, I updated my private eye to be a self-effacing, Dungeons and Dragons–playing computer specialist at a Southern California law firm—Nerdlock Holmes. I grew up next to a drive-in movie theater and I have a real love for the films of the 1970s. It seemed natural to make Holmes's client an actress from that period, and when my wife received a strange deepfake spam email, the story came together. It was especially thrilling to hear the actor Hugh Dancy read the story live for the *Selected Shorts* anniversary show.

Other Distinguished Mystery and Suspense of 2022

Manuel Ramos
   Northside Nocturne. *Denver Noir*

Marko Realmonte
   Paris. *Cupid Shot Me*

Travis Richardson
   Power at All Costs. *Low Down Dirty Vote, Volume 3*

Eric Rutter
   The Trailhead. *Alfred Hitchcock's Mystery Magazine*, March/April

Bev Vincent
   Death Sentence. *Black Cat Weekly*, no. 51

David Heska Wanbli Weiden
   Colfax and Havana. *Denver Noir*

ABOUT

MARINER BOOKS

MARINER BOOKS TRACES its beginnings to 1832 when William Ticknor cofounded the Old Corner Bookstore in Boston, from which he would run the legendary firm Ticknor and Fields, publisher of Ralph Waldo Emerson, Harriet Beecher Stowe, Nathaniel Hawthorne, and Henry David Thoreau. Following Ticknor's death, Henry Oscar Houghton acquired Ticknor and Fields and, in 1880, formed Houghton Mifflin, which later merged with venerable Harcourt Publishing to form Houghton Mifflin Harcourt. HarperCollins purchased HMH's trade publishing business in 2021 and reestablished their storied lists and editorial team under the name Mariner Books.

Uniting the legacies of Houghton Mifflin, Harcourt Brace, and Ticknor and Fields, Mariner Books continues one of the great traditions in American bookselling. Our imprints have introduced an incomparable roster of enduring classics, including Hawthorne's *The Scarlet Letter,* Thoreau's *Walden,* Willa Cather's *O Pioneers!,* Virginia Woolf's *To the Lighthouse,* W. E. B. Du Bois's *Black Reconstruction,* J.R.R. Tolkien's *The Lord of the Rings,* Carson McCullers's *The Heart Is a Lonely Hunter,* Ann Petry's *The Narrows,* George Orwell's *Animal Farm* and *Nineteen Eighty-Four,* Rachel Carson's *Silent Spring,* Margaret Walker's *Jubilee,* Italo Calvino's *Invisible Cities,* Alice Walker's *The Color Purple,* Margaret Atwood's *The Handmaid's Tale,* Tim O'Brien's *The Things They Carried,* Philip Roth's *The Plot Against America,* Jhumpa Lahiri's *Interpreter of Maladies,* and many others. Today Mariner Books remains proudly committed to the craft of fine publishing established nearly two centuries ago at the Old Corner Bookstore.

EXPLORE THE REST
OF THE SERIES!

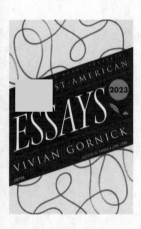

On sale 10/17/23
$18.99

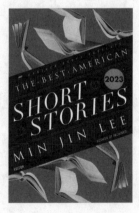